BREWER'S PRIVATE WAR

A SEA NOVEL

Brewer's Private War

by

James Keffer

www.penmorepress.com

ISBN-13: 978-1-957851-20-4Paperback)
ISBN - : 978-1-957851-19-8 (e-book)

BISAC Subject Headings:
FIC014000FICTION / Historical
FIC032000FICTION / War & Military
FIC047000FICTION / Sea Stories

Editing: Chris Wozney

Cover Illustration by
EMILIJA RAKIĆ PR EMILYS WORLD OF DESIGN

Address all correspondence to:
Michael James
Penmore Press LLC
920 N Javelina Pl
Tucson, AZ 85748

ACKNOWLEDGEMENTS

Thanks to Cindy, for marrying into the family.

Thanks to Bo, for some well-timed encouragement and advice.

Thanks to Michael James and all the folks at Penmore Press for believing in me and sticking with me all this time.

Most of all, thanks to Christine, who is nothing less than the other half of the sky in my world.

PROLOGUE

Letter of Marque: A license or commission granted by a state to a private citizen to capture and confiscate the merchant ships of another nation during time of war or conflict.

Letters of Marque are supposed to become null and void at the end of the current war or conflict.

Or that's what we thought...

CHAPTER ONE

The calendar rolled into the month of October, in the year 1819. William Brewer, commander of the sloop HMS *Revenge*, remembered the stories his mentor Captain Bush had told about the boredom he and his shipmates endured when they were on blockade duty during the Napoleonic wars; privately, Brewer had come to the conclusion that routine patrols during peacetime were almost as bad. Escorting merchant vessels to various ports in the Caribbean was necessary, but he quickly decided that it would be much better for everyone if something happened every so often to break up the routine. There were days when he would pay anything to have Blackbeard rise from the dead and plunder the Caribbean Sea.

He realized that the only way to get around the malaise that was affecting his crew was to keep them busy. Sail drills and dry firing training on the guns were held almost daily, along with frequent shore leaves on whatever uninhabited islands they came across in an attempt to keep the crew from losing their edge.

Of course, that was fine for the crew, but he needed something more specific to keep his own focus sharp. So it was that he found himself on the foc's'l with one of Alfred's wooden training swords in his hand as he practiced once again against his diminutive servant. Alfred stood poised across the deck, his sword at the ready, and Brewer was pleased to see a droplet of sweat run down the side of his face. They had been going at it for nearly two hours, and Brewer's own shirt was soaked with sweat. Training with Alfred was always a grueling affair, and the captain was certain he had the bruises to show for it. He still had not managed to lay a stroke on his instructor, which baffled him. At the very least, one would think he'd get lucky and Alfred would trip somehow and run into his sword. The only consolation he had was the undeniable fact that his swordsmanship was getting better; in fact, he thought he just might be the second-best swordsman on the ship now.

"Ready, Captain?" Alfred called. "Begin!"

Alfred abruptly switched his sword to his left hand and moved in that direction. Brewer was surprised by the move, but he determined to make the most of what just may be the best opening yet. He darted forward, careful to keep inside of Alfred's sword, which he blocked to the outside with his own. A smile grew on his face. He was just about to bring his sword down on the little man's arm and across his neck, scoring his first-ever point against his adversary. However, before he could move the blade, he felt Alfred's fist hit him in the ribs, and he knew he'd been "stabbed" in the chest and was "dead".

Alfred stepped back, and the crowd applauded. Brewer couldn't help but feel disappointed.

"You did well, sir," Alfred told him. "But don't forget that most men have two hands."

The captain saluted with his sword. "Yes, well, I shall try to keep that in mind." He handed the practice sword back to his teacher. "Thank you for the lesson."

Alfred bowed, more of an exaggerated nod. "My pleasure, Captain."

"Yes," Brewer replied with a wry smile, "I imagine it was."

The captain made his way below to his cabin, where he

toweled off and put on a clean uniform shirt. He remembered Bush telling of Hornblower's turns under the pumps, but he could never quite bring himself to try it out. He heard Alfred come in while he was dressing; by the time he finished and stepped out into the main cabin, lunch was on the table.

"Tell me truly, Alfred," Brewer said as he sat down at the table, "am I getting any better?" Lunch was a plate of cold ham left over from the night before, along with cheese, fresh fruit, and a glass of wine. Brewer dug in with relish.

"You are, sir," Alfred replied. "I find myself having to go to great lengths to defeat you. That was not the case not very long ago."

Brewer picked up a piece of meat and chewed it thoughtfully, wondering whether or not he had been insulted and deciding it was better not to ask.

Mac came in and began straightening the cabin. "Quite a show you put on today, sir," he said. "I thought you had him there at the end. Too bad you ended up dead."

Brewer stopped chewing stared at his coxswain, who had the good sense to look embarrassed. He shrugged and said, "Just a figure of speech, in your case, sir." When that didn't improve his situation, he sighed. "Sorry, sir."

Brewer swallowed his mouthful. "Don't worry about it, Mac. In fact, next time Alfred and I are training, you can step in for me and show us all how you would have done it." The captain looked around at Alfred, standing in the pantry door. "All right with you, Alfred?"

The servant looked to Mac and smiled. "A pleasure, Captain."

Mac gave them a weak smile and knuckled his forehead. "Aye, sir."

Brewer resumed his meal with a quiet smile. After a few minutes, Mac approached him.

"Excuse me, sir, but I wanted to return this to you." He

reached into the large pocket he had sewn onto the side of his tunic and pulled out a copy of *Robinson Crusoe*.

"Thanks, Mac," Brewer said as he set the book beside his plate. "So, what did you think of it?"

"A little slow at the beginning, sir," he replied, "but after he was shipwrecked, I couldn't put it down." He shook his head somberly. "Some of what he accomplished on the island is a difficult for me to believe."

The captain smiled. "Didn't I tell you? I read somewhere that the book is based on a true story."

The coxswain stared at him. *"What?"*

The captain nodded. "It seems that the author actually met a man who went through a similar ordeal, and he turned the man's account into this book." He tapped the novel with a forefinger.

Mac blinked. "Well, that's something! Every tar should read that book, Captain! Just in case, you understand."

"Not a bad idea, Mac, but we have a problem."

"What is that, sir?"

Brewer leaned forward. "Mac, how many of your own mess can read? Not many, I'd wager. What do you think the rest of the ship is like?"

The coxswain's brow furled. "Didn't think of that, sir. Would it be possible for me to borrow the book again some time and read it to them?"

"That sounds like an excellent idea, Mac." Brewer slid the book across the table to his coxswain. "Just bring it back when you're done."

Mac's face lit up. "Thank you, Captain!

The coxswain scooped up the thin volume and stuffed it back into the pocket before returning to his work. The captain watched him out of the corner of his eye. He was pleased at the way Mac had taken to reading; all it took was finding a book that held his interest. Now he wanted to read to ship messmates. Brewer wondered if he would have to open a lending library on their next voyage.

Brewer finished his meal and went up on deck. When he stepped onto the quarterdeck, he found the doctor in conversation with the sailing master and the first lieutenant.

"Good afternoon, gentlemen," Brewer said.

The men touched their hats. "Good afternoon, Captain," Mr. Greene replied, then asked, "Sir, may I ask how you are feeling?"

Brewer looked confused. "How am I feeling?"

The first lieutenant threw a nervous glance at the doctor. "Well, sir, it's just that I saw you sparring with Alfred this morning, and... sometimes you come out of those sessions a little worse for wear, shall we say?"

The captain saw a glimmer of mirth appear in the eyes of the doctor and sailing master. "I'm fine, Mr. Greene, thank you for asking. You know, for a moment I thought I had him."

"Too bad you died," the doctor said. "Still, that would have been a nice thought to have as you go out into eternity: 'For once in my life, I bested Alfred!'. Mr. Greene, be sure to mention that at the captain's funeral."

Brewer stared wide-eyed as the others turned away to hide their amusement. "So that's how it is? You know, I think some others on this ship could do with a few sessions of Alfred's tutelage. Yes! I might even sell tickets!"

Greene touched his hat. "My apologies, Captain. If you'll excuse me, I have business forward."

The premier turned and moved off, and Doctor Spinelli stepped up. "You shouldn't tease him so, Captain. He was concerned, that's all."

"Yes, I know. Besides, *you* were the one who made a

comment about me dying."

Spinelli gave an apologetic bow with his head. "And how *are* you doing?"

Brewer clasped his hands behind his back. "No worse than usual," he said. "That is, until that last thrust when I 'died'." He rubbed his ribs. "I think he enjoyed that one."

Spinelli smiled. "As you say, the usual. Chess later?"

The captain smiled. "Dine with me, and we'll play afterwards. Turn of the first dog watch."

"Very well, Captain."

The days passed, and Brewer continued to be concerned about the tedium of routine barely broken despite his best efforts. But one evening Brewer came up on deck one to find Mac sitting in front of a group of perhaps fifty men the fo'c'sle.

"What's going forward?" he asked Mr. Sweeney.

The sailing master cast a glance over his shoulder. "Oh, that. You haven't noticed that before? This is the third or fourth time they've gathered. It seems that when Mac started reading his book to his mess, any hands who happen to pass by and overhear sat down to listen. Soon nobody could move on that part of the deck due to the crowd. So, Mac agreed to do the reading on deck where there was more room. He even started over from the beginning, and no one complained. Every time he reads, he has a few more men attending. The men look forward to it."

"Well," Brewer said, "I had no idea."

Mr. Sweeney stepped closer. "There is one other thing, Captain."

"Yes?"

"I don't like the look of the weather, sir. I've seen this before, and it's never been a good sign."

"Seen what?"

The sailing master frowned as though searching for a word. "I can only describe it as a calming in the winds, sir, but that's not exactly right. You know how sometimes changes in the currents can forecast a rogue wave? Well, this is along the same lines, only with the winds." He shook his head. "We're in for trouble, Captain; I'm sure of it."

Brewer looked at his sailing master. "Very well, Mr. Sweeney. Pass the word for all officers and warrants to meet in my cabin in fifteen minutes. As soon as Mac is done reading, we'll get the ship ready for a storm."

The captain was soon facing his officers and warrant officers gathered around the table in his cabin. "Let me come straight to the point," he said bluntly. "Mr. Sweeney says we're in for a storm. It's the right time of year for a hurricane to hit the Caribbean, so we need to get ready. Mr. Sweeney, have the quartermaster and a mate go to the gunroom and check the wheel ropes. Have him grease the gooseneck and sweeps while he's there."

"Aye, Captain."

"Rig rudder tackles and detail men to man them. Double-man the wheel, beginning with the next watch."

"Aye, sir."

"Mr. Tyler, set up the portable compass. Rig a lubber line and life-lines."

"Aye, sir."

"Mr. Reed and Mr. Hodges," Brewer said to *Revenge's* senior midshipman and gunner, "make sure all the guns are secure. Lash them alongside. Choke the trucks with a hammock on each end. Hopefully, that will help prevent any movement. Take the ready ammunition below."

"Aye, sir!"

"Mr. Tyler, make sure the anchors are secured."

"Aye, sir."

"Sir," Sweeney interjected, "may I suggest we rig the lifebuoy to the lead-line and secure the reel aft? Just in case."

"Of course," Brewer said solemnly. He felt a stab of shame that he hadn't thought of it himself; it would be the best way to try to save anyone who was washed overboard in the storm.

"Mr. Greene, detail some men to check the drain holes in the boats and rig the covers. Have them make sure the deck-gripes are hauled tight."

"Aye, Captain," the premier replied. "Shall we prepare a sea-anchor?"

Brewer had been struggling with that question. If it were prepared, it might break free and career down the deck, but if it wasn't prepared, it might be needed in a pinch. *Well,* he thought, *better to err on the side of caution.* "Yes, Mr. Greene, I think that would be best."

"Aye, sir."

"Mr. Ringold," he said to the carpenter, "get the pumps ready. I'm sure we shall need them before this is over. I want the wells sounded hourly, beginning with the change of the watch."

"Aye, Captain."

"Mr. Greene, prepare to bring down the royals and upper stuns'ls on my command. Topgallant yards and masts, too."

"Aye, sir. Shall I detail men to tighten the lanyards?"

Brewer thought for a moment. "Not yet, and only if we have time after attending to priorities. The best we may be able to do is to tauten up the stays." Greene nodded, and the captain continued. "Once the weather worsens, I intend to scud under foresail and reefed main topsail. Rig a quicksaver for the foresail. Mr. Snead," he said, addressing the bosun, "I want the rigging checked. Every lift, truss, and rolling-tackle is to be inspected."

"Aye, sir."

"Let's see, have we forgotten anything? Mr. Greene, make sure the men are fed and the cook has his fires put out before the storm hits, if you please. Also, detail runners for the quarterdeck."

"Aye, sir."

"Anything else?" He looked around the table, and nobody spoke up. "Very well. Let's get to work."

The work began in earnest and proceeded throughout the rest of the day and into the night. Brewer ordered all sail while the work was proceeding, the idea being to make use of what wind they could manage and be closer to a friendly port before the storm hit. He worked with Mr. Sweeney regarding the best course, and they made for Martinique. When dawn finally approached, bearing the dreaded red taint to its skies, the captain finally ordered sail to be taken in on the appointed yards, tops and sails brought down and stored.

"Well," Brewer said as he stood on the quarterdeck with the first lieutenant and sailing master, "I think we're as ready as we can be. Is there *anything* we've forgotten?"

Sweeney shook his head. "Not that I can think of, sir. I will admit, I don't look forward to riding out a hurricane is a ship as small as this one. Tis going to be a lively ride, that's for sure."

Brewer pondered. "Do we have topmen detailed, in case we need to send them aloft?"

"Aye, sir."

Brewer looked around the deck, taking in the lubber line, running from the bow to the fantail to help men get forward or aft. This was crossed by several life-lines, which would give a hand swept off his feet by a wave a chance to grab hold before he was washed overboard. That thought made him turn to see that the lifebuoy was indeed lashed to the lead line, ready in case of need. He saw that the wheel was manned by four sturdy hands as opposed to the usual two, each of them tied to the wheel by a rope. The hands detailed to the rudder tackles were similarly secured, as was the hand manning the lifebuoy, and the quarterdeck runners. It dawned on the captain that about the only men on the quarterdeck who were *not* secured were the first lieutenant, the sailing master, and himself. That was fine with him. Now came the hard part.

"Now, we wait," he said.

When it came, the storm broke with all its intensity like a lightning bolt. Less than twenty minutes took HMS *Revenge* from a calm sea to cresting waves big enough to crush her. The wind howled and shrieked, seeming to laugh as the little ship was tossed about by the ever-growing waves. Several hands on the deck were thrown from their feet when the ship crested a wave and literally dove into the trough that followed. Wave after wave broke over the bow and swept across the deck, blown by screaming winds and taking anything that would move over the side with it. Brewer and his crew held on as best they could. He watched in horror as a particularly strong wave swept across the ship from larboard bow to starboard quarter, bearing away one of the rudder tackle men. Brewer was clinging to the lubber line as the water washed over him, threatening to rip his arms from their sockets as he struggled to hang on. When he looked up, he saw that one of the lines supposed to secure those men had snapped. The man had vanished over the side. Brewer gripped the rope, helpless; there was no way to lower the boat for a rescue in a storm like this.

A sudden shift in the wind brought a wave slamming broadside from starboard. *Revenge* was practically picked up and thrown to larboard, only to land mostly upright and be thrown forward all at once. Mr. Sweeney was swept from his feet and washed aft, his life saved by the quick reactions and fierce grips of his captain and first lieutenant, who hauled him up and wrapped his arms around a life-line.

The three men felt another wave strike aft. They turned and realized the rudder had taken control of the ship's movement, which meant the water had struck it hard enough to throw it to one side, as though it had been put hard-over by the captain. Only this time the process worked in reverse; the wheel itself was spun so hard that two of the hands manning it were sent airborne by the force. A third man on the downward side was pulled inward and was beaten to the ground, his neck snapped by the force of the wheel's spin. Greene left the safety of the ropes and grabbed the two who had been thrown across the deck. He dragged the dazed men across the bucking deck to the mizzenmast and lashed them to it with rope wrapped loosely around the mast for just that purpose.

The worst was yet to come. The wave that hit the rudder had turned the ship, and she was now buffeted by a powerful gust of wind on her larboard quarter that snapped the mizzenmast at a height of about ten feet and tossed the mast, rigging and all, over the starboard beam and into the sea. The ship rolled alarmingly to starboard, and for a moment Brewer wasn't sure she would come back, but somehow *Revenge* righted herself and bobbed defiantly across the raging waves.

Three hours later, the wind and the waves seemed to mellow a bit, allowing Brewer and Greene to organize teams to carry wounded below and search for those who might be injured and unable to respond. Brewer looked up to see Alfred and Mac emerge from below. Alfred was carrying a basket covered by a towel.

"Excuse me, sir!"

Brewer bent over, and Alfred shouted into his captain's ear to be heard above the winds. "The pantry is a disaster, but I scrounged about and found some cold ham, fruit, and biscuit. I brought it up for you and the men on the quarter-deck, sir!"

"Thank you!" Brewer shouted back. He reached in and pulled out an apple. Alfred presented the basket to Greene and Sweeney, and each man gratefully took something. Alfred moved on to feed the rest of the men. Brewer motioned to Mac.

"Go with him and make sure he's not washed overboard!" he shouted.

Mac smiled, knuckled his forehead and went after Alfred and his basket.

No sooner had they gotten the wounded below to the sickbay, and Alfred had gone below with his basket, when the next wave front of wind, rain, and waves struck. Mac stayed on deck and positioned himself very close to the captain and his party. Just as he got a firm grip on the life-line that cut across the quarterdeck, HMS *Revenge* was pooped by a tall wave that broached the ship and threatened to roll her over. Mac grabbed Brewer and both men held on to the lines for their lives.

"Mr. Greene!" Brewer cried. "The sea anchor! Put it over! Help him, Mac!"

The two men crawled up the deck to where the sea anchor was lashed against the rail. They cut the lashings with their knives and struggled to get the anchor over the side and into the water. Two of the hands left their positions on the rudder tackles to help, and together they heaved it up and over the rail. Almost immediately, it pulled the ship level again. Brewer took heart, but he also wondered how bad the damage was below deck. Then a tremendous shriek made them look forward just in time to see the mainmast broken in two by a sharp gust of wind and carried over the side, taking most of the rigging with it. Fortunately, the foremast stood firm with her shrouds and stays intact.

After that, the winds and rain faded, slowly but surely, until all that was left was a minor squall that blew itself out just before dawn. Brewer and Mac surveyed the damage. Greene and Sweeney were ordered below and to bed once it was obvious that the worst was over. There were no dead bodies on the deck, but several men lashed to the stumps of the main and mizzen masts were injured and were taken below to Dr. Spinelli. Brewer was relieved to be informed that all of their armament survived; not a single cannon or carronade had been lost overboard during the storm. Since storm-borne cannons tend to crush and kill hands, and also inflict severe damage on the ship, this was doubly to the good.

After taking reports from officers and warrant officers, Brewer let go of the life-line and took a step, only to promptly stumble, his legs quivering like rubber. Only Mac's iron grip on his arm kept him on his feet.

"Come on, sir," the big coxswain said, "let's go below and to bed."

"Not yet," Brewer said. "I need to see sickbay first."

"But sir—"

Brewer silenced him with a look. "Sickbay, Mac."

"Aye, sir."

Mac half-helped, half-carried his captain below.

Some of the wounded were sitting outside, leaning on the bulkheads. The lucky ones were sleeping. Brewer stepped inside and found the doctor.

"Adam," he said.

Spinelli turned. He looked almost as haggard and tired as Brewer felt. "Captain! You look terrible! Are you hurt?

Mac, take him to bed!"

"What's the bill, Adam?"

Spinelli sighed. "I'm not sure yet. I don't know how many we lost over the side. Eleven brought down to me have died. I have some men sewing them in canvas." He pointed off to his left, then his arm just dropped to his side. "Thirty-seven more are hurt, mostly bruises and broken bones. I think they'll be all right." He looked at his captain. "Please, William, get some rest."

Brewer looked around helplessly. "I will when you do."

"I have, let me see… five more to tend to, and then I will lay down for a nap. Mac, take him to his cabin and put him to bed."

"Aye, aye, Doctor. Come along, Captain."

"Take care, Adam."

"And you, Captain."

Mac escorted Brewer to his cabin, which miraculously had survived the storm. Mac pulled off his captain's boots and poured water out of each one, then remove the socks and wrung each one out before laying them out to dry before helping Brewer into his hammock.

"Goodnight, sir," he said, but the captain was already asleep.

Brewer got six hours of sleep before Alfred woke him, a cup of hot coffee at the ready. The captain rolled out of his cot and stood for a moment on the deck, steadying himself. Alfred handed him the coffee, and he sipped appreciatively at the hot, reviving liquid. He began to feel life return to his tired limbs.

"Do you know, Alfred," he said between one swallow and the next sip, "I hurt more now that after a battle."

"No doubt, sir," the servant replied. He pointed toward

the captain's sea chest. "I have managed to gather a uniform that is both clean and dry. I will attend to the one you have on after you change. Mr. Greene is awaiting your arrival on deck; I understand he has a damage report ready for you, sir."

"Thank you, Alfred. Please pass the word for Mr. Greene and Mr. Sweeney to join me in my cabin instead, and have coffee ready for them. The doctor, too, if he is awake. I shall join them as soon as I change."

"Aye, Captain."

By the time Brewer was dressed and came out, the three were seated at the table, drinking coffee. They started to rise as their captain entered.

"Keep your seats," he said. He took his seat at the end of the table, and Alfred refilled his cup. "All right, Benjamin; what's the damage?"

"Could have been much worse, Captain. We lost the main and mizzen masts, but the foremast seems to be stable, as is the bowsprit and jib. Thanks to Mr. Reed and Mr. Hodges, we did not lose a single gun over the side, which may be a first in the history of the Royal Navy. Mr. Ringold reports that the pumps are operational, and the levels in the wells are steadily dropping, so we did not spring any major leaks during the storm. The foresail, however, was shredded; the men are hanging a new one as we speak. We should be ready to move soon."

"Good. Any idea where we are, exactly, Mr. Sweeney?"

"A pretty good idea, Captain," the sailing master said as he put his cup down. "We had a break in the cloud cover, long enough for me to get a sighting. The storm blew us off our course to the north. The closest port where we can make repairs is still Martinique. Or would you rather risk the longer journey back to Port Royal?"

"No, I think we head for Martinique. I don't like sailing

with only one mast out of three doing all the work. How long until we get there?"

"Several days, sir."

"I guessed as much. Well, let's do the best we can, but keep the old girl in one piece please."

Sweeney smiled. "Aye, Captain."

"Now, Doctor," Brewer asked, "how bad is it?"

Spinelli answered somberly. "We lost five men over the side. Add that to the eleven who were gone when you came to sickbay, and the two who died after you left, and we lost eighteen dead, with thirty-five wounded. Two of those I'm watching to see if I have to remove a limb. I'll keep you informed, Captain. As soon as possible, I'd like to move some of the wounded up onto the deck for fresh air and sunshine."

"Of course," Brewer replied. "Coordinate with Mr. Greene if you need help." He paused while Alfred refilled their cups. "Now then, our immediate concern is to get the ship to Martinique in one piece, then get her put back together to the point where she can make Port Royal for a full refit. Any problems anticipated, Mr. Greene?"

"I hope not, Captain," the premier replied. "I shall ask Mr. Snead and Mr. Ringold to give the foremast their undivided attention."

"Good idea. Has the cook been able to relight the galley fires yet?"

Greene shook his head. "Not yet, sir, at least not enough to feed the crew; most of the wood was soaked in the storm and is slow to dry out. The crew was fed with the last of the cold leftovers. Cook said he should have the fires going in time for a hot supper."

"Let's hope so." Brewer rose, and the others followed suit. "All right, gentlemen; let's get to work."

For the next several days they were blessed with good weather, other than a rolling fog bank on the morning of the fourth day. The foremast was reinforced, and *Revenge* was able to keep a slow and steady pace. Most of the wounded were brought up on deck, and Mac read to them. The pumps were put away on the morning of the fourth day, once the level in the well held steady for twelve hours without them in operation.

Finally, the day came when, just as the sun began to set, HMS *Revenge* slid slowly into the harbor at Martinique.

CHAPTER TWO

Brewer rose and breakfasted early before putting on his dress uniform and heading up on deck. He had to make his appearance before the governor and ask for use of Martinique's maintenance facilities. He put Mac to work readying the launch and left Mr. Greene instructions to come up with a definitive list of repairs. He was just about to step over the side when he heard someone call his name. He turned to see the doctor.

"Permission to come ashore, Captain?" he asked.

"I should be glad of the company, sir," the captain replied, "only promise me you aren't planning to pick a fight with an entire tavern again!"

Spinelli shook his head. "No fights this time, Captain, I promise. No, I only want to visit a pub and drink to a certain lady's memory." Brewer knew the doctor was referring to a woman named Mary. Before their last visit to Martinique, Spinelli had received a letter from a friend informing him of the lady's death. The doctor had hoped to marry her when they returned to England. "Will you join me?"

"Gladly, as soon as I conclude our business with the governor."

The two men rode in the stern sheets of the launch as Mac conned the boat to the jetty. They made their way to the governor's mansion, where the doctor waited in an anteroom while the captain had his interview. The meeting was brief, with the governor pledging to provide all aid needed to get *Revenge* seaworthy again. Satisfied, Brewer tendered his thanks and rejoined Spinelli. The two men departed the residence and went in search of a tavern.

Brewer and the doctor found one to their liking, stepped inside, and took a seat in the back corner off to the side of the bar. Brewer thought the place homey enough, the paintings on the walls a hopeful testament to the lack of brawls in the establishment.

The barmaid stepped up. "What'll it be, gents?" she said with a smile.

"Two pints, my dear," the doctor answered. The barmaid nodded and left on her errand. The doctor looked around and nodded. "They've decorated since we were last here."

The barmaid returned and deposited two pints on the table, and the doctor fished two coins from his pocket and dropped them on her tray. The two officers raised their tankards in salute and drank. Brewer looked around again, concentrating on the people this time, but there was nobody who attracted any particular notice.

"How long do you think it will take to put *Revenge* to rights?" the doctor asked.

Brewer shrugged. "The governor said we would be the first in line when space became available." He took another swallow. "The ship currently occupying dry dock should be fit to be refloated in four or five days. After that, two or three weeks to make necessary repairs."

"Well," the doctor said as he lifted his tankard, "I can think of worse places for shore leave while your ship is being repaired." He winked and drained the pint.

Brewer was about to answer when a voice drifted through the general din of the place. It sounded vaguely familiar, something from his past, and he set his tankard down and tried to trace it to its source.

"William?" Spinelli said. "Is something amiss?"

"Shh," Brewer chided him. He thought the voice came from a group at the bar. "I'll be right back, Doctor. Stay here."

Without another word, he slipped from his seat and approached the bar cautiously, homing in on the voice until he stood behind three men who were belly up to the bar. The voice came from the one in the middle. He wore a long coat with a high, stiff collar of the type that was popular during the Napoleonic Wars. His hat, which hid his hair from view, was salt-stained, but his boots seemed of good quality. The men on either side of him were dressed as merchant sailors would be.

"Michael Underhill!" Brewer said loudly.

The voices went silent and the head snapped up and stared straight ahead. His companions on either side backed away, giving the Voice room to turn and draw his pistol if necessary. It was not; the head sagged forward and began to shake from side to side. Brewer heard a chuckle.

"Now, there's a voice I've not heard these fifteen years or more," he said as he turned around. "William Brewer!"

Brewer stepped forward and shook hands, but Underhill pulled him in and wrapped him in a great bear hug. When he let him go, Underhill still held him by the shoulders. "As I live and breathe! You've done right well for yourself, me boy!" Underhill noticed the single epaulette and whistled. "Master and Commander now, is it? Congratulations, old son!" He hugged Brewer again before letting him go. One of his friends nudged him on the arm. "Oh!" Underhill said. "Where are my manners! This here's Chauncey and Pete. They're part of my crew."

"Pleased to meet you," Brewer said as he shook hands. "Why don't you all join me at our table? The next round is on me."

Underhill slapped Brewer on the shoulder. "How can a man turn down such a gracious invitation? Lead on, mate!"

Brewer led them to the table, where Spinelli was already on his feet. "Allow me to introduce Dr. Adam Spinelli, my ship's surgeon. Adam, this is Michael Underhill, and these two are Chauncey and Pete. Michael and I served together on the old *Kent* when I was a raw midshipman."

"Indeed!" Adam exclaimed.

"Aye," Underhill said. He sat down beside Brewer. Chauncey and Pete sat on the doctor's side of the table. "I tell you truly, Doctor, your captain was fair bewildered when he came aboard the *Kent*! I taught him everything he knows!"

"Is that so?" Spinelli looked to his captain.

Brewer nodded. "Michael here was a petty officer who was kind enough to take me under his wing and teach me my craft. I'm just glad I was smart enough to listen!"

Underhill clapped Brewer on the shoulder and laughed heartily. "He caught on quick enough, Doctor, don't let him fool you. Tell me, William, how's life been treating you?"

"Can't complain," Brewer said as he signaled the barmaid to bring another round. "I'm in command of a sloop of war, HMS *Revenge*. She belonged to Jean LaFitte until we took it from him. The navy bought her, and the admiral gave her to me. We were out on patrol when we were overtaken by a storm and lost our main and mizzenmasts. We limped in for repairs; this was the closest port."

"Well, I'm glad it was!" Underhill raised his tankard and drank.

"How long did you serve together?" Spinelli asked.

"Nearly three years," Brewer replied. "Then our ship pulled into Plymouth. Boney had just torn up the Treaty of Amiens, and we needed to take on water before heading out to join a blockade squadron." He addressed Underhill now. "I spoke to you on the fo'c'sle the next afternoon. I remember, because you seemed upset in a way I'd never seen before. You played it off, but I knew there was something you were not telling me. Then the morning came, and you were gone. No explanation. Not even a note. Now, after all these years, I get to ask, *What happened?*"

Underhill's head dropped and he stared into his drink. Brewer saw his eyes shifting back and forth across the liquid's surface, and then his great shoulders rise and fall in a sigh. He drained the glass and set it down before turning to Brewer.

"William," he said slowly — almost sadly — as he rested his forearm on the table, "that day changed my life. That night when we pulled in to harbor, I went to see the first lieutenant about becoming a midshipman. I had passed the test a few months before, and I was anxious to take the first step toward becoming an officer and a gentleman." He snorted in derision. His eyes filled with sadness and bitterness. He drew a deep breath and let it out slowly; the memory obviously still hurt. "We all - most of us, anyway - have that one thing in our past that we simply can't overcome. It haunts us forever, reappearing to ruin any chance for happiness. Mine showed up again that night. The first lieutenant took me to see the captain. I had no idea what was coming; I thought my past was all behind me, dead and buried. How wrong I was!"

He hunched over further. "The captain told me that night that my skeleton doomed me to never walk the quarterdeck. He was apologetic about the matter, in light of my years of service and passing the exam, but he claimed his hands were tied. The word came down from on high, he said, and there was no changing."

Underhill tapped the table with his tankard, and the barmaid made her way over.

"This one's on me," Brewer said, but Underhill wouldn't hear of it.

"Nonsense," he said. "'Tis my story, so I'll do the buying." He gave the order to the maid and dropped his payment on the tray. She was back quickly, handing out fresh drinks and scooping up the empty tankards. After she left, Brewer asked, "But Michael, what had you done?"

Underhill smiled sadly over his drink and shook his head. "Ancient history now, me lad. 'Twill do nobody any good to bring the tale to life again. Suffice it to say that when I left the captain's cabin, I knew my naval career was over. I went up on deck and stared at the town, trying to figure out what to do. That's where you found me, William. You see now why I couldn't say anything. I wasn't entirely sure myself what I would do, where I would go. And you were safer kept in the dark."

Brewer shook his head. "You should have told me, Michael. Maybe I could have helped."

"What could you have done?" Underhill said, ancient frustrations creeping into his voice. "You were a skinny midshipman still wet behind the ears! You had no influence in high places!" He shook his head and calmed himself. "No, better you were safely out of it. After you left, I decided to jump ship. I made it to shore that night and stowed away on a lighter that left before daylight for Portsmouth. I made my way ashore and disappeared. Within a week, I had discharge papers and I booked passage for America."

Spinelli spoke up. "You got valid discharge papers a week after you deserted?"

Underhill shrugged. "Anything can be bought, Doctor, if you know where to look."

"What rock to turn over, you mean," Spinelli spat.

"Adam!" Brewer cut him off.

"It's all right, William," Underhill said, "I was none too happy myself at the time, but I had to create a new life for myself, and I sought out someone who could help me. I made it to our old colonies and made my living working on coastal shipping. I admit I was bitter at the way it turned out. I saw myself as captain of a frigate winning a mountain of prize money for victories against the French and then getting my own flag. All that was denied me. Then the war came in 1812, and I saw my chance to get my revenge. I outfitted a privateer and bought a Letter of Marque from their government, and I went to war against the British Empire."

Brewer stared into his drink, not knowing what to think or say. He'd wondered many times what happened to his friend; now he knew. There was nothing he could do about the desertion or Underhill's forged discharge papers, but to hear that he'd fought against the land of his birth was almost too much to bear.

Underhill went on. "We had decent success prowling the Caribbean and the gulf. We started out with a tiny brig and moved up every time we took a suitable prize."

"And what were you sailing when the war ended?" Spinelli asked.

"A large sloop we took in '14," he replied. "Still have her. *Oliver Cromwell,* that's what we call her. She made us a lot of money, let me tell you."

"I'm sorry to hear that you felt you had to leave the navy under such circumstances, Michael," Brewer said quietly. "I wish you had told me before you left."

"You couldn't have done anything," Underhill said.

"Maybe not, but you would have known you weren't alone. Maybe together we could have come up with a better plan than desertion."

"Ah, William," Underhill sighed. "No, my lad, I couldn't trust you with my plans. No, that's wrong; I couldn't *involve* you. If I disappeared, and they discovered that you knew I was going to run and did nothing to stop me — or did not report me to the first lieutenant — well, what do you think they would have done to you, eh?" He shook his head. "No, I couldn't ask you to bear that burden."

Brewer signaled the barmaid for another round. He knew his friend was right. He had been questioned by the first lieutenant after Underhill was discovered missing, and he had truthfully answered that he knew nothing about the disappearance. Had he known... Brewer shook his head, uncertain what he would have told the first lieutenant.

The barmaid arrived, passed out the fresh tankards and collected the empties. Brewer dropped some coins on the tray. She smiled at him and headed for the bar. Brewer turned to his friend and raised his tankard. Underhill smiled and did the same.

"The past is gone," Brewer said. "Here's to the future."

"The future," Underhill repeated. They touched tankards all around the table and drank deeply. "Well! It's been good to see you, William, but we must be getting back to the ship. We sail on the tide."

Brewer rose and shook his friend's hand. "You never did tell me, Michael, what are you doing now?"

Underhill picked up his hat before looking at the captain. "More of the same, William," he said simply. "Why change a good thing?" He nodded farewell to the doctor, and he and his men walked out into the cool of the evening.

Brewer sat back down to finish his drink. Spinelli looked at the door for a long time before turning to his captain.

"William," he said, "do you have any idea what he meant by that?"

Brewer's eyes went from the doctor to the door to his drink. "No, Adam. At least, I hope I don't."

Two weeks went by before HMS *Revenge* was ready for sea. In that time two new masts were stepped and most of the damage from the storm was repaired. The day before they were to sail, Brewer went ashore again to visit the governor and thank him for his help. Governor Donzelot received him in his study rather than his office as in previous visits. Brewer looked around the room as the valet closed the door behind him. The governor stood before an empty hearth, staring at a portrait of the Emperor Napoleon. Brewer was surprised to see him wearing his military uniform, complete with the gold trim and the star of the Grand Cross of the *Légion d'Honneur* on his left breast. He stood erect, his black hair pulled back in the ponytail style favored by French officers under the Empire and tied with a black ribbon. Brewer stood at ease, his hands behind his back, and waited for the governor to speak.

The governor sighed and rubbed the bridge of his nose with a thumb and forefinger. "My apologies, Commander," he said. "I sometimes come in here to pay private homage to the Emperor, hence my garments. As you knew His Majesty, I allowed you entrance."

Brewer bowed. "I thank you, Governor." He gestured towards the star. "During our previous conversations, you did not mention that you had one of those."

"Ah," came the reply, the governor's fingers reflexively touching the star. "The Emperor presented me with this before my ship left for Corfu. I never wear it except when I honor the Emperor."

"I will share a secret with you," Brewer said. "I have one as well."

Donzelot's eyes opened wide. "One of *what*, Commander?"

"The star that you wear," Brewer explained, "I have one."

The governor's fingers again went to the star. He swallowed hard. "May I ask when and where you got it?"

"The Emperor presented me with the one from his own uniform," Brewer said solemnly, "at our last meeting on St. Helena."

"I see." The governor looked at his guest for a moment before going to a small table containing several decanters and glasses. He poured a glass for each of them and then led his guest to two overstuffed leather chairs before a picture window with a grand view of the harbor. Governor Donzelot handed one glass to his guest, and the two men sat. They raised their glasses to each other and drank.

"You intrigue me, Commander," the governor said. "There seems no end of your depths."

Brewer nodded. "Thank you, *M. le Comte.*"

"Your ship? You are ready to sail?"

"Yes," Brewer nodded in gratitude. "That's one reason why I have come — to thank you for your assistance in expediting repairs to my ship."

"You are most welcome." The governor's head tilted to one side. "*One* reason? And what is the other?"

Brewer smiled. "I ran into an old friend in town the day I arrived, Michael Underhill. Do you know him?"

The governor's eyes turned to saucers. "*This* man is a friend of yours?"

Brewer shrugged. "He was a petty officer on the same ship when I was a raw midshipman. He took me under his wing and taught me about seamanship and working with men."

Donzelot grunted. "He came to our attention during the last difference of opinion your nation had with the Americans. He obtained a letter of marque from their government and proceeded to outfit a privateer. It seems he was successful at plundering your country's shipping." The governor shrugged. "We believe he was responsible for the disappearance of French and Spanish ships as well."

"And after the war?" Brewer asked.

The Comte frowned. "We have no proof of anything against Mr. Underhill, although we suspect him of being responsible for the disappearance of several ships, French and otherwise. Unfortunately, we have yet to catch him. What did he say to you?"

Brewer tapped his glass with his forefinger as he stared at its amber contents. He pursed his lips and said, "I asked him what he was up to since the war ended, and he said he was doing more of the same." He looked up from his drink. "How often does he come to Martinique?"

The Comte considered. "Perhaps two or three times a year. He never stays more than a few days."

"And you have no evidence connecting him to anything? He's never brought a ship here to sell its cargo?"

Donzelot shook his head. "Never."

Brewer frowned. Could it be that Michael had been joking about the whole thing? He had been known to play practical jokes on the *Kent*... No, it just didn't fit. He never got the feeling that his friend was joking.

HMS *Revenge* left Martinique on the morning tide. Captain Brewer came up on deck and made his way to stand next to the premier and sailing master.

"Mr. Reed!" he called. "Take us out, if you please."

"Aye, sir!" The young gentleman's voice cracked slightly, ample evidence of how nervous he was to be observed by the captain and first lieutenant.

He turned forward and drew a deep breath. "Stand by the capstan! Loose the heads'ls! Hands aloft to loose tops'ls!"

The deck exploded with activity. Hands brought the bars to fit into the capstan, which they began to turn at the senior midshipman's command. The captain found himself impressed; Reed's commands were crisp and well timed, better than he had anticipated. When the anchor cleared, the ship slipped to stern. Reed ordered the wheel hard over and for hands to draw the heads'l sheets, and the ship came around nicely.

"Hands to braces!" Reed cried. The sails began to fill with the first gusts of wind. HMS *Revenge* slid forward and gained momentum. Brewer looked to Greene and nodded his approval.

"Well done, Mr. Reed," he said aloud for all to hear. "We'll make a lieutenant of you yet!"

Reed blushed. "Thank you, sir."

"Mr. Reed has the deck," the captain announced. "Mr. Greene and I will be in my cabin. Call me if I am needed."

"Aye, sir," Mr. Reed answered.

The first lieutenant followed his captain below. They ended up in the day cabin, where Brewer handed his hat, coat and sword to Mac, then called to Alfred for coffee. The two officers sat on the settee.

"Does anyone ever ask you about your choice of beverage, Captain?" Greene asked after Alfred brought the coffee.

"What do you mean?"

"Well, to be blunt, sir, we're British, and the British drink tea, not coffee. Yet in all the time I've known you, I think I can count on one hand the number of times I've seen you drink tea."

Brewer chuckled. "Well, I sailed the Caribbean as a young midshipman. I was introduced to coffee on my first or second voyage, and I fell in love with it. Once I found how plentiful it was in this part of the world, and how easily obtainable, I was glad every time I was sent to these waters."

Greene took a cautious sip of the steaming brew. "I was

just wondering, Captain. Now, what's on your mind, sir?"

The captain's cup stopped as it neared his mouth, and his eyes stared through the steam at his premier. He thought about denying it, but Greene knew him too well. He lowered the cup and smiled. "Is it that obvious?"

"Let's just say it is to me," Greene said. "I understand from the doctor you ran into an old friend on Martinique?"

Brewer nodded. "Michael Underhill. He was a petty officer on my first ship as midshipman." He paused for a drink. "He befriended me and made sure I knew learned what a good midshipman needed to know. Then he suddenly disappeared. The doctor and I ran into him and two of his men in a tavern just off the harbor. Didn't the doctor tell you about it?"

"Yes," Greene said, "but I wanted to hear what you would say about the meeting. Doctor Spinelli said this man was a privateer for the Americans during the late war." Brewer nodded, and Greene went on. "He also says he's still at it today."

Brewer drew a deep breath and stared at the deck beams above them, his lips pressed into a tight line. "That is the very question I've been wrestling with, Benjamin. This man was a second father to me when I needed one badly, and even though he deserted, even though he fought against the country of his birth and against his king, that bond is still there. I don't want to believe the worst about him, even if the evidence points that way."

Greene thought for a moment. "The doctor said he commanded a large sloop now?"

"That's what he said."

"There was only one ship of that description in the harbor, and we got a good look at her," Greene said. "Had *Oliver Cromwell* across the stern."

Brewer nodded. "That's his."

Greene grunted. "I counted ports cut for ten or twelve guns down the side. Probably about the equal of *Revenge* for firepower, although we didn't get a look at her cannons." He drained the dregs of his cup and set it on the table. "So, what are we going to do?"

The captain looked Green in the eyes. "I honestly don't know." He looked to the deck beams again and sighed. "If he's still fighting that war, if he's still taking his revenge against the Royal Navy, then he must be stopped." He swallowed hard and turned to his first. "I have to stop him."

Greene looked down at his hands, folded in his lap. "Why you, may I ask?"

Brewer drained his cup and rose to pace. "Because he's my friend. Because I never had the chance to thank him, to repay all the kindness and teachings he gave me on the *Kent*." Brewer stopped and turned to Greene. "Because maybe he'll listen to me, where any other captain would simply blow him out of the water." Brewer resumed his seat, elbows on his knees and his head buried in his hands. After a moment, he rubbed his face and sat up. "I have to know, Benjamin. I owe it to him to give him one more chance to... to..."

"Surrender?" Greene prompted.

"God, I hope not," Brewer said in a voice that was almost a whisper. "Michael would never surrender. He'd die first."

Greene pursed his lips as he considered the options. "So, what's our next step?"

Brewer shrugged. "I don't see any choice. I have to speak to the admiral as soon as we pull into Port Royal."

Greene stared at the deck before him, his eyes darting back and forth as ideas flashed through his mind. Finally, his eyes closed in defeat. "Agreed."

Brewer rose. "I want you to step up gun and sail drills for the crew. If we meet *Oliver Cromwell* on the open sea, it may well come to a fight."

"Aye, sir."

"Now, if you'll excuse me, I need to make sense of all this for my report to the admiral. I'd appreciate it if you and the doctor would join me for supper."

Greene grinned. "A pleasure, Captain." He picked up his hat, came to attention smartly, and departed.

Brewer made his way to his desk and took out his cross of the *Légion d'Honneur*. He held the piece, wondering what it's previous owner would do. He shook his head; Corsicans had strange rules regarding family — real or imagined – so he wasn't sure they applied here. He put the cross away and sighed. He had the dread feeling that this was about to get very messy.

The dinner turned out to be a less than stellar affair. The captain spent much of it staring at his plate, leaving Mr. Greene and the doctor to carry the dinner conversation. The two men exchanged a concerned glance that went unnoticed by their captain. In fact, Brewer did not stir until Alfred came in to clear the dishes.

"A wonderful meal, Alfred!" Greene said heartily. "Don't you agree, Captain?"

The captain looked up suddenly, startled at hearing his name. "What? Oh, yes, of course. Excellent as always, Alfred."

"Thank you, gentlemen," the servant replied. He threw a concerned look to his captain's guests before he gathered the dishes and left the room.

Greene rose. "If you'll excuse me, sir, I'm needed on deck."

"What? Yes, of course, Benjamin. Thank you for coming."

The captain's head went back down, and his eyes

dropped his hands folded on the table. Greene nodded to the doctor and made his way out.

Doctor Spinelli sat there still, his captain completely oblivious to his presence. After a couple minutes, he rose and stepped over to the pantry door and asked Alfred for two glasses of Madeira, then he went to the captain's desk and retrieved the chess set. He brought it to the table and dropped it on the table inches from the captain's hands. Brewer jumped and looked up.

"Adam! What do you think you're doing?"

"So!" the doctor said in mock surprise. "You are alive! I was about to examine you to see if you were comatose or dead." He sat and began setting up the pieces. Brewer straightened up and rubbed the back of his neck. Alfred brought the wine, and Brewer patted him on the arm. After the servant departed, the captain leaned forward with one elbow on the table.

"I guess I'm not very good at hiding what I'm thinking, am I?"

Spinelli grunted. "No, Captain mine, I would not list that as one of your strengths." He held out two fists, and Brewer chose the right. The doctor opened it to reveal a white pawn. Brewer replaced the piece and made his move. The doctor countered by bringing out his king's knight. "This business with your friend has really upset you, hasn't it?"

Brewer didn't look up from the game. "It's that obvious, is it?" He moved his queen's pawn forward two squares. "I suppose there's no denying it. All those years ago, I never knew what happened. Now I wish I still didn't."

The doctor moved a pawn. "There was nothing you could have done to help him, William."

Brewer castled to his king's side. "I know. I just wish he hadn't run." Brewer looked up and caught his friend's eye. "I am only saying this to you, because you were there."

"Understood." The doctor's eyes flashed to the pantry door. "Alfred?"

Brewer shook his head and moved his rook. "Discretion personified. Anyway, I guess you can tell it's tearing me up inside. I want to turn my back and forget the whole thing, but I can't."

The doctor nodded as he took a pawn with his bishop. "I know."

The captain frowned and moved a knight. "As much as I don't like what he did during the war, I can tell myself that it is over and done, and it was done according to the rules of war. But I can't ignore what he's doing now — if indeed he still is. It's piracy, Adam."

"I know." The doctor castled. "I presume you want to go after him yourself?"

Brewer nodded. "That's what I intend to ask the admiral. My hope is that Michael will talk to me, that he'll listen to me and give it up."

Spinelli looked at him in disbelief. "Are you serious, William? Everything I observed, both of your friend and his men, *nothing* led me to believe they would surrender! He is bent on revenge, and that's an appetite that is rarely satisfied."

Brewer shook his head, a sort of I-don't-know movement. "I know what you say is true, Adam, but if *I* track him down, at least he'll get a chance to see that nobody dies. Anyone else who finds him would simply blow him out of the water, no questions asked."

The doctor had to grant his captain's point. Knowing Brewer as he did, he knew that his captain would give Underhill every chance to do the right thing, but he also knew that William Brewer would do his duty, even with tears in his eyes. "Do you know what you're going to tell the admiral? Or should I say *how* you're going to tell him?"

Brewer looked up briefly. "Not yet."

In the captain's cabin on the sloop *Oliver Cromwell*, Michael Underhill sat at his table and stared at a dagger. His meeting with William Brewer at Martinique bothered him more than he cared to admit. The dagger had been a present from Brewer. He'd dug it out from the bottom of his sea chest — yes, he still carried his old sea chest around after all these years — and laid it on the table, as though staring at it would help him see into the younger man's mind. Unfortunately, his efforts had so far proved unsuccessful. With a grunt of disappointment, Michael wrapped the dagger back up in its protective cloth and sat back.

He closed his eyes and tried to silence the voices in his head. Running into his old friend so unexpectedly had dredged up many old memories — memories he wished had never seen the light of day. He wasn't particularly proud of what he had done back then, but leaving Brewer the way he did had always hurt the worst. The boy was like a son to him, and he deserved better.

Underhill frowned. He'd wanted to take the boy with him, but Britain had been at war, and there was only one punishment for desertion during wartime, and that was an early morning date with the hangman. He shook his head at the thought; there was no way he would risk the boy's life.

His frown turned into a scowl as he surrendered to the bitterness rising in his soul. He had been forced to leave Brewer behind, just like he had been forced to leave the Royal Navy. He bolted from his chair and began to pace, his head down and his left hand behind his back as he gestured wildly with his right. *Forced*, that was the only word for it. He would never have deserted of his own accord. He'd loved the navy, and he'd looked forward to serving under Brewer as the midshipman advanced and eventually got his own ship.

Then that blasted lieutenant took it all from him, him and his cowardly cur of a captain. *Nothing personal,* he'd said. *Just following orders,* he'd said. *Sure you were,* he spat out bitterly. *Seven years of exemplary service should have bought more loyalty, even if I was only a petty officer.*

Leaving the navy was the hardest thing he'd ever done. He'd realized almost at once that he could not remain in England. The navy had rejected him, and to his mind nation and service were synonymous. He'd secured his newfound freedom by purchasing forged discharge documents and boarded the first ship bound for America. He wanted to find work doing what he knew, but he also knew he had to stay off the high seas due to the British habit of stopping American ships and impressing seamen — especially ones they suspected of being British. He'd found work on a coastal schooner and settled down into a new life.

He'd almost forgotten his bitterness until his past came roaring back to overwhelm his present. America had finally had enough of being bullied by the British and declared war in 1812. Underhill outfitted a small brig as a privateer, purchased a letter of marque from the American government, and went to war against his hated enemy. He and his crew became rich from prize money during that war, but it was just as the war ended that he realized the true instrument of revenge he had in his possession.

This was one memory that brought a smile to his lips. He for one hadn't been pleased that the war was ending. He considered his revenge incomplete; Britain still had many ships that he could plunder. It was only his right, after all — he would have made all this and more besides if he had been allowed to remain in the Royal Navy. He remembered sitting in this very cabin reading his letter of marque and contemplating his future when his eyes lit on the last line of the letter: *"This commission to remain in force during the pleasure of the President of the United States for the time being."* His letter gave him the authority to continue until the President himself sent word that it was no longer in effect!

He had called Chauncey, his first mate, to the cabin and showed the terms to him, and the first mate had agreed that was what it said. "But with the war over," he asked, "will the United States still buy our prizes?"

That made Underhill stop and think. Even though he still had the letter, would they still be able to do business? Surely the ships and cargo would be easily recognizable as English, so it was probable that neither the French or the Spanish would touch them. That left only one place that was both lawless enough and rich enough to fulfill his needs — New Orleans. And so it proved; he sold prize ships there and made enough money to keep his crew happy. Although he had recently begun to hear rumors that the United States was going to pacify New Orleans and turn it into a major port for the government. *Ah, well,* he shrugged, *perhaps I can sell ships in one of the South American ports.*

Underhill blinked away the memories and tried to focus on reality. He stopped his pacing and took several deep breaths. He had a gnawing suspicion that Brewer was on to him. He realized now his mistake in answering Brewer's question about what he was doing now; he should have played it off by telling him he was working for an exporter trading here in the Caribbean. Underhill knew that even that lie might not work if Brewer or one of his officers got a good look at *Cromwell* and counted the gunports.

He took a final deep breath and let it out slowly. He would simply have to hope that Brewer would leave him alone and go about his business. He couldn't see that happening, not if Brewer has suspicions, but he would hope nonetheless. His eyes went to the deck above as he heard a call coming from the lookouts about a strange sail on the horizon. He picked up his hat. He took one last look at the dagger as he headed for the door.

CHAPTER THREE

Captain Brewer walked slowly from the wharf toward the admiral's office. If he was totally honest with himself, he would admit part of him wanted to turn around and take *Revenge* back to sea. But duty ruled today.

He knocked on the door, and the admiral's steward let him in. Brewer gave him his hat, and the steward led him down the hall to the study. He knocked three times and opened the door. He stepped in and announced Captain Brewer. Brewer marched in to the office and stood at attention while he awaited his admiral's attention.

Three feet in front of him, Admiral Lord Hornblower was seated at his desk, signing his name to a report. He set the quill down and stood. "William!" he exclaimed as he came around the desk to shake hands. "To what do I owe the pleasure?"

Brewer followed his mentor to his favorite chairs before a window with a view of the harbor. Each man sat, and Hornblower signaled for refreshments to be brought. "I trust all is well with the ship?"

"Yes, My Lord," Brewer replied. "We had some damage from a storm, but we made Martinique in order to make repairs. It's that visit that brings me to you."

Hornblower waited while the steward brought each man a glass of brandy. When the man departed, the admiral looked to his guest and motioned for him to continue.

"My Lord," the captain said, "a question if I may, before I start. Since the war ended with the Americans, have many British ships gone missing?"

"A strange question," the admiral replied. "If memory serves, something on the order of five to eight British merchant ships per year have fallen victim to piracy."

"And have you any idea about the totals for French or Spanish shipping?"

Hornblower's eyes narrowed as he wondered about the reasons for his protégé's questions, but he trusted Brewer enough to know he had a reason. "To my knowledge, their losses are only a fraction of ours."

Brewer gazed out the window, his face a hardened mask and his lips pressed into a firm, thin line. He blinked and turned back to his host.

"I don't believe the losses are due to piracy, My Lord," he said, "at least, not what we normally consider piracy. While at Martinique, I met an old acquaintance, Michael Underhill. He was a petty officer on HMS *Kent* when I was a raw midshipman, and it was he who taught me how to be a naval officer. I think he had the makings of a fine officer himself. Then one day he simply disappeared."

"Deserted?" the admiral asked.

Brewer shrugged. "I never knew. The first lieutenant let it be known discreetly that the subject was not to be brought up, and we never did." He looked out the window and sighed before continuing. He chose his words very carefully. "Over drinks he told me that he left the Royal Navy after being informed that he would never be allowed to advance beyond his present rank, that something in his past counted against him. In any case, he said he left the navy and the country and made his way to America. There he made a new life for himself. Then he said that when war came in 1812, he outfitted a privateer and purchased a letter of marque from the American government."

The scowl on his mentor's face told Brewer exactly what Hornblower thought about that. He took a deep breath and forged on. "He claimed to have enjoyed a successful wartime career, and this was more or less corroborated by the French governor when I interviewed him before we left."

Now it was Hornblower's turn to turn to the windows while he thought. Brewer saw him frown twice before he turned back to the room. "And so?" he demanded.

"My Lord," Brewer said, "I believe that Underhill did not cease his privateering activities with the end of the war in 1814."

The admiral stared at his guest from hooded eyes, his face a mask of stone and his lips pressed into a thin line. After a moment, he rose and began to pace back and forth before the empty hearth. Brewer was familiar enough with his chief's habits to know that he should remain seated and quiet while Hornblower thought through what he had heard. Back and forth the admiral paced, seven steps, turn, seven steps, turn, as if he were on the deck of his ship again. He head was down, chin to his chest, eyes on the floor one step ahead of him. Not for the first time, Brewer wished there was a way to hear what was going on inside his head during times like these.

Finally, the admiral stopped pacing at the far end of his run. He straightened up and stretched his back before returning to his seat. After reaching for his glass and taking a long drink, he set the glass on the table and studied his guest.

"I can't say I'm surprised by what you say, William," he said. "I've heard speculations and rumors, but we never had any proof that privateers were still active. Are you sure?"

Brewer shrugged. "My Lord, I must admit I have no proof, other than when I asked him what he was doing now, he said he was doing the same old thing."

Hornblower grimaced. "That's thin."

"I agree, My Lord, and I almost didn't bring this to you." Brewer stopped. He had done his duty; if he let the matter stand as it was, the admiral could dismiss this as yet another unsubstantiated rumor. And yet.... "I have nothing to offer as solid proof, but every instinct tells me he is a pirate. I discovered quickly that I could still read him, just as I used to do. He's guilty, My Lord; I'd stake my reputation on it."

"We may both be staking our reputations on it, Commander," the admiral said coldly. He took another drink from his glass and let out a long, slow breath. "William, I've known you long enough to believe two things. One, if you are convinced of something, it's at least worth looking into. And two, if you bring something to me, you already have a plan you wish to suggest. What is it?"

Brewer smiled. "I want to be relieved of escort duty to go after him, My Lord. I think there's a chance Michael may listen to me, and if he does I may be able to talk him into surrendering, or at least some form of truce that will avoid bloodshed."

Hornblower looked dubious. "William, I realize that this man was a friend of yours, even a mentor; but if you're right, his activities since the end of the war have branded him a pirate at best and a traitor at worst, both of which are crimes punishable by hanging. What makes you think Underhill will listen to you?"

"I don't know, My Lord," Brewer replied, a note of despair in his voice. "Something else occurred to me, My Lord; will the Americans protect him, seeing as how he's operating under their letter of marque?"

The admiral considered for a moment. "I don't think so. We're not talking about actions that happened during time of war; our only concern is for ships that were taken after the treaty was signed and the war was over." Hornblower picked up a bell on the table and rang for more refreshments. "I don't know if you've heard or not, William, but there are rumors that the American president, Mr. Monroe, will soon issue a document declaring the entire western hemisphere to be under American protection from European political interference."

"Can they do that?" Brewer exclaimed. When the admiral raised an eyebrow, he hurried on, "What I mean to say, My Lord, is, do they have the capability to enforce a decree like that?"

"Well," Hornblower mused aloud, "I think we can say the Americans are in a position now where they can deal with any French or Spanish objections to such a decree, especially in the Caribbean. As for ourselves, I don't think the king would mind terribly if the Americans took over the job of policing this hemisphere. Parliament's main concern is that our trade routes and treaties are upheld, and the Americans would honor these."

"As you say, My Lord," Brewer commented. He had his doubts of the Americans' ability, not to mention their intensions, when it came to the protection of British trade in the western hemisphere. "In any case, My Lord, may I pursue Underhill?"

Admiral Hornblower did not give his consent immediately. In fact, he said nothing at all, choosing instead pick up his glass and study its contents. Brewer opened his mouth to repeat his request, but he wisely decided to close it again without uttering a sound. Better to wait for his master to speak.

"William," the admiral said, "even if I believe your assertions — and I'm not saying I don't — we need proof of some kind or other before we go off and charge a British national with what amounts to piracy. We need more information, chief of which is whether or not the Americans will protect

Underhill on the basis of the letter of marque. I'm almost positive they won't, given the time involved, but we must make sure." Hornblower looked out the window as he rubbed his chin between a thumb and forefinger. Soon he turned back to Brewer and said, "We need an answer from the Americans on this. William, I'm sending you to Washington City. I have seen two or three of the American letters of marque, and if I remember correctly, they were signed by their Secretary of State. I want you to go and speak to this secretary or their naval department. Find out if the Americans will protect Underhill or offer him asylum should he ask for it. Is *Revenge* ready for sea?"

"More or less, My Lord. We made sufficient repairs in Martinique to make her sea-worthy if not quite battle-worthy."

Hornblower tapped the side of his leg with one long finger. "How long to finish the job?"

Now it was Brewer's turn to look out the window while he ran down the lists in his head. He turned back and said, "Three days, My Lord. Four at most."

"Done." The admiral rose. "Go to sea as soon as your repairs are completed. Your orders will be delivered to you on board tomorrow. Go to Washington City and speak to the American government. What are you grinning at, young sir?!"

"Apologies, My Lord," Brewer said, trying his best to put on a straight face. "I was just relishing the idea of going to Washington City in December."

"As well you should, William," the admiral agreed. He patted his protégé on the arm. "Take your cloak, there's a good man."

Brewer went back to his ship and asked Lieutenants Greene and Tyler, Mr. Sweeney, and the doctor to join him in his cabin. Alfred served the refreshments in the day cabin and went to stand at the pantry door. Mac was in his usual place just inside the cabin door.

Small talk drifted through the cabin, and Brewer could tell it was forced. He smiled; they all wanted to know what had happened during his meeting with the admiral. He called the meeting to order by rapping on the table with the bottom of his glass.

"I'm sure you all want to know what the admiral said today," he said, "but before I tell you that, it is necessary for me to tell you of a meeting the doctor and I had on the island of Martinique." He about meeting Underhill in the tavern, including what Underhill meant to him and why. He also told them of his suspicions regarding his friend's activities since the end of the second American war and his decision to inform Admiral Hornblower. He ended his tale with the admiral's decision to send them to Washington City to sound out their government's position on Underhill and any others like him.

"Any questions?" he asked, looking around the room.

Mr. Sweeney shivered. "I for one do not look forward to the Virginia seaways in December. Colder than a witch's elbow!"

That drew a breath of laughter. The captain spoke up. "Nor I, Mr. Sweeney; still, it could be worse." The look on the sailing master's face told his captain what he thought of the veracity of that statement. "Anyway, we've got three days for sure, four in a pinch, so I suggest we make good use of them. Mr. Greene, get with the bosun and the carpenter. I want this ship as battle-ready as we can make her in the time allotted. Mr. Tyler, get with the gunner and make sure we are ready. If we do manage to catch *Cromwell* on the high seas, I want to be able to fight."

"Aye, sir," the two lieutenants said.

"Mr. Tyler, see that you check with the purser as well," Brewer added. "He should have time to go ashore and lay in store whatever we'll need. See that Alfred and Old Smoot get a chance to go ashore if they wish." Old Smoot was the gun-room steward and known to be almost as good in the kitchen as Alfred.

"Aye, sir," Tyler said with a grin. "I'm sure they'll want to take advantage of the chance to do some shopping ashore."

"I'm sure," the captain added. "Any other questions? In that case, thank you, gentlemen."

Greene rose and the rest followed suit. They came to attention and filed out of the cabin. Brewer noticed that his two lieutenants already had their heads together, making plans to best use the time given them. He turned to see the doctor still in his seat, and somehow he wasn't surprised.

"Something I can do for you, Adam?"

Spinelli shook his head. "No, sir, I was just wondering how you're doing these days."

"You mean, do I feel as though I've betrayed an old friend based on a hunch?" The doctor remained silent, and Brewer grunted. "Part of me does, as a matter of fact, but not the part that matters. Not the part that does its duty." The captain leaned forward, put his elbows on his knees, and leaned forward, staring at his hands. "I don't like what I have to do, Adam, but I can't ignore it. I can't shirk my duty. If Michael is still raiding British shipping, he's got to be stopped."

"And you have to be the one to stop him?" The doctor raised an eyebrow when he saw the captain wince at the question.

Brewer nodded, not taking his eyes off his hands. "Yes."

The doctor pursed his lips for a second before picking up his glass and tossing the remainder down his throat. He stood and said, "In that case, Captain, I'm with you. Goodnight, William."

"Goodnight, Adam."

For the next two days, HMS *Revenge* was a beehive of activity. Every inch of the rigging was gone over again, along with the tackling, until Mr. Snead was satisfied. Spare cordage and yardarms were laid in store. Lieutenant Tyler and Mr. Reed assisted the purser, Mr. Allen, in inspecting and rotating the foodstuffs. Afterwards, Tyler was pleased to report to the captain that Mr. Allen's records were up-to-date and accurate. Alfred and Old Smoot were rowed ashore. Brewer was sure each had a list, but he wouldn't want to wager who had more money to spend!

It was just as the ship's bell rang eight times to announce high noon that a knock sounded at the captain's door, and the sentry admitted Mr. Short. The midshipman marched into the cabin and came to attention. "Mr. Abbott sends his respects, sir, and says to tell you there's a boat approaching."

Brewer rose. "My compliments to Mr. Abbott. I shall come at once."

"Thank you, sir!" The midshipman came to attention again and scurried from the cabin. Brewer smiled and followed.

He stepped out on deck to find Mr. Greene already present on the quarterdeck with a glass to his eye. He touched his hat and handed the glass over at his captain's approach.

"I believe that to be the admiral's barge, Captain," he said, "but I don't see the admiral."

"No," Brewer said as he scanned the boat. "The admiral's not there, but his aide is. Pass the word for the doctor, if you please!"

Lieutenant Greene was confused by the request, but he turned and gave the order.

"Lieutenant Gerard was first lieutenant under Captain Bush on the old *Lydia*. We took a cruise on her in the Med and fought the Barbary pirates before I joined HMS *Defiant*. Gerard was badly wounded, and Dr. Spinelli was the surgeon at Gibraltar who treated him."

"Ah," Greene said.

"You sent for me, Captain?" Spinelli said as he came up on deck.

"Yes, Doctor. It seems we have an old friend of yours about to board."

Spinelli took his place behind Brewer and Greene near the entry port. The admiral's barge arrived, and an officer stepped up on deck. He stood ramrod straight and saluted. Brewer returned the gesture and came forward with his hand extended.

"Gerard! Wonderful to see you again!"

"Captain, it's my pleasure!" Gerard shook his friend's hand warmly.

"Allow me to present my first, Mr. Greene, and you remember Dr. Spinelli, of course."

"Indeed I do! Good to meet you, Mr. Greene. Your captain has bragged about you to the admiral. Doctor! Good to see you!" The two shook hands warmly.

"What can I do for you, Gerard?" Brewer asked.

"I came to deliver this." He handed the captain a message. Brewer saw it was sealed with wax and the admiral's seal.

"I see," Brewer said. "Let's go down to my cabin to open this."

"You may do so here, Captain," Gerard said. "It's nothing serious, I assure you. Pardon me while I speak to the doctor." Gerard took the doctor by the arm and stepped across the deck.

Brewer broke the seal and unfolded the paper. He read it twice and smiled.

"What is it, sir?" Greene asked.

"Well," Brewer said, handing the note to his premier, "it seems you and I have been invited to dine with the admiral tonight."

Brewer and Greene stood before the great hearth in the admiral's formal dining room, drinks in their hands as they watched the admiral across the room. He was in conversation with a small group of men and women in evening dress. Brewer frowned slightly at the thought that the evening dress worn by the admiral's other guests made the dress uniforms worn by Greene and himself look like a pauper's Sunday-go-to-meetings. The captain watched the other people in the room; there were about fifteen altogether, but Brewer knew only Hornblower.

"Sir?" Greene whispered in his ear.

Brewer saw the admiral excuse himself and head their way with another man in tow. The two officers came to attention (as best they could with drinks in their hands) at their admiral's approach.

"Gentlemen," Hornblower said, "may I introduce to you Lord Montagu, 5th Duke of Manchester and Governor of Jamaica." He turned to the duke. "Your Grace, may I introduce Commander William Brewer, captain of His Majesty's sloop-of-war *Revenge*, and his first lieutenant, Benjamin Greene."

The two officers bowed, and the duke nodded. "A pleasure, gentlemen," he said.

Hornblower addressed his officers. "Gentlemen, after we dine, I would like to invite you both to meet with the duke and myself in my study."

"An honor, Admiral," Brewer said.

"Good," Hornblower said. "Until then? Your Grace?" The two men went to mingle with the admiral's other guests.

"What was that about?" Greene asked softly.

"We shall soon see," Brewer replied, "but offhand, I'd say our mission has attracted some very important eyes."

The meal was a formal affair. Brewer found himself seated three seats down on the admiral's left with a plantation owner on his right and a pleasant, plain-looking woman on his left. The duke was seated at the admiral's right hand and seemed to dominate Hornblower's conversation. Lieutenant Greene was on the opposite side from Brewer in the next-to-last seat. Brewer smiled as his premier tried his best to make small talk with total strangers. The food was exquisite, but he wondered what Alfred could do with a kitchen like the admiral's.

Brewer struck up a conversation with the gentleman to his right, a man named Whipley who owned a sugar plantation.

"I say, Commander," the man said suddenly, "could you do me a favor? Could you speak to the admiral about the piracy in the area? Why, just last month I had an entire cargo stolen by the devils, brig and all!"

"Really?" Brewer replied, wondering if Hornblower had known this and arranged the seating accordingly. "If I may ask, what happened to the crew?"

"That was the oddest part! Cast adrift in a boat, if you will believe it! Complete with food, water, oars and a compass. The pirate also provided them with a heading for the nearest port."

The man now had Brewer's full attention. "May I ask, what was the nearest port? Where did he send them?"

"Eh? Oh, Martinique."

"I see." Brewer paused to take bite of the excellent pheasant. "Did the pirate identify himself in any way?"

Whipley took a bite of the oxtail and chewed while he thought. "No, I don't believe he did. Why do you ask?"

The commander shrugged. "It always helps if we know who we're dealing with. It may even help us to anticipate where he might strike next."

"Ah!" Whipley said with a swallow. "Well, I can make the master available to you, if you wish."

"He's in port?" Brewer couldn't believe his luck.

"Yes. He's due to sail next week. Would you like to meet him? Shall we say ten tomorrow morning? My house is called Canna. I shall send a carriage for you at the dock offices."

"Thank you, Mr. Whipley," Brewer said. "I look forward to it."

When the meal was over and the guests adjourned to the billiard room for drinks and cigars, four men quietly stole away and met in the admiral's study. A steward was present with four drinks and a box of cigars; each man helped himself. Brewer noted that Hornblower had the furniture rearranged so that a couch was now placed opposite the two overstuffed chairs in the center of the room, and there was a low table in between. Hornblower and the duke led the way and sat in the two chairs, leaving Brewer and Greene to take up their places on the couch.

To Brewer's surprise, it was the duke who took the lead. "Commander, I asked Admiral Hornblower to arrange this meeting after he told me certain details of your last meeting together."

Brewer leaned forward. "How may I help Your Grace?"

"The admiral here says you believe you know who is behind the disappearance of so many British ships in recent years?"

"Yes, Your Grace," the commander acknowledged. "Well,

many of them, at any rate."

"A British ex-patriot by the name of Michael Underhill," the duke continued.

"Yes, Your Grace."

Manchester looked to the admiral. "And you believe him?"

Hornblower held the duke's eye. "If Commander Brewer says so, that's enough for me to look into it."

The duke nodded. "Very well. Commander, my interest in this is diplomatic. I don't know if you are aware, but British ships aren't the only ones that have gone missing. We have reports of French and Spanish ships being raided as well. If it turns out that Underhill is responsible for any of those, then we may have a diplomatic disaster on our hands. I sincerely doubt whether the French or Spanish governments will care that Underhill was carrying out a vendetta against His Majesty's government — or at least his Admiralty — under cover of an American letter of marque." Manchester paused for a deep breath and a drink. "Lord Hornblower says you will leave soon for Washington City to confer with elements of the American government regarding Underhill."

"That is correct, Your Grace," Brewer said. "We sail the day after tomorrow."

The duke addressed the admiral. "When he returns, I need a report on the diplomatic aspects of this. Attach your views to it and forward it to me."

"Yes, Your Grace," Hornblower replied.

Manchester rose. "Well then, God be with you, Commander. Lieutenant, a pleasure to meet you. Admiral, thank you for a fine evening. I bid you all a good night."

The officers bowed. "Good night, Your Grace," Hornblower said.

"Come with me," Hornblower said after the duke had

departed. Brewer and Greene followed the admiral back to his library. The admiral closed the door behind them and poured each of them a drink. The admiral sat in an over-stuffed chair, while Brewer and Greene took the couch opposite. Hornblower sipped his drink and stared off into the distance. Brewer nursed his and waited for his chief to speak.

"William," he said, "the duke's business is secondary. I doubt whether you will be able to tell very much about how this will play diplomatically from your visit to Washington City. While you are gone, I shall try to gather more information from other sources. Your primary mission is still to feel out the Americans as to where they will stand when we take Underhill."

"Understood, My Lord."

Hornblower set his glass down and sat back. He rested his elbows on the arms and steepled his forefingers. "You sail the day after tomorrow?"

Brewer looked to Greene, who set his own drink on the table.

"Yes, My Lord," the premier said. "We need the day to finish provisioning, and the lighter is scheduled for the afternoon. If you would like, we can be ready by nightfall."

Hornblower considered for a moment before shaking his head. "No, the morning will be fine."

"My Lord," Brewer said, "during dinner I struck up a conversation with a Mr. Whipley. He's the owner of a brig that was commandeered recently, cargo and all."

"I remember that," Hornblower said. "The crew was put adrift."

"Correct, My Lord. I have an appointment tomorrow morning to speak with the brig's master."

Hornblower looked intrigued. "You hope the man will point you toward Underhill as the thief?"

Brewer My Lordmet his mentor's eyes. "We shall see, My Lord."

The admiral's eyes narrowed. He made to speak but didn't; in the end he rubbed his chin with the back of his fingers while he thought. "Very well. The day after tomorrow is fine for you to sail. Stop by tomorrow after you meet with the brig's master and let me know what was said." He rose. "Now, I believe we need to rejoin the party."

The three men made their way back to the billiard room. Brewer noticed that Whipley was no longer here, so he and Greene got themselves drinks and mingled.

The next morning, Brewer stepped from his gig up onto the wharf at precisely ten o'clock. The sun was rising, and it promised to be a warm day despite being nearly December. He made his way to the dock office, where he found a carriage waiting. The footman stepped down.

"Commander Brewer?" he asked. He opened the carriage door. "Right this way, sir. Mr. Whipley is waiting."

Brewer stepped up, and the footman closed the door behind him. He slid back into the seat as the carriage took off down the road. They made their way through the town and into the countryside. Brewer enjoyed the view so much he lost all track of time. Then his ride came to an end and the footman was at the door.

The commander stepped down and stood before a manor house, an estate larger than any he had seen in the Caribbean or in his native Kent. He looked over his shoulder to watch the carriage roll away, then he made his way up the front stairs. He knocked on the door, which was opened by a manservant who stood back to allow him to enter. At the other end of the foyer stood Mr. Whipley.

"Commander," he said, "So good to see you. Follow me, please." Brewer followed his host down a long hallway that terminated at an outdoor patio. A table stood off to the left, right where it caught the morning sunlight. Seated at the table, a steaming cup before him, was a short, stocky man with an old fashioned tricornered hat. He rose to his feet when he heard the two men approach, and bowed to Whipley.

Whipley made the introductions. "Peter Burke, may I present Commander William Brewer, of the Royal Navy. He has questions about the *Mary Alice*. Gentlemen, let us sit."

The three men sat, and house servants brought fresh cups of steaming hot tea to all. Once they had withdrawn into the house, Whipley nodded to Brewer.

"Mr. Burke," Brewer said, "thank you for seeing me. I am investigating incidents of piracy against British shipping. I met Mr. Whipley last night while dining at the admiral's house, and he told me what happened to the... *Mary Alice*, was it?" Brewer looked to Whipley, and his host nodded once. "The *Mary Alice*, and I asked him to arrange this interview. Exactly where was your ship when she was attacked?"

"Approximately two days' travel west of Martinique," Burke replied. "Our course was for Port Royal."

"Thank you. Please tell me what happened."

Burke shifted in his seat and took a drink of his coffee. "We were five days out of Barbados. It was about six bells of the forenoon watch when we sighted a strange sail to the sou'west. I immediately ordered every stitch the old girl would carry. The *Mary Alice's* always been a fine sailer, very swift in the right winds, and I thought we'd have no trouble in leaving this stranger behind." He grunted and drained his cup. "I was wrong. I've never seen so swift a craft as this one. She was in range to open fire on us within six or seven hours." He shook his head in disbelief, even now.

"Describe the ship, please," Brewer said.

Burke looked to the bright sky. Brewer could see his jaw working back and forth as he searched his memory. "She was a sloop, I'd say, but a huge one, make no mistake. Her lines were as clean as I've ever seen outside a rich man's yacht. Holed for maybe six or seven guns to the side, plus the bow chasers."

Brewer's brow went up. Burke was obviously a man who noticed details. "They put a shot off your bow, I take it?"

"Aye. We hove to, of course; what else could I do? They had us for sure."

"A wise move on your part, I assure you," Brewer said. "So, you were boarded?"

Burke nodded. "Two boats, maybe twenty men in all. One man of them stepped forward and started giving orders. Said if we cooperated, nobody would get hurt. He sent men below to search the hold and get the manifests from my cabin. When they came back and showed him what they found, he looked from his mate to me and back again, then he stepped away to the rail and stood alone for a time. I guess he was thinking about what he was going to do."

"Did you notice anything about him?" Brewer asked. "Can you describe him?"

"Well, he was taller than I am, but not as tall as you, Commander. Stand up, please." Brewer did as requested. Burke stood as well. "I guess he might come up to your shoulder, maybe a tad taller." Both men sat, and the master continued. "Grizzled face, blonde hair — what I could see of it. Oh, one other thing, he had a strange kind of hat."

"Hat?"

"Aye, like the one Boney wears in the pictures I seen."

"I see. Tell me, did he have a scar on his face?" Brewer a finger across his cheek.

Burke thought for a moment and shook his head. "No, Commander. I didn't see no scar."

Brewer nodded. Underhill had no scar. "Please

continue."

"The leader came back to us and told his men to provision two of the ship's boats with food, water, and a compass. *I'm taking your ship,*' he says, *'Your crew can take to the boats. A course of due east should bring you to Martinique in a few days.*' Then he turned and walked away. Never said another word to any of us. We were put over the side and into the boats, and his men took the *Mary Alice* and sailed off."

"What direction?" Brewer asked.

"That's the strange thing," Burke said. "*Mary Alice* went NNE, but the pirate ship went north."

Brewer made some notes and rose. "Thank you, Mr. Burke. You've been most helpful."

The two men shook hands. "I hope you catch them," Burke said.

"We will. Mr. Whipley, I thank you. Good bye."

Brewer made his way out and found the carriage awaiting him at the bottom of the stair.

"Where to, sir?" the footman asked as Brewer boarded.

"Admiral Hornblower's residence, if you please."

"Aye, sir."

The ride back into town passed quietly. Brewer had too much on his mind to enjoy the scenery this time. He was jolted from his reverie when the footman opened the door. Brewer dismounted.

"Will there be anything else, Commander?"

Brewer shook his head. "No, thank you."

"Very good sir. Good day." The footman stepped up on the rear of the carriage, and the driver whipped up the horses. Brewer turned to the house and made his way up the steps. He knocked and was admitted by the admiral's steward.

"If you please, Commander," the steward said, "the admiral is in a meeting but should be finished soon. Perhaps you'd like to wait in the library?"

"That will be fine."

The servant escorted him into the library, closing the door when he left. Brewer toured the room, reading titles and occasionally taking a book down from a shelf to read a few pages before replacing it. He'd made two full circuits before he heard a hand on the door. He was surprised to find it was not his host who opened the door, but his aide.

"Gerard!"

"Commander!" Gerard exclaimed. The two shook hands warmly. "Good to see you! The admiral begs your indulgence and says he won't be much longer. Did you discover anything in your interview with the brig's master?"

Brewer's eyes narrowed a bit, but he remonstrated with himself; of course Gerard knew of his appointment. "Nothing much," he said. "Did you know Underhill?"

"No, I did not," Gerard replied.

"The ship the master described was very close to Underhill's ship that we saw at Martinique, and his description of the pirate leader who boarded his ship could have been Underhill."

"I see," Gerard said. "Have you written a report?"

"No, I came straight here from the interview."

Gerard led Brewer to a desk by the window. "Please take a seat and write it out now." Brewer shot a questioning look at him, but Gerard just shrugged. "The admiral's request."

"Ah." Brewer seated himself, took a page from the pile and uncapped the ink well. He dipped a quill and began to write. Gerard took a book from the shelf and sat in a chair. He did not move from there until he saw Brewer sign his name to the bottom of the report, set the quill down and close the ink well. The commander handed him the pages , and Gerard glanced at them to ensure all was well.

"The admiral will see you now, Commander."

Brewer stared as his friend calmly turned and left the room. It took a moment for Brewer to come to his senses and follow.

"Gerard," he said quietly when he caught up, "do you mean to tell me that we have been waiting for me to finish my report? Why didn't you just say so?"

The aide smiled apologetically. "Sorry, Commander. Admiral Hornblower's orders. I'm afraid you'll have to take that up with him."

They found the admiral seated behind his desk, writing. Gerard announced Brewer and left the room. Brewer waited silently until his mentor set his pen down and looked up.

"Thank you for coming, William," he said. "Please, sit. I imagine you are wondering about Gerard's behavior. Yes, I thought you might. He was following my orders, which were to observe you while you were writing your report. I had to be sure that you would not be swayed by having to go after your old friend."

Brewer's control slipped only to the extent of an eyebrow rising a fraction, but inside he was outraged. "And?"

Hornblower sat back and smiled. "All is well. By Gerard leaving the room as he did, I know he saw nothing to cause him any concern. Forgive me, but I had to be sure, and now I am. Do you have anything you wish to say to me before we proceed?"

Brewer looked down at his hands in his lap, his lips pressed into a hard line while he buried his outrage. He looked back to his mentor. "No, sir."

Hornblower nearly said something, but he decided to let the moment pass. "Very well. Tell me about your interview with the brig's master."

The admiral listened as his protégé took the next hour to recount the details of the interview, interrupting twice to ask a question. When Brewer was finished, the admiral rose and stepped over to a table in the back corner of his office and returned with two cigars. He handed one to his guest.

"So," he said as he puffed his cigar to life, "this Burke seems an observant fellow, wouldn't you agree?"

Brewer shifted uncomfortably. "He seems so, My Lord."

Hornblower blew a cloud of smoke toward the ceiling. "And it seems like the man and the ship he described would be Underhill and his sloop."

"I believe so, My Lord."

"Why?"

Brewer took a long drag on his cigar and blew the smoke heavenward before answering. "First, the ship sounds exactly like the one we observed in the harbor at Martinique, but the ace in my hand was the hat."

"Hat?" Hornblower looked intrigued.

"Yes, My Lord. You will admit that while we were on St. Helena, Bonaparte's hat was distinctive. I asked him about it one day. He said he wore it *'en bataille'*, meaning parallel to his shoulders. This was different from nearly everyone else and made him instantly recognizable. Underhill wore the same hat in the same manner in the tavern on Martinique."

"Would you consider that conclusive?" the admiral asked.

Brewer chewed on the end of his cigar while he considered. "Not in and of itself, My Lord, but it's enough to cause me to investigate further."

"Good." Hornblower rose and came around the desk. Brewer rose and followed his mentor to the door. "Gerard will give you your orders," the admiral continued. "As we discussed, you are to go to Washington City and speak to whomever you can in the American government regarding Underhill. We must know if they will protect him in any way, based on the letter of marque. Report straight back to me afterward."

"Aye, aye, My Lord." The two men shook hands.

"Good luck, William."

"Thank you, My Lord. Please give my regards to the Lady Barbara."

CHAPTER FOUR

HMS *Revenge* slipped out of the harbor with the morning sun and turned east. Brewer swung around the eastern tip of Jamaica and headed for the Windward Passage. He was careful to hail every British ship he came across, hoping for news, but none said they saw a ship resembling *Oliver Cromwell*.

Once through the passage, and having made their way north through the Bahamas, Brewer set course for the entrance to Chesapeake Bay. It was past the hurricane season in that part of the world, so the sea was mostly calm as they continued northward. The biggest change they noticed was the worsening cold. Brewer did not know from experience, but December in that part of the United States was rumored to be as cold or colder than England on its worst day. The captain ordered additional clothing to be issued to the men after shivering himself on the quarterdeck. Unfortunately, stores proved insufficient to meet the need, so men who were off watch usually stayed below in an attempt to keep warm.

The captain determined to be seen on deck on a daily basis; he considered it important that the crew know he was willing to share their hardships due to the increasingly biting winds. Lieutenant Greene or the doctor were frequent and sometimes unwilling participants, keeping their captain company.

It was at the end of one such watch when Brewer spoke

to Lieutenant Tyler, who took over the watch, and motioned for the doctor to follow him below to his cabin. The two men stepped in to find the day cabin comfortably warm; Mac had appropriated one of the portable heaters that were used on the berthing deck. Brewer and the doctor gratefully sat and warmed themselves.

"Alfred!" the captain called. The servant appeared. "Coffee, if you please."

Alfred could only shake his head. "Sorry, sir."

"What?"

Alfred looked embarrassed. "We could not buy any before we left, sir. Port Royal had not a pound available; it seems they were awaiting shipments from Columbia. We didn't have time to search the countryside before we sailed."

Brewer frowned. "What do we have, then?"

"Tea, I'm afraid, sir."

The captain sighed. "Better than nothing, I suppose. Well, at least it's hot. Very well, Alfred, tea will be fine."

Doctor Spinelli smiled as he rubbed his hands together to warm them. Captain Brewer's aversion to the Royal Navy's staple in favor of the coffee preferred by their American cousins was well known. Behind his back, many of Brewer's fellow officers sniggered at him and wondered if he were really from the colonies.

Alfred brought the tea, and the doctor gratefully let the hot cup warm his hands. He sipped and smiled.

"What are you smiling at?" Brewer asked.

The doctor shrugged. "Just thinking about the holidays, Captain. Christmas and all that."

"Oh," the captain replied. "Yes, well, are you up for a game?"

"Now that my hands have thawed, yes. I'll get the set."

Spinelli went to the captain's desk and brought out the

chess set. He was mystified by his friend's dismissal of Christmas. True, it was a subject they'd never talked about, but still... He made a mental note to look into it more.

He never got the chance. Over the thirteen days it took for HMS *Revenge* to make the voyage to Washington City, Spinelli never got his captain to open up about the Christmas holidays. The doctor went so far as to question Mac and Alfred, but neither man had ever heard their captain so much as mention the holidays. So, the mystery deepened.

They anchored in the bay outside the American capitol, which was still rebuilding from being burnt by the British army in 1814. Brewer considered for a moment whether or not it would be wise to appear on the city streets in his uniform, but he decided that since the war had ended five years ago, his uniform would do fine. Lieutenant Greene objected when informed of his captain's decision and begged him to take some bodyguards along. When Brewer declined, Greene urged him to at least take Mac. Brewer sighed and put his hand on the premier's shoulder.

"I'll be fine, Benjamin," he said, and that ended the matter.

Mac conned the gig to the wharf, and the captain stepped out. They had at least convinced him to wear the cape he had purchased at Port Royal by pointing out the threat of snow in the air.

"I'll be here when you return, sir," Mac said.

"Keep the crew together, Mac," Brewer urged his coxswain. "If you go to a tavern to get out of the cold, nobody gets drunk. You might get some hot cider or the like to warm yourselves."

"Aye, Captain," Mac replied as he knuckled his forehead.

Brewer walked up the wharf to the city beyond. He stopped at the dock office to ask directions.

"Where do you wish to go, Commander?" the clerk at the desk asked.

"I need to speak to someone at the State Department and the Navy Department."

"You're in luck then, because they're still in the same building. Another month and you'd have to go an extra three miles to where the new State Department building is located." The clerk provided directions, and Brewer thanked him.

He stepped out into the cold December air only to find that the snow that had been prophesied had arrived. He pulled his cape tighter around him, glad now that he had relented and agreed to wear it. He knew his friends had urged it on him as a way of concealing his uniform, but it had turned out to be a blessing.

The city was more pleasant than he'd expected; his compatriots had been more circumspect with their arson during the war than he had been led to believe. The tea shops and cafés were reminiscent of Portsmouth or Southampton, and the people seemed friendly enough. If it weren't for the abominable weather, he might actually enjoy himself.

The clerk's directions were good, and Brewer was soon being shown upstairs to the office of the United States Secretary of State. It was only a matter of minutes before he was shown into the secretary's office.

"Mr. Secretary," the clerk said, "allow me to introduce Commander William Brewer of His Britannic Majesty's ship *Revenge*. Commander, this is Secretary of State John Quincy Adams."

The two men shook hands. "Welcome, Commander," the secretary said. "Please, sit. What can I do for you?" Adams indicated two chairs before a window. The men sat, and a steward brought two glasses of wine. The secretary handed one to his guest before taking the second for himself. He raised his glass. "To your very good health, sir." Brewer reciprocated, and they drank.

Brewer set his glass down. "Pardon me, Mr. Secretary, but I'm curious. Are you any relation to the President?"

Adams gestured with his glass and smiled. "That I am, Commander. He's my father."

"Ah," Brewer nodded his comprehension. "I admire your father greatly."

"You've met?" Adams asked.

"Purely by accident," Brewer replied. "It must be nearly two years ago, now. I was first lieutenant on a frigate that put into Boston. I was able to get a few hours' shore leave to look for a book store. I wanted to get a biography of your General Washington. While I was at the counter with the book in hand, your father stepped up and struck up a conversation. He said that he'd known General Washington for many years. We talked for a while, and he invited me to have dinner with him at the inn where he was staying." He smiled at the pleasant memory. "I even met your brother when he came to escort your father back to his rooms."

"Thomas?"

Brewer considered. "I believe that was his name." He took another swallow. "I didn't know who your father was until the innkeeper told me after he was gone."

Adams threw his head back and laughed heartily. "That sounds like him. Thomas has been taking care of him for the past several years."

The commander raised his glass. "Your father makes a very powerful impression."

The secretary raised his and nodded. "That he does. So, Commander, what may I do for you?"

Brewer set his glass down and folded his hands in his lap. It was time to get down to business. "Mr. Secretary, does the name Michael Underhill mean anything to you?"

Adams search his memory before shaking his head. "No. Who is he?"

"A British ex-patriot who left England and the Royal Navy over ten years ago and came to the United States. When the war broke out in 1812, he outfitted a privateer and purchased a letter of marque from your government."

"Common enough during a time of war," Adams commented.

"Yes, sir," Brewer agreed, "but it has come to our attention that Underhill may not have ceased his privateering when the Treaty of Ghent was signed."

"Ah. I see." The American leaned to one side and rubbed his chin between a thumb and forefinger. His eyes were hooded, and Brewer waited until his host spoke. Adams lifted a bell on the table and ordered another round from the servant who answered the call. After their glasses were refilled, Adams said, "May I ask why it has taken this many years for the Royal Navy to come to this conclusion?"

"I ran into Underhill at a tavern in Martinique recently," Brewer explained. "He was a mentor to me, although I have not seen him since before he came to America. He and two of his men join me and my ship's surgeon at our table, and we caught up on what had happened since we last saw one another. He told me of his privateering during the war. When I asked him what he was doing now, he said he was doing the same old thing." Brewer shifted in his chair. "Mr. Secretary, I was looking right at him when he said it and the moments right afterward. It was a slip, the kind when the truth comes out unbidden and is immediately regretted. I believe he is still raiding British shipping.

"Before I left Jamaica, I heard about a British merchant brig that had recently been taken by pirates, or so it was thought. I was able to interview the master of the brig before

I left the island. He described a raider that matched Underhill's vessel, a large sloop with ports cut for at least seven guns on each side. He named the ship *Oliver Cromwell*."

Adams' brow rose. "After the killer of a king? Why do I think your friend has a grudge against his homeland?"

Brewer smiled grimly. "I will confess that to be part of his motivation, Mr. Secretary."

"A part?" Adams smiled. "Very well, Commander."

"Also, sir," Brewer continued, "the brig's master described the pirate leader to me. The man described fit Underhill's general description, but the clincher was his hat."

"Hat?"

"Yes, Mr. Secretary. When I met him in Martinique, Underhill had on what is popularly known as a 'Bonaparte Hat'. Do you understand what I mean? Across the shoulders rather than fore-and-aft? I'd never seen another man wear one until that day in Martinique; it is not a popular style. The brig's master said the leader of the pirates wore one."

Adams leaned forward. "So, he's a pirate now?"

Brewer grimaced. "That's where things may get tricky, Mr. Secretary. I believe he's still operating — rightly or wrongly — under his letter of marque, or at least using it as justification for his current activities."

Adams looked confused. "But his letter of marque should have expired with the Treaty of Ghent."

"So one would assume," Brewer agreed. "Tell me, do you have a copy of the letter issued to Underhill?"

"Unfortunately, no," Adams said. "I'm afraid we lost a lot of our files when your countrymen burned the city."

"Yes, well, not our best moment, in my personal opinion," Brewer lamented. "Even Bonaparte never did that to anyone."

"What about Moscow?"

"No," Brewer answered absently. "He told me the Russians burnt it to deny it to his forces."

Adams' eyes opened wide. "He *told* you? What do you mean, Commander? Have you met Napoleon Bonaparte?"

It dawned on Brewer that the American had no idea of his background, so he proceeded to give him a brief history of his service with Lord Hornblower on St. Helena and his interactions with the former Emperor of France. When he finished, Adams leaned back in his chair and stared.

"How extraordinary!" he exclaimed. "How I would love to have a conversation with him!"

Brewer nodded. "Now would be the time, Mr. Secretary."

"What do you mean?"

"I mean he is much more amenable to conversation than he was when he was in power, more willing to admit his faults and missteps. St. Helena has brought him down to the level of a mere mortal, I'm afraid. Unfortunately, you will not have the chance."

"What? Why not?" Adams demanded.

"Forgive me, Mr. Secretary," Brewer said quickly, "but I believe I misspoke." When he saw Adams would not relent, he sighed and said, "Sir, you must remember that this, too, is a personal opinion and in no way reflects my government's positions. You see, there was a change within the government in London, and men were brought in who were not favorable to Bonaparte. They undid many of the measures put in place by Lord Hornblower to make like easier for his prisoner, and did what they could to turn St. Helena from exile to a prison. I think it highly unlikely that anyone in the Foreign Office will approve your request to visit the island."

Adams frowned as he stared into space for a moment. He blinked and looked to his guest. "That is a shame. I imagine you're right about the political situation. Still, it is something to hope for."

Brewer nodded. "I agree, Mr. Secretary. I would love to visit him again myself." He sighed and said, "Sir, I am charged by Admiral Lord Hornblower to come to your city and ask you this question: Will the American government offer any protection or asylum to Underhill and his men on the basis of the letter of marque?"

"No, Commander, we will not." Adams rose and extended his hand. Brewer rose and took it.

"Thank you for seeing me, sir," Brewer said. "Please convey my greetings to your father, and tell him from me that I loved the book."

Brewer left the State Department and made his way down the hall to the Navy Department, where he was able to get an interview with the newly appointed Smith Thompson. He was shown into the secretary's study where he found Thompson awaiting him. The secretary was a tall, spare man, maybe an inch or so taller even than Lord Hornblower, and thin to the point of emaciation. His face was dominated by a prominent nose and squinty eyes, topped by a receding hairline. His hair was cut close on the sides, and a distinguished goatee completed his appearance. He stepped forward with his hand extended.

"Commander Brewer," he said as the two shook hands, "how may I be of help?" He indicated a chair before the desk, which Brewer took. Thompson resumed his seat behind the desk.

"I am here at the behest of Admiral Lord Hornblower, commander of the West Indies Squadron of the Royal Navy. We are investigating a British ex-patriot named Michael Underhill. During the war, he outfitted a privateer and obtained a letter of marque from your government to raid British shipping."

"I see," Thompson said. "The name is unfamiliar to me, Commander, and my government issued thousands of those letters of marque during the war. I myself operated under one in the waters around Nova Scotia."

"Mr. Secretary, we believe that Underhill is still raiding British shipping under his letter of marque."

Thompson's eyes went wide in surprise at the accusation. "Really? How extraordinary! But, Commander, my government is not responsible for any such activities after the peace treaty was signed."

"Of course, Mr. Secretary." Brewer considered for a moment, trying to choose his words carefully. "Then the United States government would no longer purchase any ships taken by a privateer under a letter of marque?"

Thompson shook his head. "No, Commander, it would not."

Brewer asked his next question slowly. "In that case, Mr. Secretary, where *would* Underhill be able to sell these ships?"

Thompson drummed his fingers on the desk as he considered. His eyes narrowed even more than usual. "Commander," he said, "what I can tell you regarding this is both personal and private and in no way reflects the position of my government in any way."

"I understand, Mr. Secretary."

Thompson's long middle finger tapped the desk . "To my knowledge, there are only two places he might be able to sell such a cargo. One would be Havana; the Spanish Governor-General has been known to look the other way for a percentage." Brewer nodded, and the secretary continued. "The other is New Orleans."

Brewer frowned. "But isn't New Orleans now part of the United States?"

The secretary rubbed the bridge of his nose. "Technically, yes, it is part of the territory of Louisiana. But I must tell you, Commander — again this in my own opinion — that between the business interests and the heavy influx of immigrants and refugees from the Caribbean, it is a lawless place. My government has not yet been able to take sufficient control of the region. I think smugglers would be happy to buy a merchant ship with no questions asked as to where it came from."

"It would be a greater distance to sail, but possibly less scrutinized than Havana's port," Brewer said. "Thank you, Mr. Secretary. Is there anything else you can tell me?"

"Only that this Underhill can count on no help or sanctuary from the American government." He rose and extended his hand. Brewer rose and shook it heartily. "Good day, Commander."

"Good day, Mr. Secretary. And thank you."

Out on the street, Brewer headed back toward the wharf. He was thinking about his conversations with the two secretaries, so he might be forgiven for not hearing a carriage pull up beside him. He only looked up when he heard his name.

"Commander Brewer?"

Brewer saw a man driving the carriage he did not know. "Yes?"

"May I offer you a ride, sir?" the driver asked.

"No, thank you," Brewer replied warily. "It's a lovely day; I think I'll walk."

"Commander," the driver said sternly, "please get in the carriage."

Brewer heard a pistol cock and lowered his gaze to the window of the carriage. There was a pistol pointed at him not three feet from his head, and he recognized the face behind it.

"Hello, Chauncey," he said.

"Hello, Commander," Chauncey replied. "Get in." The door was opened from the inside, and Brewer stepped up and sat across from *Cromwell's* first mate. As soon as the door was closed, the driver whipped up the horses and they took off down the road. There were heavy curtains on the windows, so Brewer had no idea where they were going, but from the way he was bounced around the cab, he was pretty sure they weren't in the city anymore. Chauncey was steadier, being used to the ride; the pistol never wavered.

Finally, the carriage came to a stop. Chauncey motioned toward the door. "Out."

Brewer got out and found himself in front of a small hut. There was a man on either side of the door, each with a pistol pointed at his chest. Chauncey got out behind him and pressed his weapon into the captain's back. "Inside," he growled.

Brewer stepped through the doorway and into the dark hut. It was a single room with a round table in the middle. There was a lamp on the table, and seated within its glow was Michael Underhill.

"Hello, William," he said. There was a bottle on the table; Underhill poured them each a drink and pushed one toward an empty chair. Brewer hesitated for a minute before sitting. Underhill raised his glass in silent salute, and he returned the gesture. Underhill took a drink, but Brewer set his on the table untouched.

"Why am I here, Michael?" he asked.

Underhill grunted. "Still straight to business, eh? I guess some things never change." He drained his glass, set it down on the table with a bang, and sat back in his chair. "Very well. I was afraid that, after our meeting on Martinique, you would feel the need to investigate my... business dealings, shall we say. I imagined you would report your suspicions to the West Indies Squadron commander at Port Royal, but I didn't think it would really go any further than that. Then I hear that your ship has appeared here, and you came ashore.

It wasn't hard to figure where you'd gone."

"So, it's true, is it?" Brewer said. "The war never ended for you, and you're still privateering, so to speak, raiding British shipping under the letter of marque the Americans gave you."

Underhill poured himself another drink and downed it in a single draught. "Let's just say that revenge is an appetite that is never really satisfied."

"Michael, this is madness!" Brewer exclaimed. "You must know that the British will declare you a pirate, and when that happens, it is either death in battle or a date with the hangman."

Underhill shrugged and poured himself another drink. "That's probably been my destiny since the day I walked off the *Kent*."

"Michael," Brewer pleaded, "why not end it now and walk away? Before the authorities can find you and bring you to justice?"

"What justice? I'm smart enough to know that I've burned all my bridges in that regard. All you need to do is to go back to Jamaica and tell them you were wrong, that I've done nothing wrong since the war ended. Just forget all about me, William."

"That's not going to happen," Brewer said. "Listen to me. It will take a month or six weeks for me to report to the admiral at Port Royal and then for the squadron to take up positions to try to trap you. By that time, you and your men can disappear. I would imagine you can live quite comfortably on the South Seas islands with what you've got right now. You might even start a profitable business in Australia. Better that than facing British frigates. And it will come to that, Michael, sooner or later the Royal Navy will catch up to you."

"Thanks to you." Underhill took Brewer's untouched drink and tossed it down. He nodded, and Chauncey stepped up silently and slammed the barrel of his pistol into Brewer's temple. Underhill saw Brewer's head hit the table hard, and a trickle of blood drip down past his ear. He put the glass on the table and said to Chauncey, "Let's get moving. You know what to do."

It was the combination of the pounding in his head and a rooster crowing somewhere that brought Brewer back to consciousness. He tried to open his eyes and rise, but the room spun and his head screamed violently, so he laid back down again until the sensations subsided. He felt around with his hands and came to the conclusion that he was on a cot of some kind. He opened first one eye and then the other and waited for his vision to clear. When his eyes adjusted to the dim light, he turned his head slowly and saw that he was still in the hut where he had met with Underhill, only now he was alone. He took a deep breath, held it, and gritted his teeth before attempting to rise again. He moved very slowly and incrementally this time, but eventually he was seated upright on the cot. He stayed there for several minutes while he waited for the pounding in his head to ease. He tenderly probed his head with his fingers. He found it was bandaged. The skin and hair below the bandage were covered with dried blood, so he was hopeful that he could make his way back to the doctor.

He rose slowly and staggered over to the table where he grasped a chair back for support. He saw that Michael had been kind enough to leave the bottle and a glass for him, and he poured himself a generous portion and drank thirstily. He poured himself another and drank slower this time. He sat in a chair and waited for the alcohol to ease the pounding in his head.

When he thought it was safe to move, he rose slowly and made his way outside. The rising sun told him it was morning — he'd been in the hut overnight. He grunted; Mac must be going crazy by now. He saw a horse tethered to the porch railing. It was saddled, and there was a note pinned to the reins. He took the note off and read it. It was directions to back to town. It ended thus: *"No more mercy. Give it up, William. It's best for all of us. U."*

Brewer put the note in his pocket and mounted the horse. His head screamed and the alcohol in his stomach threatened to come back up, but he managed to stay in the saddle until the discomfort subsided enough for him to move. He followed the directions slowly back to town.

CHAPTER FIVE

Captain William Brewer stood at *Revenge's* fantail, staring out over her wake. His ship was on a course of SSE to the Bahamas and then on to the Windward Passage, which in turn would take them to Jamaica and Port Royal. His hands were clasped behind his back, and his eyes were narrowed against the wind as he tried to make sense of everything he had learned while at Washington, both from the secretaries and also from Underhill.

He smiled grimly as he remembered the look on Mac's face when he finally showed up at the wharf. Brewer found out later that the coxswain was operating under orders from the first lieutenant when he had two men take his captain by the arms and forcibly secure him in the gig as they pushed off for the ship. Mac had then taken him directly to his cabin and held him there until Dr. Spinelli arrived to examine the bloody bandage around his head. When the doctor pronounced himself satisfied and had changed the dressing out for a new one, Mac had finally relaxed and allowed his captain to have his say again.

Brewer had ordered the ship to sail on the first available tide. In the meantime, he'd ordered Mr. Reed — who was reputed to have the best eyes on the ship — into the tops along with extra lookouts to see if they could spot the *Oliver Cromwell* anywhere in the anchorage. Two hours later, a negative result had been relayed to the captain. Brewer had sighed in resignation; Underhill was too smart to hang around after kidnapping an officer of the Royal Navy.

Now, standing at the fantail, Brewer was more convinced than ever that his pursuit of Underhill would end in bloodshed. There was no doubt in his mind that his crew would prove superior in a battle, but he did not relish the idea of commanding the instrument of his friend's execution. But it was Underhill's choice and not his own that dictated what happened from here on. He sighed and closed his eyes; this wasn't the first time his duty demanded he do something he didn't like.

He realized at that moment that he was no longer alone. He turned his head (which still hurt slightly at the motion) to see the doctor standing beside him.

"Sorry to disturb you, Captain," Spinelli said. "I just want to ask how you are recovering."

"The same as I was the last time you asked, Doctor," Brewer replied. His shoulders heaved with a deep breath he hoped would calm him. He turned and realized that everyone on the quarterdeck was looking at him. He almost snapped off a curt order to get back to work, but the doctor's hand on his arm stayed him; he knew they were concerned for him after his adventure, and he needed to show them he was none the worse for it. He stood up straighter and raised his chin. The doctor dropped his hand and stepped back.

"Mr. Sweeney," Brewer said, "steady as she goes." Then he raised his voice and called out, "Midshipman of the watch!" He regretted this immediately, as the pounding in his head increased exponentially.

Mr. Short appeared beside him and saluted. "You called for me, sir?"

"Yes, Mr. Short," the captain said in a quiet voice. "Please pass the word. I would like Mr. Greene, Mr. Tyler, Mr. Reed, Mr. Sweeney, and the doctor to join me in my cabin for a meal tonight. Say, the turn of the second dog watch. You will have the deck while we are meeting in my quarters, Mr. Short. Think you're up for it?"

Short's eyes went wide. "Me, sir? Oh, yes, sir! I'll take good care of her for you, Captain!"

"Very good," Brewer said. "Off with you, now."

Short snapped off a salute and ran for the companion-way stairs.

"Mr. Short!" Sweeney yelled.

Short knew exactly what he wanted; he skidded to a halt and walked as quickly as he could to the stairway and disappeared below. Brewer smiled at the sight while Sweeney and the doctor chuckled.

"Mr. Short will have the deck?" Sweeney asked.

"I'm sure he'll do a good job," Brewer replied, "especially after you whisper a few words in the quartermaster's ear about keeping his eye on the boy."

Sweeney grinned and nodded. "Aye, Captain."

"I'm going below," the captain announced. "Call me if I'm needed. Doctor, if you'll come with me?"

"Aye, Captain."

The two men went below and turned aft to the captain's cabin. Spinelli debated whether or not to remind his captain about keeping his head down; one good whack on a deck beam might reopen his wound. To his relief, Brewer remembered and kept his head down.

In the cabin they surrendered their hats and coats to Mac and went to the day cabin. Brewer did not see the concerned look his coxswain shot at the doctor or the doctor's shrug in return. They sat down on the settee.

"Doctor," Brewer said, "May I trouble you to call for Alfred and order us wine?"

"I'll go take care of that now, sir." Spinelli rose and went out to the pantry. "Two glasses of wine, if you please."

Alfred set about getting the drinks. In a low voice he inquired, "Is he all right, Doctor?"

"No," Spinelli answered, "but he will be before we reach Jamaica. He just needs time, Alfred. By the way, he needs to see you about supper tonight."

Alfred dutifully followed the doctor back to the day room and waited. Spinelli handed the captain his drink and sat down.

"Yes, Alfred?" Brewer asked. The servant looked to the doctor, who leaned in and spoke into his captain's ear.

"You wanted to tell him about tonight's meeting."

"Ah, yes. A total of six for supper tonight. Can we do it? Turn of the second dog watch."

The servant closed his eyes while he went over his mental inventory. At last he said, "Aye, Captain. As long as the admiral will not be in attendance, that is."

Brewer smiled. "Thank you, Alfred."

The servant bowed and left the room.

The doctor raised his glass toward the pantry. "That man is probably the greatest blessing we could have aboard this ship."

Brewer raised his own glass. "I've certainly never had anyone like him on a ship before."

Both men drank and set down their glasses. The doctor rose and stood before the captain.

"What are you doing?" Brewer asked.

"I want to check your head before your guests arrive," the doctor replied.

"You've got hours yet."

"Not when you take into account the amount of time wasted before you agree. Now, hold still."

The captain grunted, but held still as the doctor gently

removed the bandage from his head. He glanced at the bandage after the doctor dropped it on the seat beside him and was pleased to see only a scant amount of blood. He could feel the doctor probing and reached up to feel for himself, only to have the doctor push his hand away.

"If you don't mind!" the doctor said as a warning. He pulled a fresh bandage from his coat pocket and began to wrap the wound. "It seems to be healing nicely. All it needs are time and proper care. Tell me truly, are you having any headaches, especially with stabbing pain when you move any certain way?"

"Headaches, yes," Brewer reported, "but not as badly as yesterday, and no, no stabbing pains."

"Good. You must tell me if that happens."

"Yes, Doctor." Brewer slouched on the settee so his head rested on the back. "Now, if you don't mind, sir, I shall rest until my guests arrive. You may stay or go, as you wish."

"Oh, I'll stay. Who knows when I might get another chance like this?"

The captain opened one eye and peered silently at his friend. He thought about asking what he meant by that, but he ended up closing his eye without asking. Sometimes, he thought, it was better not to know. Brewer hoped to catch a quick nap before his guests arrived, but a noise soon roused him. It took him a moment to realize the doctor was humming some tune.

"What are you humming?" Brewer asked.

"What? Oh, sorry. Actually, I was thinking about Christmas and found myself humming one of the carols we always sang in our village." Spinelli stretched and crossed his arms over his chest. "You know, this will be my first Christmas in the Caribbean." When the captain made no reply, he tried again. "What about you?"

"Yes," Brewer said stiffly, his eyes still closed. "Mine as

well."

The doctor stood, his hands now clasped behind his back as he bounced on his toes and looked over the captain's library. He turned back to the captain, who had not moved. "Well, he went on, "I supposed we shall have to improvise, don't you think?I mean, not having everything we had at home and all." He stared out into space, searching for a memory and completely oblivious to his captain's increasing discomfort.

His guests arrived at the appointed hour, and Brewer wasted no time getting them seated around the table. Alfred, Mac, and the stewards brought out the feast, modest by Alfred's usual standards but still able to challenge the best establishments in Port Royal. Brewer smiled as he watched Tyler's and Reed's eyes go wide at the sight of the platters and bowls, the rising aromas which signaled the delights to come. When the procession was complete, and Alfred had bowed and retreated to the pantry, the captain rose.

"Thank you all for coming," he said. "I have a report to make regarding our mission to Washington City, and I know that, like me, you would appreciate every opportunity to avail yourselves of Alfred's talents!"

"Here! Here!" Greene and Sweeney cried.

"Now," Brewer continued, "I would be the first to say that there are times when business must come before pleasure. However, I don't think this is one of those times! Gentlemen, let us eat while the food is hot."

He reseated himself and took a slice of ham from the platter before him before urging Mr. Greene on his right to do the same and pass it along. Soon every plate was filled and small talk was muted by full mouths and chewing. It was near the end of the meal, as the last mouthfuls were being swallowed, that the doctor spoke up.

"You know, It's almost a shame to leave such nice

Christmas weather and head back to the warmth of the Caribbean. Don't take me wrong — I like the sun as much as the next man, but when it comes to Christmas, I think it should be cold and snowy."

"I agree," Mr. Tyler said. "Our village in Northumberland always had a foot or more of snow by Christmas Day."

"I remember a few times that Liverpool got that lucky," Sweeney remarked.

"The best thing about Christmas at our house was family dinner," the doctor went on. "My mother and sisters would spend the entire day Christmas Eve and all morning Christmas Day in the kitchen baking. They made a pudding and a cake that were absolutely extraordinary!"

Sweeney spoke up. "It sounds like your mother and mine learned from the same woman." He rubbed his hands together as if in anticipation. "We would wake up Christmas morning and the whole house would smell like the best bakery in Liverpool!"

"Yes, well," Brewer interrupted, "I'm sure we all have our memories, but now that the meal is over, it's time for business." He told them of his visits to the American secretaries of state and the navy, keeping to himself the information about New Orleans. He also told then about his kidnapping and interview with Underhill, being knocked unconscious, and awaking to find the horse and directions into town.

"So," the doctor said when he had finished, "there is no doubt now."

"No," Brewer replied, "none at all. We are on our way back to Port Royal, where I shall report to the admiral. He will most likely declare Underhill and his men pirates. I will ask that he assign us the task of going after them."

"Any particular reason?" Spinelli asked.

"I have my reasons, Adam," the captain said. "I shall update you all when I have more information, most likely after

I speak to the admiral. Now, if you will excuse me, I will bid you all good night."

His guests looked at each other, stunned by this sudden dismissal. Lieutenant Greene cleared his throat loudly and rose. He nodded and said "Goodnight, Captain," looked around the table, then made his way to the door. The others got the hint and rose as well, bidding their captain goodnight and thanking him for the meal. Only the doctor kept his seat.

When they were alone, Brewer said, "Is there something I can do for you, Doctor?"

"You can tell me what's bothering you."

"What makes you think something's bothering me?"

"William, please!" Spinelli cried. "Tell me it's none of my business, or tell me the truth, but don't put me off like that!"

Brewer reached out and began running his fingertip around the rim of his glass. The doctor recognized it as an effort to retain self-control.

"What is it, William?" Spinelli said quietly. "Let me help you."

Brewer did not look up from his glass. "If you will excuse me, Doctor, I have work to do."

The doctor looked at his friend, but the captain's eyes never left the glass. He rose, bade his captain good night, and left the cabin.

Brewer spent the rest of the night in his day cabin, holding a glass of wine and trying to distract his mind with *Robinson Crusoe*. With a sigh of disgust, he closed the book and tossed it on the settee beside him. He took a drink of his wine and leaned his head back. He rose and took several slow, deep breaths to bury the frustration and regain control of his emotions. He began to pace the width of the cabin, five strides and turn, five strides and turn, his chin on his chest and his hands clasped behind his back. He was angry with himself for the way he'd treated his guests at supper, and even more so for the way he treated the doctor afterward. It wasn't their fault; how were they to know? He paused his pacing and sighed. He went to the cabin door and opened it, asking the sentry to pass the word for the doctor to please come to his cabin. Then he went to his desk and got out the chess set and set it up on the table for a game. He was about to call Alfred, but he remembered that he'd sent his servant off to bed, so he went into the pantry and came out with a decanter of Madeira and two glasses, which he set beside the chess board. Satisfied that all was ready, he took his seat and waited.

A knock at the door was followed by the doctor's entrance. Brewer could see he was still upset at his treatment earlier. Who could blame him?

"You sent for me, sir?" Spinelli asked.

"I did," the captain replied. "I apologize for my rudeness earlier this evening. And before you ask, yes, I will be apologizing to my other guests tomorrow. But for right now, I don't know about you, but I need to play a game or three." He gestured toward the decanter. "Will you do the honors?"

The doctor's chin rose slightly at the captain's words. He poured the wine and handed one glass to his host. He sat in his chair, and the captain moved a white pawn. Spinelli silently moved his queen's knight out.

"Thank you for coming, Adam," Brewer said as he moved a bishop. "I guess I got a little overwhelmed and had trouble controlling it."

"This business with Underhill?" Spinelli asked.

Brewer shrugged. "That's part of it. He could have killed me, Adam, and nobody would have found my body. The only way I can repay him for sparing my life is by forgetting the whole thing, but I can't do that." He made a move and sat back. "You heard us at the inn. He was a second father to me. He took me under his wing and taught me how to survive in the navy. He showed me how to deal with men. Now I have to hunt him down like a dog."

Spinelli castled. "I'm truly sorry for you. It must be difficult to put duty first at times."

Brewer leaned forward and advanced a pawn. "That's not the only thing that was on my mind, Adam." Brewer refilled their glasses and took a long drink before setting the glass on the table and continuing. "You know that my father disowned me for my decision to join the navy." The doctor looked up sharply, and the captain took a deep breath before continuing. "What you don't know is, that all happened on Christmas Eve." Spinelli's eyes grew wide at the revelation. Brewer leaned forward again and moved his queen. "I've never celebrated Christmas from that year to this. Every year, all I can think about is that this is the day I lost my family."

The doctor lowered his eyes to gaze at the chessboard. "I'm sorry, William. I didn't know."

"I realized that," Brewer smiled apologetically, "but only about an hour ago. So, now you know what was really bothering me: Christmas."

"My heart aches for you, my friend," the doctor said. "Christmas is supposed to be a time of joy, of redemption, a time with those you love. Your father ripped all that away from you in a moment of anger. I wish there was something I could do to make it all right for you again."

"Thank you." Brewer moved his rook. "I wish it was that easy to fix."

The doctor brought his queen sweeping down from across the board to capture his captain's knight. "Perhaps we could concentrate on improving your game in the meantime? Checkmate."

Two games later, the doctor bade his captain a good

night and headed up to the deck. He wanted to take a turn or two around to see if the cool night air would help clear his head. When he stepped from the stair, he saw Lieutenant Greene talking with Mr. Sweeney and a quartermaster's mate. Spinelli stepped over to the fantail and gazed at the stars in the sky. It wasn't long before Greene and Sweeney joined him.

"How is he?" Greene asked. The lieutenant had been in the sickbay with the doctor when the word came of the captain's summons.

Spinelli turned and leaned against the rail, crossing his arms over his chest. He considered saying nothing until he was alone with the first lieutenant, but Greene obviously considered Sweeney trustworthy, and in any case, the captain had not asked him to keep the information to himself. He spoke in a low voice. "He's better. He apologized for his rudeness toward me earlier, and he said he would apologize tomorrow to all who were present at supper. We were partly right; he is conflicted about having to go after Underhill in view of what the man meant to him when they knew each other before. But there's something else as well." He told them about Brewer's last Christmas Eve at home and how it tarnished the holiday for him ever since. "I think for now, it's better that this information stay with us."

"Agreed," Greene said, and Sweeney nodded his agreement.

The doctor noticed the look on the sailing master's face. "Mr. Sweeney?"

Sweeney pursed his lips for a moment before answering. "If we are to help the captain, we're going to need help."

HMS *Revenge* inched into the harbor at Port Royal as the pilot guided her to the spot where she could drop anchor. Brewer thanked him before departed the ship, then went below to his cabin. There he found Alfred had laid out his best uniform for his meeting with the admiral. He had just finished dressing when Lieutenant Greene was admitted to the cabin.

"Mac's got the gig ready for you, sir," Greene reported.

"Thank you, Benjamin," the captain replied. He turned and presented himself to Alfred for inspection. The manservant looked his captain over with the eye of a Savile Row tailor. He pulled a speck of lint from the left shoulder of his captain's coat before pronouncing himself satisfied. Brewer thanked him, and Alfred bowed and left.

"What do you think the admiral will say?" Greene asked.

"I expect him to declare Michael Underhill a pirate. I also expect him to order me to hunt him down," Brewer replied.

Greene saw plainly the sadness on his friend's face. "I'm sorry, William," he said simply.

The captain looked up at the use of his first name, but the look on his premier's face held his eyes. He nodded gratefully. "Thank you, Benjamin."

Brewer hooked on his hanger, picked up his hat, and walked from the cabin. Lieutenant Greene was hard on his heels. On deck Brewer looked over his men before making his way to the entry port.

The ride in to the pier was mercifully smooth and quiet. This was one visit with his mentor that Brewer was not looking forward to, but he set his face like a proverbial flint and determined to do his duty.

He walked through the town, just another officer to those townspeople he passed, none of them guessing the weight that he carried on his shoulders. He was admitted to the admiral's house and taken directly to his mentor's office rather than the parlor as on his other visits. Obviously, Hornblower was aware of his arrival and had ordered his steward to show him in immediately upon his arrival. He found the admiral writing at his desk.

"Bear with me a moment, William," he said without looking up. "I want to finish this thought."

"Take your time, My Lord," Brewer said.

Hornblower's pen scratched on the paper for a few seconds more before he put the period at the end of the sentence and set down the quill. He rose and came around the desk with his hand outstretched. Brewer took it and felt better at once.

"William," Hornblower said warmly, "it's good to have you back. I was just answering a letter from the Lady Barbara, and she asked how you were."

Brewer blushed. "Please give her my regards, My Lord, and tell her I am well."

Hornblower indicated the chair before his desk. "Sit, William, and tell me how your trip went. Do you have your report?"

"I left it with your aide, My Lord."

"Ah," the admiral said as he took his seat. "That's fine. Tell me what you learned."

"Aye, My Lord." Brewer shifted in his chair and told the admiral of his meetings with the American secretaries of state and the navy. Hornblower listened closely, interrupting twice for clarification. When he finished, he swallowed hard to steel himself before launching into the events of his kidnapping and meeting with Underhill. He watched the emotions close his mentor's face, first surprise, followed by anger and relief. When he finished, Hornblower's eyes were hooded and dark.

"First," he said, "I am pleased that he still cared enough about you to spare your life. William, I am going to ask you a question, and I do not want you to think you must agree. I want you to understand I will not think poorly of you if you refuse. Do you understand? Good. Now, the question is this: are you able to go after Underhill and bring him to justice if I give you the assignment?"

Brewer answered immediately. "Yes, My Lord."

Hornblower rubbed his chin between his thumb and forefinger. The look in his eyes spoke of his struggle in coming to a decision in the matter. Finally, he said, "I will be frank with you, William. I am not worried about you pursuing Underhill and running him to ground. I am concerned that when you come to grips with him, you will remember him from the past and you will hesitate just long enough for him to kill you." The look of concern mixed with trepidation was the most sobering thing Brewer had ever seen.

"I have thought about that, My Lord," Brewer said, "and I have made my peace with it."

Brewer held his mentor's eye until Hornblower rose and walked over to a window that offered a good vantage point of the harbor below. When he turned and walked back to the desk, with his head on his chest and his hands behind his back, for a moment Brewer imagined this to be what Bush had seen so many times on the quarterdeck of their ship. Hornblower sat on the corner of the desk nearest his guest.

"Commander, I am detaching HMS *Revenge* from her current duties, and I am ordering you to pursue the pirate Michael Underhill and put an end to his plundering of British shipping. You are authorized to use any and all measures you deem necessary to accomplish this task. Is this understood?"

"Yes, My Lord."

"Good. When can you sail?"

"Two days, My Lord."

Hornblower nodded. "Very well, Commander." He went around the desk and resumed his seat. "William, I must warn you. Be careful. Memories are powerful things. Do not hesitate to pull the trigger; I guarantee you he won't. From what you've told me, Underhill already knows that if he sees you again, it's because you have been sent to take him prisoner or destroy him. He will kill you if he gets the chance. Don't give it to him."

Brewer answered somberly, "I have no intention of doing so, My Lord."

Hornblower held a hand up to interrupt his guest while he picked up a bell on his desk and rang it. When the steward answered the summons, he ordered drinks for them both. "You were saying, William?"

Brewer shifted in his seat and crossed his legs. "Actually, I was thinking of our mutual friend on St. Helena, My Lord. Wouldn't the Corsicans consider this a blood feud of some sort? Wouldn't you or I be obligated to kill Underhill for treason under it?"

The admiral's eyes went wide. "I have no idea! I believe I can say one thing with certainty, and that is that he would admonish you to put your feelings aside and do your duty in this matter. Be the wolf, not the serpent."

Brewer nodded. "Understood, My Lord."

Hornblower rose, signaling the end of the meeting. Brewer followed suit, and the two walked to the door. Hornblower shook his protégé's hand warmly. "Take care, William. Come back to us in one piece. Barbara would never forgive either of us otherwise."

Brewer laughed. "Tell her I hear and obey! Thank you, My Lord."

"Your orders will be delivered to your ship tomorrow," the admiral said. "You sail with the tide the day after."

Brewer came to attention. "Aye, My Lord." He turned and marched from the house.

While the captain was meeting with the admiral ashore, Lieutenant Greene was meeting with the doctor and Mr. Sweeney in *Revenge's* sickbay. They were joined by Alfred and Mac. Greene addressed the newcomers.

"I've asked you both here because we've discovered the captain needs our help. Doctor, will you repeat what you told Mr. Sweeney and me on deck earlier?"

Spinelli's expression was uncommonly stern. "I trust you will both agree that this information not leave this room, and certainly not be repeated amongst the crew." Alfred and Mac readily agreed, and the doctor related what the captain had told him about his last Christmas Eve at home and how that memory had poisoned the holiday for him ever since. Mac frowned at the revelation, while Alfred close his eyes and bowed his head for a moment.

"How can we help?" Alfred asked.

"You two have information we don't have," Greene said quietly. "You've seen the captain alone in his quarters. You've seen him on a personal level probably more than any-one else on the ship. Has he ever said anything to either of you about his family?"

It was Mac who spoke up. "The last time we were in Port Royal — not before our run to Washington, but the time be-fore that — I remember he got a letter from his mother. He smiled at the beginning of the letter, but by the end the smile was gone."

"That's not good," Sweeney opined. "More about his fa-ther, do you think?"

Greene shrugged. "Who knows? All we know is, the cap-tain can't enjoy Christmas anymore because that's when he was cast out of his family by his father."

Alfred spoke up. "So we give him a new one."

"What do you mean?" Greene demanded.

"We give him a new family," Alfred said. "We are his

family now. All of us, here on this ship, we are his family now."

The four looked at each other and then back at the little man before them. "Well?" He demanded. "What about it?"

Greene looked to the sailing master. "What do you think?"

Sweeney' brows rose high on his forehead and he shook his head at the thought. "Can we try it? Certainly. Will he accept it in the spirit and for the purpose it is offered? Well now, that's quite another question altogether, isn't it?" He paused to look at his co-conspirators. "I mean, we are asking him to put aside his darkest secrets. I don't know too many men whose first question would not be *'And just how do you know about that?'* How do you propose we answer that, Doctor?"

"He never said I was to keep this private," Spinelli said.

"Oh, that's how it is, is it?" Sweeney went on. "Then I must remember never to say anything to you, sir, that I may wish kept quiet! I might forget to point it out to you!"

Greene intervened. "Just a minute, I'm sure he didn't mean any indiscretion."

"Aye, but it's not our opinion we need worry about, is it?" Sweeney shook his head. "What I'm saying is, this thing has to be done right, or we shall drive the captain right out of this new family we're creating for him. Do any of you have any ideas on how we should do that?"

Nobody did.

Lieutenant Greene stood. "That's what we need to think about, then. Remember, do not talk about this with anyone, not even amongst ourselves unless you're sure you're not going to be overheard. If the captain gets wind of this before we're ready to spring it on him, we're doomed. In the meantime, we prepare. We can be ready to sail in two days, so I bet that's when we'll go. Try to get ashore tomorrow. Buy a

Christmas present for the captain. Buy some for others as well, or to send home to your family. That way, if the captain hears of it, well, what's more natural at this time of year? We'll meet again in a few days. You two," he pointed to Alfred and Mac, "keep your eyes and ears open!"

"Aye, sir!" Mac said.

Back in the captain's cabin, the two conferred in the pantry.

"Any ideas?" Mac said softly.

Alfred shook his head. "Not a one. The hard part will be putting the idea to him without his feeling betrayed or offended. I don't know how to do that."

Mac frowned. He didn't either.

Captain Brewer returned to his ship and called a council of war that night. The doctor, Lieutenants Greene and Tyler, and Mr. Sweeney were in attendance. Mac took his usual post just inside the door.

Once Alfred distributed the refreshments, the captain called the meeting to order. He relayed to them the admiral's orders that they pursue and capture or otherwise eliminate the pirate Michael Underhill. He tactfully left out the admiral's warnings about coming to grips with Underhill. Brewer did not consider it relevant. Besides, he knew something the admiral didn't — Mac and Alfred would be guarding his back.

"So," Brewer said when he finished, "there you have it. Comments?"

"What's our first step?" Sweeney asked.

"Do we waste weeks searching the Caribbean," the doctor asked, "and hope we get lucky?"

"There must be a better way," Tyler said.

"Perhaps there is," Greene said. "Captain, what was it the

American naval secretary told you? Didn't you ask him where Underhill might sell his prizes?"

"Yes," Brewer replied. "He said there were really only two possibilities: Havana and New Orleans."

"There you have it!" Greene said. "Which do we hit first?"

Sweeney shrugged. "Havana is on the way to New Orleans, is it not?"

Brewer smiled. "Agreed. Havana it is, then."

CHAPTER SIX

The second dawn found HMS *Revenge* making her way slowly from the harbor, bound for the open sea. Once free of the harbor's confines, Brewer ordered his ship west and then northwest so as to pass west of the Cayman Islands. From there he would pass through the Yucatan Channel, round the western tip of Cuba and make for Havana.

Brewer stood on his quarterdeck, enjoying the warm Caribbean breeze despite the lateness of the season. Privately, he hoped the admiral would not send them north again until at least March or April; the quick trip to Washington had been quite enough to remind him of his dislike of cold weather.

He ordered the course change to the west before beginning to pace across the fantail. Disturbing as it was, the conversation with the doctor had made him think about Christmas. No matter his personal feelings, his crew to a man cherished the holiday, whether for personal or religious reasons, and he felt he had no right to deprive them. He realized that if the crew got wind of how he felt, they would forego their own celebrations to avoid offending him.

Brewer frowned. He could not escape the feeling that that was not right and that he had to do something to encourage his crew to go on with their celebrations. But how, when doing so would only dampen his own spirits? Surely the crew would see it on his face, and he didn't think he would be able to hide in his cabin until the holidays were safely past. A feeling of dread came over him when he realized that he needed to play chess with the doctor again. He ceased pacing and walked over to the wheel.

"I shall be in my cabin," he said. "Mr. Reed has the deck. Call me if I'm needed." He turned to Reed. "Please pass the word for the doctor to join me."

"Aye, sir."

Just then, Mr. Short came up and saluted. "How did I do, Captain?" he asked, referring to his stint in command.

"Very well for your first time, Mr. Short," the captain replied. "In fact," he turned to Mr. Reed. "Mr. Reed, I want you to take Mr. Short under your wing, so to speak, and teach him about ship handling."

"Aye, sir," Reed replied. He winked at the boy, and Short beamed.

"Mr. Short," Brewer said firmly, "your job is to listen and learn. It may be years before you are in charge of a watch again. Don't look so sad, sir! I assure you it was that way for me, and I was much older than you are now! As I said, listen and learn all you can." He leaned in to speak to the boy privately. "I am very proud of you, William. You couldn't have a better teacher than Mr. Reed. Take advantage of it and learn from him."

"Aye, aye, Captain!"

Brewer straightened up and nodded to his youngest midshipman and went below. As soon as his head disappeared below deck, the smile he had been restraining broke out. It was youngsters like Mr. Short that gave him the most joy in being captain, and he tried his best to encourage them at every turn.

Alfred met him inside the cabin door to take his hat and coat.

"The doctor should be arriving any moment," Brewer

said. "Can we have two cups of coffee?"

"Right away, Captain."

Brewer went to the desk and took out his chess set. He was almost done setting up the pieces when the doctor arrived.

"You wanted to see me, Captain?" he said, then he noticed the board. "We're playing?"

"Yes, Doctor. I need to talk to you, and I seem to think better if we play while we talk. Thank you, Alfred." The servant set two steaming cups on the table and withdrew without a word. Mac came in and came to attention before stepping into the day cabin to straighten it up. It was something he'd begun doing recently, and Brewer didn't mind. Besides, he liked having the big Cornishman around.

The doctor took his seat and chose white. He moved his king's pawn and sat back for a delightful drink of Alfred's coffee. The captain responded with his move, and it was several moves before either man spoke.

"So, Captain," Spinelli said, "what's on your mind?"

"Doctor," Brewer said softly as he moved a knight, "I have been cursing your name."

"Really? Whyever for?"

"Christmas."

"Ah," Spinelli said, trying his best to remain calm. He moved a bishop and took a pawn. "And why is that?"

"Well, this is my first Christmas in command, and it has occurred to me that everyone on the whole ship except me celebrates Christmas." He castled. "I don't want my attitude toward the holiday to put a damper on everyone else's celebrations."

"I see." Spinelli took his captain's rook, which drew a frown. "What did you do on your previous ships?"

"I more or less avoided the subject. I wasn't in command,

so even as a lieutenant I was able to keep to myself. I volunteered to take watches. Sometimes I resorted to staying in my quarters to avoid the festivities." He picked up his cup and sat back. "I no longer have that luxury."

"No," the doctor said. "I can see that. Do you have any idea what you will do now?"

The captain studied the board with a frown fixed on his face. "No."

Spinelli sat back, cup in hand, and studied his captain over its brim, but Brewer only frowned at the board and said nothing. The doctor debated whether or not the time was ripe to try to open the broader topic. He was still undecided when Mac stepped back into the room.

"Begging your pardon, Captain," he said, "I'm done. Will there be anything else?"

"No, Mac, thank you." Suddenly, Brewer stiffened. "No, wait, Mac. Let me ask you a question. How many other ships have you served on?"

"Three, sir. *Lion*, *Elephant*, and with you on *Defiant*."

"And how did your captains on those ships celebrate Christmas aboard?"

The captain's eyes were still on the board, so he did not see the glance that Mac threw at the doctor, or the latter's shrug in reply.

"Well, sir," Mac said, "Captain Glynn on *Lion* went all out. He allowed the messes to set up small Christmas trees on their mess tables, and gifts were exchanged between messmates. He also had the hands on deck to sing Christmas carols on Christmas Eve. One year, he had the marines go hunting in the days before Christmas, and they shot enough geese that he was able to feed the entire crew a wonderful Christmas dinner. Now, Captain Summers on *Elephant*, he didn't go nearly so far, but he still allowed the men to celebrate the holiday. On *Defiant*, I didn't serve with Captain

Norman during Christmas."

"I see. Thank you, Mac. You may go."

Mac swallowed. "Aye, sir." He turned and left.

The captain moved a bishop. "Check." Spinelli countered, and the captain brought out his queen. "Check." The doctor blocked with a pawn, and the captain advanced a rook. The doctor took advantage of the respite to attack with his own queen. Three moves later, he brought up a rook to finish the job.

"Checkmate," he said. The captain sat back and stared off into space.

"William?" Spinelli said. "What's on your mind?"

Brewer blinked and took a deep breath. "Christmas. I can't seem to get away from it."

"Bad memories?"

The captain shook his head. "Good ones, actually. I've been remembering the holidays when I was a boy, and the fun we had when we were lucky enough to have snow. I remember my father hitching our horse to the sleigh, and we would pile in the back, with him and my mother in the front, and ride to church on a crisp winter morning, then home for a dinner of roast goose and pudding."

Spinelli smiled. "I'm glad you have such memories. Between us, William, I was afraid that your father had stolen those from you as well."

The captain's eyes snapped to his companion. "What do you mean?"

Well, Spinelli thought, *in for a penny...* "William, I know this time of year is difficult for you; it marks a traumatic experience in your life. As a result, you've cut yourself off from everything to do with Christmas. The problem with that is, you've also cut yourself off from all the joyful things that come with it. Forgive me, but I want to suggest to you that maybe it's time for you to put that aside."

The doctor slowly sipped from his cup and waited. His captain stared at him with hooded eyes and an unreadable expression on his face.

"It's easy for you," the captain said softly. "You've never been cast out because of a choice you made. I thought my father would be happy with my decision, that he would give me his blessing and wish me well. Instead I heard him condemn me in no uncertain terms and banish me from his property and family." He paused and swallowed hard in an effort to keep control of his emotions. After a moment, the captain leaned forward and asked, "Do you know what it's like to be without a family, Doctor?"

"I beg your pardon, sir."

Brewer spun in surprise to see Alfred standing in the pantry doorway. The servant stepped forward, his hands folded in front of him. "Excuse me for interrupting, Captain. You know it is not my habit, but I felt it necessary. You are wrong, Captain, when you say you have no family. You have a hundred men in your family, every man of this crew. To a man, we all feel that way. I know, because Mac and I have asked them." He paused, but the captain didn't say anything, so he continued. "I'm sorry for what happened to you, and especially for when it happened, but you need to know that you are not alone. To a man, the crew of this ship is with you and would charge the gates of Hell itself at your command." He looked down at his hands before concluding. "Captain, Christmas is meant to be celebrated with your family. Your family wants to celebrate with you."

Alfred bowed his head and retreated into his pantry. Brewer stared at the doorway for a moment before looking down at his hands folded in his lap. The doctor sat silently and waited to see what would happen. After a few minutes, the captain sighed loudly and shuddered.

"Alfred!" he called.

Spinelli tensed as the servant emerged from the pantry and stood before his captain. Brewer rose from his seat and faced his steward. After a moment, he put out his hand. Alfred searched his captain's eyes and, finding no animosity there, took it.

"Thank you," the captain said simply.

"You're welcome, Captain," Alfred replied. He bowed and returned to his pantry.

Brewer watched the doorway before retaking his seat. After a moment, he looked to the doctor. "Thank you, too, Adam."

The doctor nodded, not trusting his voice.

Alfred returned with more coffee. When he had refilled both cups, he turned to leave. He paused and turned back to his captain.

"Merry Christmas, Captain," he said.

Brewer saluted with his steaming cup. "Merry Christmas, Alfred." The steward bowed and retreated from the room, and the captain took a drink of his coffee.

Suddenly, the captain's expression turned stricken.

"Captain?" Spinelli asked, "what's wrong?"

"It just occurred to me," the captain said. "I don't have a present for anyone!" The doctor laughed, and a smile came to Brewer's face.

"Alfred!" he called. The servant appeared. "I'm afraid I don't have presents for anyone. Can we at least provide a Christmas supper for seven or eight?"

To his surprise, Alfred's eyes didn't close. He smiled and said, "Already planned, Captain. Just say when."

Alfred retreated to his pantry, and Brewer looked to the doctor.

"Remind me to send a thank you note to Jenkins."

Spinelli laughed.

HMS *Revenge* glided into the harbor at Havana. Captain Brewer stood on his quarterdeck and scanned the busy harbor with a telescope.

"I don't see *Cromwell*," he said as he lowered the glass. "Mr. Greene, send Mr. Reed into the tops to scan the harbor. I want to know if any old friends are about, and one in particular."

"Aye, sir." Greene passed the word for Mr. Reed and posted the senior midshipman to the tops for his task.

"Mr. Tyler has the deck," Brewer turned to his second lieutenant. "Keep your eyes open, especially on the harbor entrance. I want to know at once if *Oliver Cromwell* arrives."

"Aye, Captain," Tyler said.

"I shall be in my cabin," Brewer said as he headed for the stairway. "Mr. Greene!"

"Right behind you, Captain!"

They reached the cabin to find Alfred and Mac laying out his best uniform. Mac turned to take his captain's hat and coat. Brewer picked up his coat with gold bullion on the lapels, then hesitated.

"Sir?" Greene said.

Brewer set the coat down. "Benjamin, let's do this a little differently. I want you to return to the deck and relieve Mr. Tyler. I will write a note to the Governor-General asking for an audience at his earliest convenience. Have Mr. Tyler deliver it. Best uniform. He is to wait for an answer. Mac, ready the gig. Hands in their best uniforms. We want to make a good impression."

"Aye, sir," Greene replied. Both he and Mac headed for the door.

Brewer turned to his steward. "Alfred, the uniform looks

better than the day I bought it."

"Thank you, Captain,"

Brewer sat down at his desk and wrote out a quick note to the Governor-General before beginning a letter to his mother. In a harbor as large as this, he reasoned, they might be able to find a ship bound for England who would carry a mail bag home for them. He was into the second page when he heard Lieutenant Tyler depart on his errand. Brewer tapped his nose with the feathered end of his quill and wondered what the governor-general's response would be. *You can never tell with the Spanish,* he thought.

He signed the letter, then folded and sealed it with wax. It was a letter he never thought he'd write, informing his mother of all that happened to him lately and wishing her a merry Christmas. He hoped it would bring a smile to her face.

It was nearly three hours later that he heard the boat return. A knock on the door was followed by the entrance of Mr. Greene and Mr. Tyler. Greene held a note in his hand, which he handed to the captain. Brewer read the invitation for *Capitan* Brewer to meet with Jośe Cienfuegos, Governor-General of Cuba, at ten o'clock tomorrow morning.

"Excellent!" Brewer said.

The next morning found him seated beside Mac in the stern sheets of the gig. The wind had kicked up overnight, and he wore a cloak against the spray. It was no great distance to the pier, but the crowded harbor made a direct route impossible. By the time he reached his destination, Brewer had counted ships from no less than ten nations.

He was pleased to see a carriage awaiting him at the end of the pier. A liveried footman held the door of the open carriage, and the driver whipped up the horses as soon as his passenger was seated. The ride was a pleasant one, and Brewer was surprised to find Havana to be quite a modern city — he passed coffee houses and restaurants that could have been transported from Jamaica or Martinique, and there was a park he thought was absolutely beautiful.

They finally pulled up to the governor's mansion; it was on a hill outside of the town overlooking the harbor. The lane approaching the mansion was lined with beautiful trees and opened to a fountain in front of the residence. The footman sprang from his place to open the door, and the captain thanked him as he stepped down. Another servant stood in the doorway at the top of the stairs. He closed the door behind them after Brewer stepped inside.

"*Capitan* Brewer?" he said. "I am Simon, the governor's aide. Welcome to Havana, sir. Please allow me to take your hat and cloak. Thank you. If you will follow me, the governor awaits."

Brewer followed Simon through the house to a courtyard where he found the governor-general seated at a table. Cienfuegos rose as they approached. Simon made the formal introductions, then he bowed to his master and departed.

Brewer came to attention while the introductions were made. After Simon left, the governor-general stepped forward and offered Brewer his hand. The captain shook it and found it to be firm. Cienfuegos was nearly as tall as Brewer himself with a stocky build, the only things betraying his age being a receding hairline and age lines on his face.

"*Capitan,*" he said, in reasonably good English, "it is good to make your acquaintance. Will you stay and dine with me?"

"Your excellency is most kind," Brewer replied as he took the seat offered by his host, "but I'm afraid this is not a social call."

The governor-general smiled. "I like a man who is not swayed by pleasantries. How may I assist you?"

"I am here on the orders of Admiral Lord Hornblower,

commander of the West Indies Squadron, to inquire about a British ex-patriot named Michael Underhill. He emigrated to the United States and then outfitted a privateer for use against us in the late war. The problem is, we have evidence that he did not cease his privateering after the treaty was signed. Has he tried to sell any of his prizes here?"

Cienfuegos rubbed his chin as he studied his guest. He picked up a bell on the table and rang for refreshments. The governor raised his glass in silent salute before taking a long drink. Brewer reciprocated, but only allowed the liquid to barely touch his lips. He set the glass on the table and waited for his host to respond.

"Capitan," the governor said at last, "I am sorry for the trouble this man is causing you. I admit that I have heard his name, but he has not had dealings here in quite some time. In fact, if I remember correctly, he tried to bring a ship here to sell just after I arrived — that would be just over two years ago, *Capitan* — and I refused him entrance. I said I had no wish for trouble with either England or France. You see, one of my staff who was of long service warned me that he plunders not only British but also Spanish and French ships. I would not be surprised to learn he has been back since for, shall we say, recreational purposes, but I have no direct knowledge of this."

Brewer drained his glass and set it on the table. "I thank Your Excellency for this information. I thank you for your hospitality, but I will take up no more of your time." He rose, and the governor followed suit.

"Capitan," the governor said, "I must warn you. I know that Señor Underhill has many friends, both here in Havana and elsewhere, who benefit from his activities. As you proceed they are likely to hear of you, and they may attempt to foil you. You must take care."

Brewer rested his right hand on the pommel of his

sword. "Always, Your Excellency."

"What will you do now?" the governor asked.

"My information, now that Havana has been eliminated, is that Underhill is selling his prizes at New Orleans. So," he said, as they moved toward the door, "that will be my next port of call."

The two men shook hands. "I wish you luck," Cienfuegos said. Brewer bowed and left.

The ride back to *Revenge* was a silent one as Brewer went over his interview with the governor-general in his mind, taking it apart and putting it back together again, and trying to decide whether he could take what the man said at face value. For his part, Mac could only risk the occasional sideways glance at his captain. He said nothing; not only was it not his place, but he also knew Captain Brewer well enough by now to know that he needed time to go over things and sort them out in his head. Mac knew that his part would come when the action began.

Brewer was met by Lieutenant Greene when he stepped up on the deck.

"How did your meeting go?" the lieutenant asked.

"I'm not sure yet," Brewer admitted. "I'm still processing it all." Brewer took a step, and then turned back. "Benjamin, how many American ships are there in the harbor?"

Greene raised his eyebrows in surprise. "Several, sir. Why do you ask?"

"Several? And we're sure *Oliver Cromwell* is not among them?"

"To the best of our knowledge, yes. Mr. Reed knows the ship from Martinique, and he says he did not recognize her in the harbor."

The captain thought for a moment before nodding. "Very

well. Please, pass the word — I would like to see you, Mr. Sweeney, and the doctor in my cabin at..." he pulled his watch from his pocket, "four bells."

"Aye, sir." Greene touched his hat and went to speak to Mr. Sweeney, and his captain went below to his cabin.

"Alfred!" he called when he arrived. The servant appeared. "Can we have coffee for four in a half-hour, please?"

"Aye, Captain."

His guests arrived as the ship's bell rang four times, and Brewer led them into his day cabin. They found their seats, and Alfred served the coffee. Each man savored his first drink.

"Pardon my curiosity, Captain," Sweeney said, "but I've wondered about something ever since you took command on the *Defiant*."

"And what is that, Mr. Sweeney?" Brewer said.

Sweeney held up his cup. "Coffee. You seem to like it as much as some Americans do. Come to think of it, I don't think I've ever seen you drink a cup of tea on board when coffee was available."

Brewer chuckled. "Guilty as charged. I developed a taste for it when I was young, and I much prefer it to tea. I'm afraid the East India Company will never forgive me."

"Lucky for you Alfred is a magician with the bean," Spinelli commented.

The captain raised his cup in agreement. "No argument there. I have been truly blessed." After an appreciative sip, he got down to business. "Gentlemen, I have called you here to let you know how my interview went with Governor-General Cienfuegos went and to discuss our next move." He spent the next twenty minutes describing his meeting with the governor, his guests listening intently. When he finished, Mr. Greene spoke up.

"Captain, do you think the governor is credible?"

Brewer grinned, pleased that his premier had picked up on his own doubts. "Why do you ask?"

Greene shrugged. "I have run into Spanish authorities in the past who, shall we say, had no trouble with telling us what they thought we wanted to hear rather than the truth."

"My dear lieutenant!" Sweeney said in mock outrage. "Are you saying that a representative of the Spanish monarchy would *lie* to a king's officer?"

"Let's just say he would phrase his words so he kept out of trouble," Greene clarified.

"What a shock!" the doctor said.

"Yes, well," Brewer said, "to answer your original question, Lieutenant, I am not at all ready to declare the governor as absolutely credible. Let's say the jury is still out on that one."

"Do you believe him when he says that Underhill is no longer selling his prizes at Havana?" Greene asked.

"Strangely enough, I do," the captain replied. "He seemed sincere in his desire to avoid any problems with the French or ourselves."

"So," the doctor asked, "where does that leave us?"

"We go to New Orleans," the captain said, "and hope we have better luck. Benjamin, when can we sail?"

"We are ready now, sir, but I have had requests from both Alfred and Old Smoot to go ashore before we sail. It seems there are delicacies available here that would be hard to pass up."

Brewer considered the request. Any delay could conceivably allow a ship to carry a warning to New Orleans; on the other hand, if Cienfuegos was credible, waiting until the morning to depart seemed worth it.

"Very well," he said. "Have Mac take them ashore this

afternoon. I want him to stay with them at all times, just in case."

"Aye, sir," Greene nodded.

"Thank you, gentlemen," Brewer said by way of dismissal. "We sail with the tide in the morning."

The assembly rose and made their way out of the cabin, but somehow the captain was not surprised to see the doctor remain behind.

"Something I can help you with, Adam?" the captain asked.

"No, not really. I just wanted to see how you're doing?"

The captain sighed and faced his friend. "I'm fine, Doctor. Really, there's nothing to be concerned about."

The doctor stood his ground. "What about the question of who in Havana is in Underhill's pay? Isn't that what the governor warned you about?"

Brewer shrugged. "Yes, but I don't see any way to find that out before we sail. Hopefully, we can find out more when we reach New Orleans."

"William, let me be blunt. Are you sure, or will you soon be, that you can point a gun at Underhill and pull the trigger?"

The captain looked at the deck below with his jaws clamped shut. Spinelli could see his jaw muscles clenching and unclenching. Finally, Brewer looked up. "Yes."

The doctor nodded. "Good enough. Good day, Captain."

Brewer watched his friend go out without another word, and he wondered if what he'd said was really true.

Captain Brewer stood silently on his quarterdeck and watched as Lieutenant Tyler conned the ship out of Havana's harbor and settled her on a western course toward the Gulf of Mexico and New Orleans.

The captain stepped over to the wheel, where Lieutenant Tyler was talking to Lieutenant Greene and the sailing master. The three men saluted as he approached.

"Well done, Mr. Tyler," he said. "Havana has something of a reputation of being a difficult harbor, but you handled it well."

"Thank you, Captain."

"Mr. Greene, I think it best to keep the men at their drills," Brewer said, "both aloft and gunnery. I am very much afraid we will need them at their best before this mission is over."

"Aye, Captain."

"Mr. Sweeney, steady as you go. Call me when it's time to change course for New Orleans. That should be some time tomorrow, correct?"

"Aye, Captain," Sweeney agreed.

"Mr. Greene has the deck," Brewer announced. "I am going below. Call me if I am needed."

"Aye, Captain," Greene said.

Brewer went to his cabin and sat down at his desk. He pulled out his log and brought it up to date. Then he took out a sheet of paper and began his report to the admiral. He hesitated in his description of the governor himself, because he had no direct evidence to back up his feelings. In the end, he left the description in with an appropriate caveat. Two hours later, he finished the report, and signed it. He folded it and made a notation in the corner before dripping hot wax and impressing his seal upon it. He set it aside to dry and stood to choose a book to read. He ate his supper alone, after which he took a turn on the deck and had a very interesting conversation with Mr. Reed regarding the best methods to train young midshipmen such as Mr. Short.

The next morning, Brewer was up on the deck with the dawn, pacing the lee rail of the quarterdeck before his breakfast. He went below for a delicious meal of eggs, oatmeal, and coffee. He was about to start another letter to his mother when there was an insistent knock at the door. The sentry admitted Mr. Short.

"Mr. Greene's respects, sir," he said hurriedly, "but would you please come on deck? We have two strange sail aft."

"Let's go, Mr. Short." Brewer grabbed his hat and coat and was out the door in a flash, followed closely by his midshipman. Mr. Greene met him on the deck with a telescope.

"There, sir." He pointed aft.

Brewer walked to the fantail and raised his glass to his eye. Two brigs came into focus, each carrying every stitch she could, and they were closing. He saw no colors.

"Mr. Greene," he said, "call the hands. Make all sail."

"Aye, sir." He picked up a speaking trumpet and bellowed, "All hands! All hands make sail! All hands make sail! Lookout! Is either of those the *Oliver Cromwell*?"

"Don't think so, sir!" came the reply. "Sails are all wrong!"

Brewer never took his eyes from the newcomers, but he could hear the bare feet of his men pounding the deck and then climbing aloft to unfurl every sail *Revenge* possessed. The captain hoped the increase in speed would allow them to outpace their pursuers until he could find a way to elude them. Soon the wind filled the new sails, and Brewer felt the ship leap forward, but it was in vain as it quickly became apparent that the enemy ships were continuing to close.

Greene joined him at the fantail, silently watching as the strangers approached. Brewer lowered his glass and turned.

"Mr. Sweeney?"

The sailing master shook his head. "That's all we've got, Captain."

The captain nodded and turned back in time to see one of the brigs veer a few points to starboard. Brewer saw at once they were trying to box him in by an attack on each side, but the really troubling thing was that the slight change in course put the brig on a better point of sailing, and as a result she was soon ahead of her consort. The captain lowered his glass and pursed his lips.

"Friends of Underhill, sir?" Mr. Greene asked.

"If so, I think it means we now know whose side the governor-general is on," Brewer said bitterly. "No, that's not quite fair. It may be one of his servants who's in Underhill's pay. He may have overheard and reported it."

Greene looked at the sky. "I think they'll have us before nightfall, sir."

Brewer looked at the sky and grimaced. "I agree. You may clear for action, Mr. Greene."

"Aye, sir." Greene turned from his captain and began bellowing the orders that would begin the transformation of HMS *Revenge* into an instrument of war. In a few minutes, he was back by the captain's side. "Orders, sir?"

"As an old friend of mine once said, when you are outnumbered, it is better to play the wolf than the possum." Brewer lowered his glass. "The ship coming up our starboard quarter has pulled ahead of his consort and also opened a wide gap between them. It may be possible for us to jump on him and damage him significantly before his friend can come to his aid. Beat to quarters! Load the starboard battery with grape over ball and run them out! Mr. Sweeney! On my command, I want to turn seventy degrees to starboard to cross the enemy's bow. We shall fire a broadside into her bows, cross her, then come hard to starboard again and put another broadside into her as we pass."

"Aye, sir!" Sweeney replied. He went to the wheel to relay the plan to the quartermaster and his mates.

Brewer turned to see Mac and Alfred standing there, both armed with pistol and sword. Mac held the captain's hanger and a brace of pistols. The captain quickly put them on and thanked him. Brewer turned back to business, knowing they would be close by if needed.

"Stand by!" Brewer cried. He looked to the near brig on his starboard quarter and wondered what that captain thought of his position. He was in for a surprise. "Now, Mr. Sweeney!"

HMS *Revenge* turned hard to starboard and straightened up on the course ordered. Brewer could see activity on the enemy quarterdeck. *Good,* he thought, *looks like we surprised them.* "Mr. Greene! Fire as you bear!"

Greene made no reply but waved to show he heard the order. Brewer watched as he ran forward to make sure those gun captains did not fire too early. A quick glance at the enemy brig showed they were desperately trying to get out of the way of what was coming, but it only made them lose wind and become an easier target. In the next instant, he heard his own guns erupt. There were three distinct broadsides, the guns going off in sections as they made sure their aim.

"Mr. Sweeney!" Brewer ran to the wheel. "When we're clear of them, turn hard to starboard and reduce sail. Mr. Greene! Reload the starboard battery with chain! Aim for her rigging!" He looked to starboard, but the smoke blocked his view. "Lookout! Let's hear you!"

"He's badly hit, sir!"

Brewer felt the ship swing around to starboard and the orders go out for the hands to reduce the sail. As they came out of the smoke, Brewer turned to see the enemy battery out and ready to fire.

"All hands down!" he cried. *"Get down!"*

The broadside was not as disciplined as their own; some guns went off early or flew over the deck because the gun captain didn't make sure of his target. Brewer jumped up from the deck.

"Fire!" he cried.

Three or four of his guns managed to get their shots off before they were carried past the enemy brig. Brewer looked down the deck and was relieved to see Mr. Greene and Mr. Tyler on their feet directing the guns.

"Mr. Sweeney! Bring us around to larboard. Mr. Reed, find me that other brig!"

"Aye, sir!"

Revenge came around slowly to larboard. Brewer could see the damage done by his broadside, but the enemy could still fight. His second broadside had not been nearly as effective as the first, and the enemy's starboard battery was still dangerous.

Their turn was completed and they were closing on the brig again. Mr. Short came running up. "Mr. Reed's respects, Captain!" he cried. "He says the second brig is on the far side of this one and looking to pass ahead of him!"

"Thank you, Mr. Short! Return to Mr. Reed!" Brewer turned to Tyler, who was directing the larboard battery. Tyler waved to show all was ready.

"Turn to starboard, Quartermaster!" the captain called. "Bring us alongside. Mr. Tyler, fire the broadside when you bear!"

"Aye, sir!" the quartermaster replied. Mr. Tyler waved.

Revenge came alongside the enemy, and both ships' broadsides went off together. Brewer flinched against the wind and buffeting of the incoming shot and heard the screams of the wounded. He felt a hand on his arm and turned to see Mac beside him.

"Captain? Are you hurt?"

Brewer shook his head. "I don't think so. Take Alfred and

see if you can help the injured."

"Aye, sir." He turned and signaled Alfred to follow. Both men headed forward.

"Captain!" Brewer saw Mr. Short come running up to him. "Mr. Reed's respects. Sir, he says the other brig is about to clear this one!"

Brewer's eyes flew to their larboard bow, and he heart sank as he saw the other ship begin to pull clear of the damaged ship. "Mr. Sweeney! Hard to starboard!"

He watched the sailing master leap to the wheel, and only then did he realize that three of the quartermaster's mates had fallen in the last broadside. Brewer ran to the wheel and threw his weight into the turn along with the sailing master and quartermaster. Slowly the ship came around and headed away from the enemy. Unfortunately, three men belatedly doing the work of four was just not fast enough; the second brig cleared his consort and fired.

All three at the wheel were thrown to the deck by the impact. Brewer jumped to his feet and helped Sweeney to stand. They got the wheel put back over to help the ship get to safety. He looked around and saw Mr. Short staggering to his feet.

"Mr. Short!" he called. "Tell Mr. Reed to come down!"

"Aye, sir!"

The captain went to the fantail to assess their situation. The first brig was down a mast and looked to be badly damaged, but the second one had swung around and was following them. He turned forward to see Lieutenant Greene coming aft.

"Damage report!" Brewer demanded.

Greene saluted. "Two guns out of action in the larboard battery, one in the starboard. We are trying to get them back into action. Injuries have us down one or two gun crews per battery. We can work that out."

"Load the starboard battery with grape over ball!" Brewer said. "I will throw back the mains'l and put the wheel hard over to starboard. When that happens, fire as you bear; don't wait for the command!"

"Aye, sir!"

Brewer's eyes followed Greene forward, and he was relieved to see Mac and Alfred on their feet and helping, Alfred helping the wounded to get below while Mac appeared to have taken over as a gun captain. A quick glance aloft told him the sails, though damaged, were still serviceable. His eyes came down to the deck to see Mr. Reed approach.

"Mr. Greenie's respects, Captain," Reed shouted. "He's ready."

Brewer nodded and indicated Reed should stand by, then he went to the wheel.

"Mr. Sweeney, I want to back the mains'l and put the helm hard over to starboard. Mr. Greene has a surprise for our friends."

Sweeney grinned wickedly, and he bellowed out the orders before joining the captain and the quartermaster on the wheel. They waited until the ship's speed dropped before putting it hard over to starboard. Again, the ship came around too slowly for the captain's plan to come off as planned. The enemy was able to turn to larboard, causing most of Greene's broadside to miss. The brig fired in return, and Brewer heard a devastating crack. He looked up to see the mizzenmast shot away about twenty feet above the deck.

"Bosun's mate! Get a party to cut away that wreckage!" The mate waved his acknowledgment and knuckled his forehead. He ran to get axes and jumped on the lines with three or four hands. Thirty minutes later, the wreckage fell away into the sea. Sweeney quickly issued orders to trim the ship's sails to compensate for the missing mast.

"Hard to larboard!" Brewer shouted. "Mr. Tyler! Fire as

you bear!"

Revenge caught a puff of wind that brought her around faster this time, and Tyler's broadside slammed unanswered into the brig's starboard bow. One lucky shot took the bowsprit. Brewer's ship continued past the brig only to walk into a broadside from her larboard battery. Brewer's left shoulder was sliced open by a splinter, and he went down to one knee.

"Captain!" Mac came running back to the quarterdeck. "How bad?"

"Take the coat off and look," Brewer said.

The coxswain slid the torn, bloody coat off and ripped the captain's shirt open. "There's no exposed bone, sir. Looks like a clean tear to the muscles. I don't see any wood in there."

"Then bind it up for now. I'll keep the arm in a sling."

Mac hesitated for a second before getting to work. "Aye, sir."

Lieutenant Greene appeared. "Four guns out of action in the larboard battery, six in starboard. Casualties are beginning to hamper our efforts to fight and sail."

Brewer nodded and panted heavily. What could he do now?

"Captain!" Mac called. "Look!" He pointed to a squall that had developed off the starboard bow.

Brewer looked to his premier and nodded.

"I understand, sir," Greene said. "Mr. Sweeney, put us in that squall! Mac, take the captain below."

The captain made a weak attempt to protest, but he gave in as Mac supported him and guided him to the stairway.

Greene watched them disappear below deck, then he turned aft to gauge the distance from the pursuing brig. He set his jaw and nodded to himself.

"Mr. Sweeney," he said, "give her all the sail you think she'll carry. Once we're fully in the squall, change course. I don't care where, as long as we stay hidden until they get tired of looking for us. Pass the word, we're going to enter a squall. Lash down everything you can. You have the deck; I'm going forward to see for myself, then I'm going to check in with the doctor. After that, I shall return."

"Aye, sir," Sweeney said.

Greene went forward and inspected the damage. What he saw confirmed that he was doing the right thing in removing *Revenge* from the battle. Hurriedly he made his way below to the sickbay. Once there, it took a moment for his eyes to adjust to the relative darkness before he could spot the doctor working on the captain's shoulder.

"Doctor," he said when he stepped over, "what's the verdict?"

Spinelli finished dressing the wound and said, "The splinter sliced some muscle but missed the bone. He should recover full use of the arm in time."

"Good. Doctor, can you spare Mac?"

"You mean my best nurse?" the doctor said sarcastically, then motioned toward the door with his head. "Take him."

Greene motioned for the coxswain to follow him as they stepped outside the sickbay. "Mac, find Alfred and get to work on the captain's cabin. I've no idea how badly it was hit, but he's going to need to rest for a few days. Also, stop by and see Old Smoot. Have him make up a cabin in the gunroom, in case the captain has to rest there for a few days. Report to me after you've had a look at his cabin. I'll be on the deck."

"Aye, sir." Mac left on his task, and Greene considered going back in but decided against it. He called for Gator, one of the doctor's loblolly boys. The young man had got the strange nickname because he claimed to have spent time in Spanish Florida, where he learned to wrestle with those deadly reptiles.

"Aye, sir?" Gator knuckled his forehead.

"Gator, please pass the word to the doctor to come up on deck and see me when he's done. Let him know if he needs more hands, all he has to do is ask."

Gator nodded. "Aye, sir." He saluted again and disappeared inside.

Greene made his way back to the quarterdeck. He looked aft and saw they were barely keeping their distance from their pursuers. Suddenly, he heard a report from aft and saw two white puffs from the brig — she was firing at them with her bow chasers. One landed just short of their starboard quarter while the other missed wide to larboard by about ten yards. He turned to see Sweeney standing beside him.

"Definitely not up to naval standards," he said to the sailing master. "Wouldn't you agree?"

"Yes," Sweeney said, "and that means they're pirates. Or privateers."

Greene stepped over to the compass, and Sweeney followed. "What's our course?" the premier asked. "Nornor'east? Once we're hidden, make our course due east. Keep us in the soup, Mr. Sweeney." He looked down the deck. "I think the old girl's given us all she has for one day."

Sweeney nodded. "Agreed, Mr. Greene."

Revenge entered the squall. Ten minutes later, Sweeney swung the ship around to the east. The rain that lashed the deck made it difficult to see the bow, so Greene felt relatively sure the ship was safe for the moment. Mac had reported to him during the interval that the captain's quarters would require a day to make right if they had a little help. Greene sent over a carpenter's mate and one other hand. Now he left Mr. Tyler in charge of the deck and went down to see the damage for himself.

He stepped below and heard someone call his name. The

doctor appeared out of the darkness.

"There you are," he said.

"What's the butcher's bill, Doctor?" Greene asked.

Spinelli sighed. "Seven dead, twenty-seven injured, including the captain. What's the situation up top?"

"We've taken refuge in a squall. After they've given up looking for us, we'll make our way back to Port Royal for repairs. Mac and some hands are making repairs to the captain's cabin. For now, we have a space for him in the gunroom."

"That'll do," Spinelli nodded. "Whatever you do, keep him off the deck for a few days. His shoulder should heal, but he lost a lot of blood, and I'm worried about infection."

"Understood, Doctor. I'll assign Mr. Short to keep an eye on him."

Spinelli frowned. "What will Mr. Short do if the captain decides to leave the gunroom?"

Greene smiled. "Why, Doctor, he'll go get Mac."

Spinelli chuckled, then said, "I have to get back. It'll probably be a few hours before I'll be ready to move the captain to the gunroom."

"Understood, Doctor. Do you need more help?"

"Not just now. When we're out of the squall, we'll need to bring the dead on deck and sew them up."

Greene nodded. "Let me know."

The doctor patted him on the arm and turned to go. Greene made a mental note to see that the doctor got eight hours' uninterrupted sleep as soon as was practical. He entered the captain's cabin.

The larboard quarter had taken the worst damage. The captain's sleeping cabin on the starboard side was relatively intact and could probably be made ready in twenty-four hours.

Mac and Alfred stepped over. "Not too bad, eh, sir?"

Greene shrugged. "We're lucky that this ship, despite her size, was built with a frigate's layout rather than that of a traditional sloop. The gunroom is but lightly undamaged, so we can bunk the captain there for a day or two." He looked around at wreckage. "So, how long?"

Mac took a deep breath. "We can't repair it at sea, sir," he said. "The damage is too great. Once we get out of the squall, we should be able to make it livable, but that's about all."

Alfred agreed. "If the weather turns bad, it may be better that he stays below."

Greene looked around and sighed. "Well, do your best. I'm sure the captain will understand. Alfred, as long as the captain's below, I'd appreciate it if you'd help out Old Smoot whenever you can."

"Of course, sir."

Greene left them to their work and went to the gunroom to fetch his cloak. The storm was heavy, and he needed the protection from the driving rain. He stepped up on deck and found Mr. Sweeney near the wheel. The rain was still heavy, hiding them like a blanket.

Greene got right up to the sailing master's ear. "Are we still due east?" he shouted. He felt Sweeney nod vigorously. "I have the deck!" he shouted. "Go below and get something warm to eat or drink. I shall send Mr. Tyler below as well! One of you relieve me in two hours!"

Sweeney patted the premier's arm to show he understood. Greene watched him make his way carefully to the stairway and disappear below. Then he passed the word for Mr. Tyler and sent him below as well. He pulled his cloak more tightly around him, wiped away the rain that lashed his face, and hoped for the best.

CHAPTER SEVEN

They sailed out of the squall about 3:00am. Greene made the decision to keep the ship on her easterly course for now. By the time dawn pinked the sky they were making a steady four knots, and Greene changed course to the so'east to head down the north coast of Cuba. From there, he hoped to use the Windward Passage to get back to Jamaica unmolested. Mr. Tyler stepped up on deck as scheduled; Greene went below to snatch a couple hours' sleep himself, but he was back on deck with the sunrise. Eight bells of the morning watch had barely sounded when Mr. Short appeared on deck with the message that the captain wished to see him in the gunroom.

"Mr. Short?" Greene said, "you left the captain unattended?"

"Oh, don't worry, sir! I told Old Smoot that if the captain made for the door, he should sit on him!"

Greene closed his eyes and tried not to laugh at the absurd picture that popped up in his head. "Very well, Mr. Short. Let us go rescue the captain!"

They arrived below to find the captain seated at the gunroom table, his arm in a sling and coffee steaming before him. Old Smoot appeared. "Coffee, sir?"

"Yes, please. How are you, Captain?"

"Better, thank you. I managed to get several hours sleep, which helped. The doctor says I was very lucky the splinter missed severing the artery. If I can avoid infection, I should recover full use of the arm in six weeks or so."

"Glad to hear it, Captain. Oh, thank you, Smoot. Our course is so'east. Cuba is just out of sight to starboard. I hope to get back to Port Royal for repairs."

Brewer nodded. "Ship damage?"

"We suffered damage to the deck and uppers, but Mr. Ringold says the hull is intact. Mr. Sweeney and the quartermaster are nursing us along at an average speed of four knots, not bad without the mizzen. Mr. Snead and his men got to work on the lines with first light; I should hear a report from him within the hour."

Brewer's took a drink of his coffee. "And the bill?"

"Last time I spoke to the doctor, which was nearly twelve hours ago, we had seven dead and twenty-seven wounded. All those who can be moved will be brought up on deck as soon as it's feasible for the sunshine and fresh air. I also ordered the doctor to bed."

Brewer's eyebrows went up. "How on earth did you get him to agree to that?"

Greene smiled. "I told him if he didn't go voluntarily, I would send Mac down to pick him up and carry him to bed."

Brewer threw his head back and gave a bark of laughter, followed immediately by a wince and gasp of pain, his hand going to his bad shoulder. "Oh, Benjamin, that is a picture I shall treasure for some time! Well, as long as it worked. Who has the deck now?"

"Mr. Sweeney was coming on when Mr. Short arrived. Mr. Reed will relieve him for the afternoon watch."

Brewer nodded again as he held very still and took several deep breaths to calm his shoulder's throbbing. "I'm finding the timing of this attack very suspicious, Benjamin."

"As do I, Captain," Greene replied. "Coming as it did after your conversation with the governor-general in Havana, it's almost as if Underhill was listening to the whole exchange."

Brewer frowned. "But neither attacking ship was *Oliver Cromwell*."

Greene shrugged. "I'm not surprised. I shouldn't think he'd risk his own neck or ship against us. Didn't the governor tell you that he had many friends who profit from his activities?"

"Yes, he did."

"There you have it, then. Even if the governor is correct, even if Underhill is not welcome to sell his prizes at Havana anymore, he still has ears in the governor's office and friends who are bold enough to organize an attack on a Royal Navy ship within twenty-four hours' notice."

Brewer didn't like what he was hearing, but he couldn't argue it. "And my cabin?"

"Well," Greene said, "there's good news and bad news."

Brewer steeled himself with a deep breath. "Let's have the bad news."

"It looks like we took two hits in the larboard quarter. Your desk was destroyed, and your writing set along with it."

Brewer flinched. He had bought the writing set for himself when he was made first lieutenant on HMS *Defiant*. "And the good news?"

"Your chess set survived," Greene said, "as did your cross for the *Légion d' Honneur*. Alfred has them safely stored away."

Brewer let out the breath he'd been holding. "Thank God," he whispered. "I'll need pen and paper to work on my report for the admiral. I'll need a report from you covering the events after I was taken below through, say, dawn this morning when repairs began in ernest, then the usual daily logs until I resume command."

"Aye, Captain."

Brewer looked at his cup. "Thank you for the bed space here, Benjamin. I assume you've spoken to Alfred about helping Smoot while I'm here?"

"Already done, Captain. Alfred was only too happy to help."

"Good," Brewer said. "As one of the walking wounded, so to speak, I shall go up on deck tomorrow for my share of the sunshine and fresh air."

Greene laughed. "I'm sure the men will enjoy that, sir."

True to his word, the next morning Brewer, assisted by Mr. Short, made his way up on deck and to the fo'c'sle where several of the wounded were either lying on stretchers or sitting on the deck or in makeshift chairs. Some of them tried to rise or knuckle their foreheads when they saw him coming.

"Never mind that," Brewer said. "I think we can pass on formality this once. How's the weather up here?" He sat in an empty chair and rested his good arm on the breech of a 12-pounder.

"Never better, Cap'n," said one of the hands lying nearby. "All we need now is some daffodils and petunias."

Those who could, laughed. Those who couldn't coughed or slapped the deck. Brewer said with mock seriousness. "I'll see what I can do when we reach Jamaica."

"Say, Captain," this one was in a chair across deck, his head wrapped like a Muslim turban and one arm in a sling, "if it's not out of line, do you know what that was about? Why did those brigs attack us?"

Brewer rubbed his chin, then winced in pain as he tried to adjust his seat. "I suppose you have a right to know. We are on an assignment for the admiral. We were... we are searching for a British ex-patriot named Michael Underhill.

He served in the Royal Navy during the war, but he deserted and went to America. During their last war with us, he outfitted and captained a privateer, and he was very successful. He took many prizes in the Caribbean and surrounding waters. Recently, we have discovered that he did not cease his privateering when the war ended."

The hands around him looked at each other in disbelief. The nearest one leaned toward his captain.

"Do you mean to tell us," he said slowly and deliberately, "that some no good deserter went to America, and then not only fought against us in the last war, but the damned traitor is *still* raiding out shipping?"

Brewer sighed and looked down. "Yes."

The hand stared at him in outrage, and Brewer could see the disbelief turning to rage on his face. The man opened his mouth, but he was saved by a blunt statement from the man next to him.

"You knows him."

The first hand turned to the second. *"What did you say?"*

The second nodded toward the captain. "He knows the bloke."

They all turned to the captain. Brewer looked them over before nodding. "It's true; I know him. Michael Underhill was a petty officer in the same ship when I was a new midshipman. He taught me a lot before he deserted."

The first hand jumped in. "Wait a minute! You were there? When he deserted?"

Brewer replied in a steady voice. "I talked to him that afternoon, and in the morning he was gone."

"And he never told you he was going to run?" the second asked.

Brewer shook his head. He wasn't sure where this was going, but he thought they had a right to know why their shipmates had died. The hands went silent; they looked one to another to another as though trying silently to come to a consensus about how they felt about this. Finally, they all looked at the first hand, who nodded and turned to the captain.

"We're with you, Captain," he said. "Underhill deserves to hang."

They all nodded their agreement.

Brewer looked them over, his eyes meeting each man's. God, he was proud of these men!

"Thank you," he said.

HMS *Revenge* sailed southeast past the western tip of Cuba, just out of sight of land. She turned east toward Jamaica. Brewer continued to sit on the fo'c'sle with the other wounded. They talked about home, hunting, cooking, anything that any of them thought of. The men who had the use of their hands whittled or spliced ropes. Brewer tried to teach one or two of them chess, but none seemed to take to the game. When the captain suggested Mac come up to read to them, they scoffed at the idea, so he called the coxswain up to read to him. Naturally, nobody objected to the captain's wishes, and soon they found themselves listening as well. Alfred and Old Smoot were invited to take part in the discussions on cooking, and recipes were willingly and joyfully exchanged.

Eventually, they arrived at Port Royal, and the ship slid into the harbor. Though his injury was healing, slowly but surely, and he had so far avoided infection, Brewer still found certain movements painful. He was frustrated that the doctor wanted to wait another fortnight before allowing him out of the sling and beginning to exercise his shoulder to restore strength and range of motion.

The morning after their arrival, Brewer submitted to

Mac's ministrations as he helped his captain into his dress uniform for his meeting with Admiral Hornblower, and soon they were in the stern sheets of the gig, making their way toward the shore. He walked with as much dignity as he could manage to the admiral's office, where he was shown into the admiral's presence by a steward.

Hornblower looked up in shock as Brewer made his way gingerly into the office. He came around the desk to help.

"William!" he said. "What happened?"

"It's all in my report, My Lord," Brewer explained as he slid gently into the chair the admiral indicated. "A splinter tore through my shoulder, but fortunately there was only muscle damage. The doctor said I will need to exercise, but he thinks I should regain most if not all of the strength and movement."

"That's good to hear," the admiral said. "Tell me what happened."

Brewer spent much of the next hour recounting his meeting with the governor-general and the subsequent battle against the two brigs the next day. Hornblower listened without interrupting, his hooded eyes the only indication of what was going on inside his head.

"So," he said when his protégé was finished, "it appears this business runs much deeper than we first imagined."

Brewer adjusted in his chair. "Indeed, My Lord. Either Governor Cienfuegos himself is complicit, or someone high up in his government is on Underhill's payroll. That's the only way those two brigs could have come upon us as quickly as they did."

"Agreed," Hornblower said. He rose and straightened his tunic. "Ha-hm!" he said, and, after motioning for Brewer to remain seated, he began to pace before the empty fireplace. "On the surface, and without any hard evidence, the good governor may have committed an act of war against the

British Empire. However, as I have said, we have no proof of those charges. How badly is *Revenge* damaged?"

"We lost our mizzen," Brewer said. "There's also a great deal of damage to the deck and aloft. The hull is sound."

Hornblower made a turn and stared out ahead of him, searching his prodigious memory. "There's a dry dock coming open the day after tomorrow. HMS *Prometheus* is scheduled for a refit, but I shall order *Revenge* take precedence. If nothing else, Commander, your adventures have shown me that we are on the right track, and our inquiries are striking very close to home. Underhill now considers you a serious threat to him and therefore you must be removed from the equation." He paused; there was a grim smile on his face. "No doubt, the commander of those brigs will have a hard time explaining to their master why it is that you are not dead or standing there before him."

Brewer grunted. "The way matters stand, if I were there, Michael would shoot me himself."

The admiral was at that moment behind him, so Brewer did not see his head snap around in surprise at his words. Hornblower recovered quickly and marched to his chair. "Ha-hm!" he said. "No doubt, which is all the more reason for him to be taken at the earliest possible occasion. Do you have a damage assessment and estimate for repairs?"

"Aye, My Lord," the Commander replied. "It is included in my report. I gave it to the aide outside. I believe it said less than a week, provided a new mast were available immediately."

"Very well," Hornblower said. "As soon as you are ready for sea, your original orders still hold. I presume you will head for New Orleans?"

Brewer inclined his head. "Yes, My Lord. I'm not fully convinced that Underhill is unable to sell his prizes in Cuba, if not Havana itself, but Secretary Thompson indicated that

New Orleans was a more likely place for such transactions. Even though it is a possession of the United States, its remote location apparently opens the door, at least at this present time, to nearly any sort of lawlessness that can be purchased." The commander shrugged and winced. "It seems the logical place to search next."

The admiral stared off into space for a moment as he bounced his fingertip gently on his lips. "Agreed," he said finally. "I want you to be careful, William; we know now that Underhill will have no mercy nor give any quarter."

"I shall, My Lord."

"Good. I shall have your wounded transferred ashore while *Revenge* is repaired; your doctor can go with them to oversee their care. Any declared fit by the time you sail can rejoin the ship, the rest shall have to remain here until you return." The admiral escorted his guest to the door. "In the meantime, William, I want to invite you to stay with me while your ship is repaired."

Brewer was taken completely by surprise by the request. "My Lord, I am honored, but I feel I should be with my ship."

"Nonsense," the admiral replied. "Your first lieutenant would feel as though you don't trust him to do his job, not to mention the look on your doctor's face when he discovers you intend to stay aboard without him. Besides, I confess to feeling a bit lonely during the holiday season, and you are the closest thing I have to family in this hemisphere."

Brewer surrendered as gracefully as possible. "Thank you, My Lord. I accept. With your permission, I should like to return to my ship for clothing and to inform Lieutenant Greene of these new developments."

"Of course, William," Hornblower replied. "Supper is at 8:00pm."

Brewer raised an eyebrow and smiled. "8:00pm, My Lord? Not the turn of the second dog watch?"

The admiral shrugged. "The price for having to deal with civilians."

Brewer laughed and came to attention before taking his leave. Out on the street he stopped at a sidewalk café just down from the admiral's office where he ordered a cup of his favorite strong Jamaican coffee and a pastry with a name he could not pronounce but which was a specialty of the house. He pulled a small book of poetry from his pocket and began to read while he waited for his order. He was so engrossed by the book that he did not hear a man approach.

"Hello, William."

Brewer looked up to see Michael Underhill taking a seat across the table.

"Michael? What are you doing here?"

Underhill shrugged. "Why not? Nobody knows what I look like, except you. So long as I don't bring *Cromwell* into any British harbor, no one's the wiser." He looked around casually before returning to his host. "Did you enjoy your visit to Havana?"

Brewer's brows furled and his eyes hooded in anger. "So it was you who sent those brigs after me."

Underhill shook his head. "Afraid not, old chum. I wasn't in the city. That was done by a man who works for me — or *worked* for me, I should say. Personally, I wouldn't have trusted the job to only two brigs. Not against you."

The conversation lapsed as Brewer's order was delivered. The commander sipped the coffee.

"What do you want, Michael?" Brewer demanded.

Underhill leaned forward with one arm on the table and picked up the pastry. "I want you to leave me alone," he said as he took a bite and set it down on the plate. "I had hopes that our last meeting would convince you, but I see I was mistaken. You know, in a way I'm proud of you; I had high hopes for you all those years ago when I knew you on the

Kent. Now I see how well you've turned out, I wish I'd been wrong, because you're using your skills against me."

Underhill noticed that Brewer's eyes were looking past him, so he turned to look over his shoulder and saw a group of British soldiers coming up the street. He turned back to Brewer with a deadly serious look on his face. "William, let me warn you. Look off to my left. Do you see that young couple sitting at that table, sipping their tea? I have a pistol in my belt. If you say or do anything to attract the attention of those soldiers — or anyone else, for that matter — I will fire my pistol at that table. I guarantee you, one of those people will die. Now, can we agree to have a nice, civil conversation here?"

Brewer sighed, his face set as stone. "As you wish."

"Good," Underhill said. He brought his other hand up from his lap and leaned it on the table as well.

Brewer looked at his friend's hands. "So, are you going to kill me now? That won't help you; I hope you know that. Hornblower will just send a frigate after you."

Underhill leaned back and waved his friend's threat aside. "Oh, I know that, William. Believe it or not, I'm trying very hard *not* to kill you." He leaned forward again, both elbows on the table and hands folded. "The trouble I'm having, you see, is that you're quickly advancing to the point where you're leaving me no choice." looked down at his hands, and Brewer thought he saw a look of regret cross his face, but when Underhill looked up again, it was gone. The only thing on his face was a terrible resolve. "William, you are threatening to undo more than ten years' work. I cannot allow that, no matter what you once meant to me. If I see you again, I will kill you. If I come across your ship on the high seas, I'll destroy it without hesitation. Do we understand each other?"

"Perfectly." Now Brewer leaned forward. "Now you listen. One, I'm not so easy to kill. If we do meet again,

Michael, know that I will do my duty to the best of my ability, without hesitation and without remorse."

"Just as I taught you," Underhill said. "I would expect no less."

"Two," Brewer continued, "you chose this life. It was not forced upon you by anyone. You didn't have to do this, you chose to. Don't pretend otherwise." Underhill opened his mouth, but Brewer cut him off. "Three. Somehow, I don't know how or even when, but you've taken the most decent and honorable man I knew and turned him into nothing more than a bloody pirate." Brewer leaned back in his chair. "Do we understand each other?"

"Perfectly." Underhill rose now, and Brewer could see the pistol tucked into his waistband on his left side. "I'll be leaving now. Before I go, I want you're promise you won't alert any authorities of my departure."

"Why?"

Underhill smiled. "Two reasons. One, the moment I see, hear, or even *think* someone is closing in on me, I will draw my pistol and kill the first innocent bystander I see. And two, I know that if you give me your word, you will keep it, no matter how distasteful it is to you."

Brewer looked around and saw the midday crowd growing, and he knew Underhill would fulfill his threat. "Very well. You have my word."

"Thank you." Underhill bowed and turned to leave.

"Michael!" Brewer called. Underhill turned back, and Brewer nodded to the pastry. "Take it."

Underhill looked from the pastry to Brewer and back again, then snatched it up.

"Generous to the last," he said. "Good bye, William."

"Good bye, Michael."

Brewer drank his coffee, then ordered another and another pastry. When he was finished with them, he rose and made his way to the wharf where Mac was waiting for him. He said nothing of his encounter with Underhill on the way back to *Revenge*, nor when he stepped up on deck to be met by Lieutenant Greene and Mr. Short. Brewer invited Greene to join him in his cabin, and asked Mr. Short to pass the word for Mr. Sweeney and the doctor to join them.

Once the four of them were seated in the captain's cabin and Mac was in his usual place by the door, Brewer told them of his meeting with the admiral. True to Hornblower's prediction, the good doctor was pleased to hear the wounded would be transferred ashore during repairs, and he objected strongly when he learned the captain would not be joining them. He relented upon learning that the captain would be recuperating with the admiral himself instead of staying aboard ship. After the doctor settled down, Brewer took a deep breath and told them of his meeting with Underhill.

"But how did he get to shore here?" the doctor asked.

Brewer shrugged. "As he said, there's really nobody who knows what he looks like besides me, and possibly you. If he keeps to himself, he's perfectly safe to walk the streets."

"I hate to ask this question," Sweeney said, "but, *Why didn't he kill you?*"

The captain shook his head. "I don't know, but I don't think I'll ask him, either. I will tell you one thing: I don't think we can expect such mercy next time. The line has been drawn."

Brewer met each man's eyes to make sure they understood. Each man did.

He dismissed the doctor to oversee the transfer of the wounded ashore and went over the repair lists with Greene one last time. "The admiral said the dock would come open the day after tomorrow, Benjamin. In the meantime, let's do what we can. I want you to go ashore tomorrow and schedule as much as you can regarding the stepping of the new mast, supplies, etc."

"Aye, sir," Greene said. "What about shore leave?"

Brewer thought for a moment before answering. "I shall leave that to your discretion. The work on the ship takes precedence, naturally."

"Naturally, sir," Greene agreed. "I'm sure that I can motivate the men."

Brewer smiled. "I'm sure." He turned to watch Alfred pack him a bag for a week or two with the admiral.

The servant looked up. "Which books would you prefer, sir?"

Brewer looked at his bookshelf and rubbed his chin. "Hmm. That's a question, isn't it? Just put my Bible in the bag. I'm sure the admiral will give me the run of his library."

"Very good, sir."

Brewer turned back to his premier. "Send me reports, if you please, Benjamin. I want to keep current on the state of repairs."

"Aye, sir. Daily?"

The captain shook his head. "Not unless you think it to be necessary. Let's just say updates as needed."

"Aye, sir. Have a good rest, Captain," Greene urged. "We'll take care of things here. You concentrate on getting well. We need you at full strength when we go out after Underhill."

Brewer smiled and patted his friend on the arm. "Thank you, Benjamin. I shall do my best."

Greene came to attention and left the cabin. Brewer watched him go, thankful once again to have him as his first lieutenant. It eased his mind to know that he could take a medical leave and know his ship was in such good hands.

There was a knock at the door, and Mac came in. "Gig's

ready to go, sir. May I take you bag?" He picked it up and paused. "Sir, won't you please change your mind and let me or Alfred accompany you? What if Underhill changes his mind and comes after you?" Mac stepped closer and lowered his voice. "Captain, I'd much rather protect you than have to avenge you."

"I appreciate that, Mac," Brewer said reassuringly, "but I'll be fine. Michael won't come after me, but neither will he forgive me if I choose to pursue him further."

He didn't like the answer, but the big Cornishman didn't argue, either. Instead, he came to attention and left the cabin with the bag.

Two hours later found Brewer standing in his bedroom at the admiral's house. The room was a large one with a four poster bed against one wall and a fireplace opposite with a chair and table set to one side. A washstand stood in one corner beside the bed, and there was a large dresser next to a wardrobe where he could hang his uniforms. The steward who met him at the door and showed him to his room said that Lord Hornblower sent his apologies at not meeting his guest in person, but he was called to the governor's house unexpectedly.

"His lordship did say that I was to show you to the library as soon as you were settled," the man said. Brewer indicated the door, and the man led him down the hallway and up the stairs at the end to the second story library. It was a large single room with bookshelves covering the two long walls and the short wall at the far end of the room. The admiral's desk dominated the far end, and the small wall at the near end contained a large fireplace with two overstuffed leather chairs placed in front and a table between. Above the fireplace was a large hearth with a stone bust of Napoleon Bonaparte.

Brewer stepped forward and looked around the room. He noted that the stairwell they had ascended had a twin in the opposite corner at the far end of the room. His eyes came around to take in the fireplace with the bust atop, and he couldn't help but wonder why a house in the Caribbean had such fireplaces — after all, it wasn't as though Jamaica saw temperatures like those he'd endured on his recent visit to Washington City. He shrugged and decided to appreciate the beauty of the piece. He turned back to his guide.

"Impressive," he said.

"His lordship thought you might approve," the steward said. "I believe his exact words were for you to 'enjoy yourself'." He smiled. "Dinner is at eight, Commander."

Brewer stepped into the dining room just as a clock somewhere in the house struck eight and found the table set for three. The same steward who had showed him the library — a Frenchman whose name turned out to be Claude — entered from another door, carrying a tray that held a decanter and glasses.

"Welcome, Commander," he said. "His lordship and Mr. Girard will be joining you directly." He set the tray on a small table near a window and departed by the same door.

"Commander Brewer!"

Brewer turned to see Lieutenant Girard enter the room. He went and shook the older man's hand.

"Girard! It's good to see you!"

"The pleasure is mine, sir, I assure you," Girard led him to the tray, filled two glasses, and handed one to his guest. "His lordship will be down directly; I'm afraid he was rather later than he wished in returning from his meeting with the governor. Your health, sir." The two men drank, then Girard said, "I understand you have been given a particularly distasteful assignment."

"How do you mean?"

Girard looked at him over his drink. "I understood Michael Underhill was your friend."

Brewer looked out the window. "That is true. He was a mentor to me when I was a young midshipman on the old *Kent*. But I will do my duty."

Girard took a sip of his drink. "Yes, well, I cannot say I envy you your assignment. Is that how your ship came to be attacked?"

"Yes. At least, that is our working theory. I interviewed the governor-general of Cuba in Havana, and two days out from Havana harbor we were attacked by two brigs." Brewer shrugged. "What other conclusion could we draw?"

At that point, a door opened and Hornblower walked in. Both officers came to attention.

"William! A pleasure to welcome you. Are you settled in? Splendid! Has Claude shown you the library?"

"Yes, sir, thank you."

Hornblower smiled. "I thought you would appreciate it." He accepted the glass Girard offered. "Thank you, Girard. You know, William, in my opinion, a library need only have one set of books to be fully stocked."

Brewer kept his expression serious. "Gibbon, sir?"

"The only book worth reading," the admiral confirmed. "In fact, the next time you're there, if you look you will find all six volumes on the shelf behind the desk." He shrugged. "If you're interested, that is."

Brewer traded a quick, knowing glance with Girard. "Thank you, My Lord."

Claude stepped into the room. "I beg your pardon, My Lord, but dinner is served."

The three officers found their places. Brewer was pleased to find himself seated on the admiral's right, the place of honor at a supper table. The stewards brought plate after platter after bowl and set them on the table. There was a roast chicken, a bowl of baked potatoes, a small pitcher of lime juice, fresh baked bread with marmalade, and an assortment of local vegetables cooked together with aromatic spices.

"By the way, Commander," Hornblower said, "I mentioned to the governor that you were staying with me, and he has invited us to dine with him tomorrow at noon. I trust you will be available?"

"Of course, My Lord."

"Good." Hornblower picked up his knife and fork. "In that case, gentlemen, I suggest we do justice to this feast before us!"

Hornblower carved the chicken while Girard helped himself to the vegetables and Brewer made a claim on the potatoes. Soon each man's plate was full, and the conversation was limited to between mouthfuls. The admiral told them of a letter he recently received from his wife about a Christmas pagent that would take place in Smallbridge. When the meal was done, Admiral Hornblower sat back in his chair and pushed his plate forward.

"There's nothing better under Heaven for improving a man's disposition that a fine meal," the admiral said at the conclusion of supper. He wiped the corners of his mouth and tossed the napkin on his plate. "I am glad to have you two gentlemen with me, especially at this most festive time of the year. Girard, you have been with me for well over ten years now, and you, Mr. Brewer, barely more than three, but the two of you are the closest thing I have to family on this side of the world. I would give anything for Barbara and Richard to be here with me, but, absent that, I know not of any I would rather have around me."

"Thank you, My Lord," Brewer answered for them both.

"It has been our pleasure to serve with you."

Hornblower rose. "I apologize for the early night, gentlemen, but there is an Admiralty courier leaving on the morning tide, and I must write to my wife before I go to bed. I shall see you at breakfast."

Brewer and Girard rose. "Goodnight, My Lord."

The admiral left the room, and Brewer turned to his friend. "An excellent idea, Girard. With your permission, I too shall write a letter to be sent home on the courier. If you'll excuse me?" He paused by the door. "I almost forgot - how is Mr. Phillips doing?" Lieutenant Phillips went from serving on Brewer's ship to being an aide to Admiral Hornblower after being wounded in battle.

"Quite well," Girard replied. "In fact, the admiral sent him as a courier to the Admiralty in London. He may be back by the time you return next."

"I hope so. Thank you for the evening."

"Of course, William. Good night."

Brewer made his way back to his room. He was pleased to find writing materials in the desk. He sat and picked up the quill, pausing for a moment before dipping it in the inkwell to order his thoughts. He wrote again to his mother about his recent change of attitude toward Christmas, knowing she would be pleased. He also wrote her about the recent battle — though not the reasons behind it — and the wound he'd received. He wrote of the invitation of Lord Hornblower to stay with him and convalesce while his ship was being repaired, and of his lordship's words at supper. He closed with a promise to come see her the next time he was in England and signed off with his love.

He sat back and reread the missive. He thought about changing some of the wording but in the end decided to leave it as written. He folded the paper, sealed it with the wax that was provided, and wrote his mother's name and address on the outside. He went to find Claude and gave him the letter; the servant promised it would go with the admiral's mail in the morning.

Brewer breakfasted early and went immediately to the library. He searched the stacks until he found a book about Lord Nelson and his great victories. He poured himself a glass of water from the pitcher in the corner, sat in one of the chairs before the hearth, and began to read. He was still there hours later when the admiral found him.

"Well, Commander," Hornblower remarked, "I cannot say I am surprised to find you here."

"Claude did say you said I should enjoy myself, My Lord," Brewer replied. "I have been doing just that." He held up the book. "I pray you'll forgive me for preferring this over Gibbon."

Hornblower waved away the apology. "Ha-hm! Well, never mind that," he said with a grin at the corner of his lips. "I still have hopes for you. But I came to remind you about our engagement with the governor. You just have time to dress."

Brewer set the book aside and rose. "Thank you, My Lord. I shall meet you down stairs."

He returned to his quarters and dressed hurriedly, wishing he had allowed Mac to accompany him, if only to be here to help him get his coat on. He checked his appearance one last time in the mirror before leaving the room. The admiral was awaiting him at the foot of the stairs.

They rode in the admiral's carriage in a thoughtful silence. Brewer grew uncomfortable at withholding his meeting with Underhill from Hornblower, especially considering they were on their way to dine with the island's governor — a man who made it a habit to be unusually informed. He took a deep breath.

"My Lord, I need to tell you something before we meet with the governor." The admiral turned to him, and Brewer related the story of his encounter with Underhill at the café. When he finished, Hornblower looked out the window without so much as a word. Brewer knew this was his chief's method of processing information, but still it made him uncomfortable.

"I apologize, My Lord," he said, at a loss to say anything else.

Hornblower looked back from the window. "Sorry, William? Whatever for?"

Brewer shrugged. "I honestly don't know, but I think I should have done something to apprehend him."

The admiral shook his head. "Nonsense! You acted in the only manner open to you, given the circumstances. To do anything different would have put civilians in danger." He shrugged. "You did right, William; you had no choice. Let's keep this information to ourselves for the present. Understood?"

"Yes, My Lord."

They finished the trip in silence, which suited Brewer fine. *So now we're keeping information from the governor?* He cast a surreptitious glance at the admiral, who was again watching the scenery outside the window. *You know something I don't, don't you? What would that be, exactly, and when did you learn it?* He looked out his own window, pursing his lips as he turned things over in his mind. *When we get back, My Lord,* he decided, *we need to talk, and this time I'll listen.*

They arrived at the governor's mansion outside the city. As they came up the drive, Brewer was surprised to find the governor himself awaiting them at the top of the stairs.

"Welcome, gentlemen!" he called as they alit from the carriage. "Come! Come! We have much to celebrate!"

"And what would that be, Your Grace?" Hornblower asked as they climbed the stairs. The two officers came to attention when they reached the top, but the governor merely nodded and shook both men's hands. He waved them in the open door.

"Need you ask, Admiral?" Montague said as the servant took their hats. "We have the Christmas season upon us, sir, and if that were not enough, we have the commander's safe return from a difficult battle!"

The duke led them down the hallway and into a study that Brewer thought was furnished perfectly for informal meetings. Two leather settees facing each other with a long, low table in between dominated the near half of the room. There was also an overstuffed chair at the far end off the table. The other half of the room held a small ornate desk on one side with two chairs in front of it, while the other corner of the room held two chairs with a table in between set apart for a private *tête-à-tête*. The far wall held two large windows covered by curtains, and the walls were decorated with tapestries and paintings, including a large portrait of the king. The governor waved them to one of the settees before sitting on the settee opposite them. "Refreshments for three, if you please, John," Montague said. The servant bowed and left.

"Commander," the duke began, "the admiral and I have discussed your mission to Havana in general terms, and I have read your report. Still, I should like to hear your personal account of the battle."

"Yes, Your Grace." Brewer took a deep breath and gave the governor a synopsis of the encounter. Montague listened, interrupting once with a question and again for an explanation from Hornblower of a particular battle maneuver. Brewer finished just as the servant arrived with three glasses of wine, which the governor handed out. The duke saluted his guests and drank deeply from his glass before making himself more comfortable.

"Well, Commander," Montague said, "it seems to me you acquitted yourself well against two-to-one odds. You and your people did well to come back alive. You're sure neither of the brigs which attacked you was the *Oliver Cromwell*?"

"Quite sure, Your Grace. Neither ship was known to us."

Montague looked to Hornblower. "It would seem that Governor-General Cienfuegos is compromised."

"Perhaps," the admiral replied, "but have you met the man? No? I have, once when my ship put in at Havana for emergency repairs. I found him charming in a diplomatic sort of way; I must say that I would not believe anything he says without independent confirmation."

The duke smiled and nodded. "Yes, I know the type. I shall bear that in mind in dealing with him. In the meantime, what happens next?"

"HMS *Revenge* is in dock at this moment for repairs," Hornblower explained. "Commander Brewer is my guest while he recuperates from his injuries. I have transferred his wounded to the naval hospital ashore, accompanied by the ship's doctor. Lieutenant Greene, *Revenge's* first lieutenant, is overseeing the repairs to the ship. When repairs are completed, I am sending Commander Brewer to New Orleans to complete his original mission."

"I see." The duke swirled the wine in his glass. "I hope this does not come out wrong, but do you think it safe to send *Revenge* out alone again?"

Brewer replied, "Never fear, Your Grace. We shall be careful. We're not talking about a professional navy, remember; Underhill is still only a privateer. He has learned the hard way that two brigs cannot best a ship like *Revenge*, and I very much doubt he has either bigger or more numerous resources at his command. I also don't think Cienfuegos will commit any Spanish resources to aid Underhill. I believe the governor-general was telling the truth when he said he did not want trouble with Great Britain or the Royal Navy."

The governor nodded and drained his glass. "From what you tell me, there seems to be very little I can do to help you on the diplomatic front. Admiral, every resource will be available to you, of course." A bell rang somewhere in the house, and the governor rose. "Now, gentlemen, dinner is served."

He led them to the dining room, where three places were set at the table. The commander was seated on his host's left, while the place of honor on his right went to the admiral. The servants poured their drinks and withdrew.

"I hope you gentlemen are in good appetite. The main course this afternoon is a smoked ham. I confess it to be a favorite of mine, and one I do not get very often out here." The platter containing a large ham along with a carving set was placed before the governor. Potatoes were also brought, along with several kinds of vegetables, fresh hot bread, and marmalade. The governor rose.

"Gentlemen," he said formally, "I wish you both a Merry Christmas, and offer my personal thanks for all you do to keep the sea lanes safe for His Majesty's ships."

"Thank you, Your Grace," Hornblower answered.

The Duke bowed and picked up the carving knife and fork. "If you gentlemen will permit me, I shall carve this ham, and then you can help yourselves. Have either of you ever had a ham smoked before? No? You are in for a treat, I assure you!"

The three men filled their plates and dug in with abandon. Brewer had never had a "smoked" ham before, but he made a mental note to get the recipe for Alfred. The bread was fresh, and nothing was more welcomed by a sailor than fresh baked bread. He eagerly helped himself to seconds.

The governor smiled. He turned to Hornblower. "I take it

fresh bread is a treat for sailors, no?"

The admiral pursed his lips. "Tell me, Governor, have you ever had ship's bread on one of your voyages?"

The duke laughed. "I see your point. Sorry, Commander; a silly question."

Brewer smiled and took another bite.

The ride back to the admiral's house was quiet, right up to their walking through the door and handing their hats and coats to the servant. Hornblower was making to go upstairs when Brewer stopped him.

"My Lord, a moment, if I may?"

Hornblower stepped down off the stair and looked at his protégé. "I could use a drink, William. You?"

"Yes, My Lord," Brewer replied. "Thank you."

The admiral led him down the hall to his study and poured them each a drink. They settled into the two chairs before the window.

"A question, My Lord," Brewer said. "Forgive me if I am blunt, but why did you not want the governor to know about my encounter with Underhill?"

Hornblower took a deep swallow. Then he set his glass down and sat back. Brewer got nervous when the admiral looked at his hands and not at him.

"William," he said, "I wasn't going to tell you, but I suppose you have the right to know. The governor has a reputation of interfering, and I prefer to keep him as far from this Underhill business as possible. To tell the truth, I'm not sure Governor Montague is safe."

"Safe?" Brewer questioned. "You mean, from Underhill?"

Hornblower nodded. "I have heard rumors that it was information from Montague's office, not Cienfuegos', that sent those brigs after you outside Havana."

Brewer stared at him with mouth agape. "My God!" he whispered.

"Yes," Hornblower agreed. "Exactly. When you are ready to sail, I shall tell the governor that I have new information regarding Underhill, and I am sending you back to Martinique." He sighed in disgust. "I hope that will leave you safe to go to New Orleans unmolested. Of course, if the *Oliver Cromwell* is seen in the area of Martinique, we'll know the truth about the governor — or at least his office."

The admiral rubbed his eyes and rose. "If you will excuse me, William, I shall retire. I shall see you in the morning."

"Good night, My Lord," Brewer said. Once Hornblower was gone, he drained his glass and went to his room. He was pleased to see a report from Lieutenant Greene waiting for him on his desk. He sat down and opened the report to read that repairs were proceeding apace, the only problem being the availability of a new mast — or rather, the lack thereof. It would be a week before one was available to be stepped. Repairs to the ship itself were almost completed, including the rebuilding of the captain's cabin. Greene hinted at certain unspecified improvements incorporated at Alfred's direction. Greene begged his captain's forgiveness, but he was not at liberty to give any details, having been sworn to secrecy by the captain's steward. All the guns had been repaired or replaced, and Greene estimated that by the end of the week they might be able to vacate the dock and be moved to a berth where they would be available to the sheer hulk when it came time to lift the new mast into place. He closed with a line or two about going to hear Mac read to the men on the fo'c'sle and how he hoped the captain was not straining himself too badly in the luxury of his recuperation. Brewer laughed and refolded the report. He shook himself out of his uniform and did his best to hang it up neatly with one arm, then he took himself to bed.

The next morning, he breakfasted with the admiral. The subject came around to Christmas Day, now only two days away.

"I must say," Brewer said around a mouthful of eggs, "I can't imagine a Christmas Day with so much perspiration."

The admiral laughed. "I'm afraid that goes with the Caribbean, William. This shall be my third Christmas here, and I hope my last. I confess to missing the seasonal weather at Smallbridge."

"Do you get much snow there, My Lord?"

Hornblower shrugged. "Some. I think the last letter I got from Lady Barbara said there was a small accumulation on the ground. The village children enjoy it greatly. One year when I was home at Christmas, I was asked to judge a snowman contest! Nearly all the children of the village participated."

"Marvelous, My Lord! Who won?"

Hornblower sat back and smiled at the memory. "Believe it or not, it was a young girl. Let me see, what was her name? Eliza? Alice? No, it was Emma. She was a tiny thing, only eight or nine years old, as I recall, and small for her age. Her snowman was only half as tall as some of the others, but she'd shaped the face into a comical expression, and she'd found a wonderful hat and put it on the snowman. When I saw it, I laughed and decided then and there she was the winner. I got such a hug around my leg from her that I was sore for two days!"

The two men laughed. Brewer said, "I remember playing in the snow when I was young. Sometimes I wish I could go back to those days."

Hornblower picked up his coffee. "I can understand that longing, but believe me, William, it's better to look forward." He sipped gingerly at the hot liquid. "The past is locked, for better or worse, and there's nothing we can do to change it. The future will be what we make it. You should never allow the past to ruin your future. If you think about it, that's exactly what Underhill has done."

Later in the library Brewer thought over what his mentor had said, both with regard to Underhill and also to himself. *He's right,* Brewer concluded. *Right about both of us. Michael is either unable or unwilling to get past what happened to him on the Kent all those years ago. It has directed his steps ever since, right down to his privateering during the war and his piracy afterward. And me?* Brewer shrugged. *I suppose so. I spent over ten years hating Christmas because of what happened at home. Now, thanks to my new "family", I see things differently, but what is that going to do for my future?* Brewer shook his head at the unanswerable question. *What am I doing? I remember how to celebrate Christmas!* He nodded to himself, satisfied with the plans forming in his mind.

Michael Underhill swung peacefully in his cot in his cabin on board the Columbian-flagged merchantman *Esmerelda.* It was his usual mode of travel when he did not want to take *Cromwell* to sea. Nobody expected him to travel this way, and it had worked well for the last three years. He could go to Jamaica or St. Kitts or Martinique, and nobody knew him from Adam. He travelled under an assumed name on the ship's passenger manifest, and never the same name twice. On this trip, he was plain old John Smith, a resident of New Orleans heading home.

Underhill truly enjoyed traveling this way. He had no duties to perform, and the gentle motion of the ship rocked him to sleep like a baby. It also gave him time to think; sometimes a good thing, sometimes bad, but always necessary and profitable. This time, he was thinking of his run-in with

William Brewer in Port Royal. Underhill had traveled there to arrange for the sale of some wine he had taken off a recent prize, and it had been on his way back to *Esmerelda* that he'd seen Brewer come out of the admiral's house.

He'd thought about ducking down an alley and making his way to the boat awaiting him at the pier, but somehow he could not deny himself the pleasure of one final peaceful meeting before the fight began. He wished once again that he had handled their original meeting in Martinique differently and not given William any cause for suspicion. As it was, he'd drawn exactly that attention to himself which he had successfully avoided for the last ten years.

Underhill raised his arms and interlaced his fingers behind his head. He sighed, hoping Brewer would take to heart his warning to leave him alone but knowing all the while he would not. Underhill closed his eyes in dismay; now he would be forced to kill the lad — strange how he still thought of Brewer that way — or else Brewer would be forced to kill him. Underhill shifted; better to die at sea than to be brought back to Port Royal for a date with the hangman. He felt a tug at his heart, and he had to admit to himself he did not want to kill Brewer. There had been a day, still not forgotten, when he would willingly have given his own life to save the lad's, but that time was done. He swallowed hard and set his face like a flint. He left the choice to Brewer; he would decide their destiny. He would do what he had to do, no matter what the consequences.

Time in the library — this was something Brewer thought he could really get used to. The calmness, the silence, it was almost too good to be true. He made the decision right then and there that he would have one in the house he would build one day. Bookshelves from floor to ceiling, large windows to let in copious amounts of sunlight, and a large hearth at one end dominated by a full size portrait of his wife, whomever she turned out to be.

His tranquility was shattered this particular morning by a familiar voice coming up the stairwell.

"William? William, are you up there?"

He closed his book and rose in time to see the head of Dr. Spinelli emerge from below. "Adam? What are you doing here?"

"What? Oh, there you are!" the doctor exclaimed as he crossed the threshold of the library. He looked around in wonder. "Sweet mother of God!" he whispered. "How will we ever get you back aboard ship?"

Brewer laughed as he shook his friend's hand. "Have no fear, my friend! Although I am determined now to have a library in my house when I retire. How did you find me?"

"A steward met me at the door and showed me to your room, but you weren't there, so he took me to this incredible winding staircase and said you were most likely up here."

"That would be Claude." Brewer led the doctor to the chairs before the hearth. "So, tell me truly, how are the men coming along?"

"Well enough, for the most part," Spinelli said, as he settled into his chair. "After a few days, they began to get restless, so I sent to the ship and asked Mr. Greene if he could spare Mac and a book for a few hours. He agreed, and Mac brought... let me see, what was it? Oh, yes, it was *Ivanhoe*. Anyway, they took to it like a baby to mother's milk. He comes by every other day or so, as his duties allow, and they absolutely love it! But enough of that, let's talk about you. How are you?"

Brewer shrugged. "It seems to hurt less, but I think what pain I feel now is from the arm being stiff, if that makes any sense."

"Absolutely," the doctor said as he rose. "Stand up. I

want to see the wound." Brewer rose, and the doctor began removing his shirt and then the bandage that was still around his shoulder and chest. He went and got the pitcher of water and basin from across the room and proceeded to wash the shoulder. He dried it gently and then began his examination. Brewer hissed as the doctor moved his arm incrementally this way and that. Spinelli nodded and let the arm rest.

"I think it's coming along nicely," he pronounced happily. "The color is good, indicating good blood flow to the area as well as the absence of any infection. What we need to do now are exercises to restore your strength and range of motion. I warn you, they will hurt at first, but they must be done if you expect to regain use of the arm."

Brewer slid the arm back into the sling and relaxed. "I'll work on it."

"You'd better," Spinelli warned, "or you'll be doing sword drills with Mr. Short in the future. Now, come with me." He led his patient to the desk at the far end of the room. "A table would be better, but this will do. William, I want you to lean on the table with your good arm, like this. See? Now, allow the injured arm to hang loosely, like so. Now rock it like a pendulum." The doctor demonstrated, setting his arm to swing back and forth. "Not much at first, back and forth, then side to side. Twenty of each. Increase the range of the arc each day, a little more than the day before. After a few days of this, I want you to do a circular motion, like this. Easy at first, then make the circles bigger. Understand? Now you try it."

Brewer took his position and allowed his arm to hang. He began to swing the arm back and forth, but found the pain would only allow him to go a few inches in each direction. He looked to the doctor in concern.

Spinelli shook his head. "That's about normal for the

first time or two, William. I warned you it would hurt. Now try side to side."

Brewer complied, but again found it painful to go beyond a few inches. Sweat broke out on his forehead, and he had to bite his lip to keep from crying out by the end.

"Good," Spinelli said. "I want you to do five sets of each, morning and evening. I shall be back in a few days to check on you. Also, I want you to quit using the sling unless it's absolutely necessary. Let you arm hang naturally when you walk or sit. If it hurts, you can put your hand in your trouser pocket."

Brewer looked at the doctor as if he had grown a third eye. it sounded as if his friend had stepped right out of the Spanish Inquisition! Spinelli saw the look on his face and smiled devilishly.

"Of course," he said, "if you find that you have trouble with my instructions, I suppose I could ask Mr. Greene to dispatch Mac or Alfred to help you."

"No!" Brewer exclaimed. "Don't you dare! I would end up shooting Mac, and we both know the admiral would figure out a way to secure Alfred for his own kitchen, and that's the last we would ever see of him!"

Spinelli shrugged. "True enough. I know it hurts, but exercise is the best course you have, Captain. Don't think for a minute I won't go to the admiral with my report on your rehabilitation, should you fail to keep up with your exercises."

Brewer gave him as evil a look as he could muster, but the doctor was totally unphased. He surrendered. "Very well, Adam; you win."

"Good," Spinelli said. "Er, you didn't think to bring your chess board, did you?" Brewer shook his head, and the doctor grunted. "Thought as much. Oh, well, that will just leave you more time for your exercises." He stepped back and came to attention. "Now, I'm going to check on Mr. Girard, another old patient of mine. Goodbye, my dear Captain!"

Brewer watched his friend saunter across the library to disappear the way he came, and he muttered every curse he could think of under his breath.

Dinner that night was a rather informal affair. Brewer was surprised to find the table set for only two. The admiral joined him, and Brewer asked after Girard.

"It turns out that our Mr. Girard had a visit from an old friend this afternoon," Hornblower said. "Your doctor, I believe."

"Yes, My Lord."

"It seems Girard was a patient of his at, Gibraltar, wasn't it?"

"Yes, My Lord. Both Captain Bush and Lieutenant Girard were wounded — Girard seriously, it turned out — and I had to assume command. When we reached Gibraltar, I had Girard transferred immediately to the hospital ashore. Dr. Spinelli was the doctor who treated him there."

Brewer reached for a slice of bread and winced at the effort. He saw the admiral looking at him inquiringly. Brewer sighed. "The good doctor took advantage of his visit to start me on some exercises to restore the range of motion to my shoulder. I confess that the cure seems worse than the condition."

Hornblower laughed.

Two weeks came and went, and Brewer's recuperation proceeded apace. The doctor came by twice in that span and gave him new and more demanding exercises. By the time he was ready to return to the ship, Spinelli had given consent for him to begin training with Alfred to strengthen his shoulder and prepare for battle.

Brewer celebrated the holidays for the first time since he'd entered the navy. He spent Christmas Day with the admiral enjoying the fellowship of the season and listening to a choir of children who came by to sing carols. The best part of the day was a knock at the door just after the children departed. Brewer wondered why Hornblower himself answered the door, and was surprised to see Mr. Greene, Mr. Sweeney, Dr. Spinelli, Mac, and Alfred walk in.

Greene shook his captain's hand energetically. "Good to see you again, sir!"

"If you'll excuse me, sir," Alfred said to the admiral, "but where is the kitchen?"

"Claude!" Hornblower called, and the servant appeared. "This man will show you. Claude, see that he gets whatever he needs."

Claude bowed, and the two men left. Brewer watched them go, then turned inquiringly to Hornblower.

"He agreed to cook us a Christmas feast," came the explanation. The admiral addressed them all. "If you will please follow me?" He led the way into the study. "Mr. Greene, if you would be so kind?" He motioned toward the table in the corner with refreshments. Mac took up his usual place beside the door, but the admiral objected. "Not today, faithful coxswain; you will join us this day!"

Brewer watched as they found seats before the fireplace and felt a happiness he had not experienced for years. It was like he was with his family again when he was young. He excused himself to go to his room and returned with several boxes and Alfred in tow.

"You don't know what this means to me," he said to them all. "Some of you know that my father cast me out of my family on Christmas Eve when I told him I was joining the navy. For years that soured me on Christmas, but you have recently shown me that I was mistaken to feel that way. So, to mark my return, so to speak, I have a present for each of you. I was going to give them to you later on the ship, but now seems as good a time as any. I only ask that, for the next few minutes, we set rank aside and just consider ourselves family."

Heads nodded all around the room.

He picked up the first box and handed it to Mac. "Thank you, sir, for loyalty and care of the first order," Brewer said. The coxswain blushed and opened the wrapping to reveal a fine edition of *Gulliver's Travels*. Brewer clapped him on the shoulder. "Now you have a book of your own to read to the men!"

He picked up the next box and handed it to Mr. Sweeney. "Thank you, sir, for your guiding hand." Sweeney raised a eyebrow and opened his gift — a meerschaum pipe with the white bowl carved into the head of Neptune, god of the seas.

"Thank you, Captain," was all he could say.

The next box went to the doctor. He opened it and pulled out a bottle of twenty-year-old Scotch.

"Captain!" he gasped. "I don't know what to say! Wait! Is this the only way you think you can win at chess?" The room erupted in laughter.

"No, Doctor," Brewer replied, "but I think it an appropriate way to thank you for your friendship."

The doctor made to answer, but no words came, so he closed his mouth and smiled.

Brewer turned to the door and whistled. Claude came in carrying a sword in its scabbard. The hilt was gold, shaped in the basket style, with several rubies and emeralds embedded. Brewer took it and thanked the faithful servant, then he turned and held it out to Lieutenant Greene.

Greene's eyes went wide with amazement. "Oh, Captain! I..."

"Nonsense!" Brewer cut him off quietly. "Benjamin, you have fought at my side longer and more faithfully than anyone. You have saved my life more than once. Money cannot repay the debt I owe you for your friendship and your service. This is the closest I can come. Please accept it with all the thanks from a grateful heart."

Greene took the sword, but when he looked up, words failed him. His eyes misted over. Brewer smiled, nodded, and patted him on the arm.

Next, Brewer picked up a long rectangular box and gave it to Alfred. The servant opened it and pulled out a long, wooden rolling pin, fully four inches in diameter.

"Thank you, Captain," he said, a little bewildered at the gift.

"Oh, that's not for cooking, Alfred," his captain explained. "That's for dealing with Mac. Pull the right end off to reveal your gift."

Alfred pulled and twisted until the pin came apart. He tilted it, and out slid a dagger with a gold, jewel-encrusted hilt and a six-inch blade.

"Captain..." he said in amazement.

"Thank you, sir," Brewer said, "for all you have done for me and what you have meant both to my ship and to me personally. Your training has saved many lives, including mine more than once." Brewer placed his hand on Alfred's shoulder and squeezed lovingly. "But, by all means, feel free to use the pin on Mac whenever he needs it."

"Captain!" Mac exclaimed, and the room rolled with laughter again. Brewer enjoyed it, reflecting that this is how Christmas was supposed to be.

He picked up the last box and walked over to the admiral, who rose to meet him.

"William," he said, "you don't have to give me anything. Just watching you grow, personally and professionally, has given me the joy I thought lost forever when my son, Horatio, died."

"My Lord," Brewer said, "I owe you everything. It was you, at Captain Bush's suggestion, who gave me my chance to prove myself. I can only give you this as a token of my affection and gratitude."

Hornblower opened it to find a copy of Plutarch's *Life of Caesar*. "William, I don't know how to thank you. But this shall have a place of honor in the library."

Brewer turned to the group. "As I said, I owe you all more than I can say. Thank you, from the bottom of my heart."

When the Christmas feast was over, they gathered again in the study. The admiral broke out a bottle of Bordeaux given him by Napoleon himself on St. Helena and poured each man a glass. Alfred was there with them. He'd wanted to help clean up after the feast, but the admiral had insisted that his stewards knew how to wash dishes. Again, Mac tried to take up his usual post, but a look from the admiral cowed him into taking a seat with the rest. Lastly, Claude made the rounds with a box of cigars. Each man took one and puffed them into life.

"Doctor," Brewer spoke up, "how are the wounded coming along? Will we have to leave any behind?"

"Only one, Captain," Spinelli replied. "Old McGivern. One of the original hands from *Defiant*, I believe. I had to take his left arm when infection set in at his elbow. Let me tell you, he is not happy about being left behind."

"What was his job aboard ship, Doctor?" Hornblower asked.

"I'm not sure." Spinelli looked to Brewer and Greene.

"He was a steward, My Lord," Greene said. "Formerly he was a topman, but he's too old now for that kind of work, but he continues to mentor the young hands, so we made him an idler. He was trying to learn to be a sailmaker's mate, and he helps out Alfred and Old Smoot — he's the gunroom steward, My Lord — whenever he can."

Brewer saw the look in his mentor's eyes. "Admiral, might it be possible that you would have a place for an old hand of so vast experience?"

Hornblower looked at him and smiled. "Yes, I think I have need of just such a man. Perhaps you could visit him before you leave, Commander, and put it to him? Thank you. If he agrees, ask him to come to see me when he is released from the hospital."

"I shall. Thank you, My Lord."

Hornblower nodded in gracious acknowledgement and turned to Brewer's first lieutenant. "Mr. Greene, what is *Revenge's* status?"

"Nearly ready for sea, My Lord," Greene replied. "We finished the repairs two days ago, and the last of our provisions were stowed yesterday. We are scheduled for a visit from the lighter tomorrow; once that's done, we are ready to sail on your order."

"Good." Hornblower turned to Brewer. "Captain, I would have you sail at your earliest convenience. Your original orders still hold; you are to go to New Orleans in search of information regarding any activities by Michael Underhill, then report back here to me."

"Yes, My Lord."

The admiral arose, and the rest followed suit. "Mr. Greene," he said, "return to your ship and make ready to receive your captain. Return to the pier one hour after you arrive at the ship, and you should find your captain there waiting for you."

"Aye, My Lord." He came to attention. "Thank you for the meal, My Lord. Let's go, men!" They followed him out of the room, but Spinelli caught his captain's eye and understood he was to remain behind.

"Thank you, My Lord," Brewer said. "For your hospitality, all of this. I've never had a nicer Christmas, and I believe your library actually helped my recovery! Please give my best regards to your dear wife. I hope to see her again one day."

"You are always welcome at Smallbridge, William," Hornblower said. "Doctor, please do your best to keep him in one piece."

"He does make it difficult, My Lord," Spinelli said.

"Perhaps," the admiral admonished, "but believe you me, you do not want to have to explain to my wife why you failed."

The doctor's eyes widened, and Brewer chuckled. "I understand, My Lord," the doctor assured him.

The two men left and stopped at the hospital to see the man McGivern. He was obviously weak and still recovering from the amputation, but he struggled to a sitting position when he saw his captain approach.

"Good to see you, Cap'n," he said.

"And I'm glad to see you recovering, McGivern. I'm sorry you won't be able to go to sea with us."

"Aye, bad luck, an infection like that," the hand said wearily. "Lucky for me, the doc here was able to take the arm and save me life, though I don't know what good I am now to anyone, what with one wing gone."

"Well," Brewer said, "I may have a solution for that. You and I are blessed, McGivern, in that we serve under an admiral who does not believe in allowing talent and experience go to waste."

McGivern looked bewildered. "How's that, sir? What's that ye say?"

Brewer squatted down to look the man eye to eye. "I'm

saying that Admiral Hornblower doesn't believe a man is worthless, even with 'one wing gone' as you put it. Do you remember Lieutenant Phillips? He was with us in *Defiant*."

McGivern thought for a moment before it came to him. "Weren't he the young boy of a lieutenant? Aye, I remembers him. Good lad, he was. Too bad." He shook his head. "He lost a wing as well, I remember."

"That's right," the captain said. "Only that's not the end of the story. Lieutenant Phillips went to work for the admiral. He's an aide in the admiral's office now."

McGivern looked surprised at the news. "Do tell? Good for him. But I don't need no charity."

"And the admiral doesn't give any," Brewer said, "but he does have a place for navy men who want to work. Lieutenant Phillips is at this moment in London delivering reports from the Admiral to the Lords of the Admiralty as his official aide and representative. Does that sound like charity to you?"

"Nay!"

"And it would be the same with you! We told the admiral of your experience on board ship, and he said he has a position for a man like you. What do you say?"

McGivern looked at them suspiciously. "No charity?"

Brewer shook his head. "None. As the Bible says, if you don't work, neither will you eat. Think about it! One arm is gone, but you can still do so many things! The admiral wants to make use of your experience. What say you?"

McGivern brightened up. "I'm in, sir. When do I start?"

Doctor Spinelli spoke up. "I've spoken to the staff here. It will be a few more weeks before you're ready, but as soon as you are, they have orders from the admiral to send you to him."

"Thank 'ee, Cap'n," McGivern said. "And you too, Doctor.

It's good to be wanted. Tell the admiral I'll be there in no time."

"Good luck, McGivern!" The two men waved as they left the hospital.

CHAPTER EIGHT

HMS *Revenge* sailed out of the harbor at Port Royal looking smarter than the day she was taken into the Royal Navy. Captain Brewer stood on the quarterdeck and watched as Lieutenant Greene conned the ship out to the open sea and set her on an westerly course. The new sails and rigging filled and the ship picked up speed. Brewer looked around the deck and was proud to see everything in its place. He saw Mr. Reed and Mr. Short in the mainmast shrouds, and an idea came to him.

"Mr. Greene!" he called, and the premier stepped over and saluted. "I've an idea, and I would like your opinion. How close do you think Mr. Reed is to being ready for a board?"

Greene's brows rose. "Mr. Reed, sir? Let me see... He arrived with recommendations from HMS *Clorinda*, and he's done fine work since his arrival. But as far as his knowledge to get past a board, I'm afraid I don't know, sir."

Brewer nodded. "Look into it, please. You and Mr. Sweeney sit down with him in the gunroom and find out what he knows. Mr. Tyler's commission was granted back before we began this Underhill business, and it's high time we got the next man ready, don't you think?"

Greene smiled. "Indeed I do, sir. I'll see to it at once."

"By the way," the captain added, "how's the new man settling in?"

Both men looked at the third figure on the mainmast shrouds — a ten-year-old boy whose name was Jimmy. The admiral had asked Brewer to take the boy aboard. His parents were both found dead during the last smallpox breakout, and it had been feared for a while the pox might take the boy as well, but somehow he pulled through. He had been living on the streets for several months when the admiral found out about him and made temporary arrangements for his care. Now the admiral wanted to see how the boy took to naval life, and he'd asked Brewer to take him aboard as a ship's boy, with the possibility of making him a midshipman in the future. The boy sat in the shrouds to the side and just below Mr. Short, who was pointing things out and naming ship's parts.

"He seems to be adjusting well, sir," Greene replied. "Mr. Short is quite pleased at having the youngster aboard and has almost adopted him as a younger brother."

"I see," the captain mused. "Well, keep an eye on him. He may have picked up some bad habits living on the streets."

"Aye, sir; I'll see to it."

"Thank you. I'm going below. Call me if I'm needed."

"Aye, Captain."

Brewer made his way below and entered his cabin to the welcoming smell of fresh brewed coffee. Alfred heard him come in and appeared in the pantry doorway.

"May I get you anything, Captain?"

Brewer gave him a wry look. "How can you ask me that with a straight face when I plainly smelled the coffee when I came in?"

Alfred smiled. "I'll bring a cup, sir."

"Thank you. Where's Mac?"

Alfred brought a steaming cup to the captain's desk. "I'm

not sure, sir. Shall I pass the word for him?"

"No, I can wait until he arrives."

"As you wish, sir."

"Alfred, I did want to talk to you," Brewer said. "The good doctor has given his blessing on my resuming training. What do you suggest, as far as strengthening the shoulder and getting ready for battle again?"

"Hm," Alfred said. "It's the left shoulder, yes? Thought so. Well, sir, I think the best thing to do is take up your training again and deal with any weaknesses that appear. What do you think?"

The captain nodded. "I'd rather have you discover the weakness and correct it than for it to show up when we find Underhill. Very well, Alfred, we'll start tomorrow."

"Aye, Captain."

In the mainmast shrouds, Jimmy sat with his legs through the ropes as Mr. Short had showed him, but he still held on for dear life. The movement of the ship beneath him thrilled and terrified him at the same time. He'd only been aboard for a few days, and this new life was unlike anything he'd ever experienced. In truth, he'd never thought of going to sea at all, let alone joining the navy, but Admiral Hornblower said it was the best decision he ever made. And he'd not had a lot of options; even at ten years old, some things are self-evident. The smallpox that took his parents had for some unknown reason spared him, leaving him alone and trying to answer the inevitable question of why.

He'd met Mr. Short almost immediately upon coming aboard HMS *Revenge*. He'd that his first name was William, but because he was a midshipman, Jimmy had to call him Mr. Short. Jimmy wasn't exactly sure why yet, but he figured he'd find out sooner or later. And the midshipman had been very kind to him so far, explaining everything about this new life, sometimes several times over. The food would take some getting used to, but it was better than starving by far, and he had every hope of mastering the art of staying in the hammock on the first attempt any day now.

Everything on HMS *Revenge* was new and exciting to Jimmy. Even going to the bathroom the first time or two had been an adventure! Mr. Short told him that soon Mr. Greene, the first lieutenant, would assign him a job on board. Everyone had one — some hands had two or three — and together they made this ship the best in the West Indies Squadron! Jimmy wasn't exactly sure what that meant, either, but he was definitely eager to learn.

Jimmy looked up at his two friends. On the far side of Mr. Short was Mr. Reed. He was the senior midshipman, which Jimmy guessed made him Mr. Short's boss. He seemed like a man who was very sure of himself and knew what he was doing. Mr. Short had confided in him privately that he was trying his best to learn from Reed and someday to take over from him as senior midshipman. Jimmy wondered if he would ever be a midshipman as well, or whether he would get a different job.

Jimmy looked around the deck, careful to keep his hold on the shroud. He saw the captain and first lieutenant talking together on the … what was it Mr. Short called that part? The quarter horse? No, the quarter-deck! Yes! That was it, the quarterdeck! Jimmy wondered what they were talking about — it certainly looked very secret. Jimmy watched amazedly the two hands manning the wheel. Mr. Short said that was how they steered the ship. Jimmy had no idea how that worked. He knew a little how to drive a horse-drawn wagon and how to steer that, but how that wheel turned the whole ship was beyond him.

He looked up at the small square platforms farther up the mast. Mr. Short said those were the "tops" where the lookouts were stationed. They watched out over the ocean to spot any other ships on the waters. The thought made Jimmy look all around him at the open ocean, and sure enough, they had the whole ocean to themselves. He wondered if the lookouts had much to do at all. He looked up at the tops again and shivered. Maybe one day he'd have the courage to climb all the way up there. Mr. Short said it was just a matter of getting used to it.

"Come on, Mr. Short, Jimmy," Reed said. "Let's get to work."

His companions pulled themselves up to climb down, and Jimmy did his best to imitate their movements. Mr. Short stayed with him until he was on his way down.

"Thanks for waiting for me," Jimmy told him.

"No problem," Short replied. "You did well. Come on."

The two ran to catch up to Reed, who was heading down to *Revenge's* small cockpit. When they got there, Reed sat at the small table while Short jumped up on a bunk. Jimmy just stood there, not sure what to do.

"We need to give you a job, Jimmy," Reed said. "Traditionally, when a new boy comes on board a ship, he's made a servant for a year or two and then moved on to the yards."

"You mean climbing and working the sails?" Jimmy asked. "Why can't I do that now?"

"That's not how it works, Jimmy," Reed said patiently. "There's a lot to learn about handling sails."

"Did you have to be servants?" Jimmy demanded. Both his companions nodded. Jimmy sighed and surrendered. "Right oh, but that in *not* what I thought I'd be doing."

Reed chuckled. "It wasn't what I thought I'd be doing when I signed on either." He rose and punched Jimmy in the arm playfully. "You'll do fine. I'll speak to Mr. Greene and let you know as soon as I get an answer." He waved at them both and went out.

Jimmy looked at Short on his bunk with a frown.

"Don't worry!" Short assured him. "You'll love it here! *Revenge* is a great ship!"

Captain Brewer sat in his cabin with a book in his lap. He was trying to read to pass the time, but his mind kept going back to Michael Underhill. The time spent with him back on the *Kent* kept flooding his mind. Good days, days full of learning, of enduring hard lessons through Underhill's steady guiding hand. Days that laid the foundation for what he was today.

Then came that awful day when Underhill just wasn't there anymore, and soon even Brewer had to accept the fact that his friend and mentor had deserted. The dark days that followed almost ruined his career in the navy; the first officer refused to believe he had no idea that Underhill was going to run and accused the young midshipman of assisting him in his flight. It was only after the second lieutenant and the senior midshipman stood up for him that the premier backed off.

"You need to be very careful, William," the senior midshipman had told him later, in the cockpit. "The first lieutenant still thinks you may have helped Underhill to run, but he doesn't have any hard evidence to convict you. Mind yourself; don't talk to anyone about Underhill in any way. It's the only way you'll be safe."

The young Brewer had just nodded and taken the advice to heart. He hadn't spoken to anyone about Underhill or his desertion until meeting the man himself that fateful day in Martinique. Now the shoe was on the other foot, so to speak, and he was leading the hunt to bring Underhill to justice. Part of his brain — a small part, barely heard from the deep recesses of his memory — begged him to let Underhill go, but Brewer slammed the door on that line of thinking, immediately and firmly. Underhill had made his choice, and now Brewer chose his duty.

A knock at the door interrupted his brooding, and the sentry admitted the midshipman of the watch. The young gentleman came to attention. "Mr. Tyler's respects, sir, and could you please come to the deck? There's a strange sail on the horizon."

"I'll come," Brewer said, and the midshipman came to attention and departed. He closed the book and set it on the table beside him. He rose with a sigh and put on his coat, grabbed his hat, and headed out the door.

He was greeted by his second lieutenant when he stepped on the deck.

"Hello, Captain," Tyler said. He handed the captain a telescope and pointed off the larboard beam at a white dot on the horizon. Brewer put the glass to his eye, but at this distance it only made the dot bigger. Tyler continued, "The lookout sighted him about fifteen minutes ago. He can't make out what type yet. Shall we alter course to investigate?"

Brewer frowned at the speck on the horizon as he debated within himself. Finally, he shook his head. "No," he said, "maintain your course for New Orleans, Mr. Tyler."

The lieutenant's face betrayed his confusion and disappointment, but he wisely refrained from allowing it to reach his lips. "Aye, Captain. Quartermaster, maintain your course!"

"Aye, sir!"

Brewer handed the glass back to his second. "Call me if he comes any closer, Mr. Tyler."

"Aye, sir."

Brewer went to return to his cabin, but he stopped when he saw Mr. Sweeney standing beside the wheel. He stepped over to sailing master. "Care to walk with me, Mr. Sweeney?"

"A pleasure, Captain."

The two men stepped forward as Brewer made a cursory and impromptu inspection of the larboard battery. Sweeney could see something was on his captain's mind, but determined to wait him out. He didn't have to wait long; midway up the deck, the captain leaned his head in.

"Mr. Sweeney, have you ever had a memory that caused you to doubt, or at least made it difficult to do your duty?"

So, there it is, Sweeney thought, careful to keep his eyes on the deck in front of him. "Aye, sir. I imagine we all have at one time or another."

"I never have," Brewer admitted, looking around to be sure no hands were within earshot, "until now, that is."

"I see," Sweeney said softly. "Underhill, I take it?" He felt more than saw his captain's nod. "It must be hard for you. What can I do to help?"

Brewer shrugged. "Just know that the only thing I value more highly than your advice is your discretion."

"Understood, Captain." The two walked in silence a few steps, then Sweeney leaned in. "If it were me, the memories would be the worst of it, remembering the good days would only make it hard for me to deal with the reality of today."

A sigh beside him. "That about says it all."

"And thoughts like that can cause just enough hesitation to get you killed," Sweeney said. He saw the nod in the corner of his eye. They paused while the captain inspected the two long nines at the bow and then walked back down and looked over the starboard battery. "You've got good people around you, Captain," he said softly. "Mr. Greene, the doctor, Mac, Alfred, me — we're all watching as well. You must know the fight is coming; sooner or later we have to face the *Oliver Cromwell*. What I would suggest to you is that you throw yourself into training with Alfred and maybe Mac to get your arm back in shape."

Brewer frowned. "Why Mac?"

Sweeney stopped and faced his captain. "Is this Under-hill your size or closer to Mac?"

Brewer thought for a moment. "Somewhere in between, but closer to Mac."

"There you have it," Sweeney said. "You need to practice against a bigger opponent." He smiled. "That is Alfred's one weakness, after all."

Brewer smiled. "Thank God, it's the only one I know about."

Sweeney chuckled and nodded his agreement. "But that's only the physical part. You have to be sure in your mind that you will not hesitate, because Underhill surely won't." He met and held his captain's eyes. "Do you believe the warning that he gave you at the café?"

"Yes."

"So do I. This is not the man you knew when you were young, Captain. That man must be a different person in your mind. That will leave you free to do what you need to with the Underhill of today."

The captain frowned and his eyes darted back and forth as he considered what his sailing master had said. Finally, his head came up, and he inhaled a deep breath, long and slow, and exhaled. "Thank you, Mr. Sweeney. I see your point. Please keep this between us."

"Of course, Captain." Sweeney knuckled his forehead and went aft, leaving his captain to inspect a twelve-pounder.

The port of New Orleans was bustling with activity when HMS *Revenge* was piloted to a berth. Brewer was on deck in his dress uniform for his expected visit to the governor. After the pilot left the ship, Mr. Greene ordered Mac to ready the gig. The coxswain knuckled his forehead and went forward to get the boat ready.

"Captain?" Brewer turned to see Mr. Greene and the doctor standing behind him. Greene motioned toward the fantail. "A moment, if you please?"

Brewer met them at the fantail. "Well?"

Greene hesitated, but only for a moment. "Sir, we would like you to take Mac or Alfred with you when you go ashore."

The captain's brow rose a fraction. "Really? And why would I do that?"

Greene cast a glance at the doctor before steeling himself to continue. "Sir, we went to the American capitol at Washington, and you were kidnapped by a rogue privateer. We returned to Port Royal only to have the same privateer, whom we are hunting, accosted you at a café in the middle of town." He paused to gather himself. "New Orleans is on what the Americans would term the 'wild frontier' compared to those two places. I... *We*, think you would be wise to take along some protection in the form of an armed escort. A bodyguard, as it were. We need to, we have a duty to, keep you safe."

Brewer looked off to the side and pursed his lips for a moment, then he looked to the doctor.

Spinelli simply nodded, saying nothing.

Brewer looked back to his premier. Greene met his eyes and waited. The captain blinked, and sighed. "Very well, but Alfred, not Mac. Brief him, please, Mr. Greene. The more invisible he can be, the better. And make sure Mac's feelings aren't hurt, would you please?"

Greene and Spinelli smiled.

"Aye, sir," Greene said. He turned to Spinelli: "You take Mac, I'll take Alfred."

"Aye, sir," Spinelli tossed a wry look at his captain and departed.

Brewer felt slightly awkward sitting in the stern sheets between Mac and Alfred. Nobody said a word from the time they left the ship to the moment the three of them alit onto the pier.

"Mac," Brewer said, "keep your men together and alert. Return to the ship and report to Lieutenant Greene at the first sign of trouble." The coxswain said nothing, but his eyes went from his captain to the bodyguard and back again. "I mean it, Mac. Return to the ship at the first sign of trouble." Brewer put his hand on the coxswain's arm.

The big Cornishman swallowed hard and saluted. "Aye, Captain."

"Very well. Let's go, Alfred."

They stopped at the dock office and got directions to the governor's office. A short walk brought them to a rather nondescript two story building with a gold plate beside the door that read 'Government House'. Brewer knocked and the door was answered by a negro servant in royal blue livery complete with white lapels and collar.

"My name is Captain William Brewer of His Britannic Majesty's sloop *Revenge*. We have just arrived in town, and I have come to pay a courtesy call on the governor."

"Thank you, sir," the servant replied. "Please follow me." He led them to a small parlor off the entry hall. "If you will wait here, sir, I will inform the governor of your arrival."

"Thank you." The servant nodded and left, closing the door behind him.

"Friendly fellow," Alfred observed. "Captain, what do you wish me to do when he returns? Accompany you or stay be-hind?"

Brewer thought for a moment. "Let's see what happens if you come with me."

"Aye, sir."

The servant returned a few minutes later. "The governor will see you now, Captain. If you'll follow me?"

When both men rose, the servant shot a questioning look to Brewer. "He comes with me," Brewer said simply. The servant said nothing but turned and led them down the hall to where he knocked on the door and then entered. He announced Captain Brewer and stood to the side to allow both men entrance.

"Gentlemen!" the governor said as he came around his desk. He shook the captain's hand heartily, and he looked to Brewer as he shook Alfred's hand.

"Forgive me, Governor," he said, "to introduce my aide, Mr. Thomas."

"I see. Welcome Mr. Thomas!" The governor stood in front of them, and Brewer was amused to discover that the governor had to look up at him as much as he had to look down at Alfred. "I am Jacques Phillippe Villeré, Governor of Louisiana. How may I be of assistance?"

"My ship and I have just arrived, Governor," Brewer explained. "This is merely a courtesy call."

"I see." The governor retreated behind his desk. "Please, sit. May I offer you both some refreshment?"

"No, thank you," Brewer replied. He shifted in his seat. "I do have a question for you, Governor, if I may: Do you know a man named Michael Underhill?"

The governor's eyes narrowed at the name, and Brewer saw he recognized it at once.

"Why do you ask?" Villeré asked.

"Underhill is a British ex-patriot who deserted from the Royal Navy ten years ago and made his way to the United States. During the last war, he operated a rather successful privateer against our shipping in the Caribbean. Recently, we have discovered he is still conducting these operations."

"I see," Villeré said. "Yes, I know the name. What has this to do with me?"

"We have determined that Underhill and his men are committing piracy against merchant shipping, mainly but not exclusively British. I wondered if he brought his stolen cargos and prize ships here to be sold."

Villeré sat back in his chair, resting his head against the pillow at the top. His face looked grim, and he studied Brewer as though trying to decide what or how much to tell him. Finally, he sighed and sat forward, resting his arms on his desk and folding his hands.

"Captain," he said, "you must understand that, although Louisiana has been a state since 1812, it is still a rather lawless place, wild by European standards, a place where money rules and not governments. We are working to change this, and we are succeeding, but it will take time." Villeré frowned, then drew a deep breath and plunged into an explanation.

"Yes, Underhill has been here, and yes, he has sold his cargoes and some ships to local interests, both legitimate and illegitimate. It is the latter category of which you must beware the most. Underhill has some very wealthy, very powerful backers who buy his prize ships and resell them to pirates or merchants. I also know that he is popular with the townsfolk; he has donated portions of his ill-gotten gains to feed the poor. He will not be easy to eliminate; it may even be impossible to arrest him in the city."

Brewer sat back and frowned. "When was the last time you saw him? Is he here, now?"

"That I do not know," the governor replied. "I frequently do not know when he has been here until after he has gone and someone happens to mention to me that he was here. I imagine that this is done on purpose, but of course I have never asked him."

Villeré shifted nervously in his chair. "Between us, Captain, I wish you well in your endeavor. For New Orleans to make the transition to a great metropolitan area, rich with schools, churches, and businesses, Underhill and his ilk must be eliminated. However, I do not see how this is possible, not right now. As I said, he has many powerful friends, and that makes him powerful as well."

Brewer rose. "Yes, well, thank you, Governor, for the information. I shall return to my ship. Good day to you."

Villeré came around his desk and shook hands with his guests. "Let me be honest with you, Captain. During the war, before the Battle of New Orleans, the British overran my family's plantation and used our house as their headquarters. They stole several of our slaves and took them aboard their ships where they were declared emancipated. This caused great hardship for my family. Crops could not be harvested and sent to market, so the family's income was devastated. So you will forgive me, I'm sure, when I say that I am not entirely opposed to the private war Michael Underhill is waging against you." He stepped back and bowed. "Good day."

Brewer and Alfred stepped out onto the street and turned in the direction of the harbor.

"Lovely character, that governor," Alfred said. Brewer noted that his eyes were constantly on the move, scanning the crowds for anyone or anything suspicious.

"Yes, well, I don't suppose we can blame him," the captain replied. "I got the same attitude from those who were burned out in Washington. War has terrible consequences, Alfred. War is sometimes necessary, no doubt, but best avoided whenever possible."

"Aye," Alfred agreed, "I suppose you're right. Still, I suggest we lose no time in getting back to Mac."

Brewer nodded his agreement, and the two made a beeline for the pier where their boat was waiting. They made it without incident and were soon safely back aboard their ship.

Lieutenant Greene greeted them at the entry port and saluted. "Welcome back, sir. How did it go with the governor?"

"Very informative," the captain replied. "Get us underway as soon as possible."

"From here, we can warp the ship out of the harbor, sir," Greene said, "assuming you don't want to wait for the next tide."

"No," Brewer confirmed. "Detail the boats, if you please. Join me in my cabin afterward."

"Aye, sir."

Brewer and Alfred made their way below to the cabin. Brewer changed out of his dress uniform while Alfred disappeared into his pantry. Brewer was... disconcerted by the meeting with the governor, or at least the ending of it. As he'd told Alfred, he'd seen the same resentment from some in Washington when he was there, and he had no idea how to answer it. An apology seemed out of place; first, he hadn't been there, either at the burning of Washington or the occupation and desecration of Villeré's plantation; in fact, he hadn't been in the Americas at all during that war. And second, it was war. Things like that happened in war. He set his jaw and swallowed hard, determined to put such things behind him.

He came out to find a cup of Alfred's coffee awaiting him on the dining table — how well Alfred had come to know him in such a short time! — along with a plate of cold meat and bread. He sat down and dug in, and the plate was soon bare.

Alfred appeared to clear away the plate. "Will there by anything else, sir?"

"No, Alfred, thank you. Let me ask you a question: Do you believe the governor? What I mean is, do you consider the information he gave us to be credible?"

The little man's brows furled, and his eyes looked off to the side while he considered. "On the whole, sir, I believe I do. I think he was telling the truth about the British occupation, but I also believe some of what he said earlier was true."

"Only some?" Brewer asked.

"Yes," Alfred said. "I don't for a moment believe that Underhill entered the harbor of New Orleans and Villeré did not know about it. A man supposedly that powerful,with such powerful friends, a governor like Villeré would have men watching for his ship to arrive, or failing that, for Underhill himself to step ashore. I think the governor was trying his best to appease you without bringing any trouble upon himself." A small smile appeared at the corner of his mouth. "I also think he failed."

Brewer chuckled. "I agree with you in that regard. In fact, I will wager that a copy of my report of this voyage will be forwarded by Admiral Lord Hornblower to Secretary Adams in Washington with a strongly worded cover attached."

Brewer felt the ship being warped out of the harbor, and soon he felt the sails pick up enough wind to driver her out to sea. He rose and opened the cabin door. "My compliments to Mr. Greene," he said to the sentry. "Mr. Tyler shall have the deck. Set course for Jamaica. Pass the word for Mr. Greene, Mr. Sweeney, and the doctor to join me in my cabin."

"Aye, Captain!"

Brewer closed the door and went to the pantry. "We are expecting guests, Alfred. When they arrive, please join us in the day cabin."

"Aye, Captain."

The guests arrived and joined the captain. "Alfred! Refreshments, if you please, and pour one for yourself!"

"Aye, sir!"

Soon they were all sitting in the cabin. Brewer rapped on the table with his glass. "I called you here to update you on our meeting with Governor Villeré." The captain spent the next thirty minutes describing their meeting. He left out the part about the British occupation. He looked around the room when he finished. "Comments?"

Greene shrugged. "Sounds like more of what we heard in Havana. Odds are, we can't believe any of it."

"Well, the jury's still out on that," Brewer warned, "but on the whole I tend to agree with you. Did we see any friends in the harbor?"

"Two USN brigs," Sweeney said, "but nothing of any real interest."

"So we come away with nothing?" the doctor asked.

"Not really," the captain explained. "We know now that this is where Underhill has been selling his prizes. I intend to ask the admiral for a frigate to help us keep watch off the port, and the next time Underhill tries to sneak a captured ship in, we'll nab him."

"The Americans will protest a British force off one of their ports," Spinelli warned.

Greene shrugged. "They can't say anything if we stay in international waters."

"Mightn't the admiral contact the American navy and request some help?" Sweeney asked. "I mean, he is selling captured British ships in an American port."

"I like the idea," the captain said. "I shall put it to him when we get back. What can it hurt to ask? Anything else? No? Thank you then, gentlemen."

The assemblage filed out, except for the doctor. Brewer turned to him. "Well?"

"Do you see any scenario where this does not end in a battle?" Spinelli asked. The captain just held his eyes and said nothing. "I thought not."

He left without a word.

The voyage back to Jamaica passed without incident. During their ten days at sea, HMS *Revenge* sighted only two sail, neither of which was investigated. Brewer was determined not to be delayed or diverted into a trap, so each sighting was logged and ignored. Mr. Greene and Mr. Sweeney wondered privately about their captain's motivations, but neither man dared question the captain openly.

Meanwhile, Jimmy was assigned as a powder monkey, mainly because Old Smoot didn't want any boys making trouble in his gunroom. Mr. Reed put in a good word with the first lieutenant about how stocky and fast Jimmy was for his age, and Mr. Greene agreed to the change in jobs. Jimmy reported to Mr. Hodges, the gunner.

"Welcome, laddie," the gunner said. "You're here so I can instruct you on how to be a powder monkey. D'ye know what that is? No? Well, it means that, during a battle, you will be running powder to the guns, see? Think about it! Without you, we can't fight no battles at all! You are almost as important as the Cap'n hisself!"

Jimmy's eyes grew wide at the news. The gunner snapped his fingers to get the boy's attention again. He stepped aside and let the boy see inside the magazine.

"See these shelves? See the bags on them? Those are the powder charges for the guns. These are for the long guns, and these over here are for the carronades. Your job will be to take one or two of them and put one in here." He held out what looked like a tube of wood with a lid, with rope around it. "This is called a salt box. Don't ask me why, because I don't remember. Anyway, you will stand out here," he moved the boy outside the heavy curtains that closed off the magazine, "and we'll hand you one of these bags. You put it in the salt box and close the lid down tight. Here, let's try."

He handed Jimmy a bag of powder, and the boy took it and managed to get it into the salt box.

"Good," Hodges said. "Now slide the rope over your head. If we was in a battle, you'd be told where to bring this to. You got to run low and fast when you've got this, understand? The gun captains will be waiting for you."

"Right oh!" Jimmy paused. "What do I call you anyway?"

Hodges grinned. "Just call me Gunny."

"Right oh, Gunny!"

Brewer stood at the center of the quarterdeck as HMS *Revenge* glided into the harbor at Port Royal, Jamaica. The pilot dropped the anchor and turned to wave to the captain before leaving. Brewer nodded his acknowledgement and thanks; it was a simple job, but the pilot had done it well. He turned and looked around the crowded harbor.

"We have company," Lieutenant Greene said, and pointed to several warships flying the flag of the United States. One was a *Constitution*-class frigate, and the rest were smaller, including a couple of *Revenge's* own class. Brewer raised an eyebrow.

"I wonder if their presence has anything to do with Underhill?" Greene remarked.

"We shall find out," Brewer replied. "Have Mac ready my gig; I'll go ashore and see the admiral."

"Aye, sir." Greene saluted as his captain left the quarterdeck.

Mr. Sweeney stepped over. "Do you think the Americans are here because of Underhill?"

"I don't know," Greene replied without taking his eyes from the companionway where his captain had disappeared.

"But if they are, this whole enterprise just became much more complicated."

Brewer entered his cabin to find his dress uniform neatly laid out for him. He changed hurriedly, all the while wondering what the presence of the American squadron portended. Over the past several days and weeks, this mission to find Underhill and stop him had somehow become personal. He wasn't sure when it happened, or even exactly why, all he knew was that *he* had to be the one to finish this, one way or the other.

He hooked his hanger around his waist and pulled his vest down over it. He cast a quick glance at the glass to make sure the sword was correct. Satisfied, he donned his coat and picked up his hat. One last check in the glass, and he headed up for the deck.

He found all in readiness for him. A last word with the premier, and he stepped over the side to settle into his spot in the stern sheets. Mac joined him and barked the orders that set the oars in motion and drove the boat away from the ship. Brewer looked the big American frigate over as they passed by, remembering how the USS *Constitution* had come to their rescue when HMS *Defiant* had been badly damaged in a hurricane. Was that really over a year ago already?

He studied the big ship — he couldn't see the stern and therefore didn't know her name — and remembered the rumors and reports he'd heard from the last American war, how their ships' sides were impervious to any but the heaviest sustained firepower. One of their frigates had even earned the nickname of "Old Ironsides", a name which aptly described the entire class. Their superiority had led directly to the development of *Defiant* and her sisters.

He made his way to the admiral's offices and was soon shown into his study by a steward. When he arrived, he found Hornblower in conversations with an American officer.

"Ah, there you are, Commander," the admiral said. He rose and came around the desk to shake Brewer's hand. "Allow me to introduce Commodore James Biddle of the United States Navy's Caribbean Squadron. Commodore, this is the officer I told you about, Commander Brewer of His Majesty's sloop of war *Revenge*."

The two shook hands. "An honor, Commodore," Brewer said.

Hornblower resumed his seat and directed Brewer to the other seat before his desk, next to Biddle. "The commodore and I were just discussing common threats in the Caribbean, and the subject of Michael Underhill came up." He looked to the commodore.

"Yes," Biddle picked up the narrative. "Our mission is mainly one of anti-piracy and interdiction of the slave trade, but his lordship and I have struck up quite a conversation. We had completely forgotten about Mr. Underhill and his privateering when the war ended, that is, until your visit to the secretary brought him to our attention. We went back and reinvestigated the loss of several US-flagged ships that went missing in the Caribbean in the last five or six years. We'd attributed their loss to piracy, but now we are not so sure that Underhill was not responsible."

Brewer shifted uncomfortably. "Forgive me, Commodore, but that would mean that Underhill would have... *disposed* of their crews. I was not aware that his attacks involved such savagery. What leads you to believe it was Underhill and not pirates like El Diabolito or Roberto Cofresi?"

Biddle glanced at Hornblower before answering, and Brewer wondered just what they had discussed before his arrival.

"In three of the attacks, there were survivors," Biddle explained. "All three gave descriptions of the leader of the raids, and all the descriptions had one fact in common. We didn't understand its significance until just a few moments ago when I mentioned it to his lordship." He motioned toward Hornblower. "That common fact was a *'hat like Napoleon wore in the pictures'*."

Brewer's eyes widened for a moment before he regained control of himself. He looked to the admiral and received only a nod. He frowned and looked at his hands, folded in his lap. "That does sound like Underhill," he admitted. "He had on a hat of that sort when I saw him in Martinique."

"Precisely," Hornblower agreed. "So, the Americans have a stake in this enterprise. I have asked the commodore for his assistance in running Underhill to ground."

Brewer threw a hard glance at his mentor, but he had sense enough to hold his tongue. "Aye, My Lord."

"It may interest you to know, Commander," Biddle said, "that I have met our dear Mr. Underhill."

"Really?" Brewer was intrigued.

Biddle nodded. "It was in New York in 1814, not long before the end of the war. As I remember, he brought in two prizes he'd taken south of Newfoundland. He had a drink with me in a tavern after he'd heard that I was being considered for command of USS *Demologos*." He looked to Hornblower. "Have you heard of the ship, My Lord?"

Hornblower searched his memory. "I have heard the name..."

"A steam-powered warship, My Lord," Brewer interjected. "Designed to protect New York harbor. Not much more than a mobile floating battery, if I remember correctly. She could barely make five knots, but her sides were five-foot thick reinforced timber planking."

Hornblower gave a deep nod. "Now I remember. She missed the war, did she not?"

Biddle sighed. "Yes, sir. She wasn't commissioned until 1815, and by then I had moved on to another assignment." He shook his head at the missed opportunity. "Still, it would have been an honor to command the first steam warship in history, even if she never left New York. If you gentlemen are ever up that way, you should look her up."

CHAPTER NINE

Hornblower leaned forward. "Very well, gentlemen, we have business to attend to. Commander, please give us a report on your trip to New Orleans."

The commodore's eyes went swiftly to the admiral at the mention of the American port, but he said nothing.

"Yes, My Lord." Over the course of the next hour Brewer gave the two officers a full accounting of his observations of the New Orleans harbor and his interview with Governor Villeré. Again, he left out the governor's indictment regarding his family's plantation. When Brewer finished, the admiral's eyes narrowed, and he frowned.

"Commander, did you believe him?"

Brewer shifted. "Only in part, My Lord. I don't for a minute believe that he has no idea when Underhill makes port there. Someone he considers that important, that powerful, with even more powerful associates?" The commander shrugged. "The governor would have watchers on every pier so he'd know when his ship dropped anchor."

"Agreed," Hornblower said. He turned to Biddle. "Commodore, do you know this man?"

"Villeré? I've met him once or twice," Biddle replied. "I confess that I was not impressed by the man. In fact, I will say here and now that I agree with the commander's summation. I would not take anything he says at face value."

Hornblower nodded his agreement. "So, to summarize: we are now fairly certain that Michael Underhill and his crew are using the *Oliver Cromwell* and possibly other ships to commit acts of piracy against the merchant shipping of several nations. We are also certain he disposes of most, if not all, of his ill-gotten gains at New Orleans. Commodore, I wish to confirm that the United States government will not allow Underhill to hide behind his letter of marque?"

"You are correct, Admiral. He's covered for acts committed during the war, but the war ended in 1814. Anything after that is piracy, pure and simple."

"Thank you. Therefore, gentlemen, it is up to us to come up with a plan that will rid the seas of this scourge." Hornblower tapped the desk with his forefinger. "I am open to ideas, gentlemen."

"We have two options," Brewer said, "which are to look for him, or to wait for him. Both our squadrons can be looking for him while on regular patrols of the shipping lanes, but finding him, or better still catching him in the act, would be a wild stroke of luck. Therefore, waiting for him seems to be the surer option. The problem with that option is, it may not be any quicker, especially in the short term. We know of three ports he frequents: Havana, New Orleans, and, to a lesser extent, Martinique. If we watch those ports, sooner or later we should find him."

"That could take months," Biddle objected, "especially if he finds a new place to sell his prizes and their cargos. He could even decide to lay low until some other demand takes us away."

Brewer shrugged. "If you have a better idea, Commodore, I'm open to it." He looked to Hornblower, but the admiral was staring unfocused into space while he thought. Brewer grunted. *I'm surprised he's not pacing.*

Biddle frowned and looked out the window; apparently,

he was bereft of anything better. Suddenly, Hornblower rose and began to pace back and forth before the hearth.

"You will pardon me, I'm sure, Commodore," he said absently, "but I must think."

"Of course, sir." Biddle looked to Brewer, but the commander simply shrugged.

"He does this," Brewer explained.

"First," Hornblower said as he made his turn and paced back toward them, "I need to know exactly what forces we can put toward our plan. Commodore, I have the frigates *Phoebe* and *Clorinda*, sloops *Revenge* and *Terror*, and the luggar *Liverpool*. The remainder of my forces are out on assignment. What can the Americans contribute?"

Biddle answered promptly. "My squadron consists of the frigates *Constitution* and *Congress*, corvettes *Hancock* and *Boston*, sloops *Adams* and *Roanoke*, brigs *Reliant* and *Enterprise*, and schooners *Washington, Jefferson, Hamilton,* and *Knox*. I can devote approximately two-thirds to this enterprise for the short term. The slave trade is expected to pick back up within the next ninety days, at which point I shall have to divert more of my forces to interdiction patrols."

The admiral's chin bobbed on his breast in a makeshift nod. "Understood. That being the case, I suggest we employ your lighter forces in patrolling the sea lanes in the Caribbean and watching Martinique. They will be in a good position when the need arises to switch them to interdiction patrols."

Biddle rubbed his chin while he considered the admiral's plan. "Agreed. Thank you, sir."

"Not at all," Hornblower replied as he made another turn. "I think we can safely station *Clorinda* and *Liverpool* to patrol off Havana and the seas to the north and east. I propose we define her patrol area as the triangle defined by Havana, the southern tip of Florida, and the Bahamas."

"Agreed," Biddle said. "I suggest using my forces off New Orleans, Admiral; it might cause trouble if a British ship were seen stopping and searching American ships."

That made Hornblower stop and turn. He had not thought of that, and he silently cursed himself for his oversight. "Of course, Commodore. Thank you."

Biddle rose himself and began to pace at right angles to Hornblower, careful that their paths did not intersect. "In fact, Admiral, we may need to revise our earlier agreement regarding the deployment of my forces in the Caribbean. The problem with New Orleans — and the thing that makes it such a haven for pirates and smugglers in general — is that there are countless small bayous and inlets where a ship the size of a sloop or smaller could hide. There's no room to take a frigate or even a large sloop in to search; the waterways are too small for them to turn around or even maneuver. The only thing you can do with a larger ship is to block the entrance of the bayou to prevent escape, and even then it's a tricky proposition. I think we may need most or all my smaller ships there."

Hornblower rubbed his chin as he considered the commodore's proposal. His eyes narrowed as he turned it over in his mind, attacking it from every angle, trying to find a weakness and coming up empty. Finally, he nodded.

"Very well. Your proposal is accepted, Commodore. Let's just hope we can complete our task before your ships are needed elsewhere." He resumed his seat. "So your smaller ships will search the bayous and small inlets around New Orleans, looking for the *Oliver Cromwell* or any other ship that may be associated with Underhill. I recommend we do not inform the governor of our activities."

Biddle grinned. "No, indeed."

Hornblower continued. "The two American frigates

along with HMS *Revenge* will patrol off the port itself, ready to stop any traffic coming or going. If Underhill is found and apprehended, custody and disposition will belong to Commander Brewer."

"Agreed," Biddle confirmed with a nod.

"I shall patrol the mouth of the Gulf of Mexico with *Phoebe* and *Terror*. I am expecting the schooner *Reliable* to arrive any day; I will leave orders for her to join me immediately." Hornblower looked to the ceiling for a moment. "I think that about covers it. Commander Brewer, your orders will be delivered to your ship. In normal matters of sailing, you will follow the Commodore's lead."

"Yes, My Lord."

The admiral rose. "If you gentlemen will excuse me, I must see the governor." His eyes met Brewer's for a moment; soon, perhaps, they would know whether or not they could trust the governor.

The two officers filed out of the study and made their way to the street. Biddle noticed the way his companion scanned the street.

"Is there a problem, Commander?" he asked.

Brewer shook his head. "No, sir; it's just that the last time I was here, I stopped at that café down the street after leaving the admiral. I was joined there by Michael Underhill."

Biddle shook his head in wonder. "Bold as brass, that one." He nudged Brewer with his elbow and winked. "Them's the ones I love to hang!"

Brewer couldn't help but nod his agreement. Satisfied that Underhill was nowhere in the area, the two men set off for the waterfront.

"When can you be ready to sail, Commander?" the commodore asked formally.

"We shouldn't need more than a day or two at the most, sir; depending on how soon we can schedule a visit from the lighter."

Biddle nodded as they arrived at the pier. "We are in the same position. Signal me or send a note when you are scheduled."

Brewer came to attention and saluted. "Aye, Commodore."

Back on *Revenge*, Mr. Short was leading Jimmy aft to the quarterdeck.

"What's going on?" Jimmy asked.

"More training on your job," Mr. Short announced. "We're heading on to the quarterdeck. That's where the captain and the other officers go to command the ship. Don't talk to anyone, unless they talk to you first. Understood?"

"All right, but why?"

Short looked at him. "Because that's how a navy ship works."

"Oh." Jimmy shrugged and set it aside. "But I can talk to you, right? What are we doing on the quarterdeck?"

"You can talk to me *now*," Short clarified, "because we're training. But if I'm on duty, you can't talk to me either, unless I talk to you first."

"Yes, sir," Jimmy said, slight dejected by the reply. He perked up when he saw they were heading toward some cages at the rear of the deck. "What's this?"

The two boys squatted before two wooden cages, each holding five to seven chickens. The hens clucked and strutted around the cages and for the most part ignored the newcomers.

"What're the chickens for?" Jimmy asked.

Short admired the birds. "They lay eggs for the captain's

table. Sometimes he shares with the gunroom. Your job is to gather the eggs every morning and take them to the captain's steward."

"Mr. Alfred?"

"That's him," Short confirmed. "You take the eggs to him, and he'll tell you if any go anywhere else."

Jimmy nodded enthusiastically. Here was something that sounded fun! "Who feeds them?"

"You do," Short said. He smiled when he saw Jimmy's enthusiasm. "Here's what you do. After you are done delivering the eggs to Mr. Alfred, you go see the cook in the fo'c'sle. He will give you all the bags from the ships bread that was eaten the day before."

"Whatever for?"

Short nodded. "See, every time he opens a new bag, the cook will shake it hard. He does this to dump as many weevils from the bread as he can, and they fall to the bottom of the bag. Of course, he gets a lot of crumbs in the bottom as well. Let me tell you — chickens *love* to eat bread crumbs and weevils! You will be their favorite person when they see you bringing those bags!"

"What do I do with the bags after I feed the chickens?"

"Take them back to the cook," Short said without taking his eyes from the chickens. "He'll burn them in his oven."

"I can do that."

"Good. The only bad part of this job is that you have to clean out the cages."

"Clean out the cages?"

Short nodded. "Every three or four days, you have to clean out the old straw and chicken poop from them and put in fresh straw."

Jimmy's eyes went wide. *"Chicken poop!?!?"*

"Yep." Short pointed. "See?"

Jimmy looked to watch one of the hens caught in the act. "Yuck!"

Short chuckled, remembering his own similar reaction not so long ago. "Anyway, you start tomorrow. You gather the eggs at dawn."

Short rose and left, leaving Jimmy staring at the chickens and wondering if he would like this job or not.

When he arrived onboard, Captain Brewer went to his cabin and sent for Lieutenant Greene, Mr. Sweeney, and the doctor. Mac took up his usual post inside the door. Brewer told them about his meeting with Commodore Biddle and the admiral, the plans they had made for searching the approaches to New Orleans for Underhill, and their inclusion in the American squadron outside the port.

"But we get Underhill if he's taken?" Greene asked.

Brewer nodded. "Custody and disposition of prizes and cargoes. Of course, that means our prize crew, but I can live with that."

"I should think so," the doctor added dryly.

"And we follow the Americans with regard to our sailing?" Sweeney asked.

"Yes," Brewer confirmed. "The commodore will direct all boarding, and the Americans will board all American ships."

Greene shrugged. "Makes sense. What about the governor?"

His captain smiled. "He'll probably discover what we're doing at some point, but we're not going to tell him." Greene and Sweeney looked at each other, grins on their faces. Brewer continued. "We sail as soon as we've seen the lighter. Is there anything else we need before we sail?"

"No, Captain," Greene replied. "All provisions were accounted for and stowed yesterday. Water's all we need, although I imagine if we asked Alfred and Smoot, they would want to make one more trip ashore before we sail."

Brewer smiled. "By all means, send them ashore with Mac, if it can be arranged before we sail. I don't mind — is something wrong, Mr. Sweeney?"

All eyes went to the sailing master, who was frowning. His eyes were darting back and forth. He blinked at the captain's call, and his eyes focused.

"Beg your pardon, Captain," he said, "but it just now occurred to me — the Americans use different signals than we do. We'll have to arrange a way to send basic signals—"

A knock at the door interrupted them. Mac opened the door at admit Mr. Tyler.

"I beg your pardon, sir, but a midshipman has arrived from the American frigate with a note for you from their commodore."

The captain stood. "By all means, Mr. Tyler, show him in."

Tyler turned and called, and the American midshipman marched smartly into the cabin. He stepped up to the captain and came to attention, his hat properly tucked under his left arm.

"Sir, I am David Farragut," he announced, "midshipman of the frigate USS *Constitution*. Commodore Biddle has sent me to deliver this note to you." He pulled a folded sheet of paper from his coat pocket and handed it to Brewer.

The captain unfolded it and read, his raised eyebrows betraying his surprise.

"Captain?" Greene said.

"You won't believe this." He held the note up and read: "'*Commander Brewer, it occurred to me last night that our signals are not exactly compatible. Therefore, I have sent Midshipman Farragut to you, that he may read our signals for you. I am in the hope that you have a man that you may send to me and render the same service for me. Signed, James Biddle, Commodore.'"* He looked up. "Mr. Greene, do we have a man we can send?"

The premier thought for a moment. "I'd rather not part with a midshipman, sir; we only have the two on board. If you insist, it would have to be Mr. Reed; I don't think Mr. Short is ready yet. Other than Reed, the best to send would be Crosby." Crosby was a petty officer of the larboard watch.

"Yes, well," Brewer said, "in the meantime, it looks like Mr. Farragut will be staying with us for a while. Mac, please pass the word for Mr. Reed. We'll have him take Mr. Farragut to the cockpit and see him settled in."

"Aye, Captain."

"Do you have everything you need, Mr. Farragut?" Brewer asked.

"Aye, sir," the midshipman replied. "I brought a copy of our signal book and enough of my kit to get by."

"Good. You will be assigned to a mess, of course." A knock at the door announced the arrival of Mr. Reed. "Ah, Mr. Reed. This is Midshipman Farragut, on loan to us from USS *Constitution*. Please take him to the cockpit and see him settled in. His duty station will be on the quarterdeck to read any American signals for us."

"Aye, sir." Reed turned to the newcomer. "Follow me, please." He led him out.

"Now," Brewer said, "whom do we send to the Americans?"

The three officers looked at each other, while the doctor sat back and waited.

"I suppose we'll have to send Reed," Brewer said. "I don't see how we can do less than the Americans. Any objections?" None were voiced. "Good; that's settled. Mr. Greene, perhaps you'll inform him and send him off to *Constitution*?"

"Aye, sir." He paused and smiled. "Pardon me, sir, but you do realize that this will leave Mr. Short as the senior midshipman aboard?"

Brewer grinned. "I think we'll survive, Mr. Greene."

"Aye, sir."

Mr. Reed escorted the newcomer. "I'm Jonathan Reed," he said.

"David Farragut."

"You came from the frigate, right?"

"Yes, *Constitution*."

They arrived at *Revenge's* minuscule cockpit. "I'm afraid our accommodations are slightly smaller."

Farragut shrugged. "Doesn't bother me, mate. I spent two years on *Enterprise*. A sloop smaller than this one. This'll do me just fine."

At that moment, Mr. Greene showed up, and both midshipmen came to attention.

"Is our new man settled in, Mr. Reed?" he asked.

"We were just figuring out where to sling his hammock."

Greene shrugged. "He can have your spot. The captain's sending you to *Constitution* to interpret our signals for the commodore. Put a kit together and report to the entry port at once. You go back on the Americans' boat."

"Aye, sir!" Reed assembled his belongings quickly and was gone in five minutes. Farragut looked at the premier.

"Are there any other midshipmen aboard, sir?"

"Just one," Greene replied. "He's on the deck now. Name's William Short. He's younger than you, Mr. Farragut, but with Mr. Reed gone, he will be the senior midshipman."

"I'm sure we'll get along fine, sir."

"Good," Greene said as he turned for the stair. "Follow me."

The two emerged on the deck. "I know we're in port, but you will need to be on deck or within easy call during all daylight hours until this mission is over."

"Aye, sir."

"Mr. Short!" Greene called, and the youngster crossed the deck at a quick walk and saluted. "Mr. Short, this is Midshipman Farragut, of the USS *Constitution*. He'll be sailing with us in the cockpit and reading the American signals for us."

"Excellent! Welcome, Mr. Farragut! Mr. Greene, did I just see Mr. Reed go over the side?"

"You did indeed," Greene said. "Mr. Reed is on his way to *Constitution* to read out signals for the commodore."

"I see, sir." His eyes got wide and he glanced to Greene.

"Yes, Mr. Short," Greene confirmed. "That does indeed make you acting-senior midshipman until Mr. Reed's return." Greene stood tall with his hands behind his back. "The captain has every confidence in you, Mr. Short. I trust you will ensure he is not disappointed."

The boy perked up like a peacock showing off feathers. "Oh, aye, sir!"

Farragut chuckled and shook his head, remembering what it was to be that young. Mr. Short and the first lieutenant made their way forward, leaving Farragut alone to survey his new station. With the ship safely in harbor, there was really nothing for him to do. The commodore's instructions to him were to interpret the American signals for the sloop's commander and to learn whatever he could while he was aboard. The midshipman looked up and down the deck and wondered just how much there was to learn.

That was when his attention went to a ship's boy he saw carrying a chicken aft across the quarterdeck. He followed the boy and saw him put the chicken in a cage at the fantail.

"Hello," he said to the boy. The lad turned, saw the newcomer's uniform, then he stood and knuckled his forehead.

"Hello, sir."

The stranger looked at the cage. "My name's David. What's yours?"

"Jimmy, sir."

"I'm not on duty, so it's just David," he said. "What are you doing, Jimmy?"

"I was cleaning their cages this morning, and one of them got out," the boy explained. "So I had to chase her down and put her back before she either jumped overboard or the cook got her."

Farragut smiled at the boy's quandary. "Well, I'm glad you got to her first. I take it these eggs are for the captain?"

The boy nodded. "I gather them every morning and take them down to Mr. Alfred." He leaned in. "That's the captain's steward," he added confidentially.

"I see."

Jimmy looked him up and down. "Say, why's your uniform different?"

Farragut moved in close. "Don't tell anyone," he said quietly, "but I'm an American."

Jimmy's eyes went wide. "A *real* American?" He frowned. "What are you doing here?"

"I'm sailing with you," Farragut replied. "My commodore sent me over to read our signals and tell your captain what they mean. Mr. Reed has gone over to *Constitution* to do the same thing for my commodore." He squatted down and looked the cages over from one end to the other. "So, Jimmy, how's the chicken business going?"

"I haven't decided," the boy replied. "I've only had the job for a couple days, so I'm still getting used to it. I got four eggs out this morning, so that's good, I guess, but I don't like cleaning the cages. One of them pecked me this morning when I was sweeping!"

"Yes, well, chickens can be that way sometimes."

CHAPTER TEN

The lighters came the next morning and topped off all the water barrels for the American ships and *Revenge*. Commander Brewer's orders were delivered. They contained nothing additional. He was to act in concert with the American squadron commanded by Commodore Biddle, and he was to defer to the commodore's authority in all matters of normal sailing. Brewer recognized in the wording Hornblower's gift of leaving him the option of doing what he thought best in an emergency, but he had better be able to justify his actions afterward. He read the words over again. *So, if I act independently and save the day, I might get a medal,* he thought, *but if I act and put my ship out of position, and Underhill gets away because of it, I'll probably be sent home in disgrace and never see a quarterdeck again.*

The squadron slipped out with the morning tide. *Revenge* followed the two big American frigates out of the harbor, then came the two American brigs, one of their corvettes, and the four schooners. The other corvette and their two sloops would be sent to patrol the sea lanes to the south and look into the harbor at Martinique every few days. The British forces would sail in two days to take up their patrol positions.

Brewer stood on his quarterdeck and watched the American ships to his fore and aft. He felt strangely out of place in such company plus there was a feeling that his new allies were intruding in a fight that wasn't theirs. He remembered that they considered Underhill responsible for the disappearance of several of their own ships, but to him this was still a British matter, and what's more, a personal one.

His eyes were drawn to the big frigates up forward. *Constitution* was still rather famous amongst Royal Navy ships; she and her sisters had come as a very unpleasant surprise during the 1812-1814 conflict. British shot seemed to bounce off their walls, while their 24-pounder balls went through the British hulls like they were made of paper. Their presence had led directly to the cutting-down and repurposing of HMS *Defiant* and her sisters. Brewer grunted; too bad they never had the chance to meet in battle.

Even now, Brewer thought them a magnificent piece of engineering. For all the thickness of their hulls, they were still swift across the water; British frigates had proved unable to catch them in a stern chase. He shook his head in envy.

The captain looked around the quarterdeck. He saw Mr. Sweeney and the quartermaster supervising his mates at the wheel. Mr. Farragut was also standing beside Sweeney; he would be put to the test when they cleared the harbor and the commodore signaled the change of course to the squadron. He looked further to see Mr. Short standing beside a larboard carronade. With Mr. Reed detached to the American frigate, Mr. Short was promoted to temporary command of the quarterdeck carronades. Brewer looked approvingly at the newfound confidence with which the lad carried himself. He had no idea that all officers of the deck along with Mr. Sweeney had orders to keep an eye on Mr. Short and help out as needed. He turned forward just in time to see a signal sent aloft on *Constitution*.

"Captain," Farragut called, "the commodore is signaling an easterly course once we clear the harbor."

"Thank you, Mr. Farragut," Brewer replied. "Acknowledge, Mr. Abbott."

"Aye, sir."

"Kindly comply with the commodore's instructions, Mr. Sweeney."

"Aye, Captain."

Brewer stood there, suddenly feeling unneeded, as Sweeney swung *Revenge* around to the east in her turn. Sail was set, and Brewer left the deck to Lieutenant Tyler and went below. He passed the word to see if the doctor was free to play some chess.

"Signal acknowledged, Commodore!"

"Thank you, Mr. Reed," came the reply.

Reed stood back and watched Mr. Roberts, *Constitution's* signals midshipman, haul down and stow the commodore's last signal. He was younger than Reed, but he moved like he knew what he was doing. Roberts put the last flags away and closed the locker, then he stood up and brushed his hands together.

"So," Roberts said, "what do you think of *Constitution*? A lot bigger than what you're used to, I guess."

"I served on a British frigate before I was posted to *Revenge*," Reed replied. "HMS *Clorinda*, but she was nowhere near as big as this ship. Nowhere near the firepower, neither."

Roberts nodded. "I heard stories from hands who were aboard during the war, how the enemy's balls bounced off the hull, especially the British smaller guns. Your frigates just didn't carry guns big enough to make an impression." He looked to Reed. "No offense."

Reed waved the apology off. "None taken. I can see why you're proud of the ship. She's a beauty."

Roberts stood at his post — and Reed along with him —

until the commodore went below decks. "Now we can go below," Roberts said, and he led Reed below to the ship's cockpit. This, too, was huge compared to *Clorinda's*, let alone the tiny one on *Revenge*. "Mr. Tolliver looks after us; he's the second lieutenant," Roberts explained. "He keeps his eye on us and makes sure we're keeping the area neat, that sort of stuff. John!" he called to a midshipman seated at the center table as he led Reed over. "This is Jonathan Reed. He's from the British sloop, here to read their signals for the commodore. Mr. Reed, this is Mr. Allen, *Constitution's* senior midshipman."

Allen held out his hand. "John. Welcome."

Reed shook his heartily, impressed by the American's grip. "Jonathan. Thanks. Impressive ship you've got here."

Allen looked around. "We like it. I heard your captain knows Underhill."

Reed's eyes narrowed at the statement. "I heard the same thing, but my captain hasn't said anything, at least not to me."

Allen grunted. "We'll see."

Roberts steered Reed away from the table. Reed guessed it was to prevent the senior midshipman from starting a fight, something Reed was just as happy to avoid. He did wonder where Allen had heard that about Captain Brewer and what it could mean for this mission.

"What was that all about?" Reed asked when they were away from the cockpit.

"Don't worry about John," Roberts reassured him. "He don't mean no harm. It's just that he wants everyone to know he's in charge. The easy way is not to take the bait and sooner or later he'll forget it."

"Well," Reed said, "let's hope it's sooner."

Admiral Sir Horatio Hornblower stood in his study and looked out the window overlooking the harbor. *Clorinda* and *Liverpool* were at that moment raising anchor to sail to their patrol areas. He'd spent a solid two hours yesterday afternoon with *Clorinda's* captain, Sir Charles Bexley, trying to get the man to understand the mission and his part in it. Hornblower had come away from the meeting convinced that the man must be second cousin to the king himself — it seemed the only way he would be a post captain entrusted with a frigate. After the third time Bexley had spoken airily of stopping at Charleston in the United States (he'd heard it was a "privileged town for aristocracy") or Havana ("best cigars, don't you know"), Hornblower had told the man flatly under no circumstances short of an emergency was he to enter any port other than Port Royal. He was also forbidden to leave his patrol area except if he was pursuing the sloop *Oliver Cromwell.*

Hornblower turned from the window and crossed the room to his desk. On it were the incomplete orders for HMS *Phoebe.* She was to sail with HMS *Terror* in two days. Hornblower was supposed to accompany *Phoebe* and direct this squadron and *Clorinda's*, but now he was not so sure. First, unlike *Clorinda, Phoebe* was commanded by a very competent man who could be entrusted to carry out his instructions, and second, his meeting that morning with the governor had not gone well.

True to his earlier conversation with Commander Brewer, Hornblower had gone to the meeting determined to mislead the governor by telling him intelligence indicated Underhill would soon be operating in the general area surrounding the island of Martinique. However, when told of this, the governor declared it to be the dumbest thing he'd ever heard, and said that Underhill did not have a reputation for being stupid. Hornblower was shocked at the duke's language, but Montagu stuck by his assertion. The admiral could only say that this was what he understood to be so, and he cut the meeting short at the first opportunity.

Now, looking back on the meeting, Hornblower wondered what game the governor was playing. The 5th Duke of Manchester had a reputation for speaking his mind and not caring whom he offended in the process, but to Hornblower's knowledge, Montagu had never spoken like that before. Could it be that the governor was trying to get Hornblower not to send the two ships south without actually ordering him to do so? If Hornblower went to sea now, there would be nothing to stop the duke from visiting naval headquarters and redirecting ships as he pleased. There would be nobody present with the authority to stop him. The question was, would he move the ships away from Martinique? If so, that would answer the admiral's primary question — was the governor in Underhill's pay?

Hornblower pursed his lips and began to pace the breadth of his study. Back and forth, back and forth, turning the problem over and over in his mind, looking at it from every conceivable angle, seeking the solution that would satisfy all the variables. Finally, late that night, a thought struck that satisfied that last variable. Hornblower sat down immediately and finished the orders for *Phoebe* and *Terror*. The two ships were ordered to be gone before daylight, even if they had to be kedged out of the harbor to catch the breeze. The schooner *Reliable* had made port two days early. She was also issued orders to leave before dawn. She would carry letters to Commodore Biddle and Commander Brewer explaining Hornblower's change in plans. *Reliable* would then remain to help with searching the bayous and inlets.

Hornblower finished the orders and letters and sent them out to the ships by messenger. Once he'd handed them over, he lit a cigar and crossed to the window again. The harbor was lit by the lights of the various ships, both civilian and naval; it was a sight Hornblower never grew tired of seeing. He stood there, puffing his cigar, sure of his calculations but wise enough to know that he had to guard against the introduction of any new variables, and that was the reason he had to stay. The admiral took a deep drag, blew the smoke toward the ceiling, and smiled. This was a particularly good cigar.

Brewer sat at the table in his cabin and groaned aloud when the doctor moved his rook. They were in their third game, and the captain was now certain that someone should have created an emergency that demanded his attendance on deck.

"Check," the doctor said.

Brewer made the only move open to him, which was to block with a bishop. The doctor took it with a pawn. In desperation, the captain moved a rook to the furthest rank. The doctor raised his eyebrows, then frowned.

"I keep forgetting that you occasionally manifest suicidal tendencies," he said absently. He decided to ignore the threat to concentrate on his own attack. He moved a knight. "Mate in three, Captain."

Brewer studied the board for a minute before reaching out to move a bishop that the doctor had forgotten about or overlooked. The captain picked up the bishop and set it down in perfect position to corner the doctor's king. The doctor's brows rose again in disbelief, and this time they did not come down. Humbly, he reached out and laid his king down.

"I bet that hurt," the captain said.

"Excruciating," the doctor deadpanned. "I bet you've been waiting a while for a chance to pull that off."

Brewer grinned. "Months, actually."

The captain sat back and picked up his coffee cup only to

find the dregs had gone cold. "Alfred!" The servant appeared, and the captain held out his cup. "A fresh cup, if you please. Or a hot one, at any rate. Doctor?"

Spinelli looked up and shook his head.

"Very good, sir." Alfred departed for the pantry and returned with a steaming cup.

"Ah," Brewer said, "thank you, Alfred." The steward bowed and left. The doctor waited about a minute before he spoke.

"What's bothering you, William?"

Brewer stared at the doctor through the steam that rose from his cup. It wasn't often that his guest started a conversation with the captain's first name.

"What makes you think something's *'bothering'* me?"

The doctor sat back in his chair and held his captain's eyes. "No games."

Brewer averted his eyes and raised his cup. "I don't know what you're talking about."

"Then think aloud."

The captain blinked and lowered his cup in surrender. He sat back and took a deep breath. *"How can I kill him?"* he blurted out. *"How?"* The captain looked around for a moment, and Spinelli thought he saw his bottom lip quiver. "He saved my life, Adam. I showed up on that ship, no family, disowned by my father, and pretty damned convinced that I had nothing to live for, since I had nothing to come back to. I'm sure I would have killed myself within a year. Probably much less. Instead, here comes this petty officer, who takes a young, confused, nearly-suicidal midshipman under his wing. It didn't take him long to see what condition I was in, so he put his arm around me and showed me what I could do if I stuck around. Now I have to repay that by killing him?"

Spinelli looked past his captain to see Alfred standing in

the pantry doorway, and he signaled the steward that he would like a cup of coffee. Alfred brought the cup without a word.

Brewer never even noticed his servant come or go. He continued, "Do you know what the worst part of it is? Every time I think I have it settled, that I am determined to do my duty, even if it meant killing him, my mind dredges up a memory, and I hear a voice asking me, '*How could you kill him?*'!" He sank back in his chair, breathing heavily.

Doctor Spinelli sat perfectly still and watched his friend. The moment he feared had arrived. In Spinelli's opinion, William Brewer's one great weakness when it came to command was that he was not a cutthroat. He did not have it in him to be merciless, savage, or hard as nails, no matter the situation that demanded it. His bravery was unquestioned, and his courage proven. But he'd never been asked to hunt down a friend. No matter that this friend had gone bad, and no matter that Brewer knew exactly what he'd done and had called him a pirate to his face; that was still quite a different proposition from hunting him down and killing him. Now the time had come when that question had to be answered.

"Well, sir," the doctor said calmly, "you have a decision to make, don't you?"

Brewer looked confused. "Decision? What decision?"

"The question of whether or not you will do your duty," Spinelli stated unequivocally. Brewer made to answer, but the doctor cut him off with a wave. "Yes, yes, I know about the other times you said you would do your duty, and yet here you are at this!" He waved at his captain. "Pardon me, Captain, but this is not the look of a man who will do his duty! This is the look of a man who will hesitate just long enough to get himself and a good portion of his crew killed! Underhill will not hesitate, William; you told me that yourself. Do you believe that?"

"Yes."

"Alright then. You need to come to a decision, once and for all; will you do your duty, or will you not. It's that simple. Duty does not care about the past, and it has no place for the sentimentality of relationships."

Brewer said nothing, so the doctor set his cup down and sat forward. "Look, William; either you will or you won't. If you will, don't ever let yourself go down this road again. If you won't, turn the ship around and take us back to Jamaica before you get a lot of good men killed."

Brewer's eyes snapped up at the doctor's last words. Spinelli was surprised to see a fire there. "Well?" he asked. "What's it going to be?"

"How do I know it won't happen again?"

"The same way you know what you will drink at supper. You *decide*. It really is that simple, William. You make a decision, and the reasons behind that decision are such that you will not go back on it. Is Michael Underhill the man you knew on the *Kent*, or a pirate?"

"Michael Underhill is a pirate."

"Then what are you going to do?"

"My duty," Brewer said. "Even if it means killing him. I know I may have said it before, but now I know. I won't like it, but I will do it."

"That's what duty means," Spinelli said. With that, he drained his coffee, set his cup down, and left the cabin.

Brewer rose and went to his day cabin and stared blankly at the deck. After a spell, he shook his head to clear his mind.

This is ridiculous! he thought. *I cannot go on this way. Either I am the captain of this ship, with a duty to perform, or I give up the ship and return to England in disgrace, all because I refuse to perform said duty.* He rose and began to pace the width of the cabin. *I have to settle this. One way or the other, it has to end now.* He turned and drew a deep breath, letting it out slowly to drain the anxiety and frustration from his body.

Now, he thought as he stepped out his paces, *the basic question is, will you carry out your orders or not? Those orders are, in their simplest form, to find Michael Underhill and end his reign of terror. If he is taken alive, he will be brought back to Port Royal for trial on charges of piracy, and, if found guilty, hanged. The alternative is that we meet in battle, and either I kill him or he kills me.* Brewer pursed his lips at the thought. Here was the rub. In order to do his duty, no matter which way it turned out, he would be responsible for his friend's death. Or be dead himself.

He stood there, letting that thought go round and round in his mind until the whirlwind finally stopped on the significant word — friend. *Is he still my friend? Is this Michael Underhill my friend?* Brewer turned that question over for a minute before coming to the realization that the Michael Underhill he was pursuing today was not the same man he'd known back on the *Kent.* One would think that would be seen as obvious — Spinelli had seen it — but somehow he had never drawn the distinction before.

So, he thought as he resumed his pacing, *two Michaels. One my friend, who took me and taught me what I needed to know to survive; he even taught me that life was worth living. That Michael disappeared from my life that night in Plymouth. Now, what if we separate them, say, Old Michael and New Michael.* He frowned; Old Michael was the subject of his most cherished memories, but New Michael? Brewer shook his head; did he even *know* New Michael?

Brewer stopped and stared out the stern windows. This was where he had trouble. It had started in Martinique. The voice he heard there was *Old Michael.* The face at first was *Old Michael.* He didn't get an inkling that something was different until Underhill admitted that he was still privateering. That was when he first glimpsed *New Michael.* What confused him was the *Old Michael* he saw in the *New Michael. New Michael* had kidnapped him in Washington City, but *Old Michael* had spared his life. When they met at Port Royal, *New Michael* had threatened to kill innocent bystanders, but *Old Michael* had begged him to let him go. Looking back, he honestly had to say that *New Michael* was in charge at the meeting, and he was the one that made it clear that, should they meet again, no mercy would be shown.

Brewer blinked and resumed his pacing. He was now convinced that he was dealing — in the future as at the café — with *New Michael. Old Michael,* the man he knew and loved, the one who had more or less saved his life aboard HMS *Kent,* was dead and gone.

He halted in mid-step. Dead? *Yes,* he nodded, *my friend, my benefactor, is dead. And if he is dead, it is reasonable to presume that New Michael was the one who killed him.* Brewer looked around and noticed the bottle of wine and the single glass on the table, left there silently by Alfred some time after the doctor departed. The captain crossed to the table and poured himself a drink. He held it aloft in a solemn toast.

"Here's to you, old friend," he said softly. "I'm sorry I wasn't there to save you from, from yourself, I guess you might say. I owed you that much, and more besides. All I can do now is to make you this promise: I will avenge your death. I will take down the beast who killed you. I swear it."

He drained the glass and put the cork firmly back in the bottle.

Two days later, Brewer was on the fo'c'sle, exercising with Alfred. His workouts were changing almost daily now; he was past the point of regaining his strength and was now working on what Alfred termed *"speed under control"*. Alfred was concentrating on swift, precise thrusts and blocks of a type that Brewer had never practiced before. The first few practice runs left the captain bruised and sore from being a split-second too slow. In sympathy, Alfred changed his tactics to a repetition of the same move, over and over, to allow the captain to gain speed and confidence. He did not proceed to the next movement until the current one had been mastered. This method produced results good and bad; good in that the captain was able to master each movement before taking either Mac or Alfred on in a practice fight, and bad in that when the blows did get through his guard, Brewer smarted that much more.

The combination of sparring partners was also working very much to Brewer's advantage. Alfred would teach the captain and Mac the maneuvers, slowly at first and then increasing in speed and force, and when Brewer was fairly sure that he had the movement down, Mac was brought in and thrown against his captain. Now Brewer had to contend with an opponent who knew everything he did and was stronger to boot.

The worst failure was when Mac thrust low and forced Brewer to bring his sword down to block. What he didn't expect was for Mac to rush in behind the attack and pin him against a carronade. The coxswain yelled and threw his head forward viciously over his captain's shoulder to simulate a head-butt attack. Brewer had no doubt that in a real battle, he'd be dealing with a concussion at a minimum. Alfred shouted, and the exercise ended.

"Nice move there at the end, Mac," Brewer said.

"Thank you, sir." The big Cornishman shrugged. "Couldn't resist."

"It is something you need to guard against, Captain," Alfred cautioned. "You must be ready to sidestep the charge and let his momentum carry him past you."

Brewer sighed in disgust. He knew he'd most likely be dead if this were for real. "Understood." He stepped back to the middle of the deck and raised his wooden sword. "Shall we try that again?"

Mac took his place, and Alfred dropped his hand for the contest to begin. Mac did not immediately charge; instead he hung back and threw some powerful blows that were difficult for Brewer to parry effectively.

"Press him, Mac," Alfred called. "Don't let him dance."

"Aye, sir." Mac faked a charge Brewer failed to anticipate, and it threw the captain off balance for a moment. That was all the coxswain needed; he lowered his shoulder and charged. Brewer tried his best to spin and dive out of the way, but his attacker still caught him with an elbow. Mac slashed at his captain but missed high as his momentum carried him into the carronade. From the deck, Brewer kicked out with his foot against the back of the coxswain's knee and brought him down to the deck. The captain lashed out with his sword, catching his opponent full on his exposed chest. Alfred called the exercise.

The captain rose and helped Mac to his feet. "Are you all right?" he asked.

"Oh, aye, Captain," Mac assured him. "That was a right fancy move yerself, sir. I wouldn't have thought you had it in you."

"Nor did I," Alfred said as he hopped down from his perch. "Well done, sir. That's all for today, gentlemen."

"Thanks for the exercise, Mac," the captain said as he handed over his sword. "How goes your reading to the men?"

"Right well, sir! I should be finished with *Robinson Crusoe* in the next couple days, and then we'll start *Gulliver's Travels*. From what I hear, the men are looking forward to the next book. A couple of them have heard of it and even know a little of the story, so that's got the men eager to begin."

"Good. Let me know how it goes." Brewer hung a towel around his neck. "I'll try to remember, Mac, but the next time we put in at a good-sized port, how about you and I go ashore and see if they have a decent bookstore?"

The Cornishman's face broke out in a grin. "I'd like that right well, sir."

"Good!" Brewer turned to Alfred. "I'm going below. Can you pass the word for the doctor to join me in my cabin?"

"Aye, sir."

Brewer made his way below deck. When he was gone, Mac looked to Alfred.

"Do you think I hurt him?"

Alfred tilted his head to the side. "I don't know."

Brewer went straight to his day cabin. He sat down gently and began rubbing his injured shoulder. A knock at the door told him the doctor had arrived.

"Are you all right?" Spinelli asked him.

Brewer shook his head. "Mac knocked me off balance, and I landed hard on my shoulder."

The doctor sat beside him and helped him remove his shirt. He lifted the captain's arm and he winced. Spinelli put the arm down and felt probingly around the shoulder. Brewer hissed when his fingers dug into the back muscle.

"Hm," the doctor said, "I think you're all right. You pushed it too far, is all. Take it easy for a week or so before taking him on again. I also suggest you start winning."

Brewer grunted as he pulled his shirt on. "I'll have you know," another grunt, "he was dead at the end."

"Yes, I heard about that. Too bad he killed you before that."

Brewer shrugged, wincing from the movement. "Yes, well, there is that."

There was a knock at the door, and the new boy Jimmy was admitted. He marched up to the captain and stood at attention, then his eyes went big as he forgot how he was supposed to address the captain. Brewer struggled to keep a straight face, but the doctor turned away to hide his smile.

"Well, Mr. Jimmy?" Brewer prompted.

The boy's eyes were darting here to there, desperately searching for the words. Brewer saw fear creep in.

"Calm down," the captain said. "Jimmy, who sent you?"

"Mr. Tyler, sir."

"And did Mr. Tyler say something about sending his respects?"

The boy's eyes lit up. "Aye, sir! That were it! Mr. Tyler sends his respects, and..."

The doctor leaned forward and whispered in the boy's ear. "Tell him what Mr. Tyler told you to say."

"Oh! Aye!" The lad came to attention to try again from the beginning. "Mr. Tyler send his respects, *Captain.* He says there are American signals flying, and would you please come up on deck?"

"Much better, Mr. Jimmy," the captain said. "Please tell Mr. Tyler I shall be right up."

"Aye, Captain!" The lad spun and marched as fast as he could out of the cabin.

The doctor laughed and the captain grinned. He said to the doctor, "I'd forgotten how terrifying it can be the first time you have to report to the captain."

Brewer and the doctor made their way on deck and saw Mr. Tyler standing beside Mr. Farragut. The American was referring to his signal book as he interpreted the signals flying to and from the flagship.

"Report," Brewer said, addressing his lieutenant.

The two men saluted. "One of their ships signaled the frigate, sir, and the flag responded," Tyler replied.

Brewer turned to Farragut.

"Sir, a sloop, the *Adams*, reported a strange sail to the south heading in the general direction of New Orleans," the American reported formally. "Commodore Biddle has ordered them to investigate."

"Thank you, Mr. Farragut," Brewer said. He accepted a glass from Mr. Tyler and went forward. He stepped up into the main mast shrouds and brought the glass to his eye. The contact was hull up now; to Brewer's eye it looked like a small merchantman. Too small by half to be *Oliver Cromwell*. Brewer handed the glass back to his second lieutenant. "Let me know what they find," he said, "and of course call me for any signals with our number."

"Aye, sir."

Brewer retreated below to his cabin. Once inside, he tossed his hat on the table, more out of frustration than anything else. He felt trapped in the midst of the American squadron, and the position of his ship — at the very center of the formation — did nothing to ease this perception. In his heart, he fully expected Michael to run when he was finally found, and he was also determined that *Revenge* would be the ship to run him down, Commodore or no Commodore.

The captain crossed the room and pulled the door open. "Pass the word for Mr. Greene!"

"Aye, sir!"

Brewer closed the door and went to his day cabin. He dropped into a seat beneath the stern windows, leaned his head back, and closed his eyes. He barely had the chance for any of the tension to drain from his neck and shoulders when a knock at the door announced the arrival of Lieutenant Greene.

"You sent for me, Captain?"

"Yes, Benjamin," Brewer replied. "Sit, please. Alfred, refreshments for two, if you please."

"Aye, sir."

"I'm frustrated, Benjamin," Brewer confessed as they waited for Alfred. "We're stuck here, in the middle of the Americans — figuratively *and* literally — and I'm not sure if that isn't where the admiral wanted us to be. We are supposed to have disposition of both Underhill and his ship; I guarantee you that as soon as Michael figures that out, he will run. And when that happens, I will order our pursuit, Commodore or no Commodore. The trouble is, I'm pretty sure we can outrun everything the Americans have around us — except their frigates."

Alfred appeared with a tray carrying two glasses of wine. He handed one to each officer.

"Will that be all, sir?" he asked.

"Yes, Alfred, thank you."

"What do you propose, Captain?" Greene asked.

The captain sighed. "I'm not exactly sure. I want you to keep up the drills on the sails and the guns. The Americans need to see we take this seriously."

Greene nodded thoughtfully. "So, Underhill is discovered, and he runs. We pursue, orders or no. I take it you expect the commodore to come after us with *Constitution* at least?"

"Yes. The question is, what will he do? I would expect him to follow and observe, since it should be obvious to him that we would be chasing Underhill himself — or at least his ship." The captain let out a loud, exasperated sigh. "Benjamin, I almost wish the admiral had kept the Americans out of it." His hand swept like he was clearing a table in anger. "Just give me a frigate and let me take care of Michael, once and for all."

"That would have made the process easier," the premier agreed.

Brewer raised his glass. "Well, here's to things working out well."

Greene raised his as well, and the two men drank.

Three days later, a knock at his door interrupted Brewer's letter to Captain Bush. He set his quill on the desk and turned. "Enter."

Mr. Short came in. "Mr. Tyler's respects, sir; we have a signal from the flagship. Mr. Farragut says it reads, *'All ships heave to. Captains come on board.'*"

"Thank you, Mr. Short," the captain replied as he rose. "My compliments to Mr. Tyler. Acknowledge the signal and have Mac clear away the gig. I shall change and come up on deck."

"Aye, Captain."

"Alfred!"

"Here, sir. Your best uniform, sir?"

"Yes, thank you."

The two men worked at transforming the captain into a symbol of the might and righteousness of the Royal Navy. He passed Alfred's inspection and made his way to the deck. He was met by Lieutenant Tyler, along with the sailing master. Brewer glanced over his shoulder and saw the first lieutenant talking with Mac forward near the entry port.

Tyler saluted. "We are hove to, Captain. Mac's ready for you forward."

"Thank you, Mr. Tyler." Brewer made his way forward to the entry port.

Greene and Mac saluted. "All is ready, Captain," Greene confirmed.

"Thank you. I hope to have news when I return."

The captain followed Mac over the side and took his place in the stern sheets. The trip to the big American frigate was a short one, the low swells of the Gulf of Mexico cooperated to allow a swift and easy passage. Brewer stepped nimbly up to the *Constitution's* entry port, where he was greeted by the ship's captain.

"Commander Brewer?" the officer inquired. "I am Captain Josiah Pringle, captain of USS *Constitution*. Welcome aboard."

Brewer saluted. "A pleasure to make your acquaintance, Captain."

"The pleasure is mine, Commander." Pringle turned. "Mr. Edwards!" A young man stepped forward and saluted his captain. "Mr. Edwards will conduct you to the commodore, Commander. I shall join you as soon as the rest of the captains are aboard."

"Thank you, sir."

"If you'll follow me, Commander?" Edwards led him below decks and aft to the great cabin. The sentry outside the door came to attention before delivering two sharp raps to the door and opening it without awaiting a reply. Edward stepped inside the door.

"Commodore?" he announced formally. "Commander Brewer of HMS *Revenge*."

Edwards stepped aside to allow Brewer to enter the room, then he backed out, closing the door behind him. Commodore Biddle advanced to greet his guest.

"Commander, welcome to *Constitution*. Wilson, a drink for the commander. Thank you. Step over here for a moment, Commander." Biddle took him by the arm and steered him off from the others in the room. "One of the purposes of this meeting," the commodore confided in a low voice, "is to inform the other captains of the details of our plans for New Orleans and the taking of Underhill and his ship. I just wanted you to know that up front. I will handle any objections that will arise — and there will be one or two, I assure you — at dinner."

"Very good, sir," Brewer replied.

The two officers rejoined the group. Brewer noted the presence of Captain Pringle and presumed the gathering was now complete. "Allow me to present my officers," the commodore said. "You have met Captain Pringle. This is Captain Allen of USS *Congress*."

Brewer came to attention before shaking the proffered hand of the frigate's captain. "A pleasure to meet you, Captain."

"Yes," came the reply, and it was all Brewer could do not to blink at the effrontery. The captain nodded to the commodore and moved aside.

Biddle introduced the commanders in the room in quick fashion, James of the corvette *Hancock*, Franklin of the sloop *Adams*, Hutchinson of the sloop *Roanoke* — that name caught Brewer's ear; he remembered hearing a tale of the captain's guile and cunning in escaping a trap set for him during the late war. Commander Henry of the brig *Reliant* was next, followed by schooner captains Harrison of the *Washington*, Hale of the *Jefferson*, and Potter of the *Hamilton*. Refreshments were served by the stewards; Brewer was impressed by the Madeira.

In making his way around the room, Brewer found himself in company with Commander Franklin. "Pardon my asking," he said, "but are you any relation to the writer and diplomat?"

Franklin looked surprised. "To Benjamin, you mean?" He grunted. "No such luck. Not even distantly, so far as I know. Tell me, is *Revenge* your first command?"

"Yes."

"What do you think of it?"

Brewer took a sip of his wine. "Command, or the ship?"

Franklin shrugged with a smile. "Both."

Brewer chuckled. "I like them both fine. I have a good crew, and *Revenge* is soundly made. Of course, my ship is smaller than this," he waved his arm around the cabin, "but I have my hopes."

"Yes, well, I look forward to working with you." Franklin moved off.

Brewer wondered if he'd somehow insulted the man but decided not to worry for now. He sipped his wine and observed the Americans. They were gathered in groups of two or three, and none of them cast glances in his direction. He found this somewhat odd; he would have thought that they would be curious about his presence among them. Just then his thoughts were interrupted by a throat clearing at his shoulder; it was one of the American commanders. Brewer desperately searched his memory, trying to recall the man's name, but the American came to his rescue.

"James Henry," the man said, "of the brig *Reliant*. It's good to have you with us, Commander."

"Thank you."

"So, why are you here?" Henry's voice was low; Brewer wondered if that was due to the gathering or so the commodore wouldn't hear. Henry was a small man — more than a head shorter than Brewer — and balding on top with his temples tending toward grey. His face was narrow and clean shaven, with a Roman nose and close-set, dark eyes. The commander's wiry build spoke of a constitution founded on action. Brewer thought this was not a man to sit back and let others do the fighting for him.

Ah, thought Brewer, *the direct approach.* He smiled over his drink. "My admiral ordered me to sail with the commodore."

Henry grinned. "See you at dinner, Commander." He too

moved off to mingle.

Brewer noticed a steward step in and whisper in the commodore's ear, and that worthy rose.

"Pardon me, gentlemen," he said loudly to get everyone's attention, "but I am told that dinner is served. If you will follow me, you will find your place by name card."

Commodore Biddle was at the head of the table, with the places of honor at his right and left reserved for Captains Pringle and Allen respectively. Brewer was shocked to discover his place to be at Pringle's left hand, despite being the youngest captain present. He tried very hard not to show his surprise. Commander Hutchinson was across from him and Commander Franklin was on his left, with James of the *Hancock* across from him. All stood until every officer had found his place, then Biddle sat and the rest followed suit. The commodore rose again, and stewards entered the room to fill every man's glass.

"I know this is a little unusual," Biddle explained, "but this is an unusual occasion." He paused until the stewards finished and departed before raising his glass. "Gentlemen, I ask you to join me in a toast to the health of the President of the United States, James Monroe." All drank to the toast, including Brewer after only a moment's hesitation. The commodore continued, "And I ask you, in view of the presence of our guest and ally, Commander Brewer of the Royal Navy, to drink with me the health of His Britannic Majesty, King George III as well as the Prince Regent." All drank to that as well, and the commodore resumed his seat.

"I apologize if I got that toast wrong, Commander," he said to Brewer, "but I thought it something of the sort would be appropriate in the spirit of our newfound cooperation."

"Thank you for that, Commodore," Brewer said. Actually, he had no idea either as to whether or not it was appropriate, but he appreciated the effort.

Biddle picked up a bell from the table before him and rang it. A line of stewards emerged from the pantry, each carrying a platter, tray, or bowl. The aromas that filled the air made Brewer wonder for a moment whether Alfred was in the pantry.

"In honor of our young British commander," Biddle said, "I have endeavored to provide the very best in American cuisine for him to sample. Hollingsworth has overseen the feast before us; we have two of the best Virginia baked hams, followed by a roast turkey and a roast goose — unfortunately, they are each so small as to barely make one decent sized bird between them — fresh peas and carrots, potatoes and onions, tarts, fresh bread, beaten butter, and two kinds of marmalade. And for dessert, apple pie."

Brewer heard both groans of delight and subdued cheers at the menu, and he heartily agreed. Captain Pringle rose and began to carve the ham place before him, and Allen did the same with the turkey. Both captains served the commodore first before helping themselves, and each was kind enough to serve Brewer before passing their platters down the table. The roast goose and the other ham were taken to the far end of the table where Commanders Hale and Potter did the honors. Brewer took small helpings of everything and found he had to try very hard not to succumb to gluttony.

"Well, Commander," Captain Pringle asked him after a few mouthfuls, "what do you think of American cooking?"

"Fabulous, Captain!" came the reply. "I think I shall arrange for my ship to be blown ashore every time I pass the Virginia coast, just to get a chance to purchase a ham like this!" He paused for a bite or two. "But, to tell you the truth, this is not my first exposure to American cuisine."

"No?"

"No, sir. When I was first lieutenant in HMS *Defiant* and on my way to the West Indies Squadron, my ship put in at

Boston, and I was lucky enough to get a spot of shore leave along with another lieutenant. We found an inn not far from the docks that served thick veal chops with the most delicious gravy I've ever had in my life!" He shook his head at the memory. "That was the first time I ever contemplated deserting from the navy."

A laugh went up around the table, and a voice came from down the table.

"What you say sounds familiar, sir! What inn was that?"

Brewer sat back and looked at the deck above as he searched his memory for the name. "What was it? Let me see... red something... red bow? No, that's not it... red lion? Yes! That's it! *Red Lion Inn*!"

Commander Henry slapped the table. "I knew it! That inn is the best known in all of Boston! The owner welcomes sailors of every nation. It's said he sailed with John Paul Jones during the Revolution."

"We didn't discuss the war," Brewer said, "but he certainly took care of my friend and me right well."

The dinner conversation spun down from fabulous restaurants in big ports to the most modest cantinas in hole-in-the-wall villages where the food was absolutely fantastic. Finally, the platters were empty, and the stewards were able to clear the table and bring coffee for each man.

Captain Allen gestured at Brewer's cup and said, "I'm sorry we poor Americans are unable to provide you with a decent cup of tea, Commander."

Brewer picked up his cup and blew over the rim. "Oh, that's quite all right, Captain Allen. I for one am with your side when it comes to coffee — nothing better, in my opinion!" The table erupted with laughter while Captain Allen drank his coffee.

Biddle rose from his seat, and the conversations subsided. "It's time to tell you all what our mission is and what we're doing here. Most of you have figured out that we're approaching the port of New Orleans. Now you shall know why." He spent the next hour telling them the story of Michael Underhill, British ex-patriot turned privateer, then pirate.

Brewer looked mostly at his hands folded on the table in front of him, but his eyes darted quickly to several of his companions to gage their reactions. When the commodore finished his tale, no one spoke at first. Then Brewer noticed a sneer at the corner of Captain Allen's mouth.

"So," he crowed softly, "am I to assume that the British need our help to capture this renegade?"

Immediately, the tension level in the room skyrocketed. Brewer noticed Commodore Biddle's eyes narrow in silent disgust.

"I remind you, Captain," he said, "that American ships have disappeared as well, and the secretary believes this renegade to be responsible."

Allen waved the objection away. "Speculation," he said coldly. "We all know that piracy is alive and well in the Caribbean. What we don't know is why the British have allowed this travesty to continue for so long."

Brewer's eyes flashed. "It has only recently become known to us, Captain."

Allen shrugged. "You need to police your own, Commander."

"He didn't operate under any letter from the king, Captain," Brewer said, the edge now plain in his voice. "With all due respect, it was you who turned him loose, and now it's come back to haunt you as well. Personally, I was against any American involvement in this matter. In my opinion, we don't need you. All I need is to find the *Oliver Cromwell* and blow Michael Underhill out of the water. Sir."

In the silence that followed, Brewer realized he'd gone

too far, but he wasn't about to back down now, not with Allen waiting for a chance to pounce. Fortunately, Biddle cleared his throat loudly and retook control of the meeting.

"Yes, well," he said firmly, "let's remember that we are here because Admiral Lord Hornblower and I agreed that it was in *both* our countries' interest that this threat be dealt with as soon as possible. Any comments or concerns should be directed to me, not Commander Brewer. Is that understood?"

A chorus of "Aye, sir" and "Aye, aye" echoed softly around the room. Brewer's eyes looked from Captain Allen to his folded hands. His face was blank, and he was determined not to show weakness in this company. Still, he knew what Hornblower would expect from him.

He turned to the commodore. "My apologies, sir, if I spoke out of turn."

"Thank you, Commander," Biddle replied, "but let's set that aside for the present. Gentlemen, let us turn our attention to New Orleans." He turned toward Captain Pringle, who was also his flag captain, to take over the meeting.

Pringle rose to his feet. "As most of you know, New Orleans has several outlets into the Gulf of Mexico. We have no idea which is favored by Underhill, so we have to search them all. *Reliant* will patrol the coast to the west as far as Ship Island. I doubt you'll find him out that far, but it has to be checked. Commander Henry will also be responsible for clearing Timbalier Bay and Lake St. Denis. *Hancock* and *Adams* will take the West, Southwest and South Passes, *Roanoke* and *Hamilton* will take the Southeast Pass as well as the Pass a l'Loutre. *Washington* and *Jefferson* will take the coast north as far as the Bay of River aux Chenes. I remind you all to beware of the sandbar, which can be a hazard at times of low tide. *Constitution, Congress,* and *Revenge* will patrol the coastline at a distance of about twenty to twenty-five miles between the area north of the West Pass. Questions?" There were none, so he continued. "Remember, we are looking for the sloop *Oliver Cromwell*. Commander Brewer and his officers have provided us with a comprehensive description of the vessel, and copies will be included in your orders."

"That's hardly necessary, don't you think?" Commander Harrison said. "Won't *Oliver Cromwell* be the one that runs?"

Several commanders grinned at this. Pringle cleared his throat. "Yes, well, that is certainly a possibility, Commander, but I remind you that Underhill is not the only pirate or smuggler out there. You might just get lucky and run across one of them."

Harrison shrugged and looked vaguely disappointed. "I suppose..."

"I remind you," the commodore interjected, "*Cromwell* and Underhill are to be taken alive if possible, but we will not ask him to surrender twice."

"And Commander Brewer gets disposition?" It was Captain Allen who posed the question.

"That is my agreement with Admiral Hornblower," the commodore replied.

"I can understand that about Underhill," Commander Hutchinson added. "He is one of theirs, after all. But what about the ship? That's a lot of potential prize money to give away."

Biddle sat back and rubbed his chin as he considered the question. A quick glance told him that Brewer was staying out of the discussion. He pursed his lips and made his decision.

"Commander Brewer will have disposition of Underhill and any of his crew taken alive, along with any papers found on board the *Cromwell*. We will retain possession of the ship for American prize courts. Commander," he turned to Brewer, "I will write you a letter regarding this for you go give to Admiral Hornblower."

"Thank you, sir," was all Brewer could say. In truth, the idea of taking *Cromwell* as a prize had hardly occurred to him. His war was with Michael Underhill.

"Thank you, gentlemen," Commodore Biddle said. "Your orders will be sent to your ships. Dismissed."

The American officers rose and filed out of the room. Brewer stayed at the table. When they were alone, the commodore resumed his seat. He rang the bell, and the steward appeared.

"Coffee, Commander?" the commodore asked. Brewer nodded, and Biddle turned to the steward. "Two, please."

"Aye, Commodore." The man disappeared for a moment before reappearing with two cups on a tray.

"Commander," the commodore said, "between us, I will apologize for Captain Allen. He has all the tact of a brick. However, I must caution you to guard your tongue; he is a captain in the United States Navy."

"I apologize, sir," Brewer said sincerely. "I will be more careful in the future."

Biddle nodded. "Then we'll say no more about it. I'm sorry to take the *Cromwell* from you, but I felt I had to give them something."

"Quite all right, sir," Brewer replied. "I wasn't planning on taking it back to port anyway."

Biddle hid his smile behind his cup. "No, I thought not."

CHAPTER ELEVEN

Michael Underhill and his first mate Chauncey sat in the corner of the tavern inside Fort St. Philip on the east side of the Mississippi River, some 40 miles north of the gulf. Underhill had paid a hefty price for a hidden anchorage for *Oliver Cromwell* in the Freemasons Islands, then sailed to the Louisiana shore in a swift pinnace. The fort's tavern, commonly called 'The Inn', was as close to home as anywhere on earth for him, and it was the place where he conducted the majority of his business.

"So," he said to Chauncey, "what did Henri tell you?" Henri was their informant with connections in the governor's office. Chauncey had met with the man yesterday.

The mate shrugged. "His contacts agree that the British have taken a great interest in our activities, and in you, personally."

Underhill took a long draught from his tankard. He dropped the tankard hard on the table, his semi-inebriated eyes staring blankly before him. "Brewer!" he whispered.

Chauncey said nothing. This behavior was typical now whenever his chief drank. The mate stared silently at his own drink and waited for it to be over.

"Why?" Underhill whispered desperately. He put his elbows on the table and dropped his head into his hands. "Why was he there? At that tavern? What cruel fate brought us together?" His head shook in his hands, and his breath grew ragged. "Dead!" he gasped. "He should be dead! But how can I kill him? He was like a son to me. I tried my best to save his life when I left him behind..."

Chauncey glanced up at his captain, and his heart wrenched within him. He had been with Underhill for years — they'd sailed on together on merchant ships before the war. During that time, he'd known nothing about his chief's past. In fact, he didn't find out until he'd heard Underhill and Brewer talking in the tavern on Martinique, and it helped him understand many of his captain's actions both during the war and afterward.

"What will you do, Captain?" he asked.

Underhill drew a long, deep breath and let it out slowly before lifting his head. The eyes that looked at Chauncey were sad and resigned.

"I will do what I said I would. The next time Brewer and I meet, I will kill him."

Just then, the Inn's door burst open, and a stranger stepped in. He looked briefly around the dimly-lit room before making a beeline for the table in the corner. As he got closer, Chauncey recognized him.

"Jo Jo!" he said as the man took the chair beside him. "What brings you here?"

"Packet's just arrived from the delta," the newcomer said in a low voice. "The navy's searching the delta for you."

"For us?" Chauncey asked as he looked to Underhill.

Jo Jo nodded. "By name and by ship."

The two shipmates shared a look, and Underhill nodded. Chauncey reached into his pocket and placed a coin on the table. He slid it to Jo Jo. The newcomer scooped up the coin and departed.

"Now what do we do?" Chauncey asked.

Underhill closed his eyes and massaged the bridge of his

nose with his thumb and forefinger as he thought about it. The Americans must be here in some force if they were searching the entire delta at once. *Cromwell* should be safe for now, but the naval commander would surely enlarge the search area when they found the delta clear. "We need to leave. Return to the ship. I shall follow you presently. Our destination will be one of the ports of the northern United States or Canada, someplace we can lay low for a while until the British get tired of looking for us. Go now. Be ready to sail when I arrive. Two, three days at most."

"Aye, Captain." Chauncey drained his tankard and left the inn.

Underhill watched him go and then drained his tankard as well. He ordered coffee and began making a list of people he had to meet with before he left New Orleans.

Commander Brewer sat at the desk in his cabin rereading the orders from the commodore delivered to his ship the day before. At dawn tomorrow, HMS *Revenge* would change course for her assigned patrol area, from the Pass a la Loutre north to the Bay Ronde. He also had responsibilities to cover Breton Island and the Bristants du Grand Gosier Islands, fifteen to twenty miles to the east. The orders estimated that seven to ten days might be necessary for the squadron to search the entire delta. Brewer set the orders down and took a drink of his wine. Without knowing exactly what the coastline was like, he thought it might take two or three days to make one pass over his patrol area, and that was if it didn't take too long to search the islands to the east.

Brewer rose, and began to pace. He knew the mission was coming to a close, one way or another, and he wasn't at all sure it would end the way he wanted. He fully expected the sweep of the delta to flush out Underhill and *Cromwell*, but he only had a one-in-three chance of intercepting him and bringing him to battle. He was frowning as he turned; he didn't want the Americans to get Underhill. That would mean his getting turned over to Brewer and going back to Port Royal for public trial as a pirate and hanging for his crimes. Brewer paused and dropped his head when the thought hit him. Even Michael deserved better; he deserved the chance to die in battle. Brewer raised his head and sighed. It had to be him. Please, God, let them come east.

Two days later, Captain Brewer stood in his usual place in the center of his quarterdeck. HMS *Revenge* had just finished searching the Bay Ronde for the second time and was now heading east toward the islands. They' competed their first circuit faster than he expected – they had arrived back at the Pass a la Loutre in less than two days.

He looked forward and hid a smile at the sight of the crowded shrouds. He'd made an announcement when they first arrived on station that a reward of a gold sovereign would go to the man who first sighted *Cromwell*. The shrouds and tops had been full ever since, day and night. Not that it had done any good; it was almost as though Underhill had found a way to make *Oliver Cromwell* sail under water. Brewer slowed the search in favor of diligence over speed and used the entire third day to search the passes and Bay Ronde more carefully. As a result, the fourth day found them approaching Breton Island. The search moved quickly now, as there were only three places where *Cromwell* could be on the entire coast. The rest of the shore was marred by cliffs or shoals. Four hours found *Revenge* approaching the Bristants du Grand Gosier Islands.

"Mr. Sweeney," the captain called, "we'll search the southern portion first and work our way back."

"Aye, sir." Sweeney turned and talked with the quartermaster. Sail was taken in as they began their run, slowing the ship to allow a thorough search as they passed by.

Lieutenant Greene approached. "You know what I think would help?" he asked. "One of those big hot-air balloons the French used. Tether it to the mainmast, and we could let it rise four or five hundred feet into the air. It would expand our search radius by miles!"

"True," Brewer acknowledged, "but wouldn't it be just as easy to make wings like Icarus and send the midshipmen aloft to search?" He gazed aloft and sighed. "I wonder about the future sometimes, what wonders it will bring. I mean, think about it: a hundred years ago, a ship like *Revenge* didn't exist, nor anything like a first-rate today. What will the navy look like a hundred years in the future? I've heard the engineers are very close to putting a steam engine in a warship. That's not all — what if they found a way to strengthen the hull by sheeting it with copper all the way up to the railings? Or better yet, with iron instead of copper? Such a monster could sink any wooden ship that came against her and dominate the seas. My nightmare is, *what if the French get there first?*" He crossed his arms over his chest and shook his head. Greene stood there silently, considering what his captain had said.

Suddenly a call came from the starboard foremast shrouds.

"Ship off the starboard bow!"

Brewer and Greene went forward.

"Who called that?" Brewer cried.

"Me, sir!" It was a hand about halfway up the shrouds. "Hancock, sir!"

"I shall remember that, Mr. Hancock!" the captain waved to him. "Lookout! Let's here you!"

"Ship heading south, Captain!" the lookout confirmed. "Maybe a point or two east! About the size of a brig or sloop — can't say for sure yet!"

"Benjamin," Brewer turned to his premier, "send a runner up to the lookout. I want a report every fifteen minutes. I'm going aft to set a course to intercept."

"Aye, sir."

The captain marched aft. "Intercept course, Mr. Sweeney!" he cried when he arrived on the quarterdeck. "As much sail as she'll carry!"

"Aye, sir!"

Sweeney grabbed a speaking trumpet and began bellowing orders. The men on the shrouds either made their way to the yards or jumped clear to make way for their fellows. Soon the sky above them was filled with canvas, and *Revenge* shot forward on her new course of south-southeast.

Mr. Short approached and saluted. "Mr. Greene's respects, Captain. I'm sent to report to you. Lookout says the chase is now a point starboard and heading south. He's pretty sure she's a sloop, sir, maybe a sloop-of-war. He don't think she's seen us yet."

Brewer nodded. "Thank you, Mr. Short. Return to the lookout."

"Aye, sir."

Brewer stepped over to the lee rail and began to pace. If the chase was *Oliver Cromwell,* he would be hard pressed to close the gap before nightfall at this distance. When he made the turn aft, he lifted his eyes and scanned the horizon. There was no way for him to inform the commodore of the sighting. Brewer set his jaw, his lips pressed into a firm line. *So be it,* he thought. *I'm not letting him go.*

In the great cabin of the *Oliver Cromwell,* Michael Underhill sat at his table and sipped a cup of tea. In all his years in America, he never could give up tea for the American preference of coffee. He considered it a bitter brew. Not even cream and many lumps of sugar could save it, and he was bitter enough without it.

He'd felt the nets closing in on him even before he fled from Fort St. Philip. The pinnace had parted from the dock the moment his foot hit the deck, and the voyage back to the ship was pleasantly uneventful. Little did he know, that would be his last bit of good luck.

He'd boarded the ship only to learn from Chauncey that there had been a storm, and lightning had damaged the fore topmast and made havoc of the rigging. Two men died in the lightning strike. They did not have a suitable replacement mast aboard and would have to make do with a poor substitute, unless the captain wanted to wait for the arrival of a new mast. The bosun was already at work setting up fresh line, but the substitute mast probably would not take the stress of full sail for very long. Underhill was loath to wait for a new mast, not with the Americans looking for them, so he ordered the ship to sea. He intended to head south and then east to the Bay of Tocobaga — what the Americans were calling Tampa Bay — or one of the ports on the west coast of Florida and replace the mast there. He scowled at the thought. There was talk that the Americans would soon take possession of Florida; when that happened, those ports would most likely be closed to him as well.

He drained the dregs of his cup before they got cold. He was tired, the kind of tired a man couldn't sleep off. Seeing Brewer again — first in Martinique and then afterwards — had got him thinking of retiring before something happened. Maybe it was time to say he'd paid the British back both for what they'd done to him and the future they'd stolen from him. He rapped the table with his empty cup, and his servant appeared and poured him another. He grunted as he raised the cup to his lips. It was all well and good to think about such things — to dream about the future — but he had to get out of this mess first. Then he had to see to it that his men were taken care of; that was paramount. They'd been faithful too long to be abandoned, no matter what the cost.

South. That was the place to hide. Gran-Columbia, perhaps, or even the Argentine. He had friends there, or at least, no enemies that he knew of. Once the new mast was installed and the ship provisioned, they could sail down the east coast of Central America, taking advantage of the many hiding spots when necessary. Underhill raised his chin; yes, it could work, if the stars aligned.

His thoughts were interrupted by a knock at the door, and a boy from the deck opened the door.

"The mate's respects, Captain," he said simply. "There's a strange sail on the horizon."

Underhill made his way on deck without his coat or hat. He was met by Chauncey, who handed him a glass and pointed off their starboard quarter. He went to the rail and used the telescope to pick out a small patch of white that was slowly growing larger — obviously heading toward them.

He lowered the glass and swallowed reflexively. "How much sail can she take?" he asked.

The mate turned and studied their cloth. "Some, maybe, but not much more."

Underhill handed the glass back. "Give her everything she'll take. If that's an American, we may be able to bluff our way out of this. But if it's Brewer, there'll be a fight if he catches us before nightfall."

Chauncey turned and began calling out orders to the crew. Underhill paid no attention — he knew from vast experience he could trust his mate's seamanship. He leaned on the rail and stared at the approaching ship, trying his best with his mind's eye to see who was on that quarterdeck. It troubled him that, all the while, the pit in his stomach was growing.

"They've seen us, Captain!" came the shout from the lookout. "They're running!"

Brewer made his way to the larboard rail and raised his glass to his eye. Sure enough, the chase was putting on sail. The sailing master stepped up beside him.

"Studs'ls?" Brewer asked.

Sweeney shook his head. "I'd advise against it, Captain. In this wind, they'd actually slow us down, believe it or not."

A quick glance at the clouds told him the sailing master was right, and he closed his eyes briefly in self-recrimination for not seeing this himself.

"Yes, of course," he said. "You're right, Mr. Sweeney. Thank you. Put her on her best point of sailing, if you please. I want to catch them before they have a chance to escape in the darkness."

"Aye, Captain. I'll do my best."

"I know you will," Brewer said kindly. "Carry on."

Sweeney saluted and made his way back to the wheel, where the quartermaster was waiting for him. Brewer turned and was surprised to see the doctor stepping up from the companionway.

"What brings you on deck, Doctor?" he asked.

"Curiosity," the doctor replied. "I felt us pick up speed earlier, so I came up to see what's going on." He nodded his head forward. "*Cromwell?*"

"I think so," the captain admitted. "She's certainly running, which is what I'd expect *Cromwell* to do."

"So what now?"

Brewer sighed. "Now, we chase her. Hopefully, we can close the gap enough before nightfall to bring her to battle. If not, it's a hundred-to-one against our being able to hold on to her overnight."

Spinelli pulled out his watch and opened it. "Call it eight

hours of daylight, maybe eight-and-a-half at this time of year. Can we do it?"

The captain shook his head uncertainly. "Maybe, but we'll probably need help."

Michael Underhill had not moved in the past two hours. His gaze was constantly aft, toward the slowly growing patch of white that would soon be hull-up from the deck. A quick glance to set the position of the sun in the sky told him he had about seven hours of daylight left. He knew his best chance was to survive until nightfall and then to lose his pursuer in the darkness. But, could they last that long? If that mast gave way, their speed would drop drastically, which would allow their pursuer to close the gap.

He turned and stepped forward. "Chauncey!" he called. When the mate arrived, he said, "Is there any way to strengthen that mast so we could add more sail? That ship out there is gaining on us, slowly but surely, and I'm not sure we can make it to nightfall."

The big mate shook his head. "I set the carpenter to that the minute you decided we had to leave, and he's done the best he could. It's braced better than a broken leg and wrapped with one-inch line to keep it that way. There's nothing more we can do."

Underhill turned back to the chase and leaned on the rail. "Put her on her best point, whatever the wind. What we need today is distance, not direction."

"Aye, Captain."

It was two bells of the afternoon watch when Alfred came up on deck. He waited until the captain was finished with his conversation with the sailing master before he approached.

"Yes, Alfred?" the captain asked.

"I was wondering what you would like to do about lunch, sir. The men ate some time ago, but you haven't left the quarterdeck in hours."

Brewer was about to order him below when his stomach growled a warning. He hesitated, caught between desire and duty.

"Excuse me, sir," Alfred saw his difficulty, "but would you like me to bring you a cold tray up here? I could do an assortment of meats and cheeses, for example, and a glass of wine to wash it down?"

"Yes, Alfred, that would do nicely," Brewer said, the relief evident in his voice. "And thank you."

The servant bowed and went below. Soon, Mac appeared carrying a small table and a chair that he set up by the lee rail so the captain could sit and take his meal on deck. Alfred followed, a tray on one hand and a goblet in the other. He set them on the table. Brewer sat and helped himself to the sliced ham and cheeses on the tray. One slice led to another and another; he hadn't realized that he was so hungry. He drank the dregs of his wine and stood. Almost immediately, he felt overwhelmed by a wave of exhaustion. He sat back down hard and his hand went to his head. *How long since I slept?* he wondered. *Twenty-four hours? More?*

Lieutenant Greene stepped over. "Captain? Are you all right?"

"Fine, Benjamin," he said, his voice shaking a bit. "I'm just tired, I think."

"I agree, sir." Brewer saw a movement in the corner of his eye and turned to see Mac standing there. He turned back to his premier. Greene smiled. "I have the deck, sir, with your permission. May I suggest you get some sleep? You're going to be rested when we catch up with *Cromwell*."

Brewer looked up to Mac, standing silently to the side. "You're the muscle?"

Mac shuffled his feet. "Just a coxswain, sir."

Brewer looked back to Greene, and the first lieutenant shrugged. "Nothing is going to happen for the next several hours, sir. Why not take advantage of the dead time and catch up on your sleep?"

He hated to admit it, but the suggestion was sounding better and better. With his belly full, his body was crying for sleep. He nodded and stood. His strength was gone, and Mac's strong right arm helped him stand long enough to marshal the strength to cross the deck and descend the companionway on his own. Mac followed. When they got to the captain's cabin, Alfred was waiting.

"*Et, tu*?" Brewer said sarcastically.

Alfred shrugged. "I'm sure I don't know what you mean, Captain. Is there something I can do for you?"

Brewer sighed in surrender. "Call me when I'm needed." He made his way to his sleeping cabin without another word.

He awoke to the clanging of the ship's bell. He blinked the sleep from his eyes and sat up in his cot. He was still in his uniform. He looked over to see his coat folded neatly over the back of the chair; he vaguely remembered dropping it on the floor after he staggered into the room. He rolled off of the cot and stood on the deck. He stretched to work the kinks out of his back and found the exhaustion gone and his head clear.

He walked out of the cabin and wandered toward the table. Alfred appeared in the pantry door.

"Captain?" he asked. "What can I get you, sir?"

"What time is it?" Brewer asked.

"Turn of the second dog watch, sir."

Brewer sat. He'd been asleep for five hours. "Coffee, if you please, Alfred."

"Aye, sir."

"Sentry!" he called. The sentry opened the door. "Pass the word for the first lieutenant."

"Aye, Captain."

Alfred arrived and placed a steaming mug on the table. Brewer nodded his thanks and blew on the rim of the cup before taking a tentative sip. The strong brew revived him. "Perfect! Thank you, Alfred."

The servant bowed and retreated. A knock on the door preceded the arrival of Lieutenant Greene. He was followed in by Doctor Spinelli.

"Adam?" Brewer said. "To what do I owe the pleasure."

"Just checking on you, Captain. I heard you worked yourself into a state of perfect exhaustion. Feeling better now, I hope?"

"Yes, thanks to five hours' sleep and Alfred's coffee." He turned to the premier. "Report."

"We're closing on *Oliver Cromwell*, but I don't think we'll close the gap before dark.."

"We're sure it's him?"

Greene shrugged. "As sure as we can be at this distance."

"How long before we can reach her with the long nines?"

"Unknown, but it may be several hours yet. The weather looks to be closing in."

"In for a storm, are we?" the doctor asked.

"A bad one, I fear," Greene confirmed. "Possibly within the hour."

Brewer finished his coffee. He rose and picked up his hat. "Let's go."

He stepped up on deck and was met by Lieutenant Tyler. "I was about to call you, sir," he said as he handed him a telescope. "We're closing the gap faster than anticipated. Apparently, *Oliver Cromwell* is not sailing very well today. We should be in range for the bow chasers within an hour at most if conditions hold."

"Good," the captain replied. He did not trust himself to speak overly much just now. Better to concentrate on the job at hand. "Have the hands been fed? No? Feed them now, if you please, then clear for action. Benjamin, once we've cleared for action, I'd like you to take station at the bow chasers. Let me know when you're ready to fire."

"Aye, Captain." Greene saluted and went forward.

Brewer went to the lee rail and began to pace. What was going on? Was Michael setting a trap for him? He must have identified *Revenge* nearly as quickly as his men identified *Cromwell*. He set that idea aside and proceeded on the assumption that something was wrong and *Cromwell* was not sailing at her best.

The captain made the turn aft, and his mind turned to tactics for the coming battle. There was no knowing how badly the enemy's problems would affect her maneuverability. Ideally, Brewer thought to get close enough to put the wheel hard over and rake *Cromwell's* stern, but he didn't think Michael would sit still and allow that. *Most likely he will turn and try to put a broadside into my bows,* he thought grimly. *I must be ready to turn opposite to counter, and even anticipate him if I can. A minute or two's advantage can make all the difference.*

When Brewer made the turn forward again, he raised his eyes from the deck and was astonished to see *Cromwell* very nearly in range. How had the gap closed that quickly? He went forward and found the first lieutenant studying the chase through a telescope.

"Ah, Captain," he said. "I was about to send for you. I think we can try a ranging shot in about fifteen minutes." He indicated a hand at the rear of the larboard gun. "Grimes here wants to bet he can land a shot on their quarterdeck."

Brewer turned to the gun captain, who was saluting him with a nearly-toothless grin.

"Really, Grimes? How many tries?"

Grimes considered for a moment. "Can we have three?"

"Done," Brewer decreed. "An extra ration of grog for your gun crew if you succeed. Mr. Short!" The midshipman appeared. "I want you to get up to the foretops. Tell the lookout we are about to fire on the chase, and he is to watch specifically for a shot to hit their quarterdeck. Understand?"

"Aye, Captain!" He saluted and was off.

Brewer watched Grimes taking a final sighting along the barrel of his gun. Once he was ready, he stood back and looked to the first lieutenant.

Brewer stepped back so there would be no question that Mr. Greene would be the one to give the order. The premier studied the chase through his glass. He lowered and glass and his eyes narrowed, and Brewer could readily imagine the calculations rolling through his mind. He raised the glass again for a moment, then lowered it and nodded to Grimes.

The gun captain stood back, lanyard in hand. He gave it a great tug, and the gun erupted with fire and smoke. The noise, being so close, was deafening, and Brewer wished again it was not considered undignified to put one's hands over one's ears. The smoke cleared quickly, but they did not see the fall of the shot.

Brewer raised his head and his voice. "Lookout! Let's hear you!"

"Shot landed just to larboard, Captain!"

Grimes and his crew reloaded the gun and checked its aim. Satisfied, Grimes stood back and held the lanyard. He looked to the first lieutenant and received a nod of permission. He yanked the lanyard hard, and once again the gun erupted. All eyes turned skyward to the lookout.

"Shot landed short by about twenty yards, sir!"

Brewer shook his head ruefully. "That's two, Grimes. One shot left."

The gun captain nodded, and he and his crew went to work. Brewer could readily tell the crew was well drilled, and privately he thought Grimes missed the shot only because he misjudged the roll. He thought to offer the advice, but he didn't want to interfere. Grimes stood back, lanyard in hand. Brewer could see by the look in his eyes he was timing the uproll. He pulled the lanyard, and the gun fired with a belch of smoke and another deafening roar. The lookout peered over the side of the tops.

"A hit! A hit, sir!"

The gun's crew cheered, shaking each other's hands and slapping backs in congratulations. Grimes stepped away from his men and saluted his captain. Brewer gave him a crisp salute in return.

"Mr. Greene," he said, "an extra ration of grog for these men. Well done to you all!"

"Aye, sir," Greene replied.

"Thankee, Captain!" Grimes said, and his men cheered again.

Brewer turned to the first lieutenant. "You may open fire, Mr. Greene. Maintain fire as long as your guns bear."

"Aye, Captain!" Greene nodded to the starboard crew, and almost immediately the gun fired. Brewer noticed that Mr. Short had returned from his mission to the tops.

"Mr. Short," he said, "the first lieutenant and I are returning to the quarterdeck. I want you to take over command of the bow chasers. You heard my orders?"

"Aye, sir; maintain fire as long as they bear."

"Very good. Take over, Mr. Short."

"Aye, Captain."

Greene fell into step with his captain as they made their way aft. "You made his day, Captain."

Brewer grinned. "He needs the experience. You've trained them well, by the way; congratulations are in order, Benjamin, and I intend to mention such in my report to the admiral."

"Thank you, Captain."

The steady fire of the bow chasers could be heard by the time they reached the quarterdeck. Brewer motioned for Mr. Sweeney to join them at the fantail. The three huddled close for a quick conference.

"Mr. Short is forward pounding *Cromwell* with the bow chasers, so I expect Michael to alter his course slightly in an attempt to throw off their aim. Mr. Sweeney, I want you to match them at every opportunity. We want to give Mr. Short as much time as possible. Pay special attention to what they do; it may give us a clue as to what's going on over there."

"Aye, Captain."

"If luck is with us, and depending on which way he turns, I intend to throw the wheel over when or if we can get close enough and send a broadside right through their stern." Brewer shook his head. "I can't imagine Underhill just standing by and allowing us to get away with that, but that's my intention."

"We'll just have to react to whatever they do," Greene said matter-of-factly.

"Agreed," Brewer said. "You may beat to quarters."

Greene saluted and picked up a speaking trumpet. In moments the hands were racing to their stations.

"Run out the guns, if you please, Mr. Greene!" Brewer shouted.

"Aye, sir! Run out the guns! Prepare to fire on command!"

Brewer turned to say something to his premier, but he was preempted by a cry from the sailing master.

"She's edging to starboard, Captain! Two, maybe three points!"

"Stay on her tail, sailing master! Let's not spoil Mr. Short's aim!"

Stinky, one of the ship's boys, arrived and approached the captain. He knuckled his forehead. Brewer recognized him, but the boy's name didn't readily come to mind. He looked to Greene for help.

"What is it, Stinky?" Greene asked the boy.

"Mr. Short's respects, sir," the boy said. "He reports the enemy appears to be rigging stern chasers. He requests permission to load with cannister over ball."

Brewer looked at Greene with raised eyebrows and received a similar look in return. The captain turned back to Stinky. "My compliments to Mr. Short. Permission granted. Also, please tell him that we shall soon be turning hard to deliver a broadside. I shall notify him by runner."

"Aye, aye, Captain!" The lad knuckled his forehead again and ran forward.

Brewer stepped over where the sailing master was conferring with the quartermaster.

"Keep your men alert," the captain warned in a low voice. "That ship out there is going to try something, and soon. Whichever way they turn, I want to be ready to cut across their stern and pour a broadside into it."

"Aye, Captain," Sweeney assured him, "we'll be ready."

Brewer nodded and stepped away from them, resuming his station in the center of the quarterdeck. He felt strangely comforted every seventy-five seconds by the report of the bow chasers throwing grape and ball into the *Oliver Cromwell*. He felt his nerves becoming more tightly strung as time dragged on; he knew Michael Underhill would not wait very much longer.

The deck shook as another ball hit; fortunately, his alteration in their course meant it only took out the head in the captain's cabin one deck below. Michael Underhill made his way quickly to the wheel.

"Another two points!" he shouted.   The mates at the wheel acknowledged and put it over two more spokes to starboard. Underhill hoped it would be enough to get them a breathing space to where he could turn the tables on his pursuers.

"No good, Captain!" came the call from the mizzen tops. "He's still on our tail!"

Underhill cursed. That ship back there was quickly forcing him into a maneuver he did not like, but there was little choice left if he did not want to be slowly pounded into pieces. The damaged mast made it impossible to outrun his enemy.

He lifted a glass again, but still could not identify anyone on the ship. She still wasn't showing any colors, but there was little doubt in his mind who was back there. It had to be Brewer; fate would not allow any other outcome. *So, this is it,* he thought as he lowered the glass and stared at the enemy ship. He saw two more puffs of smoke as their bow chasers let off another volley. Two geysers appeared twenty yards short of his quarterdeck; whoever was in charge of those guns must have misjudged the roll. *Enough. Time to end this.* He snapped the glass shut and handed it to the boy standing — shivering, actually — beside him. He patted the boy on the head and made his way to the wheel.

CHAPTER TWELVE

When the ship beat to quarters, Jimmy ran to his station down at the forward magazine. He was one of several boys and hands whose job it would be to rush powder to the guns. The gunner and his mate were inside the magazine and handed a bag of powder to each boy in turn, which was put in a leather salt box. Then they ran as fast and low as possible to the guns, handed over the powder, and ran back for another load. They'd practiced many times over the past several weeks, and Jimmy thought he had it down cold.

He was second in line to get his bag when the first volley hit their sloop. Jimmy screamed and dropped to his knees, covering his head with his salt box.

"Stand up, boy!" the gunner's mate roared from the other side of the window. "Remember what you practiced! Here, put this in yer box and get going!"

He handed a bag through the window, and Jimmy put it in his salt box and closed the lid. He ran toward the stairs, just as he'd practiced.

He stepped up on deck just as a volley came through the side farther down the side of the ship. It was the first time the lad had seen casualties. He stood frozen in horror at the sight of an overturned cannon and bloody body parts beneath.

"Jimmy! Jimmy!" It was Lieutenant Tyler shouting. Jimmy blinked and looked toward the lieutenant. "Over here!" the lieutenant waved and pointed. "Number three gun! Move! Keep low!"

Jimmy hurried over to the gun and handed over his powder. He had just turned to head back toward the stairs to get more when a ball came through the gun port of number three gun, upending the gun and killing most of its crew. The last thing Jimmy saw was a 12-pounder gun hurling through the air straight at him.

"Captain!" the lookout called. "She's turning, sir!" A quick glance forward to be sure. "Starboard, Captain!"

"Mr. Sweeney!" Brewer cried. "Take us to larboard! Cut across his stern!"

The sailing master waved his acknowledgement, not wanting to take his eyes from the chase. Brewer saw him turn and give short, crisp instructions to the quartermaster and his mates at the wheel, and *Revenge* heeled over to larboard.

"Mr. Tyler, standby!" Brewer called to his lieutenant, who was forward with the starboard battery. The lieutenant waved.

Cromwell came around sharply. That gave Brewer a precious few extra seconds; by coming around so sharply, Underhill caused his ship to heel over, and as a result he had to wait for his ship to settle on her new course if he did not want his broadside to shoot high.

Brewer decided to take a chance, even though he had thought to hold his fire until he had a true chance to rake the stern. "Mr. Tyler! Fire as you bear! Take out his quarter!"

The lieutenant waved and ran toward his forward guns. Brewer watched him talk with each gun captain and move aft, going gun to gun. A minute later, the forward carronade and the first two twelve-pounder long guns fired, followed a moment later by two more.

The captain raised his glass again and scanned

Cromwell's starboard quarter. He saw several geysers near the ship but at least two balls hit and sent splinters across the quarterdeck.

"Well done, Mr. Tyler!" Brewer called. "Keep it up! Reload with grape over ball!"

Tyler waved again to show he heard the order, but he did not take his attention from his guns or his target. Brewer watched as the last two 12-pounders and the after carronade went off together. Tyler did not wait for the results; he ran forward as soon as the guns fired, shouting the captain's reload instructions as he went. Brewer turned to say something to Mr. Greene at the larboard battery, but Mr. Sweeney gestured wildly.

"Captain!"

Brewer spun and saw *Cromwell* settle down on her new course. The next moment, her entire side erupted in flame as she let loose her broadside.

"Down!" Brewer shouted forward. "All hands down!"

He dove to the deck himself just before he heard the balls impact and the screams of the wounded begin. He counted to ten before allowing himself to raise his head and look cautiously around. He rose to his feet just as he saw Mac burst from the companionway.

"Captain!" he said. "Are you hurt?"

"No, I don't think so," Brewer said as he felt up and down his torso. "Help get the wounded below!"

"Aye, sir!"

"Damage report!" the captain cried out. Mr. Greene approached nearly at a run.

"Two guns out of action forward," he said. "Mr. Tyler thinks he can have one back in action soon."

Brewer turned to see *Cromwell* was now off their starboard quarter and heading away. "Bring us about, Mr.

Sweeney!" he called. "After her! A wide loop — bring us up on her larboard quarter! Benjamin, ready the larboard battery!"

"Aye, sir!"

Mr. Sweeney acknowledged his captain's order. *Revenge* swung around in an almost lazy loop to starboard and settled on a course toward their quarry.

"Mr. Sweeney," Brewer said, "if I know Michael Underhill, one of two things is going to happen. Either he will put his wheel over hard to larboard and put another broadside into us, or he's been damaged and will continue on his present course while he tries to make repairs. If he turns to larboard, we shall turn hard to starboard and try to beat him to the punch with the larboard battery. If he doesn't, we'll use the larboard battery to rake her stern."

Sweeney nodded. "Understood, Captain. We'll be ready."

Brewer squeezed the sailing master's arm and turned forward. "Stinky!" he called, and the boy appeared. "I want you to go to the fore tops. Warn the lookout that the enemy ship may soon turn. Stay with him, and as soon as he turns, you come and tell me."

"Aye, Captain!" the boy knuckled his forehead and ran off.

Brewer took his glass and made his way to the rail. He raised it to his eye and scanned *Cromwell's* deck, but they weren't close enough for him to make out specifics. *What are you doing, Michael?* Brewer lowered the glass, his lips pressed into a thin line. *Why don't you just take your ill-gotten booty and head to the South Seas islands?* His face was set like a flint. *So be it. Remember, you chose this.*

"Mr. Sweeney!" Brewer said. "Hard to starboard! I want to rake his stern!"

Sweeney was confused. "Now, Captain?"

"Now!" Brewer roared.

"Aye, sir!" Sweeney nodded to the quartermaster, and the wheel was put over.

Brewer looked forward. "Stand by, Mr. Greene!"

"Ready, sir!"

Brewer stood at the larboard rail as the ship turned to cut across his enemy's stern. They were at the extreme range of the carronades, but he didn't want to give Underhill any more time. Yet it seemed his old mentor still had a trick or two up his sleeve. No sooner did *Revenge* steady up than *Cromwell* healed hard to larboard. She seemed to be moving more slowly than usual, but it was still quicker than *Revenge* could move to counter it. Brewer had made a mistake in ordering the helm held hard over to starboard. His idea was to come around and meet the enemy broadside to broadside, but all he did was present his stern to *Cromwell's* waiting gunners. Her broadside caught *Revenge* fully in the stern and threw ball and grape down two decks.

Brewer himself was thrown to the deck, the impact caused his head to strike the deck and knocked the wind from his lungs so he struggled to breathe. He could hear the screams of his wounded crew through the pounding in his head. Suddenly a weight seemed to be lifted from his body and he was pulled from the deck.

"Captain! Are you all right?"

Brewer squinted until his vision cleared and he could make out the form of his coxswain. "Mac? Yes, I'm fine. It was you who knocked me down?"

"Yes, sir. Sorry."

"Don't be. I'm obliged." He looked around. "Do you see Lieutenant Greene or Mr. Sweeney?"

"Mr. Greene was forward, sir, but I think he's on his way back. It looks like Mr. Sweeney's down."

"What?" Brewer turned to see his sailing master lying in a heap on the deck. "Get him below, Mac! I'm fine, now get him below!"

"Aye, sir!"

Brewer leaned on the rail in the hope his head would clear, but it was slow going. He looked up to see *Cromwell* moving down his starboard side, her battery out again and aimed high this time. Before he could shout a warning, *Oliver Cromwell* fired.

Brewer dropped to the deck out of reflex. As he thought, the broadside was aimed high, no doubt the guns were loaded with chain and ball. Brewer sat curled up on the deck with his arms around his head as he listened to the tearing and impacts doing damage to his top hamper. A tremendous wrenching sound drew his eyes aloft again, and to his chagrin he saw the main top mast tumble over. For one moment it hung there, caught by the rigging, but Brewer knew that couldn't last. His only hope was that the mast would break away from its ropes and fall to the deck or better yet over the side.

He rose to his feet and looked around the deck. If there was a blessing in what they'd just received, it was that broadsides aimed high did not produce so many casualties on the deck. He saw Mr. Greene and Mr. Tyler working amongst their guns crews, trying to get guns back into action. Brewer also noticed the American midshipman, Mr. Farragut, was helping to take the wounded below. He made a mental note to thank him for his kindness when this was all over.

His thoughts were brought abruptly back to the situation at hand when he heard the noise of the main topmast come crashing down to the deck, bringing the mizzen topmast with it. Three men were buried under the wreckage. Brewer staggered a few steps from the rail and nearly fell as a wave of dizziness swept over him, causing him to go down on one knee and put a hand on the deck to steady himself. He looked up gingerly and saw Mac at the fore of a group of men directed by Lieutenant Tyler to clear the wreckage and rescue the men. He also saw Farragut jump into the fray with a hatchet in his hand. He looked for Mr. Short and finally saw him staying with the guns of the forward starboard battery, no doubt told to take command there by Lieutenant Tyler.

Brewer forced his way to his feet and made his way to the wheel. "Who's the senior master's mate?" he asked the quartermaster.

"That would be Mr. Cooke, Captain."

"Pass the word for him, if you please."

Cooke arrived and saluted. "You sent for me, Captain?"

Brewer looked him over. "Name?"

The mate came to attention. "Archibald Cooke, sir. Friends call me Archie."

"I am not your friend, Mr. Cooke. You are the senior master's mate?"

"Aye, sir."

"You've heard about Mr. Sweeney?"

"Aye, sir."

"For the time being, you are now the acting sailing master." He looked up and saw Mr. Greene approaching. "Come with me, Mr. Cooke."

The two stepped away from the wheel and were joined by Lieutenant Greene. Brewer introduced the two men, and they got down to business. Brewer asked Greene for his report.

"Three men are still trapped under the wreckage. We've spoken to two of them, so we have hopes of getting them out alive. We've not been able to hear from the third. We hope he's just unconscious, but we're working to get to him as soon as we can. The bosun is surveying the rigging to see what needs to be done in that respect; I am waiting for his report. The carpenter says the hull is good below the waterline, but there are three holes above the waterline that he and his mates are plugging. We have three guns out of action, one of which should be put back in action within two or three hours."

"Any word on casualties?" the captain asked.

"No, sir," Greene said. "I'm sorry, sir, but I haven't made it down there yet."

"That's all right, Mr. Greene," Brewer said. "I shall go myself soon. Now, where's *Cromwell*?"

"There, sir," Cooke said as he pointed toward the southeast. The ship seemed to be slowly pulling away from them on the starboard tack. "She looks like something's wrong. Wonder what it is?"

"Let's worry about ourselves for the moment, Mr. Cooke," Brewer said sternly.

"Of course, sir. Sorry."

"Mr. Greene, find Mr. Snead and get his report. I don't think we have anything more to fear from *Cromwell* for the time being. I'm going below to see what's left of my cabin and then to visit sickbay."

"Aye, sir."

Brewer made his way down the companionway stair without too much difficulty. His chest and back hurt from Mac's tackle during the battle, and his head still ached, but he wasn't dizzy anymore. He turned aft and was pleasantly surprised to see that his cabin hadn't fared too badly. All the walls had been down due to the battle, so the worst of the damage was to the stern windows, half of which were shattered and would need to be covered by the shutters until they could be replaced. Once *Cromwell* was away and they were safe, some hands could down and put his cabin back together again as well as bringing his furniture back up from the hold.

He made his way down to the orlop and forward to the sickbay, carrying a lantern held high to light the way. He entered the sickbay and promptly ran into Gator.

"Begging yer pardon, Cap'n!" the hand said.

"It's all right, Gator," Brewer replied. "Where's the doctor?"

The loblolly boy inclined his head. "Over there, I think, Cap'n."

"Thank you." Brewer made his way carefully to his right and soon found Dr. Spinelli seated on a stool beside Mr. Sweeney. "Doctor? How is he?"

"I don't know yet," Spinelli said. "He had a large splinter in his upper chest, just below his shoulder about here." He touched a spot on his own chest. "I removed it and cleaned the wound as best I could. I think he was lucky; the splinter was high enough that I believe it missed his lungs but low enough that it missed his shoulder joint as well. I need to watch him for infection. Barring that, I think he'll recover."

Brewer noticed that Alfred was working on a patient. "Doctor, what's Alfred doing here? Don't tell me he's a doctor, too?"

Spinelli chuckled. "I don't think so, but apparently one of his many talents is the ability to suture wounds. I've watched him do a couple, and they were nice and tight with no leakage. So, I put him to work. Let me tell you, it's freed me up to attend to more patients."

Brewer shook his head. "Incredible! I'm glad we don't have to pay him based on the individual jobs he can do. He'd make more than a fleet admiral!"

"At least we would be sure he earned all he got!" the doctor replied.

Brewer laughed and took his leave.

Lieutenant Tyler was making a survey of the fo'c'sle when he heard whimpering. He made his way around an overturned 12-pounder to find Mr. Short kneeling beside the body of young Jimmy. The dead lad's face was a frozen look of wide-eyed terror. His body didn't look too bad from the waist up, but his legs were crushed by the gun that fell on him. Tyler didn't see a great deal of blood about; hopefully, that was a sign that death had been mercifully swift.

Short was on his knees off to one side, his head down and his hands hanging between his knees, whimpering softly. Tyler squatted down opposite him, and after a minute he reached out and closed Jimmy's eyes.

"William?" he said.

Short either ignored him or possibly didn't realize he was there, so Tyler reached out and touched the young midshipman on his arm. Short jumped.

"Mr. Tyler!" he said and moved to stand, but wobbled badly. Tyler took hold of his arm and eased him back down. Short didn't resist.

"Are you hurt?" Tyler asked.

Short wiped his nose on his sleeve and shook his head. "I should have watched over him," he said. "He was just a kid. I should have watched over him. He looks like he was terrified, and I wasn't there to help him."

Tyler tried to think of something comforting to say. "William, you were the best friend he had on this ship. You couldn't have been there for him; we were in action. He was doing his duty, and you were doing yours."

Short's eyes welled up with tears. "But he was scared." He squeezed his eyes shut, and the tears slid down his cheeks.

"I'm sure he bwas," Tyler said. "I know I am, every time we go into battle. He was doing his job, William. You can be proud of him for that. He didn't run and hide; even though he was scared, he did his job and helped this ship as best he could."

Tyler noticed someone standing beside Mr. Short. They both looked up to see Mr. Hodges, the gunner, standing there, his hat in his hands.

"Mr. Hodges?" Tyler said. The old gunner pulled a dirty kerchief from his pocket and dabbed his eyes dry. He knelt beside the body and reached out to touch him. He bowed his head and closed his eyes while he breathed a silent prayer, then his eyes opened and he sighed.

"I heerd the lad had bought it," he said, "so I came up to look for 'im. He was a good one, and I'll miss 'im." He reached out and put his arm around the grieving midshipman's shoulders, and Short just fell against the old gunner. Tyler watched as the two mourned the loss of their friend.

"I'll look after the lad, if 'tis all right, sir," the gunner said, "with your permission, sir, I'll take poor Jimmy over to where me and the lad here can sew him up." He looked to Short. "It'll be our way of saying goodbye."

Short sniffed and nodded. Hodges looked to Tyler, who nodded.

"Of course. Carry on," he said. "And thank you, Mr. Hodges."

The captain made his way back to the deck and found Mr. Greene talking with Mr. Cooke. The two men saluted as the captain joined them.

"Do you have a report, Mr. Greene?"

"Aye, sir. Mr. Snead says he can repair the rigging, but it will have to be with us hove to. We can use the time to replace the two topmasts, but doing them both will leave us with no replacements available to cover future losses. The alternative is to head for a port with a dock who can do the work for us."

Brewer looked to the ship's tophamper, then brought his eyes back down to hold those of his premier.

"Order the repairs. We stay and complete the mission."

Michael Underhill sat in what was left of his cabin on the *Oliver Cromwell.* He sat in a chair with a bottle of wine on the table next to him. He looked around at his shattered ship and took a long pull from the bottle. His cabin had taken heavy damage from the raking, but the hands were able to get the walls back up. The rear wall above the rudder had taken several hits; much of the stern windows were shattered and covered by shutters, and his personal head was gone. The worst damage was on the deck. Six guns had been up-ended, but his men were able to get two back into service. The worst news was that the jury-rigged top mast had given way during that last hard turn that had allowed them to do such damage to Brewer's ship. Once the mast gave way, Underhill had been forced to abandon any ideas of finishing off the British sloop and make his way out of the area as best he could. His immediate destination was a small harbor on the east coast of southern Florida where he thought they could get the mast replaced. He'd done a favor or two for the locals over the years, and now he aimed to call them in.

A knock on the door preceded Chauncey entering the room.

"Well?" Underhill said.

"Luck is with us," the mate said. "The wind is just right to where we can make a steady four knots even with the mast down. We were able to strengthen the main topmast and rig a jib of sorts to keep us on a steady course. Pete's watching it; I gave him orders to take it down in a hurry if the wind gets too strong. "

Underhill nodded and took another swig from the bottle. He offered it to Chauncey, who accepted after a moment's hesitation. He took a deep swallow and said, "Are we headed for White Inlet?"

Another nod. "I think it's the best place for us to get the mast replaced quickly and quietly," Underhill said. "The only alternative is one of the small ports near Havana, and I'm afraid the British may be watching the area for us. We'll enter through the Martyrs — we're light enough to brave the reefs, I think, and the outer islands will hide us from British eyes all the way to White Inlet."

Chauncey wasn't happy with his chief's plan, but it offered a high possibility of success — if they could avoid having their keel ripped off by the reefs. True, they had done it successfully once before; five years ago they had avoided a Spanish frigate by entering the Martyrs and riding the coastline, but it had cost them four cannon overboard to make the ship light enough for the passage. He remembered Underhill cursing himself at the time for not taking the time to search for a deeper passage through the reefs. Hopefully, that was his plan this time.

"And after we get the mast repaired?" he asked.

Underhill looked at his mate and took a long pull from the bottle. He offered it to Chauncey again, but he declined this time. "I honestly don't know," Underhill admitted. "We could head for the South Seas Islands, but that would mean leaving everything we've taken behind." He thought for a moment before asking, "Are the books up to date?" Chauncey was surprised by the question and had to think about it for a moment. The books his captain referred to contained financial breakdowns of all prize money not yet distributed, including each man's share. Underhill had made it a practice since early in the war to keep these accounts; that way the share of a man who was lost could still be sent to his family.

"Yes, sir, I believe the schoolmaster has them current," Chauncey replied. The schoolmaster was the captain's clerk. He'd earned the nickname after offering to teach some of the hands how to read, write, and do their sums.

"I was just thinking," the captain said, "if worst comes to worst, we could write each man a letter with his share on it so he could get his money. We have enough specie on board to give each man something to start him out. Then we'd just sink *Cromwell* off shore and melt into the population."

Chauncey was surprised by the idea. "Not the worst idea I've ever heard," he said. "I mean, it beats hanging, but that's about it. Anything else?"

"I wonder," Underhill said slowly, "if it would be wise to head to Washington City and see if the Americans would help us?"

Chauncey was dubious. "Aren't the Americans the ones helping Brewer track us down?"

"Yes, but that's their navy. I plan on speaking to their politicians and see if I can't help them realize how embarrassing it would be for their government for it to come to light in the press on two continents that a ship was still operating under a letter of marque from the United States government after all these years?"

The mate stared wide-eyed. It was the single dumbest idea he'd ever heard! He wondered now if his captain had cracked, but that was not something he could bring up at the moment. "Michael, they'd laugh you out of town!"

Underhill looked hard at his friend. In all the years they'd been together, Chauncey had never spoken to him in that manner. He blinked and took another drink. "I don't think so. You don't understand politics, Chauncey. Politicians are always afraid of being smeared with dirt. And what could be worse than this? It might even be enough to cost the Jeffersonians the 1820 presidential election."

Chauncey doubted that, but he wasn't sure enough of his ground to put up an argument. "I'm going to relieve Pete and let him get some sleep. If we can keep our present speed, we should approach the Martyrs in approximately thirty-six hours. I shall keep you informed."

The mate left the cabin, and Underhill stared at the door for a long time afterward. It wasn't like Chauncey to raise objections like that, and Underhill had learned over the years to take heed whenever he did. He took another pull from the bottle and wondered if his mate might be right.

It took the better part of five days for Brewer's crew to get the two masts replaced. It would have been done in less than three, but a gale hit early in the morning before they were able to get them properly braced and tore all their work to pieces. There was nothing to do but start again. Fortunately, the masts and spars were not damaged, only blown into the water. Mac took a boat and retrieved them so the work could proceed.

Soon after the gale lifted, a lookout sighted a sail on the horizon on an approach course on the larboard quarter. Lieutenant Tyler was the officer of the deck; he quickly found the growing speck of white and sent for the captain. Brewer came up on deck, Tyler handed him the glass and pointed to the horizon.

"Lookout?" the captain called. "What can you tell me?"

"Looks like a frigate, sir!" came the reply. "Don't see no colors yet!"

Mr. Greene joined Brewer at the rail.

"Friend, Captain?" he asked.

"Don't know yet, Benjamin. Coming from that direction, the odds are strong that the frigate is American and not British. If it's the commodore in *Constitution*, I think we're all right, but if it's Allen in *Congress*, we could be in trouble."

Fortune smiled on them, for the frigate turned out to be *Constitution*. She hove to within pistol shot and signaled. Mr. Farragut was there with his book.

"Captain," he said, "it says, *'Captain come on board'*."

"Acknowledge," Brewer said. "Mr. Greene, have Mac prepare the gig. I'm going below to change."

"Aye, sir."

Brewer went below. He entered the cabin and called for Alfred.

"Sir?"

"The commodore had arrived, Alfred," he said. "My best uniform, if you please."

"I'm afraid it was damaged in the battle, sir."

Brewer frowned. This did not bode well.

Brewer stepped up onto *Constitution's* deck to be met by Captain Pringle. He saluted, and the captain reached out his hand. Brewer shook it.

"So glad we found you, Commander!" the captain said. "When you didn't make your rendezvous, we went searching for you. We ran into a Spanish ship that reported two sloops in a chase heading southeast, so we followed on, and here we are." He led the way below to the great cabin where they found the commodore standing with his hand clasped behind his back, staring out the stern windows. "Commander Brewer, sir." Pringle announced.

Brewer came to attention. Biddle turned around and smiled. "Good to see you, Commander. I was afraid you'd gotten yourself into trouble. Stand at ease."

"Not too much, Commodore," Brewer said as he relaxed. He held out the packet he brought. "Copies of my logs, sir, as well as one of our pursuit of *Oliver Cromwell*."

Biddle nodded toward Pringle, and Brewer handed the packet to the captain. The commodore indicated a seat on the settee. "Please, Commander, sit. Wilson, we'll have those refreshments now." Biddle sat in a chair off to the side, and

Pringle sat beside Brewer. Wilson entered carrying a tray with three glasses of a dark liquid. Biddle raised his in a toast.

"Your very good health, sir," he said to Brewer, and the three men drank.

Brewer was surprised at what he tasted. "Cognac?"

Biddle chuckled. "Yes. I know it's not exactly American, as one might say, but I got hooked on the stuff the first time I visited New Orleans. Now I make sure I resupply every time I visit the port." He set his glass down and sat back in his chair, elbows on the arms and hand clasped before his face with his forefingers steepled. "Now, Commander, I'd like to hear all about your encounter with *Cromwell.*"

Brewer set his glass down as well. He leaned forward and launched into a detailed account of their sighting the sloop and pursuing. He gave an accurate if abbreviated account of the battle, and then described their repairs to the topmasts. "And that's when we sighted you, sir," he said in conclusion.

"And what," said the commodore, "is you estimate of damage done to *Cromwell*?"

"Inconclusive, Commodore. We raked her more then once, so the damage from those may have been considerable, but something was wrong with the ship from the start. She wasn't sailing well at all; that's the only way to account for our being able to close the gap as we did."

"Where did you go wrong?" Pringle asked.

Brewer turned to him. "I beg your pardon?"

"If *Cromwell* was sailing poorly, how do you account for Underhill being able to dismast you and get away? Where did you make your mistake?"

"I've been thinking about that these past three or four days," Brewer said, staring at the deck before him. "The only thing I can think of is that I didn't expect him to make that last turn and reverse his course. I came around to starboard to try to rake him again. I didn't expect him to come around to larboard. I ordered the ship to continue around to starboard, my thought being to come out of the turn and meet him. When I think about it now, all I did was present my stern to his larboard battery." His eyes came up and met Biddle's. "*Cromwell* must have been damaged, or else Michael wouldn't have missed a chance to finish us off."

"No doubt," Pringle said.

Both men looked at the commodore, who sat in his chair with his lips pursed in thought, his eyes focused on the fingertips steepled before them. Brewer glanced at Pringle, whose subtle shake of the head told him everything; they were to wait for the commodore to speak.

Nearly five minutes went by before Brewer saw the commodore blink. His eyes came back into focus and his hands came down. "Commander," he said, "I believe you acted in the best traditions of the service and will note as much in the letter I shall give you for Admiral Lord Hornblower. You and your ship fought well, and I think *Cromwell* was lucky to dismast you and get away in the aftermath."

"Thank you, sir," Brewer said with relief.

"So, what do we do now?" Pringle asked.

Brewer jumped at the chance. "Repairs to *Revenge* are nearly complete. Allow me to pursue Underhill and finish this, once and for all."

Biddle thought about this for a moment before shaking his head. "I'm sending you home, Commander. Your Admiral Hornblower may wish to regroup, and in any case he needs to hear what you've told us here today."

"Home, Commodore?" Brewer asked, slightly confused. He shook his head. "No, sir, please... You must let me finish this! This is my war!"

Biddle's left eyebrow rose, something Brewer immediately recognized as a warning, and he hurriedly backtracked.

"Forgive me, Commodore. I apologize for my outburst, but, sir, this is my mission!"

"I believe that's Admiral Hornblower's decision," Biddle said flatly. "Will you obey my order or not, Commander?"

Brewer's back was against the wall, and he wisely decided to surrender graciously. "Yes, sir. I shall obey your orders."

"Good." Biddle visibly relaxed and called for more Cognac. Once the venerable Wilson had refilled their glasses, the commodore asked, "Do you have any idea where Underhill might have gone, Commander?"

Brewer considered everything he know or guessed about his former mentor's command style. "I think his first move will be to find a port to repair his ship. I don't think he'll head for Havana again; it's too dangerous for him now." He went on, "Do either of you know of a port, either on the coast of Florida or in the Bahamas where he could see to his ship? It would likley be someplace small and out of the way, someplace where he would not be discovered and could elude pursuit by larger ships."

The two Americans searched their memories, but neither could think of a suitable location in that region. "It's impossible to nail down," Pringle lamented. "There are just too many places where a good crew could make repairs to a ship the size of a sloop."

"I was afraid you'd say that," Brewer frowned.

"I'm sure he'll turn up," Biddle said. "Once you head for Jamaica, I shall take *Constitution* and search the Florida coast, everything from the Bay of Tocobaga southward to the keys. After that, we shall move on to the Bahamas."

Brewer nodded and kept his mouth shut, his lips pressed into a thin line. He was not happy with the situation, but he knew better than to raise an objection again. Better to head south and see the admiral; the quicker he got that over with, the quicker he could get back on the hunt. He wanted to find Underhill before the Americans did.

"When do you estimate your repairs will be completed, Commander?" Biddle asked.

"Tomorrow or the next day, sir."

"Good. Your orders will be sent to you by noon tomorrow," the commodore said, "along with my letter and reports for your admiral." He rose, and his guests followed suit. "Now, if you'll excuse me, I have work to do."

Brewer came to attention. "Thank you, sir." He followed Pringle out of the cabin.

"Good sailing to you, Commander," Pringle said as he bade him farewell at *Constitution's* entry port.

The next morning, Brewer invited Lieutenant Greene to have breakfast with him. Alfred served them eggs and ham supplemented by some leftover pudding. And coffee, lots of coffee.

"Repairs are almost complete, sir," Greene reported. "Mr. Snead is very nearly satisfied with the new rigging, and he says there's only one or two more adjustments to make. The new masts are in and secured; the yards were crossed late yesterday afternoon."

"Very good," Brewer said absently. Alfred was just pouring their coffee when the sentry knocked and opened the door. "Yes?" the captain asked.

"Mr. Tyler's respects, Captain," came the reply. "Boat approaching from the American ship, sir."

"My compliments to Mr. Tyler. Ask him to bring the orders down when they arrive."

"Aye, sir."

Presently, Lieutenant Tyler entered the cabin and presented both a packet and a letter to his captain. Brewer noticed immediately that neither was sealed, and he looked to the messenger.

"That's the way they arrived, Captain. A Mister Allen is waiting outside to speak to you. He is the Americans' senior midshipman. One more thing, sir: the commodore sent back Mr. Reed and requests the return of Mr. Farragut."

"Well," Brewer said, "show Mr. Allen in, if you please."

Tyler opened the door and motioned, and Mr. Allen marched into the cabin. He was taller than Reed, thinner, with thick brown hair, dark eyes and a large Roman nose. He came to attention.

"Mr. Allen? I am Captain Brewer. You wished to see me?"

"Aye, Captain," the youth replied formally. "Commodore Biddle directed me to speak to you and verify that he sent both his reports and the letter to your admiral to you unsealed. This was done deliberately; the commodore wished you to know that he is hiding nothing from you. He ordered me to inform you that you have his permission to read both items before you reach Jamaica if you so desire. He has included sentences in both documents so the admiral will know this as well. May I take Mr. Farragut back with me, sir?"

Brewer set his parcels on the table and rose. "You may indeed, Mr. Allen." He stepped over to the American and offered his hand. Allen was surprised by the gesture but took his hand and shook firmly. "Please convey my thanks to the commodore for all his hospitality."

"Yes," Allen said with a smile, "about that: Sir, the commodore sent some... supplies for you. I asked Mr. Tyler not to tell you."

"I see! Well, please thank the commodore for me. I hope we sail together again, Mr. Allen."

The midshipman came to attention before smartly turning and marching out the door. After he left, Brewer looked to his second lieutenant.

"Sir," he began, "the commodore has sent us two rabbits."

"Two?" Greene asked.

"Yes. According to Mr. Allen, that's all you need. He advised us not to eat them for two weeks, and after that our problems with shortages of fresh meat will be solved."

Brewer grinned widely. "Anything... else?"

Tyler looked to the deck above as he ran down the list in his head. "Let me see... one bullock, three pigs, three bushels of assorted vegetables, one barrel of lemon juice, and a barrel of apples. There is also a bottle of Cognac, Captain."

"Well!" Greene exclaimed.

"Bounty indeed!" Brewer proclaimed. "Inform the purser, Mr. Tyler. Inform the carpenter that we need a hutch for the rabbits. Also, coordinate with Alfred, Smoot, and the cook to arrange for the crew to enjoy the fresh pork and vegetables."

"Aye, sir!"

"Alfred!" Brewer called. "You heard?"

"Aye, sir."

"Coordinate the feast, if you please. Second or third night out should do, I would imagine. Tonight, Mr. Greene and Mr. Reed will dine with me. Turn of the second dog watch."

"Aye, sir."

"Thank you. Mr. Greene, will you be so kind as to inform Mr. Reed?"

"Aye, sir."

"Fine. If you will excuse me, I have a letter to write."

When he was alone, Brewer looked at the two pieces of mail on his table and wondered if he should take the commodore up on his offer to read them. Tempting as it was, he decided it would not be proper. He reached inside his desk and drew out a length of twine along with his sealing wax. He bound the packet and letter with the twine and sealed with the wax before pressing his personal seal into it. He set it aside for Myers to put with his reports for the admiral. Satisfied, he pulled out a fresh sheet of paper and began a letter to his mother.

CHAPTER THIRTEEN

The aromas that filled the cabin were familiar to two of the men who sat at the table, but for the third they were a rarely encountered wonder, a marvel that confirmed his desire to advance from the cockpit to the great cabin. Captain Brewer sat back with a light in his eye as he and the first lieutenant watched the expressions that passed over the senior midshipman's face. This was only Mr. Reed's second time to be present for one of Alfred's meals, and his face possessed an expection that familiarity had stolen from that of his companions.

The main course tonight was a chicken, dressed in a way Alfred had previously described to the captain as one "handed down from my great-grandmother." Brewer said nothing, assuming that meant the recipe was beyond reproach. All agreed they could never eat chicken again any other way, and the cauliflower and carrots served alongside completed the experience. Brewer could never figure out what made Alfred's meals so special; certainly any other accomplished cook could do a chicken with cauliflower and carrots and satisfy his audience, but with Alfred the dining experience was usually transcendental, as it was tonight. The captain had long accepted it as one of the universe's unsolved mysteries.

The meal ended, and Brewer led his guests to the day cabin. At the captain's request, Alfred brought the bottle of Cognac sent over to them by Commodore Biddle. Brewer gestured for Greene to do the honors. The first lieutenant nodded with a grin and got to work.

"Ever had Cognac, Mr. Reed?" Brewer asked.

"No, sir," Reed replied, his eyes focused on Greene's handiwork.

"You are in for a treat, I assure you."

"Aye, sir."

Greene poured and handed the glasses around. Brewer looked to his senior midshipman.

"Mr. Vice, the toast."

Reed obediently rose and held his glass out in a toast. "Gentlemen, the King!"

"The King!" the officers echoed, and all drank.

"Mr. Reed," Brewer said, "one reason I invited you here tonight, other than to welcome you home, was to ask you about your time on the American frigate. What did you think of *Constitution*?"

"She's a fine ship, sir," he said."

"You came to us from *Clorinda*, did you not?" Greene asked. The midshipman nodded, and Greene continued. "How would you compare the two?"

Reed took another appreciative gulp of Cognac, then spoke. "*Constitution's* much bigger, sir, and her 24-pounders are absolute monsters!" Brewer smiled at the look of longing in Reed's eyes. "Her walls are thick. Mr. Best, the first lieutenant, told me about them while giving me a tour right after I arrived. He said it was the southern live oak from Georgia in between oak and pine that gave the hull its great strength. 18-pounders would have a difficult time penetrating, and 12-pounders would have no chance at all."

"Well," Brewer said, "I'm glad we won't be fighting her. Tell me, Mr. Reed, what did the Americans think of having the Royal Navy in their midst."

The midshipman's shrug gave way to a smirk. "They were definitely unimpressed, sir. The general impression I got from nearly everyone other than the commodore, Captain Pringle, or Lieutenant Best was that they had been called in to clean up our mess for us."

Greene looked up sharply, but Brewer shook his head and the premier subsided. "What else can you tell us, Mr. Reed?"

"Not much else to say, sir. They didn't hold any sail or gunnery drills while I was on board." He sought his memory and raised his glass for a meditative swallow. "I can tell you the food was good. And they were all volunteers, sir."

That caught Greene's attention. "What do you mean?"

"I mean they don't have a press, sir."

Greene stared at him in disbelief.

"That's what they said!" Reed insisted. "Every man on board that ship is a volunteer, and the purser told me *Constitution's* current compliment was something close to 400 souls."

Greene s looked to his captain. "*Clorinda* has maybe 200."

Brewer rose, and his guests did the same. "Mr. Reed, welcome home. Please excuse us."

Reed came to attention. "Thank you, Captain. Please give my compliments to Alfred."

"I shall." The two officers watched the midshipman try not to stagger as he made his way from the cabin.

"I believe Mr. Reed is having a little trouble holding his liquor," Greene observed.

Brewer nodded. "Nothing a little practice won't cure. Be seated, Benjamin, and I will update you on our orders. The commodore has ordered us to return to Jamaica and report our progress to Admiral Lord Hornblower."

Greene was shocked at the revelation. "But what about *Cromwell*? What about Underhill?"

Brewer sighed in resignation, although his brows furled a bit. "He said that would be up to the admiral. Commodore Biddle assured me that he would continue the search down the western course of Spanish Florida and then through the Bahamas."

"But sir!" Greene was clearly incensed at the orders. "He can't do this! *Cromwell* is ours! Admiral Hornblower—"

"*All right, Benjamin!*" Brewer shouted. Greene stared at him, eyes wide and mouth hanging open, for a moment before managing to compose himself.

"Of course, sir. My apologies."

Brewer knew he'd gone too far, and he buried his face in his hands. A wave of shame flooded over him. He knew his first lieutenant did not deserve that kind of treatment; he was only expressing the outrage Brewer himself was unable to express on the *Constitution*. He drew a heavy sigh and lowered his hands.

"Benjamin," he said wearily, "please, forgive me. You haven't said anything here tonight that I didn't wish I could have said before the commodore. I'm truly sorry."

Greene rose. "Think nothing of it, sir. Now, if you'll excuse me, sir, I'll retire. I've got the watch in the morning."

"Of course. Good night."

"Good night, sir."

Brewer stepped up on deck and ordered a course for Jamaica. He turned forward and admired the way the moonlight lit the deck. The men of the first watch went quietly about their business, and Brewer could imagine how they were looking forward to the upcoming feast. Still, a nagging voice in the back of his mind kept reminding him that the

Americans were out to steal his victory and take Michael Underhill for themselves. Brewer tried his best to push it out of his mind, to look at the beautiful moonlit ocean and wisps of clouds that floated by, but it was no good. He went below to his cabin, but the enclosed space only seemed to magnify his frustration. He considered calling the doctor for a game of chess, but in the end he decided he didn't want to put up with the multitude of questions that would surely come. The good doctor was simply too good at reading him.

The next day, the day of the feast, brought excitement and anticipation throughout the ship, everywhere except the captain's cabin. Brewer politely declined an invitation from the gunroom to join them for supper, pleading ill health. It was a lie, of course, but he didn't want to spoil their good time. He stayed by himself in his room and tried to read a book. He released both Alfred and Mac to go and enjoy the feast. They went. Not willingly, but they went.

Brewer listened to the sounds of the merriment drifting back from the crew's messes up forward. Cheers abounded, along with several toasts to the commodore's health. Some of the messes broke into various songs, some of which were almost on key, but all of which were done with gusto. His isolation only permitted his frustrations to fester.

Dawn found him on the quarterdeck. He checked in with his acting sailing master and, satisfied that all was well, he returned to his cabin and did not emerge for three days. The officers on the quarterdeck all speculated, quietly and amongst themselves, the reasons for the captain's self-imposed isolation. In the captain's cabin, Alfred and Mac speculated as well, although theirs was silent, the communication carried on by their eyes alone. They watched as the captain went from his cot to his table to his desk to the settee and back again. They saw him take a book from the shelf to try to distract himself, only to discard it after a few pages. He sat at his desk for close to an hour at a time, quill in hand and a page at the ready, only to have no words come. Brewer tossed the quill down in disgust and returned to his cot.

Finally, Alfred had had enough and determined to do something to deliver his captain from his demons. He cornered Mac in the pantry. "Take the practice swords to the quarterdeck," he told the coxswain quietly. "I shall try to draw the captain out."

"What are you going to do?"

Alfred shook his head. "I'm not sure, but I have to do something. I only hope it doesn't get us hung for mutiny."

Mac swallowed hard and nodded, then he left to carry out his task. Alfred stepped out of the pantry and found the captain lying on the settee, staring at the deck above.

"Pardon me, Captain," he said, "but I believe it's time for your workout."

"What?" Brewer blinked his eyes into focus and looked at him. "What did you say?"

"I said, it's time for your workout, sir."

The captain turned away and resume his study of the deck beams above. "Later."

Alfred sighed but did not move. It had the desired effect, as the captain turned to him again a minute or so later.

"What is it, Alfred?" he said irritably.

"Your workout, sir?"

"I told you, later."

Alfred sighed loudly and looked at the deck for a moment, but he did not move. Eventually, the captain sat up and put his feet on the floor. He stared at his servant for a moment as he chewed his bottom lip and considered. Finally, he surrendered and rose.

"If you insist," he said. "What about the equipment?"

"Mac has it on the fo'c'sle, sir," was the reply.

"I see. Well, let's get this over with. After you."

Alfred turned and led the way forward and up the forward stairs by the galley. This led them through the crew quarters, alerting the men to what was coming. Brewer thought nothing of it; Alfred often went this way before one of their matches. Today, however, the wily servant had an ulterior motive.

They ascended to the deck to find Mac waiting with the practice swords. Brewer was already in his usual shirt sleeves, although his shirt was the same one he had worn for three days and looked distinctly disheveled. Mac handed each of them a sword and stepped back.

Brewer was momentarily nonplussed. "I'm not fighting Mac today?"

"No, sir," Alfred said. "I shall be your opponent. Shall we warm up?"

"Never mind that," the captain responded. "Let's get this over with."

"Very well, sir."

The two crossed swords and prepared for combat. Suddenly, Alfred knocked the captain's sword aside and scored a point with a thrust to his gut. Brewer looked accusingly at him but said not a word. They readied themselves again, and the captain attacked. Alfred blocked two slashes and a thrust without much difficulty before making two abortive steps forward that threw the captain off balance. He stepped quickly to his right and landed a hard blow to the captain's thigh before jumping back. The captain stepped back gingerly and rubbed his thigh. In the corner of his eye he saw a growing crowd. Not unusual for one of his training sessions, but this time he didn't want to lose before his men. He readied his sword and stepped forward again.

Alfred moved to his left, forcing his captain to have to push off his injured leg. He made a couple mediocre slashes which the captain easily blocked, then he feinted a thrust at Brewer's chest. The captain made a downward block and stepped back, which is exactly what Alfred expected him to do. The servant rushed in with a loud cry and jumped up, his sword high and coming down at the captain's head. Fortunately, Brewer's instincts took over; he dropped and twisted to the side, and Alfred's blow landed loudly on the deck. Alfred himself landed softly, only to leap onto the captain's back and touch his sword to the back of his neck. A death blow in real life, to be sure.

Brewer angrily shook him off and rose. His thigh ached mightily, and the resulting limp was hindering his movements as well as his reaction time. The wise thing to do would be to bide his time and look for a weakness, but his blood was up and anger overruled his better judgment. He launched an attack, hoping to get in close and overwhelm his diminutive opponent with his size advantage. Alfred ducked low and to his left and brought his wooden sword down hard on the back of his captain's knee. Brewer cried out in pain and went down to the deck.

Alfred stood at his feet, breathing heavily. His eyes went to the crowd, and he turned to Mac and motioned toward the onlookers with his head. Mac got the message.

"All right, you mugs," he said. "Show's over. Scatter."

"Will you be reading later, Mac?" one of the crowd asked.

"Maybe, if you clear out now!"

"We're going! We're going!"

The crowd quickly thinned out, and Alfred stepped up and knelt beside his captain's head. Brewer's eyes were squeezed tight from the pain, and his breathing was heavy and ragged.

"I'm sorry, Captain," he said in a low voice that even Mac could not hear, "but I knew you needed to get the anger and frustration out. That's why I offered you a training session, so you could release it on me. I'm sorry, but it was the only way I could think of to help."

Brewer listened, his eyes still squeezed shut as he tried his best to master the pain and bring his breathing under control. He quickly realized Alfred was right, his frustration was gone and his anger was now replaced with embarrassment at how foolish he had been. He blinked until his vision cleared and he could see his hands on the deck. He turned gingerly and looked up at his servant.

"So, I'm supposed to thank you for this beating?" he asked sarcastically. "And what will you do for my birthday?"

Alfred smiled at his captain's jest. "Mac, come, help me get him up." Together the two of them got Brewer on his feet and allowed him to test his sore knee. "Help him below, Mac. I'm going to try to find something cold to wrap around his knee." He disappeared below before either of them could utter a word.

"Can you make it, sir?" Mac asked.

Brewer nodded. "I think so. Just stand by in case I need steadying."

"Aye, sir."

After a few steps, Brewer found it necessary to hang on to Mac's arm, but the two made their way aft and down the companionway stairs. Once they were inside the captain's cabin, Mac put Brewer's arm around his shoulders and helped his captain to the settee. Alfred arrived with a cold, wet rag. He unbuttoned the bottom of the pants leg and rolled it up to expose the knee. It was already beginning to swell; Alfred wrapped the rag around it as gently as he could. Brewer winced at the effort and gritted his teeth to keep from crying out.

"Mac," Alfred said.

"Aye," Mac replied, and he headed for the door.

"Where's he going?" Brewer asked.

Alfred just looked at him, and the captain laid his head back and sighed. "Wonderful."

Mac returned with the doctor in tow. Alfred stepped aside to give the physician room.

"Well, well, what have we here?" Spinelli said. "Mac been giving you dancing lessons again?"

"I'm afraid it was me this time, Doctor," Alfred said. Spinelli listened as Alfred described the fight and the blows he'd landed. He sat on the edge of the settee and gently unwrapped the rag from Brewer's knee so he could look the injury over. "Same thigh?"

Alfred shook his head. "The other leg, Doctor."

Spinelli straightened up. "Find a towel to cover him, Alfred. Mac, help me take his pants off. I need to see both legs."

"Is that really necessary?" Brewer asked.

"What do you think?" the doctor replied, and Brewer laid back with a groan. "Mac, you lift him just above the waist while I try to slide the pants down over his feet."

As soon as the pants were off, Alfred was back and laid the towel over his captain's modesty while the doctor began probing around the growing bruise on the outside of Brewer's left thigh. His patient hissed a couple times. Finally, the doctor was done and sat up.

"Well," he said, "I don't think anything's broken, but that's one nasty bruise you've got there, Captain. I'm afraid walking's going to hurt for a while."

"Thanks," Brewer said. "And the knee?"

Spinelli shook his head. "Won't know for a few days. From what I can see, and the way Alfred described the blow, I'm hopeful there's no long-term damage. Was there any sharp pains on the way here?"

Brewer nodded. "On the outside of the knee, toward the back."

The doctor felt around the outside of the knee. "About here?"

Brewer winced and nodded. Spinelli bent over the knee and looked closely as he felt around the area indicated, causing the captain to wince. Twice.

Finally, he straightened up. "I don't think the damage is permanent, but I won't know for sure until the swelling goes down. Mac, keep him off his feet for at least the next few days, then bring him down to sick bay so I can look him over again. Alfred, keep something cold on his knee as much as possible."

"Aye, Doctor."

After the doctor had left, Alfred sent Mac after another cold rag while he stood beside his captain. "I'm sorry, sir," he said when they were alone. "I never meant to do such damage. I'll understand if you decide punishment is necessary."

"Alfred," Brewer said after a moment, "I ask that what I am about to say stays between us. It is I who should apologize to you, and thank you for looking after me the way you do. Other men may be tempted to take advantage of a position like yours, but you have proven yourself to me many times over, and I know I can trust you. What you did today shows me just how far you are willing to go to look after me. Believe me, I do not take it for granted. This goes for Mac, too, but I'll get around to telling him."

"Aye, Captain."

Brewer winced from the pain and the exertion, and he laid his head back on the bench and closed his eyes. Alfred stood silently over him before a moment before wiping a tear from his eye and retreating to his pantry.

Three days later, Mac walked his captain forward and down to the sickbay. Brewer considered sending for the doctor, but he decided he wanted to visit Mr. Sweeney while he was there. He had Mac deposit him on the bed next to the sailing master.

"How are you?" Brewer asked.

"Better every day, Captain," Sweeney replied. "The doctor says tomorrow I can get up on my own to see how I do for a turn around the deck."

"Wonderful!" Brewer exclaimed. "In fact, maybe we can convince the old quack to let me give it a try with you."

Sweeney stifled a laugh as the doctor walked up to them.

"Don't trouble yourself, Mr. Sweeney; I heard what our beloved captain said. And even if I hadn't, he'd still be in trouble. Well, my liege, do you want to endure an examination here, or shall we go someplace more private?"

"We can do it here, sir," Brewer said as he stood. "I had Alfred whip me up a new pair of trousers, very loose in the legs, which will allow you to pull them up far enough to do what you need to."

The doctor whistled when he saw what his captain meant. Brewer sat on the bed again, and Spinelli pushed the billowy pants leg up past his bad knee. The swelling had indeed gone down, leaving ugly bruises behind. "How does it feel?" he asked.

"Stiff. Hurts to move."

"I'm not surprised. Was there any sharp pains?"

"No, just stiff and achy."

"Good." Spinelli moved to the other leg and pushed the pant leg up to expose the yellow field of a deep, old bruise. The doctor placed his palm on it to feel the temperature, then he ran his hand lightly over the entire area. "How about this side?"

Brewer shrugged. "About the same. Not stiff as such, but it hurts when I use it."

Spinelli nodded absently. "Any sharp pains?"

"No."

The doctor pulled both pants legs down. "In my best medical opinion, Captain, you got lucky. Looks like nothing Alfred did to you will be permanent. Oh, don't worry," he reassured his patient, "I'll talk to him and encourage him to try harder next time."

"You're all heart, Adam." Brewer gave Sweeney a sideways look and winked. "So, is it all right if I take a walk with my wounded friend tomorrow?"

Spinelli shrugged. "I don't see why not. In fact, it might do both of you good. Take Mac with you, just in case, won't you?"

Brewer turned to Sweeney. "What do you say, Sailing Master? Shall I send Mac for you at, say, one bell of the forenoon watch?"

Sweeney cast a quick glance to the doctor, who nodded. "That would be fine, Captain. I look forward to it."

"Good!" Brewer rose gingerly. "I shall see you tomorrow, then. Thank you, Doctor." Brewer walked out under his own power. His steps were tiny and at times hesitant, but they were his own.

The next morning found the captain leaning on the carriage of one of the long nines when Mac appeared with Mr. Sweeney at the top of the fo'c'sle stairs.

"Good morning, Mr. Sweeney," Brewer called. "Ready to give it a try?"

"Ready and willing, Captain!"

"Mac, stay a step behind us, just in case."

"Aye, sir."

Brewer handed his companion a staff. "I had the carpenter make us a couple of staves in case we needed them. Quite handsome, don't you think?"

Sweeney accepted the six-foot staff and looked it over. Mr. Ringold had made them from oak, and at two inches in thickness, they could take all the weight in the world. "Looks like his usual good work, Captain."

The two men set off, heading aft past the larboard battery. They quickly fell into the habit of using their staves as though they were hiking through the woods. Sweeney looked over his shoulder to Mac, who caught the silent message and fell back a couple steps.

"So," Sweeney said, "how are you feeling?"

Brewer shrugged. "Better and better."

Sweeney's voice went low. "I didn't mean your legs."

The captain's face came up for a moment, but he lowered it again. "How did you know?"

The sailing master shook his head. "I've watched you and Alfred spar dozens of times, and I have never seen him give you a beating like that. We both know Alfred doesn't do that of his own accord, so — pardon my saying this, sir — you either deserved it or needed it. I don't know of anything you've done to earn something like that, so you must have needed it. So, I asked how you are feeling."

Brewer blushed. It seemed so obvious when Sweeney explained, and there was no use denying it. "I was frustrated and angry at the commodore for ordering us back to Port Royal to report to the admiral. I wanted to go after Underhill again, but I knew the admiral would expect me to obey orders, so we're heading for Jamaica. The truth is that I allowed myself to sink into an angry melancholy, and it got bad enough that Alfred decided he had to act in order to break me free from it. The rest you know."

Sweeney nodded. "I heard about the match from Gator and a few others. They said Alfred had no mercy and that, had it been real, you'd be dead."

Brewer shrugged. "True, every word."

The conversation ceased as they reached the quarter-deck. Mr. Greene stepped forward and saluted. "It's good to see the both of you up and around."

"How could we not be," Sweeney held forth his staff, "when Mr. Ringold has equipped us with such marvels!"

"Hum!" Greene said. "Remind me not to make you angry!" Sweeney laughed and took a playful jab in the premier's direction.

"All is well, Mr. Greene?" Brewer asked.

"Aye, sir. Mr. Cooke says we should raise Jamaica either late tomorrow or the next morning."

"Good. How's our acting sailing master doing?"

"Almost as good as the genuine article, Captain!" Greene winked at Sweeney. "A little more practice, and I'd say he could stand for his warrant."

"Thank you, Benjamin. Come and see me when you are off watch."

"Aye, sir. Good day, Mr. Sweeney."

"Good day, Lieutenant."

The two men turned forward, Mac keeping three steps behind them. Their pace slowed a bit, but the staves kept them steady on the deck as the ship rode the waves.

"So," Sweeney resumed his low tones, "We were discussing your feelings."

"I'm sure you heard about the bout," Brewer said. "First a blow to my thigh which, had it been a blade, would have bit all the way to the bone. All that did was make my blood boil, and I lost all rational control after that. He simply side-stepped my blind-rage charge and took me down with a blow to the back of the knee." He shook his head in self-recrimination. "Do you know, while I was down, he had Mac shoo the crowd away, and while he was busy with that, Alfred knelt down and confessed all to me. Of course, as soon as he said it, I knew he was right, and I was ashamed."

"So? What did you do?"

"First I forgave him," Brewer said, "then I thanked him."

Sweeney nodded, a token of understanding and appreciation. "You're lucky to have him."

"I know."

They reached the fo'c'sle stairs. "I for one have had enough for the first day, sir," Brewer said. "Same time tomorrow?"

"I'll be ready, Captain."

"Good. Mac, be so kind as to see Mr. Sweeney down the stairs to the sickbay. I'll wait for you here."

"Aye, sir. Ready, Mr. Sweeney?"

Brewer leaned against a long nine to wait. Soon he noticed Mr. Short wandering his direction.

"How are you this fine day, Mr. Short?" he asked.

Short saluted and gave him a sad smile. "Still missing little Jimmy, sir."

Brewer leaned forward on his staff. "I'm sorry for your loss. I think he would have made a good sailor."

"I can't help but think I should have been there for him," Short said. "Maybe I could have saved him, like Mac does for you, Captain. Say, that's a nice piece of wood, sir!"

Brewer proffered the walking stick. "You know how to use a staff, do you?"

"Oh, aye, sir. Me brothers and I used to fight with them when we was little. That was before I joined the navy," he clarified.

"I see. You know, Jimmy had a hard life. He was an orphan with no family. It was the admiral who arranged for him to join the navy and ship out with us. But I happen to know that he found a family here on *Revenge*."

"Really?"

"Yes, Mr. Short. I'm referring to you."

"Me, sir? How do you know that?"

"Mr. Farragut, the American midshipman, told me. He had several chances to speak to Jimmy. He said the boy told him how kind you had been to him and how you were teaching him how to be a sailor. He said you were his friend and made him feel less lonely than before he joined us."

Brewer saw the lad's lower lip poke out a bit. "You think even more now that you should have saved him somehow, right?" Short nodded and sniffed. "Mr. Short, look at me. Believe me when I say you could have done nothing to prevent his death. However, you did something even better — you gave him a friend while he was alive. Not everyone gets to have one of those. You made Jimmy happy while he was with us, and in doing so you gave him a great gift. Remember that."

The boy gave him a sad smile. "Aye, Captain. I will, sir."

"Good lad. I'll see you tomorrow."

"Aye, sir. Good day." He saluted and left. Mac appeared. "Ready, sir?"

Brewer smiled and nodded. "I am now."

The knock at the door made Brewer put down his book as Mr. Greene entered.

"You wanted to see me, sir?"

"Yes, Benjamin. First, I wanted to make sure everything was all right between us personally."

"Yes, Captain. We're fine."

"Good. Then on to other things. When we make Port Royal, I want the ship provisioned and watered in one day if possible. I'm hoping the admiral will allow us to go right back out after *Cromwell*. I want you to go ashore and make the arrangements yourself; if I send anyone less, they might not get the attention we need. Take the purser, Alfred, and Smoot ashore to shop, if they desire. I wish to be ready to go at dawn the next day."

"What about the lighter, sir?"

Brewer raised his brows. "Be persuasive, Benjamin."

Greene smiled. "Aye, sir."

"And let us hope I can be as persuasive with the admiral."

CHAPTER FOURTEEN

Brewer walked slowly, and, he hoped, steadily into Hornblower's study. He'd left his staff on the ship, thinking it was not the image he wanted to portray to the admiral.

"William!" Hornblower came around the desk and shook his hand. "It's good to see you, although I'm mystified as to why. Unless?"

"No," Brewer said, "we haven't caught Underhill. Not yet. I am here because Commodore Biddle insisted that I come back and report to you." He handed the packet over. "The large bundle contains his reports to you, and the other is a personal letter to you." He waited while Hornblower broke the seal and read the letter. The admiral stopped and reread a portion, then he picked up the package and examined the seal.

"This is your seal," he said.

"Aye, sir." The admiral looked for an explanation, so he continued. "The commodore sent both the packet and the letter to me unsealed. He even sent a midshipman with a verbal message confirming this was done on purpose and giving me full permission to read the contents before they were given to you." Brewer shrugged. "It didn't feel right to me, so I sealed them myself."

"I see." Hornblower finished reading the letter and set it aside. "Commodore Biddle speaks very highly of you, William. He says you tracked down *Oliver Cromwell*. Tell me about it."

Brewer rehearsed the battle from start to finish, including the strange way *Cromwell* was sailing. He did not gloss over his own mistake that allowed *Cromwell* to disable *Revenge* and escape. He concluded his tale with the arrival of the *Constitution*.

"Ha-hm!" Hornblower sat forward and rested his elbows on his desk. "It seems like you were doing well until you gave Underhill an opportunity, and he took advantage of your mistake. Don't worry, William; we've all done so. You were fortunate; just be sure to learn from the experience."

"Aye, sir."

"What is the condition of HMS *Revenge*?" Hornblower asked.

"She's in good shape, My Lord," Brewer said. "We got the masts repaired, and my first lieutenant is ashore as we speak to get new spares for the hold and arrange for the ship to be provisioned as quickly as possible."

"Are you in a hurry to go somewhere?"

Brewer blushed. "Commodore Biddle said he was going to search from the Bay of Tocobaga on the west coast of Spanish Florida south to the keys, then he was heading for the Bahamas. I was hoping to be allowed to continue with the mission you gave me, My Lord."

Hornblower sat back in his high-backed leather chair — a gift from his wife — and studied his protégé from hooded eyes over interlaced fingers. Brewer waited as patiently as he could.

"Very well, Commander," the admiral finally said. "You are authorized to continue. Your orders are to find Michael Underhill and the *Oliver Cromwell* and either bring them in or sink them. Your orders will be sent to your ship tomorrow. You may sail as soon as your ship is provisioned." Hornblower leaned forward and picked up his pen.

"Thank you, My Lord." Brewer rose, recognizing the dismissal and hoping he hadn't done anything to displease the admiral. He turned to go.

"And Commander," Hornblower's voice arrested him, and he turned back.

"Good luck," the admiral said.

"Thank you, My Lord. My best to Lady Barbara."

When Brewer stepped up on the deck of HMS *Revenge*, he was met by his premier. "Good to see you, Mr. Greene," he said as he returned his lieutenant's salute. "Back rather quickly, aren't you?"

"Not really, sir," Greene said. "I was able to arrange for our provisions with little difficulty, including replacement masts and scheduling a lighter to top off our water. I also stopped by the personnel office, after which I returned to the ship so I could be here when you returned. Alfred and Old Smoot are still ashore. I sent the boat back to wait for them."

Brewer eyed his first lieutenant, but Greene obviously did not wish to say anything more while they were on deck. "Very well, Mr. Greene," he conceded, "what time is it?"

"Just rang six bells, sir," Greene replied.

"Be in my cabin at the turn of the next watch. Pass the word for the doctor to come as well, and Mr. Sweeney if he's up to it. If he's not, have Mr. Cooke attend."

"Aye, Captain." Greene saluted, and the captain went below to his cabin.

He nearly called for Alfred when he did not appear, but he remembered his steward was still ashore. He poured himself a glass of wine and went to the day cabin. Alfred or Mac had opened several of the stern windows, and now there was a wonderful cross breeze through the cabin. He sat on a chair and put his feet up on the settee and drank. He set the glass on the table and leaned back in the chair. He closed his eyes, hoping to catch a quick nap, but his busy mind would not co-operate. He wondered where Underhill was hiding: on the coast of Spanish Florida, or somewhere in the Bahamas maybe? He frowned; those two areas held nearly a thousand places to hide a ship the size of *Oliver Cromwell.*

His mind was still racing when he heard the ship's bell toll eight times, and Brewer rose to prepare for his guests. He'd barely cleared the table and set out the decanter and glasses by the time a knock sounded at the door. Lieutenant Greene entered the cabin, followed by Mr. Sweeney, with the doctor right behind him and watching his every step. Behind the doctor came a midshipman Brewer did not know. The captain looked to his premier; Greene stepped forward to make the introductions.

"Captain," he said formally, "may I present Port Royal's contribution to our ship, Midshipman Jonathan Striker. Mr. Striker, this is Captain Brewer."

The midshipman came to attention, his hat properly tucked under his left arm. He was older and taller than Mr. Short, but as Mr. Greene had not introduce him as *Revenge's* new senior midshipman.

"Welcome aboard, Mr. Striker," Brewer said. "I trust you're settling in?"

"Haven't had the time as yet, Captain," Striker said. "The first lieutenant suggested I join you here."

Brewer turned to the premier, who nodded his agree-ment. "Well," Brewer said, "let us adjourn to the day cabin. Mr. Greene, if you and the doctor will do the honors?" He nodded toward the decanter.

"Aye, sir."

"Come, Mr. Sweeney," Brewer said, as he led his guests aft. "You seem to be doing better."

"Indeed, Captain. I'm finding it easier to get up to the deck than last week, and my shoulder is hurting less than before. I hope to return to duty soon."

"I'm glad to hear it." Brewer turned to see Greene and the doctor carrying in their drinks. Once they were handed out, Brewer turned to the newcomer. "Mr. Vice, the King!"

Striker cleared his throat and raised his glass. "Gentlemen, the King!" All raised their toast and drank. Brewer's eyes met Greene's; the lad had passed his first test. The captain noted the new midshipman moved off to the corner of the room. Obviously, Greene brought him for a specific purpose, and he was awaiting his time. The four officers made themselves comfortable.

"Gentlemen," Brewer said, "we have been authorized by the admiral to resume our mission to track down Underhill and the *Oliver Cromwell*. Mr. Greene, how soon can we sail?"

"Provisions will arrive this afternoon or tomorrow morning," the premier detailed, "depending on how quickly they can get the boats loaded. Mr. Snead is rigging a derrick as we speak, in case they come early. The lighter is scheduled for the forenoon watch tomorrow. That's the soonest they could fit us in, Captain."

Brewer nodded, frowning slightly at the unavoidable delay. His eyes flashed to Sweeney before he turned to Dr. Spinelli.

"Doctor," he hesitated. "Forgive me, Mr. Sweeney, for talking like this in front of you, but Doctor, when Mr. Sweeney said he hoped to return to duty *soon*, how soon is that? Do I need to get Mr. Cooke down here?"

The doctor rubbed his chin and eyed Sweeney up and down, while the sailing master simply sat there with a grin on his face. The doctor looked to the captain and said, "I suppose he's as ready as he'll ever be, assuming he takes the next bullet in the other shoulder."

Brewer shrugged. "You heard the doctor, Mr. Sweeney: I order you to get shot in the other shoulder next time."

"Aye, Captain!"

Brewer leaned forward. "We're sailing north for the Bahamas via the Windward Passage. Michael will need a place to hide *Cromwell* while they fixed whatever caused them to sail so poorly when we last met."

Brewer halted at a motion from his premier. Greene waved to Striker, who came and sat beside him. "This is why I brought Mr. Striker to this meeting, Captain. He was telling me about himself, and it turns out he's very familiar with these waters. He was a mate on a merchant vessel before the war, and he served on a British privateer during the war. I think he may be of help in searching for *Cromwell*."

Brewer looked to Sweeney, who shrugged in a *can't hurt* sort of way. "Very well, Mr. Striker, have you any ideas?"

"How large is this ship, Captain?" Striker asked.

"Roughly the same size as ours," Brewer replied.

"And what kind of repairs do you think they might have to make?"

"Mr. Sweeney?" Brewer said.

The sailing master sipped his wine and then replied, "I thought about that during those long hours in the orlop, Captain, and I believe it must have to do with their tophamper. I didn't notice them missing a yard, so my guess is a damaged topmast of some sort. Damage like that would prevent them from pushing the ship to her limits for fear the bad mast would give way."

All eyes went to Striker to see what he would do with the information provided. The midshipman rested one elbow on his knee with his chin buried in the palm of his hand. His brows furled and his eyes narrowed. Finally, he sat up with a frown on his face.

"There are many places in the Bahamas where such work could be done, but only if he had the spares with him. Quality masts and spars are hard to come by in the islands and must be pre-positioned for when they are needed. Wait!" His eyes went wide and he turned to Greene. "Is this the same ship we talked about on our way here? The one who was an American privateer during the war?"

"Yes," Greene confirmed.

"There is a place that we discovered later the American privateers used during the war for this sort of emergency," Stricker explained. "A place called White Inlet, but it's on the coast of Florida, south of the Miami River in Seminole country."

"And the Seminoles just let them use the inlet?" Spinelli asked.

"They were usually bought off, was my understanding, usually with whiskey or guns."

The doctor shook his head ruefully, but Striker shrugged. "I'd heard that the Seminole want to expel the Spanish and claim Florida for their own before the Americans can take over."

Sweeney grunted. "So, Underhill may be helping them."

"So it would seem," Brewer said, "but if he is, it is by far the least of his transgressions. Mr. Striker, do you know where this harbor is located?"

"I was there once, Captain," the midshipman said, "several years ago. I think I could find it again."

Brewer shifted. "Mr. Sweeney? The Miami River?"

"No problem, Captain."

"Good." Brewer made a gesture of salute with his glass. "We'll head there as soon as we clear the Straits. Maybe we'll get lucky."

The meeting broke up shortly thereafter, and Brewer was amused to see the doctor leaving with Mr. Striker. He heard them saying something about chess, and he wondered if the doctor had found a new victim. He turned to see Mr. Greene still seated. He refilled both their glasses and resumed his seat.

"What's on your mind, Benjamin?" he asked.

"I'm just wondering what we'll do if we find them, Captain. We can blockade the ship, or we can go for help, but we can't do both. And if we try to cut *Cromwell* out, it becomes a matter of numbers, and Underhill almost certainly wins that game."

Brewer took a drink. "So what do you recommend?"

"I think our best chance is to catch her at sea," Greene said. "She can't match us in a sea battle."

"She did well enough a few weeks ago," Brewer said.

"Bah!" Greene waved away the captain' remark. "Bad luck!"

"That's part of the game, Benjamin."

Greene shook his head. "I'd still rather sail with you than any other captain I've served with, sir."

Brewer lowered his eyes for a moment. "Thank you. It's kind of you to say that. Still, I agree with you; we need to bring *Cromwell* to battle and blow her out of the water."

The next morning found Captain Brewer reading the orders that had just been delivered from the admiral. They restored the original parameters of his mission, which were to find Michael Underhill and the *Oliver Cromwell* and either capture or destroy them. No mention of the Americans in any capacity, which suited Brewer perfectly. There was a letter enclosed asking that any British commander contacted regarding this mission render all necessary aid to Commander Brewer.

Brewer set the orders to the side and picked up his steaming cup of coffee. Alfred and Old Smoot had come to an understanding, one might say. They had gone in together on a large order of coffee, together getting a greater amount at a better price than either could have managed alone. Brewer heartily approved. He blew on the rim of the cup and took a long, appreciative sip. He sighed as he set the cup down. Alfred never disappointed.

A knock on the door heralded the arrival of the first lieutenant. "You sent for me, sir?"

"Yes, Benjamin. Have a seat. Coffee?"

Greene settled himself. "No, thank you, sir. I had some with my breakfast."

Brewer nodded as he took a gulp. "Tell me specifically regarding our stores."

"Lookouts report boats loading at the wharfs."

Brewer frowned. "So we will probably miss the tide, but we should be able to sail tomorrow morning?"

"I am hopeful, Captain."

"Good." Brewer set his cup down and said, "Benjamin, I'd like to host a dinner party this evening. I know we usually wait until after we sail to do this sort of thing, but I think the situation calls for a deviation from the norm. We can use the occasion to welcome Mr. Striker to the ship as well as informing everyone of our orders."

"You've read them, sir?" Brewer slid the papers over to him, and the premier read them carefully. There was a smile on his face when he set them down. "Looks like everything we could have asked for."

"I think so as well," the captain said cautiously. "That's what scares me."

"Sir?"

Brewer smiled. "No excuses."

"Ah!"

"Alfred!" Brewer called, and his servant appeared. "I want to do a party for, say, ten tonight. Can we do it?"

"Aye, Captain. It would be helpful if Mac could run me ashore this morning."

"Benjamin?" Brewer looked to the first lieutenant.

"I'll take care of it, sir," Greene assured him.

"What time, sir?" Alfred enquired.

The captain considered for a moment. "Can it be at the turn of the first dog watch?"

"Aye, Captain, but I would need to leave immediately."

Greene rose and passed the word to the sentry for McCleary to ready the gig.

"Thank you, sir," Alfred said, as the first lieutenant resumed his seat.

Alfred refilled his captain's cup and retreated. "For the party," the captain said, "I want all officers and midshipmen, plus Mr. Sweeney and the doctor. Am I forgetting anyone?" Greene thought for a moment before shaking his head. Brewer sat back. "See to it then, if you please. I'm thinking of a strategy for the next time we encounter *Oliver Cromwell*. Tell me what you think: three broadsides, the loads preset. The first pass would be grape over ball for all guns. The second pass would have double-shot in the 12-pounders and grape over ball for the carronades, and the third pass would have chain for all guns to take out as much of her upper works as possible. Three passes done in quick succession, as quickly as we can come about and reload."

"It has much to commend it, Captain," the premier replied. "Much will depend on the first volley; if it can be delivered to our advantage, we may well have him at our mercy."

"It would be best if we could rake him or at least catch him by the quarter with the first broadside," Brewer agreed. "Thank you, Benjamin. Think on it, if you please; I would welcome any suggestions you may have. Now, please excuse me, and I shall see you tonight."

"Thank you, sir." Greene came to attention and left.

Captain Brewer spent the time until his guests were due writing a letter to Captain Bush. Letters to his old mentor usually fell into one of two categories, the first of which dealt mainly with ship's routine and personnel tales while the second consisted of more personal matters. His current effort definitely fell into this second category. Brewer heard the ship's bell ring and put the letter away so he could make ready for his guests.

The dinner might have gone down in history as one of the strangest ever held on a British warship. Brewer got his guests seated immediately upon their arrival, and Alfred and his stewards brought out the fare. Brewer watched in amusement the expressions on the faces of his guests as the food was placed before them. He had requested Alfred to cook several Jamaican delicacies, and the captain's servant had outdone himself. The main course was a curried goat, the aroma of which was tantalizing if completely foreign to most of them. Next came roasted breadfruit, a staple of not only the Jamaican diet but also several islands of the West Indies A traditional Jamaican cassava flatbread, known locally as "bammy", was made ashore and brought aboard to be fried and seasoned by Alfred himself. The flat loaves measured ten inches across and were sliced into halves or quarters. The drink of choice for the evening was carrot juice seasoned with nutmeg and vanilla. There was considerable reluctance at first to partake of the strange feast set before them, but Mr. Sweeney and Mr. Striker, both of whom had served in the area on other ships, dug in and showed the others how to enjoy the meal, and soon conversations were springing up around the table with comments on the taste of various items and urgings to try this or that. To the memory of all in attendance, it was surely the first time that the health of the King had been drunk with carrot juice.

The captain stood as the stewards were clearing the table and Alfred refilled their glasses. "Gentlemen, to paraphrase Shakespeare, now that I have filled your bellies, kindly lend me your ears." A gentle laughter went around the table. "The purposes of this gathering are twofold. First, we are privileged to welcome a new member to our family, Midshipman Jonathan Striker." Applause and cheers filled the room. Striker nodded his thanks to all. Brewer continued, "Mr. Sweeney, I made the mistake of allowing Mr. Greene to go ashore alone again, and you know how he is when he sees a stray on the streets of a port."

Sweeney played it up, sighing heavily and nodding. "Aye, Captain..."

Brewer saw the grins appearing around the table, and he continued. "Unfortunately, this time, he was in the vicinity of the personnel office when the feeling struck him again. And somehow, now I've got a new midshipman assigned to my ship!"

Laughter broke out, and Brewer was glad to see Striker joining in with the rest of them.

"Now, Captain!" Greene protested loudly. "It weren't my fault! He looked so lost and pathetic, I couldn't help myself!"

The laughter erupted again. Reed, sitting next to Striker, slapped the newcomer on the back. A gesture of pure comradery, plainly received in the manner intended. Mr. Sweeney slapped the table, while the good doctor beside him grinned like a mad fool. Brewer allowed the revelry to die down before picking up his glass.

"I give you a toast," he said. "To Midshipman Jonathan Striker. Long may he serve his King and this ship, and may our voyages together be both successful and profitable!"

"Here! Here!" came from several throats, and all drank to the newcomer.

"Now," the captain said, "on to the second purpose for our gathering. The admiral has given us permission to sail at once and has reinstated our original orders to hunt down the *Oliver Cromwell*. I don't know if you happened to notice, but the last time we engaged her, *Cromwell* was not sailing right, and that's what allowed us to catch up to her so easily. Whatever the problem was, it wasn't obvious from our quarterdeck. Mr. Greene, Mr. Sweeney, and myself put our heads together, and the most probable we can come up with is there must have been something wrong with a topmast or a spar.

"When I last spoke with Commodore Biddle, he was going to take *Constitution* and search the west coast of Florida from the Bay of Tocobaga southwards and then make for the Bahamas. My original intent upon sailing was to head for the Bahamas and begin our search there. However, we are indeed fortunate that Mr. Striker joined us when he did. He sailed these waters on merchant vessels before the last American war, and during the war he sailed on a privateer — only he had the sense to be on our side! He knows of a small, somewhat hidden bay on the east coast of Florida, south of the Miami River, that was used by American privateers during the war for minor repairs and watering. That will be our first stop after we sail. If *Cromwell* is not there, perhaps we can gather some intelligence that might help us track her down . I want you to keep up your drills within your divisions. In all likelihood, our next meeting with result in a battle that only one of us will walk away from. I want it to be us   ."

"Aye, sir!" Lieutenant Tyler answered for them all.

"Thank you for a wonderful evening, gentlemen," the captain said. "Dismissed. Doctor, would you remain, please?"

The assemblage rose from their seats and made their ways toward the door. The doctor kept his seat as the captain went to his desk and returned with his chess set.

"I feel the need of a game, Adam," he said as he resumed his seat. "I hope you don't mind?"

"Not at all, Captain," came the reply. "I take it you've run out of the Cognac the commodore sent you?"

Brewer grinned. "How did you know? Shall I ask Alfred for coffee?"

Spinelli smiled. "You know me well."

Brewer gave the orders, and the two men sat down to play. Neither spoke for several moves until the doctor took a pawn.

"How *did* your meeting with the admiral go?" he asked.

The captain appeared to ignore him as he moved a knight. He picked up his cup and took a drink. "As well as could be expected, I think. I'm just glad he agreed to send us back out after *Cromwell*."

"You mean after Michael Underhill, don't you?" Spinelli moved a pawn. "Check."

Brewer moved a bishop to rescue his king and said nothing. They played on until the captain finally checkmated his opponent. He sat back and called for more coffee. Alfred came and refilled both their cups, and the captain took a sip as his opponent reset the board.

"I have come to terms with Michael Underhill, Adam," he said. "In my own mind, I mean. I know what must be done, and I am perfectly willing to carry out my orders."

"No matter the cost?" Spinelli asked.

"No matter the cost," Brewer confirmed.

Spinelli nodded and moved his pawn. "I was hoping you'd say that."

Reed and Short led their new messmate to the cockpit. Reed sat at the table and Short jumped up in his hammock, but Striker stood and looked around.

"Like it?" Reed asked.

"Just like home," Striker replied.

"So, where did you come from?" Reed asked.

Striker sat on the table and swung a leg. "I was the senior midshipman on HMS *Mercury*, but I got sick on the crossing. The captain put me ashore to the naval hospital in Port Royal, and the ship left without me. I got better; I was out of the hospital and waiting for a ship for about a week when I ran into Lieutenant Greene. He made me an offer, and here I am."

"I saw *Mercury* once!" Short called out from his hammock. "She's a great ship!"

"Does it bother you that you're not senior on *Revenge*?" Reed prodded.

"No," Striker said. "Some may think it a step backward, but I can live with it."

"Yay!" came from the blankets on Short's hammock. "Someone else for Mr. Reed to boss around!"

"Hush, Mr. Short!" Reed yelled at the hammock.

The hammock giggled. "Aye, sir!"

"At any rate," Reed said as he extended his hand, "it will be good to have another hand. Welcome."

Striker took the hand and shook it warmly. "Thank you."

Captain Brewer stepped up on deck and breathed deeply. Spring was dawning across the Caribbean, and the returning warmth of the sun would soon turn into the oppressive, hated heat of summer, but for now it was welcomed and enjoyed. He stepped over to the wheel, where Mr. Sweeney stood talking with Mr. Cooke and the quartermaster. The three men saluted as he approached.

"Gentlemen," Brewer greeted them. "Mr. Sweeney, it's good to see you back on deck. And I must congratulate you on the way you train your mates! When you went down, Mr. Cooke was able to step up and do his best to fill your shoes. In my opinion, he did a great job."

"Thank you, Captain," the mate said modestly.

"Not at all! You have done yourself credit, sir," the captain replied.

"If you'll excuse me, sir, I'm needed forward." Cooke knuckled his forehead and left them.

The captain watched him go. "I don't know whether to continue his training or to hide him so another ship won't poach him."

Sweeney chuckled. "Maybe I should retire and save you the agony?"

Brewer chuckled. "Once we clear the Windward Passage, set course for the mouth of the Miami River. Once we find that, I'm hoping that young Mr. Striker can lead us to this harbor."

"And if he can't?" Sweeney asked.

Brewer shrugged. "If we can't find it, we'll make for the Bahamas and resume the search there. But right now, this is our best shot. Who knows, we might even trap them in the harbor."

It took ten days for them to reach the coast of Spanish Florida, and even then they were miles south of where the wanted to be. Brewer waited until the noon sighting the day after they sighted land to call Greene and Sweeney into his cabin. Alfred poured the coffee and retreated to his pantry. Mac was at his usual post at the door.

"Well, Mr. Sweeney?" Brewer opened the meeting.

The sailing master frowned. "Captain, the contrary winds we've been fighting the last several days have blown us far to the south of our intended position. Based on the sighting I just took, I put out position about here." He rolled out a map of the Florida peninsula and northern Cuba and pointed to a spot just north of the southern tip of the peninsula. "The bay we're looking for should be north of us, but I have no idea how far."

Brewer looked up from the map. "Mac, pass the word for Mr. Striker to join us, if you please."

"Aye, sir." He opened the door and spoke to the sentry, and soon their newest midshipman entered the room.

"You wished to see me, sir?"

"Yes, Mr. Striker. We've arrived off the coast of Florida, and I hope you might help us determine our route from here."

Mr. Sweeney put his forefinger on the map. "Today's noon sighting places us here. How far north would you say the bay is?"

Striker leaned over the table and studied the map. He placed a finger on the coast north of their position and frowned. Finally, he shook his head and rose.

"Impossible to say from this map, Captain. The scale is such that I can't tell details that small." He shrugged. "All we can do, in my opinion, is to crawl north and look for it. If we reach the Miami, we'll know we missed it."

Brewer looked over to Greene, who nodded.

"Very well," he said. "Mr. Sweeney, you and Mr. Striker report to the deck. Set our course to head north along the coastline so Mr. Striker can find our harbor. Please pass the word for the doctor on your way out."

"Aye, Captain." Both men rose and came to attention before heading for the door.

"Do you think we'll find them?" Greene asked.

"I don't know," Brewer admitted. "The Michael Underhill I used to know would have taken advantage of any opportunity to hide out until the pressure died down, but that man is dead and gone, and I can't say what his replacement will do." He bent over the map and stared at it. "The problem is, there are simply too many places he could hide." He sighed in frustration. "Benjamin, if you were Underhill, what would you do?"

Greene sat back in his chair to consider while Alfred refilled their cups. Finally, he spoke up. "Captain, assuming I've repaired my ship, I would provision her for sea and make for the middle of the Atlantic Ocean. I can't think of a better hiding place, especially if I can avoid the major shipping lanes. From there I'd head south. I would resupply in the short term from any merchantmen sailing alone I encountered. I believe Brazil would be friendly, especially if I had any other papers identifying my ship as American besides the outdated letter of marque. Then after the pursuit has died down, I might even take a turn 'round the horn and head for the Galapagos Islands to help myself to one or two British whalers. Sell those cargoes in any port along the Pacific coast of South America, and I'd have enough to pay off my crew and retire. None of us would ever have to work again."

Just at that moment, a knock came from the door. Mac opened it to admit Doctor Spinelli.

"You sent for me, Captain?"

"Yes, Adam. Coffee?" The doctor nodded, and the captain called for Alfred. "Have a seat, Doctor. We're hypothesizing over Underhill's next move." Alfred brought the doctor's coffee and retreated. "Benjamin, repeat to the doctor what you just told me."

Spinelli picked up his cup and took a carful sip as he listened to the premier recount his idea. When Greene was finished, both men looked to their captain.

"What do you think?" Brewer asked the doctor.

"Sounds reasonable," Spinelli replied.

"Do you think he'd do it?" Brewer pressed him.

"How would I know?" the doctor answered. "You know him better than I do."

"That's just it, Doctor," Brewer said in frustration as he shifted in his seat. "My judgement is clouded in this regard, because of my connection to the man he used to be. You, on the other hand, have no such cloud before your eyes."

"Captain, I only met the man once."

Brewer nodded emphatically. "And that is what gives you better vision. Adam, you are one of the most perceptive people I know, and you are very good at reading people and taking their measure. Tell me, what did you glean from Underhill?"

Spinelli looked at his forefinger, tapping on the tabletop as he thought. He took a long, slow, deep breath in through his nose and expelled it forcefully from his lips. "I don't think so, Captain. What the first lieutenant describes is a very good plan, and one Underhill would do well to employ, but it simply doesn't *feel* right to me." He paused to search for the right words. "I *gleaned*, as you call it, two things from the man that night. The first was, *This man is not a runner*. He will stand and fight. If he retreats, it is done for a tactical reason only to allow him to return and reengage from a position of advantage or strength. The second was, *This man is tired*. I mean 'tired' as in 'worn out'. I could hear it plain as day in his voice while he was recounting his story to you, Captain." He raised a finger to emphasize his next point. "Mind you,

I'm not saying he's not still *driven*. One can be tired or worn out but still be driven or highly motivated." Spinelli smiled. "Captain, over the years, I've noticed two things about men who are tired. One, sometimes they can be reasoned with."

"Makes sense," Brewer replied. "What's the second."

Spinelli sat back in his chair, with a look on his face like he had an ace to take the last rubber in a game of whist.

"They make mistakes."

Michael Underhill paced in his cabin, the only light given off by a single lamp suspended from the deck beam by his head. He'd ordered *Oliver Cromwell* to sail at full dark from White Inlet. That had been nearly five hours ago, but he wished it were five days so as to put more distance between him and any pursuit. He'd driven his men hard, and they had completed the work in time to leave on the third night after arriving. Underhill cursed beneath his breath; if it hadn't been for their being becalmed for nearly a week west of the Florida Keys, they'd already be safe in their next hiding place. As it was, they'd stayed just long enough to make sure the work was properly done. Pete wanted to stay one more day to take on water, but Underhill feared being bottled up in that deathtrap. Their course was two points north of east, their destination one of his favorite hideouts from his war days: High Cay, on the eastern side of Great Abaco Island in the Bahamas. He'd hidden there often during the last war. Good source for fresh water, sheltered anchorage, and plenty of food for those willing to forage.

A knock came at his cabin door. He ignored it as best he could, but by the third time it was becoming insistent. Underhill stopped his pacing.

"What?!?!" he shouted.

Chauncey entered the room, closing the door behind him. Underhill clamped his jaws shut at the sight of him and renewed his pacing. He wanted to unleash a string of curses at him for the unwelcome interruption, but they had been through too much together, and Chauncey had saved his life more times than he could count. The mate took a seat at the cabin table and waited for his chief.

When Underhill finally stopped pacing, he looked at the ceiling as though expecting an answer to his unasked question.

"Captain," Chauncey said, "where are we going?"

Underhill kept his gaze on the deck beams above his head. "High Cay."

Chauncey nodded. "Thought so. Three days, maybe four if the wind doesn't hold."

"That was my estimate as well," Underhill confirmed. He sighed and came to sit across from his first mate. "What can I do for you, Chauncey?"

The mate did not look up from the table. "Captain, where are we going?"

"I told you," Underhill repeated, "High Cay."

Chauncey's head shook. "Not what I mean. Where are we going? What lies ahead for us?" When the captain didn't answer, the mate went on. "Most of this crew has been with us for years. They know you, and they trust you, but some of the newer men are asking questions, and none of us have any answers to give them. You know as well as I do what that can do to a crew."

"True enough," the captain admitted. "All right, Chauncey, you've got my attention."

The mate looked up and held his captain's eyes. He wanted nothing he said to be misinterpreted. "We've never been hunted like this, Captain, not even during the war. It's not just Brewer — he may have started it, but the British are on to us now, and they have brought in the Americans to help. I overheard a group of the men discussing the situation a couple nights ago on the fo'c'sle, and one of the newer hands said that we were all liable for hanging as pirates if we were caught by the British. When another reminded him of the letter of marque, he said that the war had ended a long time ago." Chauncey waited, but there still was no reaction. "Michael, these men aren't like the ones from the old days, and even they weren't driven like you for revenge on the British. In order to lead them, we have to lead them *somewhere*."

"What do you suggest?"

Chauncey leaned forward. "Call a meeting when we get to High Cay. Hear them out, and then go from there. Let them see you care."

Underhill search his friend's eyes, but saw only loyalty and concern there. "All right, Chauncey. We'll have a meeting when we get to High Cay."

"Thank you, sir." The mate rose and left without another word. Underhill stared at the door for a long time afterward and wondered if it really was time.

CHAPTER FIFTEEN

HMS *Revenge* crawled northward at barely three knots along the Florida coast, so that lookouts could scan for the harbor. Mr. Striker found a place on the larboard rail, and Mr. Short volunteered to aid him. He was in his usual spot in the bottom of the mizzen shrouds.

"Say, Jonathan," Short said as he lowered his telescope, "how will I know when I find this harbor — what did you call it?"

"White Inlet."

"That's it. White Inlet. How will I recognize it?"

Striker lowered his glass. "I'm not sure, William. I haven't been there in five years or more. The entrance may be overgrown, or floods could have changed the contours. I suppose we'll have to report anything that looks likely."

Short frowned. "I was afraid you'd say that."

Striker chuckled and raised his glass. He studied the shoreline, and something struck a chord in his memory. He lowered the glass and hurried aft. When he got to the quarterdeck, he paused to check his findings once more before turning to Mr. Greene.

"Sir!" he called. "I think I've found it!"

"Where away?" Greene demanded.

Striker handed him the telescope and pointed. "There, sir. About three points abaft the beam."

Greene saw what the midshipman was pointing at, but it didn't strike him as what they were looking for. Still, this was why Striker was on deck. He turned to the wheel.

"Mr. Sweeney, bring us around! Mr. Short! My respects to the captain, and can he please come up on deck?"

"Aye, sir!" Short hopped down from the shrouds and disappeared below. Minutes later he returned with Brewer hard on his heels.

"What is it, Lieutenant?" he asked.

"Mr. Striker?" Greene said. Striker led the captain to the starboard rail, now facing the shoreline, and pointed to the entrance. The captain took the glass Greene offered him and raised it to his eye.

"Are you sure, Mr. Striker?" he asked when he lowered the glass.

The midshipman hesitated. "I think so, Captain. It's been a while since I was last there, but this looks familiar."

Brewer studied his newest midshipman's face before making his decision. "Very well," he said. "Mr. Greene, take a boat, and you and Mr. Striker go for a closer look. Take Mac with you, and six marines."

"Aye, sir."

Orders went out for Mac to prepare the boat and for Lieutenant Smythe of the Royal Marines to prepare his men.

"Captain!"

Brewer spun to see Mr. Short in the shrouds, pointing at the shore. "Ship coming out, sir!"

Sure enough, a pinnace was emerging from the river mouth Greene and Striker were planning to investigate. Brewer raised his glass to his eye for a closer look, but he could see no colors and the pinnace itself was unfamiliar to him.

"Mr. Greene!" he called, "belay that order! Mr. Sweeney,

bring us about! Intercept course!"

"Aye, Captain!"

Brewer crossed the deck as she came around and settled on her new course to cut off the pinnace. From his position, he had an excellent view of the activity on her deck.

"She's seen us, sir!" Short called. "Looks like she's running!"

"I see it, Mr. Short," the captain replied. "Mr. Sweeney, make all sail! I want to overtake that ship!"

"Aye, sir! All hands! All hands! Make all sail!"

Brewer could hear the stampede sounds of his men racing to their stations as he focused on the pinnace, now heading north away from them at a high rate of speed. Mr. Greene appeared beside him and stood silently as he studied the chase through his own telescope. Brewer smiled to himself; this was one of the things he loved about his first lieutenant. Benjamin Greene was not one to indulge in distracting small talk or idle chatter. He would not speak to his captain unless he was spoken to or had something important to say.

Brewer felt his ship pick up speed. He looked forward again and saw the chase was two or three points off the larboard bow and moving across their bow to starboard. He lowered his glass and thought for a moment.

"Mr. Sweeney," he said as he turned to his sailing master, "Best course to intercept. I am going forward to see if I can get a better look. Mr. Greene, you're with me. Mr. Short!" *Revenge's* junior midshipman jumped down to the deck and presented himself with a crisp salute. "I have a job for you. I want you to station yourself on the fantail with your glass. Your mission is to watch the harbor where the pinnace appeared. Tell me if anything else emerges. You may also come to tell me when it is out of sight."

"Aye, aye, Captain!" Short saluted again and headed aft.

Brewer headed forward, and Greene fell in right behind

him. They arrived at the bow chasers and the captain raised his glass.

"Lookout! Let's hear you!" he called.

"We're closing, Captain!" came the reply from aloft. "Not sure if we can cut her off, though."

Brewer turned over his shoulder. "Return aft, Benjamin. Confer with Mr. Sweeney. We need a better point of sailing; either that, or the studs'ls."

"Aye, sir."

Brewer heard his footsteps fade as he went aft, and he turned his full attention to the chase. He was surprised by the circumstances; it was rare to find a pinnace that could outrun *Revenge.* He heard the call for the studs'ls and nodded to himself. Hopefully, that would do the trick. He raised the glass to his eye again and tried to gauge the distance.

"Ready the long nines," Brewer said. The crews for the two bow chasers jumped into action. Ninety seconds later, both captains raised their right hands, signifying they were ready to fire.

"Pass the word to Mr. Sweeney, *'Steer three points to starboard.'*"

"Aye, sir!" A hand ran aft, and presently the ship swung three points to starboard. Seconds later, Mr. Greene appeared.

"Remember," Brewer admonished the gun captains, "I want two in the water off her bows."

"Aye, sir."

"Fire."

Both guns went off, and Brewer closed his eyes against the smoke.

"Two geysers off his starboard bow, Captain!" the lookout called down. "She's lowering sail, sir! She's heaving to!"

"Well done, men!" Brewer congratulated the guns crews.

"Mr. Greene, take that boat along with Mr. Striker and the marines and see what she's about. Bring back the master if you think it worth our while."

"Aye, sir." Greene touched his hat and disappeared aft.

Brewer stood beside the mizzen shrouds as the boat made its way to the pinnace when he suddenly glanced back at Mr. Short, still manning his post at the fantail. He wondered what kind of officer the lad would make, assuming he lived long enough to grow into the role. He pressed his lips together, admonishing himself for the grimness of that thought.

"I'm going below," he said to Mr. Sweeney. "Please ask Mr. Greene to come to my cabin when he returns. Call me if I'm needed."

"Aye, sir."

Brewer made his way to his cabin and then to the day cabin. He sat beneath the stern windows, leaned his head back, and closed his eyes. He'd hoped to let the tension drain from his body, but the tenseness in his back and neck refused to leave. *Just my luck,* he thought ruefully, *it likes me.* His stomach growled. With an exasperated sigh, he called out, "Alfred?"

His servant appeared. "What can I do for you, Captain?"

"I seem to have missed lunch. Have you anything that could tide me over to supper?"

Alfred ducked his head. "I have just the thing: some cheese and fresh fruit."

"Thank you, that will be fine."

Brewer pulled a book from the shelf and sat at the table where a plate of food awaited him. Alfred poured a glass of wine for his captain before retreating. Brewer opened the biography of George Washington and, between bites, began to read where he had left off. Washington had just discovered Benedict Arnold's intention to betray the fort at West Point to the British, and his sense of betrayal knew no bounds. Brewer bobbed his head to the side and nodded with his chin.

Yes, I can certainly sympathize with you, General, he thought. *People you rely upon, the ones who may have helped to get you where you are today, they aren't supposed to turn on you. They cannot try to put a knife in your back and then not expect revenge to be swift and harsh.* Brewer looked up from the pages. *You didn't get your revenge, General, but I will.*

He looked down to see his plate was now empty, so he closed his book and took his drink to the day cabin.

A knock on the cabin door interrupted the captain's train of thought. There was a cool breeze blowing through the cabin, the result of his opening several of the stern windows. He looked up to see the door open and Mr. Greene lead another man into the room. Mac came in behind them and closed the door before following them into the day cabin. Brewer closed the gap to greet his guests.

"Captain," Greene said by way of introduction, "this is Thaddeus Jones, master of the *Zephyr*. Mr. Jones, this is Captain William Brewer of His Majesty's sloop-of-war *Revenge*."

"Captain," Jones greeted him as the two shook hands.

"Please, Mr. Jones, sit," Brewer motioned to the settee. "Alfred! Refreshments for three, if you please!"

"Aye, sir!"

Brewer resumed his chair and looked to his premier.

Greene paused long enough for Alfred to deliver their drinks. "Captain, per your instructions, Mr. Striker and I took a boat and boarded the *Zephyr*. A quick inspection of the ship and her papers revealed nothing illegal. Mr. Jones and his crew were nothing but cooperative. After questioning

Mr. Jones, I decided he should come back with us and speak to you directly."

Brewer looked to his guest. "I take it that means you saw the *Oliver Cromwell* in the harbor."

"Aye, Captain," the master replied. "We arrived about three weeks ago. We'd taken damage from a storm north of Cuba, and, to tell the truth, we needed a rest after a long and hard voyage. *Cromwell* was making repairs to her topmasts, and she seemed to be in a hurry to get the work done. No sooner had we dropped anchor then they sent a boat over to us. We were boarded by a party led by his first mate, a bully of a man named Chauncey. I recognized him from the war, and when he saw it was me he insisted I come back with him have a drink with his captain, Michael Underhill."

Brewer shared a look with his premier while Jones drained his glass.

"Alfred!" Brewer called for a refill. "Please, Mr. Jones, go on."

Jones thanked the captain's servant for the refill and settled back to continue his tail. "Michael was glad enough to see me, though it had been nearly six years since I saw him last. He pulled out a bottle of Cognac he said he'd got from an American and we drank to old times. I asked about his ship. He said he'd been caught in a storm in the gulf and lost his fore- and maintop masts. I asked about the Seminoles and whether he'd ,met with any since he'd arrived, but he said he'd seen nary a one, even though he'd sent parties ashore after food and water."

Brewer leaned forward. "I take it he's gone now?"

Jones nodded. "Lit out about a day or so later."

"Any idea where he went?" Greene asked.

The master shook his head. "The subject never came up. In fact, when I left Michael that first day to return to my ship, that was the last time I saw him."

"Hmm," Brewer asked his next question cautiously. "Mr. Jones, I take it you were a privateer for the Americans during the last war?"

Jones eyed him suspiciously. "That's right, Captain, but that war ended a long time ago."

"For most," Brewer replied, "not for all. I asked because I thought that was how you knew about White Inlet."

"That's right," Jones confirmed warily.

"My business, Mr. Jones," Brewer said, "is with Michael Underhill, not with you. Tell me, during the war, was there any place you used to hide? Someplace you would go when you left White Inlet?"

Jones looked from the captain to his first lieutenant and back again. He debated asking what it was they wanted with Underhill, but decided that he was better off staying out of the crossfire. "A few," he admitted. "There were a couple secluded coves on the northern shore of Cuba that we used for short periods only, so we didn't attract Spanish attention."

"Anywhere in the Caribbean?" Greene asked.

Jones shook his head. "No, there was just too great a risk of blundering into a British warship. Raids into the Caribbean were always straight in and straight out."

"What about the Bahamas?" Brewer asked. "Or Spanish Florida?"

"A few in the Bahamas, although not as many as you might think, especially if you were looking to hide for a while. As for the Florida coastline, the St. Johns River just south of American Georgia has a few suitable coves inland."

Brewer rubbed his chin between his thumb and forefinger. "And where would you go, Mr. Jones?"

Jones considered for a moment before deciding to come clean and be done with it. "Personally, I would head to Rum Cay. There's a cove on the western end of the island that wasn't too bad to hide in, and it provided decent shelter from the weather as well. But don't take what I say as gospel, Captain; it's been quite a while since I've been there."

"I understand, Mr. Jones," Brewer reassured him as he stood, "and I thank you greatly for your help. Is there anything the Royal Navy can do you for before we go?"

Jones and Greene stood as well. "Just let me go in peace, Captain," Jones replied as the two shook hands, "and don't mention this meeting to Underhill, should you meet him."

"You have my word, sir. Mr. Greene will escort you back up on deck, and our boat will conduct you safely back to your ship. Thank you again."

"My pleasure, Captain." Jones touched his forehead in a friendly gesture before following Greene out of the cabin.

Brewer followed them up on deck a few minutes later and found the first lieutenant at the rail watching the boat return its master to the *Zephyr*.

"Did he say anything else?" Brewer asked.

"Not really," came the reply. "He tried to ask why we wanted Underhill, but I'm afraid I was less than forthcoming with information."

Brewer grinned. "As soon as the *Zephyr* is gone, have Mr. Tyler and Mr. Striker take a boat and check out White Inlet. Once we're sure *Cromwell* is gone, we can make our next move."

Greene was surprised. "You think Jones may have lied to us about her being gone?"

Brewer shrugged. "I don't know, but I think it would be wise to verify his story. I'm going below. Report to me in my cabin with Mr. Tyler once he's returned."

"Aye, sir."

"Mr. Short," Brewer called to the midshipman of the watch, "kindly pass the word for Doctor Spinelli to meet me in my cabin."

"Aye, Captain."

Brewer lingered long enough to see Jones safely back aboard his ship before making his way below, which meant that the doctor met him at the door.

"Ah, there you are, Captain," he said. "I thought for a moment there Mr. Short was mistaken."

"Sorry I'm late, Doctor," Brewer said, "please come in."

They entered the cabin, the captain directing his guest to the table while he retrieved the chess set from his desk. He took his usual seat at the head of the table, and the doctor began to set up pieces on the board. Alfred brought wine and the two men played.

"So, Captain, what's on your mind?" the doctor asked, moving a pawn.

Brewer moved a knight. "We intercepted a pinnace that came out of the harbor, and Mr. Greene brought the master back. He said Underhill and *Cromwell* had been there."

Spinelli looked up. "Excuse me?"

Brewer nodded. "That's what he said. They left some time ago after repairing a couple topmasts."

"So, you were right!" the doctor said. "There was something wrong with their ship. Did he say where they went?"

The captain shook his head. "Said he didn't know. I've sent Lieutenant Tyler and Mr. Striker to check out White Inlet just to make sure."

"And if he's still there?" Spinelli moved a rook. "Check."

The captain moved his bishop. "Then," he said, "we close the door before the horse can leave the barn."

Spinelli moved his rook. "And if he's gone?"

"Then we head for the Bahamas to begin our search there." Brewer reached down and casually picked up his queen. He smiled as he set it down one space from the doctor's king.

"Checkmate."

The doctor was about to make a smashing remark when a frantic knocking at the door prevented him. Mac opened the door to allow Mr. Short to charge in.

"Captain!" he said. "Mr. Greene sends his respects and asks that you come on deck at once."

"What is it?" Brewer asked.

Short looked wide-eyed. "Lookout reports hearing gunshots from White Inlet!"

CHAPTER SIXTEEN

Captain Brewer burst from the companionway with the doctor and Mr. Short hard on his heels. "Report, Mr. Greene!"

The premier touched his hat and handed his captain a glass. "Several shots approximately eight minutes ago. Nothing since. Sir, I suggest Mac prepare the launch. I volunteer to lead a rescue team."

"Deck there!" cried the lookout. "Our boat's coming out of the bay!"

Everyone on the quarterdeck turned as one to see the boat emerge from the protected inlet. The sail was up and a blue flag was flying — the signal that there were injured on board. Brewer lowered his glass and frowned.

"Doctor," he said, "it looks like they're bringing you business."

"Yes. With your permission, Captain, I'll meet them at the entry port."

Brewer nodded. "Take Mac with you."

"I will. Mr. Short, kindly run below and warn Gator that we're going to be busy, and he'd better prepare."

"Aye, Doctor!"

"Captain!"

Brewer turned back to see several small boats emerge from the inlet in pursuit of *Revenge's* launch. He raised his telescope to his eye, but he wasn't sure what it was he saw.

Beside him, Mr. Greene was having the same trouble. "Indians?" he asked as he lowered his glass. "Seminoles? They aren't known for raiding ships in small boats."

"No," the captain said thoughtfully. "I think I know now what the Seminole were paid to allow the American privateers to use this anchorage." He turned toward the wheel. "Bring us about, Mr. Sweeney! I want *Revenge* between the launch and those boats! Lieutenant Smythe! Get your gunners to the tops! Man the rails as well! Mr. Greene! Load the carronades with grape!"

Activity exploded aboard ship. Marine sharpshooters and their loaders climbed the shrouds while their muskets were hoisted aloft. The ship came around and headed inland, passing the boat on her starboard side. Brewer had a better view of the situation now. The Seminole boats were each loaded with warriors. They carried a mixed armament; some were armed with muskets or pistols while others carried bows and arrows. Lieutenant Smythe approached and saluted.

"I've got men in the tops," he said, "and I've positioned most of the rest in the bows. What are your orders, sir?"

Brewer lowered his glass. "If they don't turn around," he said and then hesitated. "If they don't turn around before we reach them, you may open fire."

"Aye, sir." Smythe saluted and went forward.

"Mr. Greene," Brewer called, "stand by to fire."

"Aye, sir."

Revenge was closing rapidly with the oncoming Indians. Brewer began to wonder if they would turn back. He got his answer when he saw one of the braves stand up in his boat and shoulder his musket, followed by a puff of smoke.

"They're shooting at us!" Mr. Short cried in disbelief.

"So I see, Mr. Short," the captain calmly replied. He studied the situation through cold, narrowed eyes before picking up a speaking trumpet. "Mr. Smythe! You may open fire!"

Smythe acknowledged the order before turning forward to his men. Seconds later, a volley rang out from both sides of the bow. Brewer looked over the side in time to see several Indians fall into the water. The sharpshooters in the tops now went to work, the Seminoles below defenseless against their fire, but still they came on. Brewer grimaced and turned to his first lieutenant.

"Order the carronades to pick their targets," he said. "Fire as you bear."

"Aye, sir."

HMS *Revenge* plowed into the smaller boats like a bull charging into a pack of wild dogs. Brewer watched from his quarterdeck as the Seminole boats slid past. He heard the carronades fire, one at a time as they picked their targets. Of the four shots, three resulted in the destruction of one of the Seminole boats, the fourth going a bit high but still taking several of their attackers to their final rewards.

The show of force proved too much for the Seminoles; they broke off their attack and turned for the safety of White Inlet. Brewer watched them for a few moments to make sure the maneuver wasn't a feint on their part, then he picked up the speaking trumpet and ordered a cease fire.

"Mr. Sweeney, turn us about," he ordered. "Let's go get our men."

Sweeney brought the ship about smartly and they ran down on the launch, which had hove to as soon as they saw they were out of danger. Sweeney dumped the wind from their sails, and the launch came alongside.

"Sir!" Tyler shouted up from the boat, "Mr. Striker's been hit by an arrow! He's in a bad way!"

"Get that sling ready!" Spinelli shouted.

"Sir, I don't think there's time!" Tyler warned.

Without a word, Mac leapt over the side and climbed down into the boat and grabbed the injured midshipman by his lapels. Realizing what he was about to do, Tyler tried to stop him.

"Mac, you'll kill him!"

"Sir, he's dead anyway if we don't get him to the doctor right now!"

Tyler knew he was right, so he backed off. Mac heaved the injured Striker up and over his shoulder and climbed back to the entry port. Spinelli had a horrified look on his face but knew better than to interfere at that point.

"Straight to the sickbay, Mac!" he said. "Gator will show you where to put him! I'm right behind you!"

Brewer stood on the quarterdeck and watched them disappear below deck. He turned to look aft and see Lieutenant Greene keeping watch on the mouth of the inlet, just in case the Seminoles decided to try again. He sent Mr. Reed to relieve him, then crossed the deck as Lieutenant Tyler stepped up on deck.

"Mr. Greene, Mr. Tyler," he said, "you're with me. Mr. Sweeney, let's get moving. Course due east."

The sailing master nodded. "Aye, Captain."

Brewer led his officers below and aft to his cabin. The sentry closed the door behind them as the captain dropped his hat on the table.

"Sir," Tyler said, but Brewer forestalled him with an upraised hand.

"Not yet," he said quietly. "Alfred! Wine, if you please. Follow me, gentlemen."

They followed him into the day cabin, where the captain motioned for them to sit. Brewer remained standing, his gaze focused on the deck above them. Greene could see his lips moving and realized he was praying. Alfred appeared, but he paused at the door until his captain finished and lowered his gaze.

"Thank you, Alfred," he said as he took his seat and the servant passed out the glasses. The captain took a swallow, the held the glass cupped in his hands as he stared into space, before blinking his eyes back into focus.

"Alright, Mr. Tyler," he said, "tell us what happened."

Tyler took a quick sip of his wine to compose himself. "We approached the mouth of the inlet. Mr. Striker suggested we take it down the middle, as we had no idea if there were any Seminole guarding the entrance from either bank. Once inside, the channel turned about 40 degrees to starboard." He motioned with his hands so they could follow the story better. "The channel narrowed somewhat at this point, but there was still plenty of room for a ship the size of *Revenge* or *Cromwell* to get through. After three hundred yards, the channel turned about ten degrees to larboard and soon opened into the bay itself. It was empty of any shipping. I ordered a turn to starboard to go once around the bay, and almost immediately we saw boats on the shoreline. What I didn't do was pay attention to our position. We ended up drifting close enough for a flight of arrows to appear in the air heading our way. Two hit the railing of the boat and the third struck Mr. Striker. I immediately ordered a retreat and raised the sail for more speed. As we approached the entrance I saw you, so I raised the blue pennant. I saw the Indians coming after us in their boats. The rest you know."

Without warning, the cabin door opened and Mac walked in. He stared at the deck in front of him, and the look on his face showed a loss of all hope. The left side of his shirt was covered in blood from carrying Mr. Striker to sickbay.

"Mac?" Brewer said. "Any word?"

The coxswain shook his head. "I dunno, sir. I carried Mr. Striker into the sickbay, and Gator showed me where to lay him. The doctor came in right behind me and ordered me to leave. That's all I know, sir."

"Very well, Mac," Brewer said. "Why don't you step into the pantry and have Alfred pour you a glass of wine?"

"No, thank you, sir." Without another word, he assumed his usual post at the door. Brewer looked to his first lieutenant, who merely shrugged. The captain turned back to Tyler.

"Is there anything else you'd like to add, Lieutenant?" he asked.

Tyler thought for a moment, then shook his head. "I don't think so, sir."

"I need you to write up your report for me tonight and turn it in tomorrow morning."

"Aye, sir."

Brewer was about to dismiss him when a single knock sounded from the door. Mac opened it and stepped back to allow the doctor to come in. He had a towel he was using to wipe his hands, and there was blood on his shirt.

"Adam?" Brewer prompted him.

Spinelli lowered his eyes and shook his head. "I did everything I could. The arrow nicked an artery in his chest before lodging in his right lung. Mr. Striker died on the table." He raised his eyes briefly to meet the captain's. "I'm sorry, Captain."

"I'm know you did your best," Brewer said almost automatically. The tension had escalated in the room with the announcement.

"*No!*" The tragic whisper came from Lieutenant Tyler.

Brewer turned to see a wide-eyed look of complete devastation on the younger man's face, and he guessed this was the first time anyone under his command had died. A quick glance back to the doctor showed his concern for Tyler, but nobody moved.

"Mr. Tyler," Brewer said to him. The lieutenant ignored him completely. His mouth was agape and his eyes were darting back and forth, as though he was reliving everything in his mind to see what it was he should have done so that this midshipman would not have died. Brewer remembered the feeling well, and his heart bled for the man.

"Mister Tyler!"

The captain's voice was loud, authoritarian, and firm. The combination did the trick; Tyler blinked and raised his eyes to his captain.

"Jeremiah," Brewer said, softly but firmly, "I need you to listen to me right now. This is not your fault. Do you understand? From everything you told me in your report, you are not to blame for Mr. Striker's death."

Tyler's eyes narrowed in disbelief at his captain's words, then his head fell and hung, his body wracked with the ragged breaths of sobs that were fast growing out of his control. Brewer had to strain to hear his words.

"If I'd only stayed farther from the shore..."

Brewer shook his head. "Mr. Tyler..."

"Striker might still be alive..."

The captain stirred and seemed to be at a loss of what to do, so the doctor spoke up.

"They had muskets."

Tyler's head snapped up. "What did you say?"

Greene seized the opportunity. "It's true. Several of the Seminoles in the boats that attacked us were armed with muskets." He leaned in and held Tyler's eyes. "Had you stayed farther out, they would have opened fire with muskets rather than arrows. Striker would probably still be dead.

When it's your time, it's your time."

Tyler's eyes welled up with tears, and he hung his head and wept openly. Brewer looked to the doctor and silently motioned with his head toward the second lieutenant. Spinelli sat beside the young ma and put his arm around his shoulders.

"Jeremiah," the doctor said softly, "Let's you and I go down to the gunroom. Come on, up with you."

Spinelli helped the young officer to his feet and led him from the cabin. Neither man looked back. Brewer watched them go until Mac closed the door behind them.

"Do you think he will be all right?" Greene asked.

"I hope so. Time will tell."

"Did it hit you that hard? The first time one of your men died, I mean."

"I don't remember," Brewer replied stiffly.

"I see," Greene said with an exaggerated nod. "I'll check in on him tomorrow."

"Please do. Tell the doctor we'll cover Tyler's next couple watches. Bring him to see me tomorrow or the next day, whenever the doctor thinks he's ready."

"Aye, sir." Greene rose. "So, where to now?"

"The Bahamas. We'll start across the northern islands and work our way south."

Michael Underhill sat in his cabin, his head in his hand. An empty tankard sat on the table before him next to his saber. *Oliver Cromwell* was safely sconced in the little bay at the western tip of High Cay, her topmasts lowered and branches hung on her yards and along her rails to make her harder to spot from the sea.

The meeting Chauncey had suggested he have with the crew had not gone well. Many of the men had had enough of being chased by the British, and now the American navy as well. They wanted to quit, many of them. Said it was getting too dangerous. He couldn't blame them, not really; it wasn't their fault that they didn't share his motivations. In the end, they'd agreed to give him three months to come up with a plan. The trouble was, he had no idea what that should be.

He picked up the bottle from the table and made to refill his tankard when a sharp sound from the deck stopped his hand. It was the sound of a gunshot. He grabbed his sword from its hook on the wall and rushed from the cabin. When he arrived on deck, he was shocked to see his men fighting a British boarding party! Underhill didn't have time to wonder where they'd come from or how they'd got on board, for he was immediately attacked by a British sailor brandishing a saber and a dagger. He parried a thrust with the saber and ducked inside a slash with the dagger to land a punishing uppercut with his heavy fist on his enemy's chin which dropped the man to the deck unconscious.

"Michael!"

Underhill spun at the sound of that voice so familiar to see Brewer standing there, not ten feet away. He was in shirtsleeves and carried a sword.

"It's time we finished this, Michael," he said.

"I don't want to kill you, William," Underhill replied.

"Then you can stand there while I run you through!" Brewer made a thrust at his heart that Underhill barely had time to parry. The two men circled to the right as they made feints and slashes to feel each other out. Brewer made a high slash at his opponent's head and swiftly ducked inside Underhill's counter to bury his shoulder in the older man's chest and throw him back. Somehow Underhill kept his feet, although he slid backward on the blood that was swiftly covering the *Cromwell's* deck. He stood there and looked at Brewer, just beyond sword point, standing poised for battle with fury in his eyes.

"All right, William," Underhill said as he raised his sword, "let's finish this."

He attacked, but Brewer sidestepped and nearly landed his blade in the older man's thigh as he passed. Underhill turned just in time to parry a thrust and then throw a slash that made the British captain duck. Underhill kicked out with his foot, hoping to catch Brewer in the head, but the younger man caught his ankle and gave it a mighty heave. Underhill was off-balance enough that it sent him to the deck. He quickly rolled over and brought up his sword, expecting Brewer to jump in for the kill. He was in time to see Brewer raise his sword, only to have Chauncey appear out of nowhere behind him and run the British captain through. Brewer dropped to his knees beside his old friend, then fell to the deck, his eyes wide and frightening.

"NO!"

The sound of Underhill's own scream awakened him, and his head shot up from the cradle of his arms where it had been resting. He was still seated at the table in his cabin. The door burst open and Chauncey entered.

"Captain?" he said. "What is it? I thought I heard you scream."

"I'm fine, Chauncey," Underhill said slowly as he tried to blink the sleep out of his eyes. "Just a bad dream. I'll be up on deck shortly."

Chauncey stared at his captain as if to satisfy himself that the man was all right. He nodded and looked around the room before retreating and closing the door behind him.

Underhill rose and walked over to the washstand in the corner and poured some water into the basin. He splashed some onto his face and the back of his neck before drying with a towel. He rubbed his face with his hand as he wandered more or less aimlessly around the day cabin. The dream had seemed so real! He had been certain Brewer was on *Cromwell's* deck and trying to kill him. And then to watch him die, to see Chauncey run him through like that, broke his heart! It was like watching his son die!

Underhill made his way to the table, refilled his tankard from the bottle that was there beside his sword, and carried it to the day cabin. He sat under the stern windows and thought about the future. Suddenly, and without explanation, he felt very tired, and he just wanted everything to be over. The realization surprised him; after all these years, he was simply going to give up the fight and let the British Crown off the hook, so to speak? *Yes,* he thought. *I don't know why, but I have no energy left for this war. I must find a way to end this.*

This decision brought with it a whole new set of problems. He and his men were wanted by the British government — and quite possibly the American government as well — on charges of piracy for their actions since the end of the war in 1814. Simply surrendering to Brewer meant the trial and hanging of his entire crew, and he could not do that to them. Surrendering himself to the British would not guarantee that they would not continue to pursue his men. Sailing for the South Seas wasn't an option, not really; it meant leaving behind the money they had banked under false names and companies in New Orleans, which was a considerable sum, as well as forcing them to beware of meeting a British ship anywhere in the world.

The best idea seemed to be that of abandoning *Cromwell* and melting into the American countryside. Each man would receive a letter for the banks in New Orleans which should allow him access to his share of the prize money there, and they had enough coin on board, if it were divided evenly amongst the men, to give each man a good start. But would the men agree to this? He got up and paced for a while as he turned the question over in his mind. Finally, he stopped; if the men would not go for it, then he would leave them to their decision. He would take his share and disappear. Underhill sighed. Far from a perfect solution, and he knew it, but it offered the best chance for them to come out of this alive.

He went up on deck and found Chauncey and Pete conferring by the wheel.

"Make ready to sail with the first available tide," he ordered.

The mate and master looked at each other in confusion. "Course, Captain?" Pete asked.

"Washington City," Underhill replied. "I need to see a man about a letter."

CHAPTER SEVENTEEN

Captain Brewer paced back and forth along the lee rail of *Revenge's* quarterdeck. Thus far, their search of the northern Bahamas for Underhill and the *Oliver Cromwell* proved fruitless.

Striker's funeral three days ago had been a strange event that still haunted him. The midshipman hadn't been aboard long enough for Brewer to get to know him at all, but he had been instrumental in finding White Inlet and putting them on Underhill's track. Mr. Reed had asked to speak, and he'd done a fine job complimenting Mr. Striker and lamenting that he would never have his chance to make his mark in the world. Reed ended by pledging for himself and Mr. Short — who stood beside him as he spoke — that they would remember him. Brewer thought it a good speech, but it was still strange for him to preside as a body — one of his own men — slid over the side to be consigned to the deep.

Out of the corner of his eye, Brewer caught sight of Mr. Short running up to Mr. Greene, who stood on the other side of the quarterdeck with the sailing master and quartermaster. Short seemed excited as he pointed forward. Greene looked up to where Short indicated, then Short saluted and returned forward. As Greene approached his captain, Brewer stopped his pacing.

"Yes, Mr. Greene?"

"Sir," the premier said with a smile on his face, "the lookout in the foretop reports a sail on the horizon. She appears to be heading nor' nor'west."

Brewer looked forward. Could it be? "Intercept course," he ordered. "Call the hands! Give her every stitch she'll carry!"

"Aye, sir!"

The ship leapt forward and came around to a new NE course, followed a few minutes later by a change to NNE and then finally to a point east of north. *Revenge* began to overhaul the unknown ship.

"Think it's *Cromwell*?" Greene asked.

"Not sure," Brewer answered. He brought a glass to his practiced eye. "She's about the right size. Ah, there she goes! She's putting on sail — she must have seen us!"

The strange ship crowded on sail, and both ships now raced on converging courses.

"You may clear for action, Benjamin," the captain said quietly.

"Aye, sir."

"Mr. Sweeney! Two points to starboard! I want to close the gap."

"Aye, sir."

Brewer stepped to the rail and raised his glass. The ships weren't close enough yet to make out specifics, but he was sure he could see someone on the strange ship standing at the rail with a glass to his eye studying him. *Is that you, Michael?* Brewer lowered the glass and sighed. *So, is this how it ends?*

"Mr. Greene," he said as he turned from the rail, "Please go to the long nines. I want an estimate of how long it will be before we might come around to starboard, fire the bow chasers, then resume the chase with a minimum loss of speed."

"Aye, sir. Mr. Short, you're with me." The two men headed forward.

Brewer resumed his post at the rail. The chase ran out its larboard battery. He grunted; they were still out of range of each other. He blinked as he saw the guns run back in again. A message, then; a warning of what was to come. Brewer's eyes narrowed. Did he really think that would change his course of action, or make him think twice about blowing *Cromwell* out of the water? *No, Michael. This ends. Now.*

Brewer made his way forward and found his first lieutenant in conversation with Mr. Hodges, the gunner, and Mr. Short. The three men touched their hats as he approached.

The captain nodded his acknowledgement. "Well, Mr. Greene?"

Greene cleared his throat and nodded toward the gunner. "We believe it won't be long, sir. Thirty minutes, more or less, assuming they don't change course."

Brewer stepped up between the guns and raised the glass to his eye again. He quickly came to agree with his premier's estimation. He lowered the telescope and thought for a moment before turning back to his men.

"Mr. Greene," he said, "I'm returning to the quarterdeck. When you feel the ship turn to starboard, you may fire as your guns bear. Do not wait for orders. Continue to fire as long as you are able. Inform me at once when this is no longer possible. Do you understand?"

"Aye, Captain."

Brewer nodded. "You may keep Mr. Short to act as messenger."

"Thank you, sir." The three saluted, and Brewer turned aft.

His mind raced as he made his way to the quarterdeck. A

misstep now could doom his prospects for bringing this to a successful conclusion.

"Studs'ls, Mr. Sweeney," he said without preamble when he arrived.

The sailing master was obviously surprised by the order, but he knew better than to question his captain. Not now.

"Aye, Captain." He picked up the speaking trumpet and bellowed orders. In moments, the ship gained speed.

Brewer resumed his place on the rail, glass to his eye as he carefully studied his enemy. He was sure now the ship was the *Oliver Cromwell*, and he was determined not to allow her to get away again. One way or the other, this would end today.

"Mr. Sweeney!" he called over his shoulder. "When I give the word, I want you to put the wheel over to starboard. Point us right at that ship."

"Aye, Captain."

Brewer kept his eye on *Cromwell*. He knew he would have only a few minutes at most before they outdistanced his turn, and he wanted to take advantage of every second. He only hoped they were close enough to make the first shots count.

"Now, Mr. Sweeney!"

Sweeney nodded to the quartermaster, and from the rail Brewer saw the four men spin the wheel to starboard. The sailing master's eyes were on *Cromwell*, for he had to bring his ship out of the turn pointing right at her. Brewer stood by, determined not to interfere. He had confidence in Sweeney's seamanship. The sailing master pointed to the wheel and shouted an order over his shoulder, and the four at the wheel quickly reversed themselves and straightened out the ship. Brewer leaned out over the rail and looked forward; sure enough, *Oliver Cromwell* lay dead ahead.

The bow chasers barked.

"Well done, Mr. Sweeney!" Brewer called out. "You are authorized to make such corrections as are necessary to keep the long nines pointed at the enemy. Continue until you hear otherwise from myself or Mr. Greene."

"Aye, sir."

Brewer went forward hurriedly. He arrived just as the guns were being run out. "Report, Mr. Greene!"

"Lookout informed me that both shots landed short but on line," the first lieutenant replied. "I'm hoping to get off another shot, maybe two, before they turn."

"Proceed."

Greene nodded to the gunner, who gave the order to fire. The cannon went off together, and the combination of muzzle flash, explosive repercussion, and smoke made the captain flinch.

"Lookout!" Greene called aloft. "Let's hear you!"

"A hit, sir!" came the excited reply. "The second landed aft."

"Reload! Quickly!" Greene urged the gun crews. He looked towards the wheel as he felt the ship turn to larboard. One, maybe two points. Not a great deal, but enough to notice if you knew what was happening. He looked to the captain, who shrugged.

"Mr. Sweeney's helping you out."

"I must remember to thank him," Greene muttered. He nodded to the gunner.

"Oh, I'm sure he'll remind you," Brewer deadpanned.

"Fire!" Hodges cried.

Brewer was ready for it this time. He closed his eyes and held his breath until the smoke cleared. He refused to put his fingers in his ears, welcome as the action might be. Greene looked up to the lookout.

"Two hits on their larboard quarter, sir! Deck there!

Chase's turning!"

The two officers spun forward to see *Cromwell* turning to starboard. Brewer leaned toward his premier.

"Continue to fire as you bear. I'm going aft to settle into a chase. I'm taking Mr. Short with me. He will bring you orders."

"Aye, Captain."

"Mr. Hodges!" Brewer said before he left, "A hearty 'Well Done' to you and your men!"

Grins broke out amongst the crews of the long nines.

"Thank 'ee, Captain!" Hodges answered for them.

Brewer heard the long nines go off again as he made his way aft.

"They're running," he said to Sweeney when he arrived. "Try to get us one or two more shots with the long nines, then I want them on our starboard bow for the chase."

"Aye, Captain."

The bow chasers got another shot off before Mr. Greene appeared on the quarterdeck. He touched his hat as he approached.

"Yes, Mr. Greene?" Brewer asked.

"The long nines no longer bear, sir," the premier explained. "Request permission to send Mr. Reed to watch over them with orders to fire if they bear."

Brewer thought for a moment before nodding. "Granted."

Greene stepped away long enough to send the senior midshipman forward. When he returned, he asked Brewer his plans. The captain shrugged.

"For the moment, I am watching for an opening, some sort of mistake or accident that will give us a decisive advantage."

Greene nodded. "Where do you think he was going?"

Brewer's head tilted to the side as he contemplated the first lieutenant's question, then his eyes went wide as a thought hit him. Before he could reply, the voice of the lookout arrested their attention.

"Deck there! Chase's slowing!"

The two officers moved quickly to the rail to see for themselves. Sure enough, the gap to *Cromwell* was closing fast.

"Quickly, Benjamin," Brewer exclaimed, "ready the larboard battery. I am going to put the ship hard over to starboard. When I do, run the guns out and fire as you bear. Put every ball through her stern!"

"Aye, sir!" The first lieutenant ran up the battery, shouting orders to the gun captains as he went.

Brewer went to the wheel. "On my orders, Mr. Sweeney, put us over hard to starboard. I want to rake her."

"Aye, Captain." Sweeney turned to the wheel to make sure the quartermaster and his mates understood the plan.

"Deck there!" the lookout called franticly. "Chase is turning to larboard! She means to cross our bow!"

"Now, Mr. Sweeney!"

The sailing master bellowed orders and the ship came around. Brewer watched as Greene ordered the larboard battery run out and ready to fire. He marched back and forth behind the battery, stopping occasionally to check the sighting on a gun, before he stood back and looked up and down the line.

"Fire as you bear!"

The first half of the battery went off as a unit. The second five went off piecemeal. Brewer went to the rail to see the results for himself, but he had to wait for the smoke to clear. When he finally had a clear view, he estimated three or four balls had struck home from the damage he saw on the enemy's deck. Unfortunately, *Cromwell* continued her turn and was now running out her guns.

"Down!" Brewer turned and cried to the deck at large. "All hands! Down, I say!"

He hit the deck and covered his head with his arms just as he heard the sound of *Cromwell's* broadside, followed almost immediately by a *whoosh* of air over his head punctuated by the impact of a ball striking wood. Then came the screams of those not lucky enough to evade the wave of destruction.

He got to his feet and looked around. The damage looked minimal with only one gun overturned.

"Mr. Sweeney! Where's *Cromwell*?"

"There, sir," the sailing master pointed off their larboard bow.

"Bring us about!" Brewer ordered. "After them!"

"Aye, Captain!"

Orders went out, and HMS *Revenge* swung around in pursuit of her quarry. *Cromwell* was continuing to come around and would soon cross *Revenge's* bow. Brewer decided he could not pass up the opportunity.

"Mr. Greene!" he shouted. "Mr. Sweeney! Let's do it again!"

Greene waved his acknowledgement, and Sweeney gave the quartermaster the orders that put the ship hard over to larboard. Greene ran out the battery and prepared to fire. As soon as the ship steadied up, he shouted the order, and the guns erupted all along the side of the ship. By the time the smoke cleared, Brewer couldn't tell if the enemy was any more damaged than she was before, but *Cromwell* was turning away.

"Bring us around, Sailing Master," the captain said. "Put us at pistol shot."

"Aye, Captain."

They settled into a chase with *Cromwell* slightly ahead on their larboard bow. Mac and Alfred joined their captain on the quarterdeck.

"Stand by, Mr. Greene!" Brewer called. To Sweeney, "three points to starboard."

"Aye, sir." The ship edged over, and the broadside thundered. Brewer saw at least two hits.

"Well done, Mr. Greene!" he shouted.

"Captain!" Sweeney cried. He pointed toward *Cromwell*. "She's closing, sir!"

Brewer turned to see Underhill had come around to run parallel to them with the starboard battery now out. He turned to Alfred, who was now standing beside him. "Have I ever told you what my old captain used to say in times like this? He always said, *'For what we are about to receive, let us be truly thankful.'*"

Alfred merely raised an eyebrow, and Brewer shrugged.

"I know," he said, "I never understood it either."

Cromwell's broadside went high in an attempt to tear apart their tophamper. Brewer wondered if they were reloading with bar, but decided not to worry about it.

"Mr. Greene! Load the carronades with grape and the ball for the next two salvoes. Fire at will! After two salvoes, check with me about loading with bar!"

"Aye, sir!"

The next half-hour was an old-fashioned slugfest. The two sloops sailed in parallel and exchanged broadside after broadside. Brewer stood on his quarterdeck, mainly because that's what captains are supposed to due during the part of a battle when they have nothing else to do. Mr. Greene directed the battery's fire. Brewer had decided against loading with bar after the two salvoes, so the fight was on. Three of the larboard battery's guns were now out of action, and they were having to borrow hands from the starboard battery to man the guns.

"Mr. Greene!" Brewer called. "One last broadside, all guns to fire at once. I want maximum smoke."

"Aye, sir!" Greene sprinted back to his guns. Brewer saw him going from gun to gun, speaking in gun captain's ear to pass on the instructions.

"Mr. Sweeney! After this last broadside, wear ship to starboard. Continue around and cross their stern! We'll rake them with the starboard battery!"

"Aye, sir!"

The captain turned to see Greene raise his arm. The two men locked eyes for a moment, and Brewer nodded once. Greene dropped his arm.

"Fire!"

As soon as the broadside was gone, Sweeney put the wheel hard over and *Revenge* wheeled off to starboard. She steadied up on a course roughly WSW. Brewer quickly gauged their approach and turned to the sailing master.

"Two points to starboard."

"Aye, Captain."

The ship slid to the right and straightened up on a course to deal a killing blow to their adversary.

"Mr. Greene! Standby the starboard battery!"

He saw that Greene was ahead of him on this one, as he was already running the guns out and preparing to fire into *Cromwell's* unprotected stern.

"Standby!" Brewer called. He saw that Greene was watching him for the order to fire, but he was focused on delivering this blow before Underhill could slip away.

"Fire!" Brewer ordered. The guns went off, and the stern of the *Oliver Cromwell* disintegrated into shards of glass and wood. The ship seemed to stagger a bit before righting herself and coming around to starboard to settle on a course to close with *Revenge*.

Brewer stood at the fantail and studied his quarry through his glass. She'd taken a beating, but he saw nothing that indicated a knockout blow had been delivered. He also knew his own ship had taken a beating; he needed to end this as soon as possible.

He stepped forward and met the first lieutenant near the mainmast.

"Mr. Greene, I intend to put us over hard to starboard so you can put a broadside into her bows. After that, I want to continue around and down her starboard side. Reload with bar and fire when your guns bear. Your aim is to shred her upperworks."

"Aye, sir," Greene replied. "We'll be ready."

Brewer gripped Greene's arm and returned to the quarterdeck. He explained his plan to Mr. Sweeney before moving to the fantail for one last look at his intended victim. Satisfied, he stepped away from the rail.

"Now, Mr. Sweeney," he said. "Hard to starboard. Put us across her bows."

"Aye, sir!"

"Ready, Mr. Greene!"

"Ready, sir!"

"Fire!"

Fire and iron belched from the side of the ship. Brewer sometimes wished it was possible to see the balls clearly as they sailed to their targets; he wondered if their flight would be as majestic as watching a falcon swoop in on its prey. At least three impacted with the prow of the oncoming vessel, and Brewer could only hope the resulting splinters did even more damage.

But Brewer had made a mistake. He'd let *Cromwell* get too close before he cut across her bows. Now the sloop's headway carried her past the British ship as *Revenge* came around to starboard again, intending to pour another broadside into the pirate ship. As he swept past his foe, Underhill put all his experience and seamanship to good use. He put his wheel hard over to starboard so hard that the ship heeled over as she rounded the Britisher's stern. This gave his guns extra elevation, just as the pirate captain intended. *Cromwell's* starboard battery erupted, throwing well-aimed shot at *Revenge's* defenseless tophamper. Everyone on the British quarterdeck heard the sickening sound of the mizzen topmast shattering from a direct hit from a 12-pounder ball. The mast crashed down and lay across the starboard rail aft of the mainmast. The tip of the mast dragged the water and caused the ship to do a slow, tight circle to starboard.

"Bosun!" Greene called. "Send men with axes to cut that wreckage away! Hurry now!"

Brewer went to the rail and raised his glass to study *Cromwell's* quarterdeck as she sailed away to the NNW. For a moment, Brewer could have sworn he saw Napoleon Bonaparte on that quarterdeck. The hat, the coat were exactly what the ex-Emperor had worn that last time they spoke in Brewer's office, just days before he left St. Helena. Then the figure waved, and the spell was broken. He knew it was Michael Underhill who waved.

"Captain!" Greene said. "Shall I order the maintop lookout to follow their course?"

"Don't worry about them," Brewer said. "I think I know where they're going."

Michael Underhill sat in the outer office and awaited his audience. The journey to Washington City had not been an easy one, but the damage from the battle with the British sloop had been repaired enough to allow them to make decent time, and fortunately the weather and wind cooperated. He spent the first two days in harbor with Chauncey and the schoolmaster readying and signing the bank letters for the crew. They would be given to any of the crew who wanted to leave, along with an equal share of the specie they had on board. That way, anyone who wished to could leave with a small stake to start them off.

His real hopes for any future lay with the man he was waiting to see. The way he saw it, politics was his ticket to freedom. He was sure that the American government would rather help him make his escape than have it become common knowledge that a ship with an American letter of marque was still out there raiding British shipping.

He frowned at the thought; part of him despised the necessity of this course of action. Personally, he would rather take any other course of action, but this was all that was left to him. He knew now beyond all doubt that his ability to roam the seas was compromised beyond his ability to repair. There was nowhere he could go to escape the Royal Navy. Napoleon was not wrong when he said that wherever you find a foot of water, you will find the Royal Navy. He could not ask his men to fight to the death, not when there was any other way out. By this time tomorrow, any who wanted to leave would be gone. He hoped he would have enough left to work the ship, even if it meant she would be unable to fight. If they could somehow evade the British and American ships, they could sail south and try to make a new life.

He looked up to see the secretary standing before him.

"Mr. Adams will see you now," he said.

Underhill rose and walked through the door a steward held open for him and found himself in the presence of the American Secretary of State, John Quincy Adams.

"Mr. Underhill?" Adams stepped around his desk and

offered his hand. "A pleasure to meet you. What can I do for you?"

"That is a complicated question, Mr. Secretary," Underhill said as he took the seat he was offered. "I need your help, sir. To be blunt, the British are after me, and I need the protection of your government."

Adams frowned at this. "I don't understand."

"I came to your country more than ten years ago," Underhill explained. "During the late war, I ran a privateer under a letter of marque from your government. Now the British want revenge."

Adams rubbed his chin as he studied the man across the desk. Suddenly memory broke through, and he realized who this man was.

"Mr. Underhill," he said, "I've heard your name. Would you happen to be familiar with a Captain William Brewer of the Royal Navy? I see you are. Therefore I can safely say that you have been dishonest with me sir, or at the very least you have withheld a vital detail."

"And that would be?"

"That the British are after you for your piratical activities since the *end* of the war."

Underhill shrugged. "That in no way alters the fact that I need your help, Mr. Secretary."

"The government of the United States is not in the habit of helping pirates," Adams said coldly.

"I did good work for you during the war," Underhill protested. "And what the government of the United States does not need is for the world — and specifically the British Empire — finding out that I was operating in good faith under your letter of marque all these years." He leaned forward to make a point. "It would be in both our interests if you would help me out of my current dilemma."

"And how would you suggest we do that?" Adams demanded coldly. He did not care for the undertone of blackmail in the air.

Underhill shook his head. "I doubt that you can guarantee me safety at sea, so that leaves helping me to melt into the interior of your great nation."

"And why shouldn't I just arrest you and your men and impound your ship?"

Underhill smiled. "You don't want to do that, Mr. Secretary. The moment I am arrested by American authorities, a package that includes a copy of my letter of marque, with its ambiguous wording, will find its way to several newspapers. I imagine the Federalists will use that information to their advantage in the upcoming elections."

"I seriously doubt such news would sway many votes either way, Mr. Underhill. You must do what you will." Adams stood. "The government of the United States will not help you, sir. Good day."

Underhill had feared this would be the outcome, but he did his best to look angry. "You have made a grave mistake, Mr. Secretary. One that your government will regret, I assure you."

Adams shook his head. "You made your own destiny. You decided to ruin your faithful service during the war by turning to piracy after it ended. That's the only word for it — piracy! The British are welcome to you and your men. And if I had any proof that you had taken any American ships, I'd arrest you and hang you myself. Good day!"

Underhill marched out of the office, not slowing until he was on the street. He paused and took a deep breath before setting off for the docks. His head was down, his eyes seeing only the road before his feet, so it was not surprising he didn't hear someone come up behind him. The stranger announced himself by putting his pistol against Underhill's backbone.

"Hello, Michael."

CHAPTER EIGHTEEN

Underhill raised his hands. "Hello, William." He made no move as Brewer reached inside his coat and relieved him of his pistol and dagger.

"Now," Brewer said, "what say we sit at this lovely café and have something to drink, shall we?"

"After you," Underhill said.

"Oh, no," Brewer replied, pressing the muzzle into his captive's back, "you first."

Underhill led the way over to a table outside the café and sat. Brewer sat across from him, the pistol hidden under the table but pointed squarely at his old mentor's midsection.

The waitress came over, and Brewer ordered them two glasses of wine. She left with their order, and Underhill grinned.

"I suppose I shouldn't be surprised to see you," he said, an set his elbows on the table, at which Brewer cocked his pistol. The sound was unmistakable, and Underhill's face grew serious. "What do you want, William?"

"This must end, Michael."

"What must end?"

"Don't play with me, sir," Brewer remonstrated with his captive. "I have orders to kill you or bring you in for trial and hanging for piracy."

Underhill leaned back as the waitress brought their drinks. Brewer dropped several coins on her tray and she left. He picked up his drink and held it out in salute.

"Then why don't you?"

Brewer's aim and gaze never wavered. "Why won't you stop, Michael? After all this time, what more can you hope to gain?"

Underhill stared into his drink. "A good question; I wish I had a good answer. Revenge is a game that is hard to leave, William. I guessed as much when I disappeared from the *Kent*. In fact, that was one reason I didn't take you with me." He downed the glass and set it on the table. "It eats at your heart and then your belly and leaves a hole that can never be filled no matter how hard you try." He looked up at the sky and watched a bird fly past, and he envied it its freedom.

"I have to take you in, Michael," Brewer said. "Are you going to give me any trouble?"

"If I say yes, will you just shoot me now?" Underhill asked, still watching the bird. He lowered his eyes to see his captor watching him closely. "I'll make you a deal, William. You guarantee me that you will not go after my ship or my men, and I will go with you. No trouble. I promise."

"And let your men resume their trade on the open seas?" Brewer scoffed.

"They won't," Underhill assured him. "At this very moment, Chauncey is dismissing the crew. We were going to take the ship out to deep water and burn it. We'd make our way back to shore in a boat and disappear into the countryside."

"Why should I believe you?"

Underhill held the younger man's eyes. "I promised, didn't I? I know many things have changed, William, but that's one thing that hasn't. I keep my word. Always have, always will."

Brewer stared at him through narrowed eyes as he tried to decide whether or not Michael Underhill — *this* Michael Underhill — could be trusted. For his part, Underhill ignored his captor completely; he'd said what he had to say, and it all lay in Brewer's hands now.

Finally, Brewer sighed, his decision made. He would take Underhill back with him for trial. He would tell the admiral what Underhill told him — that the rest of his crew had been paid off and discharged, and that he and his mate had scuttled the *Oliver Cromwell* in deep water in the Chesapeake Bay. He stood and offered his hand.

Underhill remained in his seat, his eyes moving suspiciously from Brewer's hand to his eyes and back again. "Does this mean we have a deal?" he asked.

"My word upon it."

Underhill rose. "And I'm supposed to take you at your word?"

Brewer shrugged. "Why not? I'm sure it's as good as yours."

Underhill smiled and took the captain's hand. "Thank you, William."

Brewer nodded, not trusting himself to speak. He cleared his throat and said, "We'd better be going. My boat is at the dock." He held up his pistol. "Will I need this?" The other shook his head, and Brewer let the hammer down and tucked the weapon in his waistband. The two set off for the dock.

"Did you ever wonder what might have been?" Underhill said. "I had dreams, William. I dreamed of commanding a frigate, with you as my first lieutenant. We'd have been rich men, what with the prize money and head money from intercepting slavers! Our crew would have been first-rate, too; Do you remember that moose who was in the mess next to mine back on the *Kent*? The fellow from Berkshire?"

"Shelby?"

"Yes! Oh, what a coxswain he would have made! I—"

"So!" a voice shouted hysterically from across the street. "I was right! You've sold us out to the English!"

A man stepped out of the shadows. Brewer recognized as the third man who'd been with Underhill at the tavern on Martinique. Pete. Underhill stepped away from Brewer to draw Pete's attention.

"What are you talking about, Pete?" he asked.

Pete drew a pistol and pointed it at Underhill. "I knew something was wrong with you, *Captain*, but I couldn't put my finger on it. When I thought back, I realized it all started after we met your friend here at that bar on Martinique. You changed after that, Michael! Don't deny it! Then when we kidnapped him you only wanted to *warn* him! You were foolish! I told you we needed to kill him, but you wouldn't listen! Twice we've met his ship in battle, and twice we've had him at our mercy, only you wouldn't give the order!"

Underhill took a step forward, but Pete leveled the pistol at his captain's chest and cocked it. "We had a good thing going, Cap'n," Pete cried shrilly. "You know we did! We had enough hidden in the Mississippi delta to make all of us like King Midas hisself! And now it's all gone, do you hear? How can we get it? It's gone!"

Brewer watched for an opening to draw and fire on Pete without endangering any of the civilians who were quickly gathering to watch the commotion. Underhill caught his eye and shook his head; clearly, he wanted to try to talk Pete down.

"It's not like that, Pete, and you know it," he said. "The time has come for us to go our separate ways, that's all." He motioned toward Brewer. "The British are still after us, and the Americans too. If they take us, we can be tried for piracy. Is that what you want?"

"You said the letter would protect us!" Pete cried.

"You've been saying that for years!"

Underhill shot a glance at Brewer before answering. "Yeah, well, it seems I was wrong about that."

Brewer thought the look on Pete's face was one of absolute shock and betrayal. The gun in his hand never wavered from the center of his captain's chest.

"You know," Pete said, his face clouding over with anger, "all this would never have happened if we hadn't gone to that bar on Martinique. Even then, I remember Chauncey asking you after we left if Brewer was going to cause us any trouble. You said no." His gaze switched to Brewer, and the aim of the pistol followed. "Seems you were wrong about that as well, Michael. You should have let us kill him then."

"Pete?" Underhill asked. "What are you doing?"

"What you never had the guts to do."

Brewer's hand was going for his own pistol, but he knew he would be too late. Just as he saw the smoke from the primer pan, a blur of movement from his side caught his eye. Michael Underhill dove in front of him at the exact moment the pistol went off, taking the bullet in his chest. He fell at Brewer's feet. Pete's eyes went wide when he saw what he'd done. Brewer wasted no time in pulling a pistol from beneath his coat and firing. The impact in the center of his chest threw Pete off his feet backward to the ground.

Brewer dropped his pistol and knelt by his friend. He turned Underhill over, relieved to find he was still conscious. But a spreading stain of blood was darkening his shirt, and blood ran down his arm to stain his hand.

"Michael!" Brewer cried. "What have you done?" Underhill opened his eyes and took a moment to focus on his avenger's face. He smiled. "Hopefully made up for many years of mistakes. I'm... sorry, William." His pupils widened, and his head fell back. He was gone.

Brewer felt tears start to his eyes. He looked up when he

realized he was not alone. Chauncey was standing there with a pistol in his hand. Brewer rose.

"I'm sorry I was too late," the mate said.

"So am I."

Chauncey frowned. "I knew Pete was upset, but I didn't realize until it was too late that he had left the ship. I came after him as soon as I could. I got here just in time to see him shoot Michael, then you took him down before I could."

"I owed Michael."

The mate nodded.

"Michael told me of your plans. How many men do you have left?"

"Only a handful. I will return to the ship, and we'll take her out and burn her. You have my word, you will never hear from any of us again."

Brewer nodded. "Thank you." He looked down to the bodies. "What will you do with them?"

"They will go down with the ship."

Brewer sighed. He thought Michael would approve.

"I'll leave you to it, then." He left the scene and headed down to the dock.

EPILOGUE

Captain William Brewer sat at his desk in his cabin, working on his report for Admiral Hornblower. *Revenge* was on course for Port Royal. He took a drink of his wine, then set the glass down and stretched his back.

He picked up the dagger from the side of his desk. It was the one he had taken from Underhill when they met in Washington City, and Brewer recognized it as a gift he had given to his old mentor as a birthday present before he vanished from the old *Kent*. Brewer had been amazed that Underhill still had the blade. He would keep the dagger as a reminder of the man who befriended him when he needed it most. He set the dagger down and picked up his glass.

"Here's to you, Michael. I'm glad you made it home."

THE END

About the Author
James Keffer

James Keffer was born September 9, 1963, in Youngstown, Ohio, the son of a city policeman and a nurse. He grew up loving basketball, baseball, tennis, and books. He graduated high school in 1981 and began attending Youngstown State University to study mechanical engineering.

He left college in 1984 to enter the U.S. Air Force. After basic training, he was posted to the 2143rd Communications Squadron at Zweibruecken Air Base, West Germany. While he was stationed there, he met and married his wife, Christine, whose father was also assigned to the base. When the base was closed in 1991, James and Christine were transferred up the road to Sembach Air Base, where he worked in communications for the 2134th Communications Squadron before becoming the LAN manager for HQ 17th Air Force.

James received an honorable discharge in 1995, and he and his wife moved to Jacksonville, Florida, to attend Trinity Baptist College. He graduated with honors in 1998, earning a

Bachelor of Arts degree. James and Christine have three children.

Hornblower and the Island is the first novel James wrote, and it is the first to be published by Fireship Press. He has self-published three other novels. He currently lives and works in Jacksonville, Florida, with his wife and three children.

BREWER'S REVENGE

BY

JAMES KEFFER

Admiral Horatio Hornblower has given Commander William Brewer captaincy of the captured pirate sloop *El Dorado*. Now under sail as the HMS *Revenge,* its new name suits Brewer's frame of mind perfectly. He lost many of his best men in the engagement that seized the ship, and his new orders are to hunt down the pirates who have been ravaging the trade routes of the Caribbean sea.

But Brewer will face more than one challenge before he can confront the pirate known as El Diabolito. His best friend and ship's surgeon, Dr. Spinelli, is taking dangerous solace in alcohol as he wrestles with demons of his own. The new purser, Mr. Allen, may need a lesson in honest accounting. Worst of all, Hornblower has requested that Brewer take on a young ne'er-do-well, Noah Simmons, to remove him from a recent scandal at home. At twenty-three, Simmons is old to be a junior midshipman, and as a wealthy man's son he is unaccustomed to working, taking orders, or suffering privations.

William Brewer will need to muster all his resources to ready his crew for their confrontation with the Caribbean's most notorious pirate. In the process, he'll discover the true price of command.

PENMORE PRESS
www.penmorepress.com

BREWER'S LUCK

BY

JAMES KEFFER

After gaining valuable experience as an aide to Governor Lord Horatio Hornblower, William Brewer is rewarded with a posting as first lieutenant on the frigate HMS *Defiant*, bound for American waters. Early in their travels, it seems as though Brewer's greatest challenge will be evading the wrath of a tyrannical captain who has taken an active dislike to him. But when a hurricane sweeps away the captain, the young lieutenant is forced to assume command of the damaged ship, and a crew suffering from low morale.

Brewer reports their condition to Admiral Hornblower, who orders them into the Caribbean to destroy a nest of pirates hidden among the numerous islands. Luring the pirates out of their coastal lairs will be difficult enough; fighting them at sea could bring disaster to the entire operation. For the *Defiant* to succeed, Brewer must rely on his wits, his training, and his ability to shape a once-ragged crew into a coherent fighting force.

PENMORE PRESS
www.penmorepress.com

BREWER

AND THE

BARBARY

PIRATES

BY
JAMES KEFFER

It is said that a man is shaped by his past, and so it was with William Brewer. Before he took command of *HMS Defiant* in a hurricane, before he hunted pirates in *HMS Revenge*, Brewer endured a crucible of fire. Fresh from the tutelage of Napoleon Bonaparte on St. Helena, Brewer signs on for a cruise under Captain Bush in *HMS Lydia* to the Mediterranean to battle the Barbary Pirates. Here Brewer learns to fight, but he also learns what it means to command men in battle and what it takes to order men to their deaths. Their enemy is a Scottish renegade who is responsible for the deaths of dozens of his fellow sailors over the years and the selling of hundreds of Europeans into African slavery. Along the way, Brewer is introduced to new heroes and new devils. He also receives sage advice from no less than the Duke of Wellington himself. In the end, Brewer has to use all he's learned and going beyond to save *HMS Lydia* from destruction at the hands of pirates.

PENMORE PRESS
www.penmorepress.com

Fortune's Whelp
by
Benerson Little

Privateer, Swordsman, and Rake:

Set in the 17th century during the heyday of privateering and the decline of buccaneering, *Fortune's Whelp* is a brash, swords-out sea-going adventure. Scotsman Edward MacNaughton, a former privateer captain, twice accused and acquitted of piracy and currently seeking a commission, is ensnared in the intrigue associated with the attempt to assassinate King William III in 1696. Who plots to kill the king, who will rise in rebellion—and which of three women in his life, the dangerous smuggler, the wealthy widow with a dark past, or the former lover seeking independence—might kill to further political ends? Variously wooing and defying Fortune, Captain MacNaughton approaches life in the same way he wields a sword or commands a fighting ship: with the heart of a lion and the craft of a fox.

PENMORE PRESS
www.penmorepress.com

HORNBLOWER AND THE ISLAND

BY

JAMES KEFFER

Even as a prisoner on the remote island of St. Helena, Napoleon Bonaparte is embarrassing the British, and England is now the laughing stock of Europe. The answer is a new Governor: Lord Horatio Hornblower. The British government is betting that Hornblower's background, being so similar to Bonaparte's, will earn the Corsican's respect. Both men rose from humble beginnings to nobility by his achievements alone. Both have commanded men and lead them to victories. Hornblower's mission is simple: deal with the greatest military genius of the modern era and make him behave. Hornblower discovers a Bonaparte that history never knew, and learns the truth about the man who would be Emperor of the world.

PENMORE PRESS
www.penmorepress.com

The Dragon's Breath

by

James Boschert

Talon stared wide-eyed at the devices, awed that they could make such an overwhelming, head-splitting noise. His ears rang and his eyes were burning from the drifting smoke that carried with it an evil stink. "That will show the bastards," Hsü told him with one of his rare smiles. "The General calls his weapons 'the Dragon's breath.' They certainly stink like it."

Talon, an assassin turned knight turned merchant, is restless. Enticed by tales of lucrative trade, he sets sail for the coasts of Africa and India. Traveling with him are his wife and son, eager to share in this new adventure, as well as Reza, his trusted comrade in arms. Treasures beckon at the ports, but Talon and Reza quickly learn that dangers attend every opportunity, and the chance rescue of a Chinese lord named Hsü changes their destination—and their fates.

Hsü introduces Talon to the intricacies of trading in China and the sophisticated wonders of Guangzhou, China's richest city. Here the companions discover wealth beyond their imagining. But Hsü is drawn into a political competition for the position of governor, and his opponents target everyone associated with him, including the foreign merchants he has welcomed into his home. When Hsü is sent on a dangerous mission to deliver the annual Tribute to the Mongols, no one is safe, not even the women and children of the household. As Talon and Reza are drawn into supporting Hsü's bid for power, their fighting skills are put to the test against new weapons and unfamiliar fighting styles. It will take their combined skills to navigate the treacherous waters of intrigue and violence if they hope to return to home.

PENMORE PRESS
www.penmorepress.com

Historical fiction and nonfiction
Paperback available for order on line
and as Ebook with all major distributers

Penmore Press

Challenging, Intriguing, Adventurous, Historical and Imaginative

www.penmorepress.com

www.ingramcontent.com/pod-product-compliance
Lightning Source LLC
Chambersburg PA
CBHW060735190726
48285CB00001B/211